Elaine Hastings studied art and graphic design at the University of the Arts London. She is the Creative Lead in a communications agency and writes fiction in her spare time. She lives in Surrey with her husband, son and little black cat. *When We Were Young* is her first novel.

elainehastingsauthor.com
@ @ehastingswrites
@ehastingswrites
@ehastingswrites

When We Were Young

ELAINE HASTINGS

avon.

Published by AVON
A division of HarperCollins*Publishers* Ltd
1 London Bridge Street
London SE1 9GF

www.harpercollins.co.uk

HarperCollins*Publishers*
Macken House, 39/40 Mayor Street Upper
Dublin 1, D01 C9W8, Ireland

A Paperback Original 2025
1
First published in Great Britain by HarperCollins*Publishers* 2025

A catalogue copy of this book is available from the British Library.

ISBN: 9780008763329

Set in Sabon LT Std by HarperCollins*Publishers* India

Printed and bound in the UK using 100% Renewable
Electricity at CPI Group (UK) Ltd

FSC™ C007454
MIX
Paper | Supporting
responsible forestry
FSC
www.fsc.org

For Adrian and Sam. My little family.

Content Warning

When We Were Young, although fictional, tackles some events and issues that some may find distressing. If you'd like to find out more, please read the 'Content Warning' note at the very back of the book, but please be warned it does contain spoilers.

Chapter One

March 2016

Emily

'Cheesecake!' I yell at Liv. She can't hear me, so I roll down the window and try again. 'Cheesecake!'

Oblivious, she saunters towards the car, her eyes fixed on her phone, thumbs a blur as she types. She's got earphones in, for God's sake. I wait for her to open the car door and get close enough for me to lean over and yank her sleeve.

She jumps out of her skin and glares at me. 'What?' she says, pulling out an earphone.

'I asked you to bring the cheesecake from the fridge.'

She tuts, slams the door, and turns back to the house.

She's inside for ages. What's she *doing* in there? My fingernails dig into the steering wheel. We'll be late for dinner now, and my mother won't let me hear the end of it.

When she finally emerges, I'm surprised at how tall she is, how much older than fifteen she looks. It's as though she went in that door a child and came out an adult. I get a brief pang of sorrow. I miss my little girl.

Liv is still texting as she strolls back down the path. She gets in the car, puts the dessert box in the footwell, and fastens her seatbelt, all with her eyes glued to her phone.

'What?' she asks when she notices we're still stationary.

'How many times have I told you? No headphones when we're together. It's anti-social.'

'But I want to listen to music.'

'So, play it through the speakers.'

As I pull away, she rummages in the glove box for the cable and connects her phone to the car stereo.

'How was school today?' I ask.

'Huh?'

'How was school?'

'Fine.'

'What did you have today?'

'What?'

'What lessons did you have?'

'I dunno. The usual. Maths? English?'

I give up. She's too engrossed in scrolling through her vast music library, the phone lighting up her face. We'll be there before she chooses a song.

'Loads of kids from school are going to Beatland in the summer,' she says out of the blue.

I know where this is heading. 'You're too young for festivals, Olivia.'

'But everyone's going.'

'No way. You're only fifteen.'

'I'll be sixteen by then.'

I raise my eyebrows at her.

'I'll ask Dad then,' she says.

'He doesn't make the decisions, Liv. *I* do.'

Sensibly, she changes the subject. 'I heard the most amazing song today. I'll play it for you.'

As I flip the indicator and turn left, the car fills with music. Within the first few notes, I recognise the song and it's like a punch to the solar plexus. I can't breathe.

'Turn it off!' I croak, but my voice is drowned out as she turns up the volume.

A bird in a cage,
A butterfly on a pin,
It fills me with rage,

It's such a terrible sin—

'Liv, turn it off! Now!'

The headlights of the oncoming car dazzle me. Through the glare, I see a silhouette stark against the bright lights of a stage. I blink, and the image disappears. The car veers left, a lamppost looming in my line of vision. I throw my left arm across Liv. Brakes screech. My body strains against the seatbelt. Metal crunches. Airbags burst in my face and throw me back in my seat.

The music stops. The car is silent. I turn to my daughter, wrestle the airbags out of the way, and pray I haven't killed another person I love.

Chapter 2

April 1994

Sun streamed through the skylights in hazy beams as the first rush-hour train crawled onto the platform, so Will played 'Here Comes the Sun'. He loved busking in Uxbridge station. The acoustics in the ticket hall were amazing – you didn't even need an amp – but you had to keep an eye out for the station manager in his orange high-viz vest, otherwise you were out on your ear. Commuters swarmed through the barriers, several making the detour to throw him change, but there was no sign of the girl.

Ali popped out of his barbershop and yelled, 'Hey boy! Play "Sunny Afternoon". Then come in here and I'll give you a haircut!'

'No chance. I'd lose all my power!' said Will, but he played it anyway.

The spring sunshine had everyone in good spirits. One or two people even made eye contact, and a guy in a suit walked by but turned back to toss a pound. The station clock said five-fifteen. The next train was due in three minutes, so he played one of his own songs.

For the passengers of the 17:18, he played 'Summer Breeze' and got two nods and a smile, but no cash. Will thought he saw a flash of fluorescent orange out of the corner of his eye, but he was probably being paranoid.

Then he saw her.

She was carrying an unwieldy portfolio case and a toolbox. Last week, she'd had a canvas gathered up in a bin liner with a brightly daubed corner poking through. The week before, she'd cradled a bundle of driftwood, smiling as she went by, the turquoise smudge on her cheek only adding to her beauty.

What was in that portfolio case today? He pictured loose charcoal sketches, layered collages, vibrant watercolours bleeding into each other on thick, textured paper.

She struggled at the barriers. The toolbox jammed against the side of the machine as she reached to take her ticket from the slot. The catch caught, and the toolbox erupted. Sticks of charcoal, tubes of paint, brushes and pencils all clattered to the ground while hundreds of wispy yellow feathers danced around her, wafting aimlessly down.

Commuters piled up behind her as she scrabbled on the floor and the barrier closed, trapping her on the wrong side. No one was helping.

Will had an idea. 'Help!' he sang. 'She needs somebody. Help, come on, anybody. He-e-help. You know she needs someone . . .'

He hijacked the Beatles song, changing the odd word to draw attention to the girl. A gaggle of schoolgirls noticed what he was singing and went to help. One of them pointed him out to her. She stood up and looked over, her frown softening into an embarrassed smile. She was as lovely as he remembered.

He finished on the 'ooh' at the end of the song and smiled back, but her expression had changed. She was looking past him, frowning again. Two police officers were striding towards him. Will lifted the strap over his head and dropped the guitar into its case at his feet. He was well-practised at kicking the case shut and scooping it up in one slick move, but he felt a heavy hand on his shoulder before he could do either.

'You can't beg here,' said the more senior officer.

'I'm not begging, I'm *performing*.' Over his shoulder, the girl was deep in conversation with Mr High-Viz.

'Can we have your full attention, sir?' barked Senior, his neat white moustache twitching. 'You've been asked to move on several occasions. You're causing an obstruction.'

'An obstruction?' said Will. 'Christ, have you got nothing better to do?'

Senior scowled, veins bulging at his temples. 'I'm arresting you for causing a breach of the peace and for causing an *obstruction*.'

Will stifled a snort of laughter. Senior's eyes widened. He nodded to Junior, who manhandled Will into a pair of handcuffs.

'You're not seriously arresting me?'

The girl was still on the wrong side of the barriers, watching along with everyone else. It was his turn to be embarrassed now.

'Yes. I. Am,' said Senior.

Junior pulled Will by the elbow.

'Hang on, what about my stuff?'

'Not my problem, son,' said Junior, which was rich coming from him considering he looked like a kid playing dress-up.

'You can't do that!'

'Watch me.'

'Ah, come *on*!'

Over his shoulder, he looked back at the girl. She was through the barriers now, watching them drag him away. He'd got her attention at last, but for all the wrong reasons. Today of all days. The day when he was finally going to say something.

6

Chapter 3

March 2016

Liv

What just happened? Through the shattered windscreen, I see a lamppost embedded in the car bonnet.

Mum is saying *Are you okay?* over and over as pain seeps across my shoulder and chest. 'Liv, answer me, please! Are you okay?'

'Yeah . . . I think so. What happened?'

Blood trickles from her eyebrow in a thick red line. She drops her head into her hands, spreading the blood around, making me feel sick. 'I don't know . . . I got distracted.'

'You've cut your head,' I tell her, but she ignores me.

'That music . . . that song . . . I knew him.'

'Who? What are you talking about?'

'I can't listen to that . . .'

Steam hisses from under the bonnet. We should get out.

I stumble around the back of the car and help her out, but as soon as we reach the pavement, she sinks to her knees in tears. She's freaking me out. Maybe she has concussion.

'Should I call an ambulance?' I ask.

She's crying uncontrollably now. 'No . . . I'm okay.'

She's *not* okay.

My hands tremble as I take out my phone and call Grandad. He's calm. He tells me not to worry, they'll be here in a minute.

I find a pack of tissues in my pocket. 'Here, put some pressure on.'

I sit down beside her and put my arm around her. It's weird, me taking care of her for a change. My throat aches and I fight the urge to cry. We sit there, me rubbing her back while her shoulders shake in silence.

'Mum,' I say after a while, 'did you say you knew Will Bailey?'

Her face is a mess of tears, snot, and blood. She nods.

I open my mouth to ask the first of a million questions, but my grandparents pull up and I don't get the chance.

*

'That doesn't look like public health in the Middle Ages,' Chloe says, sitting down beside me and shoving me with her hip. I shriek and everyone in the library looks over. 'Sorry! I forgot about your ribs. How are they?'

I roll my eyes at her. 'Sore.'

At A&E last night, Mum was treated for whiplash and had her eyebrow glued. They told me my ribs and collarbone were bruised from the seatbelt, but it feels way worse than just 'bruised'.

'So, what *is* that?' Chloe asks, pointing to my laptop. I scroll to the top of the Wikipedia page. 'Will Bailey? Who's he?'

'I was playing one of his songs in the car when we crashed. Mum was crying afterwards. She said she knew him.'

Chloe scrolls to the picture of Bailey.

'He's hot. Wait, do you think she was a groupie?' She giggles. 'What does he look like now?'

'He's dead.'

She grabs my arm. 'No!'

'He was twenty-six. Says here "drowning and undetermined factors". Whatever that means.'

'That's so sad . . . How well did your mum know him?'

A sixth-form girl at the end of our table glares at us, so I lower my voice. 'I don't know. After the crash, she said she knew him and later, she said she didn't know what I was talking about.'

'She hit her head, didn't she? Maybe she was confused?'

'I asked my grandparents about him. They gave each other this look, then said they'd never heard of him.'

'What's the big secret?'

'I don't know.' I tell her. 'But I want to find out.'

Chloe reads the Wikipedia entry: 'William Oscar Bailey (25th November 1972–29th July 1999) was an English singer, songwriter, and guitarist. In 1996, Bailey released what would be his only album, *Fragments*. It reached number one in the UK and number three in the US.'

'Can you imagine my mum hanging out with someone like Will Bailey? *Not* likely.'

We tap away at our laptops for half an hour, and I've just found out what trepanning is when Chloe nudges me.

'Look at this,' she says.

My screen's filled with historical engravings of people having holes drilled into their heads, but Chloe is on YouTube with her earphones in. We must have slipped into an alternate reality where our roles are reversed. She hands me one of her earphones and plays the video.

'Is that the Pyramid Stage?' I ask, recognising its iconic shape. 'Will Bailey played Glastonbury?'

'Yeah, in 1997. It's daytime, though, he's not headlining or anything.'

The camera pans across the vast undulating ocean of people stretching as far as the horizon. It zooms in on the singer's face, his eyes gleaming as he looks out at the scene before him. He pauses before strumming his guitar and the crowd roars.

When Bailey sings, his voice is as incredible live as it is on the recorded tracks. The camera angle switches to the side of the stage, showing a group of people watching from the wings.

'There!' Chloe points to a girl dancing, her arms raised over her head.

Bailey launches into the chorus, serenading the dancing girl. She beams at him. I feel a goofy smile form on my face, but it's removed by a sudden slap of recognition.

'Oh my God!' I gasp. 'That's my mum!'

'I knew it!'

The girl remains in shot for a full five seconds before the focus switches to Bailey's fingers on his plectrum.

'Do they show her again?' I ask.

'No, that's it, but he keeps looking her way. It's her, right?' Chloe scrolls backwards, finds the shot and pauses.

'I think so.' I've never seen her look like that, happy and carefree. She's beautiful. I've never thought of my mum as beautiful before. And I can't imagine her ever going to a festival, let alone dancing in the wings of the Pyramid Stage. It can't be her. My mind's spinning.

'Will you ask her?'

'She'd say it's not her. And the way my grandparents reacted . . . they were covering something up. Why would she say she knew him one minute and deny it the next?'

Chloe plays the video again.

Bailey closes his eyes and sings:
Here she comes in a cloud of yellow feathers
Can we ever be together?
There's always something in the way.
Here she comes, all around her yellow feathers
It's an image that I'll treasure
And now they're dragging me away.

Chapter 4

May 1994

It was Will's round, and he was trying to remember what his mate, Matty, was drinking when the girl behind the bar asked, 'What can I get you?'

He did a double take. There, standing before him with raised eyebrows, was the arty girl from the station.

It had been weeks since he'd had to stop busking there, and he'd given up on ever seeing her again.

'Two bottles of Bud, please,' came a voice from his left. He was too late; she went off to fetch the drinks and by the time she came back, her colleague had already taken his order.

She caught him looking at her and asked, 'Are you being served?'

'Er, yes, thanks.'

She nodded and moved on. *Shit*. He watched her back as she scooped ice into a glass, reached up to the optics and poured a shot. She turned and stood right in front of him, topping it up with the soda gun. A strand of dark, wavy hair escaped from her ponytail and dangled onto her cheek. She was close enough for him to see a smattering of freckles on the bridge of her nose. He should say something now he had the chance: tell her he'd seen her at the station, ask about her art. But every sentence he constructed in his head made him sound like a stalker. Even when all eight drinks were paid for and sitting on a tray in front of him, he still had nothing. Absolutely nothing.

He took the tray back to his friends' table and handed out the drinks. They were only three rounds in, but they were already getting loud, all talking over each other. Will didn't sit back in the same seat; he chose one with a view of the bar instead. He took a sip of beer to swallow his frustration and vowed to go back up there when he had something less creepy to say.

'Guys, did I tell you my little brother here got arrested?' said Aidan, pulling him close and grinding his knuckles into Will's head.

'No! What did you do, Will?' asked Rob.

Aidan butted in before he could answer, 'What do you reckon? Drug dealing? Stealing cars?'

Will gave his brother a sarcastic smile.

'Well, what was it?' asked Rob.

'Busking!' Aidan was practically incontinent with laughter. 'Can you believe it? They held him at the police station for *six hours.*'

'Ah mate, that's rough,' said Rob, while the others jeered.

Will stole another look at the girl. She was making her way back behind the bar, having collected a tower of dirty pint glasses. Aidan leant in to see what Will was looking at, then eyed him with a knowing smile.

Suddenly, Aidan was on his feet. 'Will, you're so tight. Why didn't you get any crisps? Anyone want crisps?'

Everyone wanted crisps except Will, who watched his handsome, charming, older brother stalk confidently to the bar. She didn't stand a chance.

'Have you contacted any record companies yet?' asked Rob.

'What? No!'

'Why not?'

'We don't have any decent songs for a start.' Will shifted to his right to get a better view of Aidan chatting to the girl.

'"Random Anthem" is brilliant, so is "Wandering" and everybody loves "Fever",' said Rob. 'Have you recorded *anything* yet?'

'We did a crappy demo of "Wandering" ages ago.'

Matty slipped into the seat Aidan had vacated. 'It wasn't crappy!'

'You need to get a demo recorded and send it out to record companies,' said Rob.

'That's exactly what I've been saying!' Matty's eyelids were heavy. He was getting pissed.

Will sighed. 'Demos cost money, Matty.'

'Good job you've got some travelling money left . . .' Matty clinked his pint glass to Will's with a wink.

'Not much . . .' The girl was tipping her head back in laughter at whatever Aidan was saying.

'Listen,' said Matty. 'I'll ask my mum to lend me money and we'll see what we can get off Mitch—'

'You must be joking!' cried Will. Their drummer was tight as arseholes.

'Hear me out.' Matty sat forward in his seat, excited now. 'Let's record those three songs, I'll send out some tapes, make a few calls, get us some decent gigs. What do you say?'

Will thought for a moment. 'Could we get the Mean Fiddler?'

'You want the Mean Fiddler? I'll get you the Mean Fiddler!' Matty slammed his hand on the table. 'But only with a decent demo.'

'Okay – let's do it.'

Aidan returned from the bar then, dropping an armful of crisp packets onto the table. 'Look what I've got.' He waved a strip of paper in Will's face, with a smug grin. Will snatched it and looked closer. It was a till receipt and written on the back in neat handwriting was the word 'Emily' and a telephone number.

Chapter 5

March 2016

Liv

I'm at the bus stop after school listening to the Will Bailey album for the hundredth time when I get a tap on the shoulder. I turn to see our school tie and crest at eye-level. There's only one kid that tall and as I lift my chin to confirm it, my whole head ignites with embarrassment.

It's Nathan Hall.

He hasn't spoken to me since primary school, and even then, it was only to tell me to move out of the way. I pull out an earphone.

'What are you listening to?' he asks.

They're the most confusing five words I've ever heard, and I gawp at him until I come to my senses. 'Will Bailey. Have you heard of him?' He shakes his gorgeous blond head. 'This song's on the trailer for *Nostalgia*. It's all over the TV.' God, I'm such a nerd.

He points to my dangling earphone, so I hand it to him and skip back to the start, then immediately regret it – this track is six minutes long. Hyperventilating, I stand rigid beside Nathan for the entire song. I don't dare look at him but I'm dying to know if the hairs on the back of his neck are sparking too.

By the time it's over, I'm about to pass out.

'Have you heard the new Liars song?' he asks. When I tell

him no, he gestures for my phone. He types something into Spotify and the Liars track rumbles in my ear.

'It's good,' I say, raising my voice over the jangly guitars.

'If you like this, I've got a playlist you might like. We should swap numbers.'

I stop hyperventilating – now I can't breathe at all.

With The Liars harmonising in our ears, we exchange numbers then stand awkwardly waiting for the song to finish.

Nathan interrupts the middle eight. 'Here's my bus.' He pulls out my earphone and hands it back. 'You're coming to Beatland, right?'

'Huh?'

'Beatland. Festival. Everyone's going.' He jumps on the bus. My insides are doing somersaults. 'Er . . .'

'Come.' He flashes a grin as the doors close.

As the bus pulls away, I deflate like a popped balloon.

Because that's *never* going to happen.

*

Dad is waiting for me at our usual spot, leaning against a pillar of the old market building. He's always early. Sensing me coming, he looks up and beams.

'Hi Dad.'

'Hiya, Livster.' When he wraps his arms around me, he smells of soap and freshly washed clothes. He plants a million kisses on the top of my head with embarrassing sound effects.

'You'll ruin my hair,' I complain.

'I can't ruin your hair – it's perfect.' He takes my rucksack. 'Bloody hell, what've you got in here? It weighs a ton.'

'Homework.'

'Ugh!' He holds it at arm's length, like it's contaminated, then swings it onto his back as we head towards the cinema complex.

'How are your ribs?' he asks.

15

'Still painful. The doctor said it could last up to six weeks. It's worse when I laugh, so no comedies tonight.'

'Okay. Pizza first?'

'I fancy noodles.'

'Noodles it is.'

At the restaurant, a waiter takes us to a table near the window and we slide across the long benches opposite each other.

'How's your mum?' he asks, while studying the menu.

'Her face is healing, and the physio exercises are helping her neck, but she's been acting weird since the crash.'

He looks up from his menu. 'Weird how?'

'I don't know – distracted? Not herself.'

He considers this. 'Well, it was a traumatic experience – you'll both need time to get over it. Keep an eye on her and let me know if you're still worried.'

'Okay.'

I take a breath and go to ask him about Will Bailey, but he catches me off guard with: 'So, how's your love life?'

He's not being entirely serious but my cheeks flash with heat as Nathan pops into my head. 'Non-existent. How's yours? Are you still seeing Katya?'

'Sort of.'

'What does that mean?'

'It means sometimes I see Katya, and sometimes I see Lily, or Gretchen, or Camilla.'

He's making up these names, but he has had a lot of girlfriends. Katya's the first one to leave a toothbrush in his bathroom, though.

The waiter takes our order and when he's gone, I ask, 'Don't you like Katya anymore?'

'Honestly? She's a bit high-maintenance.'

I don't know what he means but I nod anyway. I've only met her a few times – she's usually leaving when I'm arriving. Everything about her is glamorous – her clothes, hair, and make-up.

16

'How old is she again?' I tease.

'I'm not sure.' She's twenty-eight – Dad is forty.

The food arrives, and we shut up and eat. Well, I do. Dad keeps dropping little clumps of rice before they reach his mouth. I'm a chopsticks expert – Chloe's dad is Chinese, and I eat at hers all the time. His food is *so* good.

'You're embarrassing me,' he whispers, giving up and using his fork.

I can't think of a way to bring up the subject of Will Bailey, so I come right out with it while his mouth is full. 'Dad, have you heard of Will Bailey?'

He splutters and swallows. 'Sorry?'

'Have you heard of Will Bailey?' I repeat, but I said it clearly the first time.

'What, the singer?' He keeps his eyes on his food. 'Yeah, magnificent voice.'

'Did you know Mum knew him?'

His eyes dart up and bore into me. 'How do you know that?'

I knew it! 'Something she said. Did *you* know him?'

'Listen.' He wipes his mouth with a napkin, places it on the table. 'Your mum wouldn't want me talking about this.'

'Why not?'

'Well, he died, she was upset – she doesn't like talking about it.'

'Was she a groupie?'

'A *groupie*?' He scrunches his nose. 'No!'

'Were they boyfriend and girlfriend?'

'They were friends.' He blows upwards to cool his sweaty forehead. 'Wow, this is spicy.' Then he changes the subject. 'Have you thought any more about work experience?'

'Not really.' That's not exactly true – I've been stressing about it because I can't decide what to do. Chloe's doing hers with her dad because she's always wanted to be a solicitor like her parents, but I think they've brainwashed her.

17

I almost wish my parents were pushy like Chloe's; at least then I'd have a plan. All I know is I don't want a boring job in a school like Mum, and I can't even draw a decent stick man so being a designer like Dad is out.

'Remember, Tom offered for you to do it at *Luminaire*.'

Dad's friend Tom works at *Luminaire* magazine. He says they play table football all day and everyone gets free pizza on Fridays. It sounds cool but what do I know about magazines? And what's a *lifestyle* magazine anyway?

'Come on, you'll love it,' says Dad. 'It's only a fortnight.'

I sigh. 'Oh, all right then.' I wish it was a music magazine. Now *that* would be cool.

'I'll text him now.' Dad taps away at his phone then puts it on the table. We go back to shovelling food in our mouths.

I'm trying to think of a way to steer the conversation back to Will Bailey, when Dad's phone buzzes.

'Tom says he'd be delighted to have you for work experience. There you go, all sorted.'

Oh God, what have I let myself in for? I'm rubbish at table football.

Dad checks his watch. 'We'd better get going, or we'll miss the trailers.'

He pays the bill, and we head out into the cinema complex.

Inside the auditorium, the lights go down as we take our seats. He takes a handful of Maltesers and passes me the bag.

I lean in and whisper, 'Do you know how Will Bailey died?'

Dad shifts in his seat. 'I know he took his own life, but I don't know the details.'

A chill ripples through me. 'He took his own life?'

'Yeah . . . such a waste . . .'

'But why?'

The trailers start, music blaring. In the flickering light, Dad pops a Malteser into his mouth and shrugs.

Chapter 6

July 1994

Will's mum gave him a stern look as he took his seat. Aidan and his dad were already tucking in to the steaming pot of chilli at the centre of the dining table.

'What kept you?' she scolded.

'I just got off the phone with Matty,' said Will. 'He's got us a gig at the Mean Fiddler.'

Having pooled their savings and recorded a demo, Matty had delivered on his promise within two months. Who'd have thought Matty would be good at that shit?

'What's the Mean Fiddler?' she asked.

'It's a music venue in North London. The Pixies have played there, and Radiohead, and The Underdogs.'

'Never heard of them,' said his dad, piling more chilli onto his rice.

'How can you not have heard of them?' asked Will, incredulous. 'You've got the Underdogs album!'

'He only got it because he fancies Christie Blackmore,' said Aidan through a mouthful of food.

'Is *that* what her band's called?' asked Dad. 'She's a beautiful voice, that one.'

'So, when are you getting a job, Will?' said Aidan. 'If you're well enough to play gigs, you're well enough to work.'

'What's it to you?' asked Dad.

'Because it's not fair. I'm giving Mum money and Will's not. I'm paying for him to sit at home playing guitar all day. How come Golden Boy doesn't have to pay rent?'

'Firstly, the money you give me barely keeps us in toilet paper,' said Mum. 'You'd hardly call it "rent". And secondly, Will can't get a job yet – he's still recovering.'

'Not this again. He had the holiday trots – everyone gets it.'

She flicked Aidan with a tea towel. 'He was in hospital for four days!'

'He's better now!'

Will was sick of listening to them talking about him as if he wasn't there. His chair squeaked against the lino as he stood. 'I'm not hungry.'

'Is it your stomach? I shouldn't have made chilli—'

'Don't worry, Mum. I'll have some toast later.'

As he left the room, Aidan was saying something about Will's stomach only hurting when you reminded him about it.

What a fucking stirrer.

Will stormed through the kitchen to the garage.

He'd planned to spend the summer island-hopping around Greece with Matty, playing covers in the tavernas for beer money. They'd been working hard to save up, but Matty spent money faster than he could earn it, so it soon became clear Will would be going on his own. Will jacked in his supermarket and pizza restaurant jobs and flew out to Corfu earlier in the year. With only a little spending money, he needed to get plenty of gigs if he was to stay the whole season. He played one gig in a tiny beachside bar before coming down with an awful stomach bug. He felt so dreadful he couldn't get out of bed. Luckily, two guys he befriended on the first day noticed he hadn't come out of his room at the hostel. He woke in hospital on a drip. The doctors said he had a viral infection and severe dehydration. It was another week before he was well enough to travel home. It had knocked him for six and he was only just starting to feel normal three months later.

Will flicked on the lights in the garage as the door slammed behind him. Matty and Will had been friends since primary school. As teenagers they'd started a band. Will's parents had agreed to let them practise in their garage on the condition they clear it out themselves. It was hard work, and it took the first two weeks of the summer holidays when they were fourteen, but they did it and the garage hadn't changed much since. They still had the shabby leather sofa they'd rescued from a skip, the same hideous Persian rugs still covered the bare floor, but back then he only had one guitar. Now he had three, all standing to attention on their stands. He chose the Strat, took it to the sofa, and sat picking out the melody that had been haunting him lately.

They had trouble with drummers. Their current drummer, Mitch, had been with them on and off forever. He was like the girlfriend you keep getting back with, even though you know she's no good for you. Mitch never practised. He was always late for rehearsals and gigs, and he was tight. Getting him to pitch in for anything was impossible. But he had a van. And they needed a van.

Will made a mental note to give Mitch a false deadline for the Mean Fiddler gig. There was no way he'd let Mitch mess this up.

Will grabbed his headphones and a beer from the mini fridge. He'd feel better when things got loud.

*

On Sunday night, Matty picked up Will for rehearsal. They rented a unit on an industrial estate once a week. It was deserted at weekends so they could play as loud as they wanted. It stank of sweat and stale beer and the toilet was god-awful, but it was what Will lived through the week for.

21

A figure was squatting by the studio door as they pulled up.

'Who's that? That can't be Mitch already,' said Will.

'It's that skinny kid that hangs around after gigs. He helped carry the gear to the van last time.'

'Oh yeah, I said he could come along to a rehearsal. Reuben? Yeah, that's it, Reu.'

Reu jumped up, went to the boot, and started lugging out the gear. For someone so skinny, he was handy at lifting heavy amps. He said little as they unloaded the car. All they got out of him was he was almost sixteen and he'd travelled there by bus, and even that was like getting blood from a stone.

As they waited for Mitch, Reu began assembling the shabby drum kit that was scattered in pieces around the rehearsal room.

'I wouldn't bother with that, mate,' said Matty. 'Mitch brings his own kit.'

But Reu carried on fiddling and had set it up in no time.

As Will played the intro to 'Wandering', Reu joined in with the bass drum.

'That's great, Reu,' said Will. 'If you can keep time for us, we can get started.'

After a few bars, Reu began playing the rest of the kit.

'You've got sticks?' asked Will.

Reu nodded.

'You play drums?' asked Matty, laughing.

'A bit . . .'

They played three songs before Mitch arrived and Reu jumped up to unload his kit.

'Who said he could come?' whispered Mitch while Reu was at the van.

'I did. Why?' said Will.

'He drove me mad at the last gig. He must have asked a million questions.'

'Give him a break. He's helping you, isn't he?'

Every rehearsal after that, Reu arrived first and helped

them set up. He sat cross-legged in the corner, tapping away on his knees, his presence a barometer for how a session was going. The more he bobbed his head and slapped his knees, the better the song. Each week, he played drums until Mitch arrived, and every time, he revealed more of what he could do.

Chapter 7

March 2016

Emily

A pile of Post-it-covered papers is waiting on my desk. Mrs Taylor, the head teacher, looms in the doorway. 'Ah, there you are. The email for the Year Three trip needs to go out this morning – it should have gone yesterday. Good Lord, Emily,' she adds, 'couldn't you have put make-up on? You'll frighten the children.'

And she's gone without so much as a 'how are you?'

She's right though, an inky purple stain has formed at the outer corner of my right eye and the eyebrow looks like one of the reception kids glued it.

I head to the kitchen. I've been working for that witch for a decade, and if I've learned one thing, it's my day will go much better if I make her a drink. Just thinking about spitting in it gives me enough pleasure to make it unnecessary.

'I made coffee,' I say, entering her office. I do an odd little curtsey to place the drink on her desk with my stiff neck.

'Glad you're feeling well enough to join us.' She keeps her eyes on her computer screen.

I'm taken aback. 'Thank you.'

'Don't forget to give Diane your doctor's note.'

'Oh, I didn't think I'd needed a doctor's note – I was off for less than a week.'

'Speak to Diane. You'll have to fill out a form.'

'Fine,' I mutter and leave before I say something I'll regret.

Back in the office, Kay is draping her jacket on the back of her chair. She grimaces at the sight of my face. 'How are you feeling?'

'Whiplash is a pain in the neck,' I joke, but her concerned look cuts right through it.

'What happened?'

I tell her Liv distracted me by fiddling with the car stereo, that I took my eye off the road. It's not exactly true, but it's what I've been telling people.

The doorbell chimes. I go to turn my head but stop short with a yelp.

Kay looks over the counter separating our little office from the reception area. 'It's your boyfriend,' she says with a wink.

I rotate the whole chair around on its wheels to see Florence Harding's dad waiting at the glass door. I groan and buzz him in. Since Kay found out he's divorced, she's been trying to set us up. I've told her I'm not interested, but she won't listen.

'I'll go – you look horrendous,' she says, standing, but I get to the counter before her, to prove how uninterested I am.

'Morning,' I say, brightly.

'Oh my God, what happened to your face?' he blurts.

'Oh – I was in a minor car accident. It looks worse than it feels.'

'Sorry. How rude am I? It doesn't look that bad. You hardly even notice it.' He stops jabbering and takes a breath. 'Apparently, I'm supposed to hand in this form about the maths workshop.'

'I can take that for you.'

'Great. Well, I hope you're okay. Get well soon.' He flashes an awkward smile and ducks out.

Kay sighs as the door swings shut behind him. 'He'll never ask you out now. He probably thinks you're a cage fighter.'

'Ha. He'd never ask me out anyway.'

'Why do you think he comes in here every Friday afternoon?'

25

I place his form in my in-tray. 'To pick his daughter up from her guitar lesson.'

'Why do you think he gets here fifteen minutes *early* every Friday afternoon?'

I stifle a smile as I sit back at my desk. 'Because he's punctual?'

'Because he fancies you.'

'Rubbish.'

*

After lunch, a boy from Year One is brought to the office looking peaky. Before I have time to call his mum, he projectile-vomits up the filing cabinet and it takes half an hour to clean up the mess.

The rest of the day drags. I stare out of the window. A gust of wind whips up a crisp packet and carries it across the playground. I used to love watching Liv playing out there when she was little. I took this job so I could spend the school holidays with her, but seeing her from my desk, knowing she was safe, was the best part. Christ knows why I'm still here, Liv left for secondary school four years ago.

I've been doodling teardrop shapes all over the page of my notebook. Large ones, small ones, some with scalloped edges, others filled with ever-decreasing duplicates. A nagging feeling tugs at my attention, then I remember. Cold dread washes over me. My limbs are heavy, weighing me down, and I fight to suppress the sob rising in my throat.

I know what to do. This used to happen all the time. *Breathe, just breathe.* I drag myself up and somehow make it to the ladies' loo. Locking myself in a cubicle, I sit and cover my face with my hands, but in the darkness his face emerges, and it's excruciating. I count my breaths like they taught us in yoga class. When I reach a hundred, the panic fades, but I count to a hundred again to be sure. As I open the door, I

26

glimpse the woman in the mirror and wonder if she has the strength to do this again.

*

Thursday is parents' evening – my least favourite day of the year. I sound like a broken record saying *Hello, what class are you here for?* every five minutes. My voice was chirpy earlier this afternoon, but it's becoming more of a squawk as the evening wears on.

Figures gather at the glass door. Florence Harding's dad is among them with his ex. He holds the door open for a group of parents while his ex comes over to check in. She doesn't make eye contact the whole time we speak and strides off to greet a friend without saying 'thank you'.

Mr Harding hangs back until everyone is signed in, then clears his throat and steps forward. 'Hi.'

'Hello. You're a bit early. Miss White has got one more before you.'

He nods but stays put. 'Your eye's healing nicely. You can hardly see it now,' he says. 'I'm still mortified by what I said the other day.'

'Oh, don't worry. That was nothing compared to what the children said.'

'Can I buy you a coffee sometime? To say sorry.'

Heat flashes to my cheeks. 'Oh, I—'

'Miss Lawrence!' barks Mrs Taylor, suddenly at my side. 'Sorry to interrupt but I need your help with something.'

'Now?'

'No, no. Pop to my office when everyone's gone.'

'At seven-thirty?'

'Shouldn't take long. You're such a whiz at PowerPoint.' She turns and heads back to her office.

Mr Harding arches an eyebrow. Either he's surprised at my PowerPoint genius or he's waiting for me to answer his question. 'Mizz Lawrence,' he says, imitating Mrs T. 'I can see now isn't a good time. Have a think about it. I'll pop back and see you after this.' He smiles. He has nice teeth.

There are more parents coming in behind him. 'Hello, what class are you here for?'

I deal with a flurry of arrivals and before I know it, the bell rings and the parents from Mr Harding's time slot are filing out of the hall. I haven't worked out what I'm going to say yet. Florence's mum sashays towards the exit. She stops in front of me and waits for him to catch up.

'So, you're picking her up at six tomorrow. Don't be late,' she says and strides off.

Out of the corner of his mouth he tells me, 'I'm never late.'

I laugh.

'So, coffee?' he asks.

'Well . . .' I begin, 'sorry, I don't even know your name . . .'

'Harding, Will Harding,' he says in a James Bond voice. 'And your name's Emily, right?'

His name is Will.

I lose my train of thought. He's waiting for me to confirm my name, which makes me look crazy. 'Yes, Emily. How did you—'

'Your colleague in the office told me.'

I squirm in my seat. 'Right.'

'And it's at the bottom of the emails you send out.'

'Of course . . .'

'So, coffee Emily?'

I was almost going to say yes. What was I thinking? 'Thanks for the offer,' I say. 'But I'm with someone actually . . .'

His eyebrows slide towards each other. He's confused or annoyed. 'Oh? Your colleague told me you were single.'

'I am, well I was. It's just . . . it wouldn't be a good idea. You know, not very . . . professional.'

'O-kaaay.' He's annoyed, definitely annoyed.

'I'm flattered,' I say. 'It's just difficult at the moment—'

'You don't need to explain.' He smiles, but this time it's gone in an instant. 'See you around.'

*

The house is dark and silent when I arrive home.

'Li-iv!' I sing.

I take off my jacket and hang it on a peg by the door.

'Liv?'

No answer.

I check my phone. No messages, no missed calls.

I dial her number; it goes to voicemail.

I send her a text: **Where are you? Call me.**

I open the fridge. The food I left for her is still there. I open the cupboard. The packet of caramel wafers is still unopened – a sure sign she hasn't been home. My heart rate accelerates.

I call Chloe but she hasn't seen her.

I call Scott, but he's not heard from our daughter either. 'Don't panic,' he says. 'She's probably at a friend's and lost track of time.'

My phone pings. 'Wait, I've got a text . . .'

I put him on speaker and read the message aloud, '"At a friend's – leaving now". Scott, I'll call you back.'

I cut him off and dial Liv. It goes to voicemail again.

'Call me now!' I shout at the phone.

Liv: **Reception is terrible. I'm in Surbiton, around the corner from the dentist. I'll get the bus, there's one every 11 minutes. See you soon x.**

Me: **DO NOT get the bus! Send me the address. I'll come and get you.**

By the time she replies, I'm already driving towards the dentist in the company car Scott lent me after the crash. I pull over to read it.

Liv: **27 Windsor Ave**

*

29

Windsor Avenue is a smart row of Victorian houses lined with beech trees. Number 27 has little lollipop-shaped bay trees on either side of the front door. I text to tell Liv I'm outside.

The door opens. Liv comes out and waves. She turns and says something to her friend, a boy so tall he fills the entire doorway. What the hell? He looks about twenty. He raises his hand in farewell and shuts the door as Liv skips down the stairs and over to the car.

She gets in, shoving her rucksack into the footwell. 'I thought you were going for a drink with Kay after parents' evening?'

'Who was that?'

'Oh, that's Nathan. We were working on a biology project.'

That old chestnut. 'How old is he?'

'Same age as me. He's in my science class.'

'What's going on, Olivia? You can't go off without telling me.'

She shrugs. 'It was a last-minute decision. You were working late and then out with Kay, so I knew you wouldn't worry.'

'It's not about me worrying, it's about you being safe. I don't want you getting the bus at this hour on your own.' My neck smarts as I check over my shoulder before driving off.

'It's not that dark yet. It's no different to me getting the bus after school.'

'There are fewer people around. And don't argue with me,' I say, heat creeping into my voice. 'The rules are: you tell me where you're going, and you answer the phone when I ring.'

'I told you the reception was—'

'For God's sake, Liv! Stop answering back!' I'm exhausted and hungry.

Liv stares out of the window, giving me the silent treatment the whole way home.

Chapter 8

September 1994

Despite giving Mitch a false deadline for the Mean Fiddler gig, he was still late picking them up in his van. When they couldn't wait any longer, they got going in Matty's mum's car. It was a twenty-minute game of Tetris getting both guitars and amps in the back and Reu had to go ahead on the tube. They got caught in traffic, then got lost trying to bypass it and arrived forty minutes late for their sound check.

Reu was waiting in the loading area looking sheepish when they parked.

'What's the matter?' asked Will.

'They wouldn't let me in.'

'Why not?'

'I don't have ID.'

Matty sniggered. 'Okay, don't worry, we'll smuggle you in the back way with the gear. Keep your head down.'

Reu carried both guitars, while Matty and Will hefted the amps. They dumped their gear near the stage where a band was doing their sound check. The singer's voice was a grating screech.

'Wait here,' said Will and headed for the sound desk.

He loitered by the sound engineer until there was a break in the racket and said, 'Sorry we're late. We're on first.'

31

The guy didn't even look up from the knobs and sliders. 'You missed your slot, mate.'

Will's heart sank. 'Ah, man – come on, we're only a few minutes late.'

The band struck up again putting an end to the conversation.

What the hell were they going to do? He'd always dreamed of playing this venue and now they were here they might have to turn around and go home again.

Will scanned the place for inspiration, spotted the bar, and had an idea.

'Do you know what the sound guy drinks?' he asked the barman.

'Andy? He drinks Guinness.'

'Pint of Guinness, then please.'

Will took the pint and waved it in front of Andy. 'Andy, can you squeeze us in? Please?'

Andy hesitated then accepted the drink. 'I'll try to fit you in after this lot, but I'm not promising anything.'

Will waited until Andy had taken a sip. 'I don't suppose you have a house drum kit, do you?'

Andy choked mid-swallow. 'You don't have a drum kit?' he asked, wiping his chin.

'We do, it's just . . . delayed.'

'No, we don't have a fucking house kit. You'll have to ask these guys if you can borrow theirs.'

On stage, two band members were locked in a vicious argument. Will didn't fancy his chances of getting them to share.

The doors from the loading area swung open and the headline band dragged in their gear. Will gave them a minute, then sidled up to the one who looked most like a drummer. 'You're Space Pirates, aren't you?'

'Space *Junkies,* actually.'

'You're the drummer,' Will ventured.

'Yeah.'

One out of two – not bad. 'Any chance we can borrow your kit?'

'Fuck off!'

Will slumped into a seat at the table where Matty and Reu were waiting. 'The Space Junkies won't let us borrow their kit.'

'Let me try,' said Reu.

Reu walked up to the drummer and started talking. Whatever Reu was saying made him nod and smile. Then they *high-fived*. Matty and Will exchanged looks.

Reu returned a few minutes later, grinning. 'He's gonna let us use it.'

'How come?' asked Will.

'I've been to a few of their gigs. I remembered stuff about his kit and the rolls he does. And I flattered him a bit.'

'Reu, you genius!' Matty gave Reu a playful punch on the arm. 'Ah, look, there's Mitch.'

Mitch was marching towards them, brow creased. 'Where the fuck were you?' he spat.

'Where the fuck were *you*?' replied Will.

'I went to your house – no one was there!'

'You were meant to be there at four – we waited ages for you.'

'You don't need *that* long to get here. It's only twelve miles!' Mitch noticed Reu standing beside Will. 'What's he doing here? Were you going to get him to play instead of me?'

'No. Reu helped with the gear, but he'd have played if we needed him to.'

'You back-stabbing bastards . . .'

'If we'd waited for you, we'd be off the bill,' said Matty.

'It's always you two against me. I'm fucking sick of it! Let him play, see how that goes. I hope you bomb tonight – at your precious Mean Fiddler. Shame there's no one here to see it.' He knocked into Reu on his way to the door.

33

'Looks like you're up, Reu,' said Matty.

All the colour drained from Reu's face.

*

Considering their new line-up, Will shortened the set list and put the songs Reu was most comfortable with first – they'd have to wing the rest. Andy didn't give them long to sound check and it sounded rubbish, and despite rushing to get there, they still had to wait a full hour before performing. They sat there hardly talking, nervous energy buzzing in the air between them.

'I just spoke to one of the Space Junkies,' said Matty after a trip to the gents. 'He told me they've got an A&R man from Island Records coming tonight,'

'Wow,' said Will. 'They must be good.'

'What's an A&R man?' asked Reu.

'Artists and repertoire,' explained Will. 'They're basically scouts for record companies.'

'Let's hope they come early enough to see us play, eh?' Matty rubbed his hands together.

Reu stood, clamped his hand over his mouth, and ran off to the gents.

*

Will's heart kicked hard against his ribs as he climbed onto the stage. He laid the set list down next to his pedals, straightened up, and squinted through the lights. People were still arriving, greeting friends, ordering drinks. He hated being the first act.

Reu was still a little pale as he sat at the Space Junkies' drum kit. Will gave him an encouraging wink and turned to his microphone.

'Hi, I'm Will Bailey, and this one's called "Fever"!'

Reu gave them more than a basic beat. He played it almost exactly the way Mitch would have. Will had given Reu a demo tape; he must have been listening to it, practising even – which was more than Mitch ever did. This might be okay.

'Fever' only got a smattering of applause, and the pause between songs made the conversations seem louder.

He had been looking forward to this gig for weeks, and what with all the drama of getting here and Mitch dropping them in it, it couldn't end with no one listening.

He turned to Matty, 'Let's do the acoustic version of "Satisfaction".'

Matty nodded.

'Reu, sit this one out.'

Reu's shoulders sagged with relief.

People continued chatting as they played the intro to the Stones song, but they got a few sporadic whoops when Will sang the first line. He hated playing cover versions, but they always grabbed an audience's attention, and it wasn't so bad if you put your own creative spin on it. Tonight was no exception – by the first chorus, people began shushing each other, and by the second, some were even singing along. When the song finished, the applause was much livelier.

But people kept arriving throughout their set. Even his brother was late. Aidan sauntered in with a girl and left her watching the stage while he went to the bar.

Just then, Reu missed his timing coming out of a roll, and it was painful there for a few bars, but once he recovered, he upped his game and came back stronger than before. His energy rubbed off on Will and Matty. The crowd was with them now and there were moments, just one or two, where it felt like he'd always dreamed it would.

They finished the set with their latest song. It was rough around the edges, but it got the biggest applause of the night.

'Thank you!' Will yelled over the cheers. 'We've got Matty on bass!' Matty raised his hand. 'And stepping in for us at the last minute, give it up for Reu on drums!'

The boy gave a bashful nod.

'I'm Will Bailey. Thank you and goodnight!'

Sweaty and thirsty, they made their way to the bar and ordered a round of drinks. Aidan joined them, shook Matty's hand, and slapped Will on the shoulder.

'Love the new song,' he said.

'Cheers,' said Will.

Aidan came to all his gigs. He often showed up late, but he never failed to make an appearance. Complimenting him on a song was new, though. What had him in such a good mood?

Aidan stepped aside to introduce the girl he'd brought along. 'Will, this is Emily. Emily – Will.'

It was the girl from the station.

The girl he guessed must be an art student.

The girl that got off the train at 17:18 every Wednesday.

He should say something, not stand there with his mouth open. Aidan hadn't mentioned her since he got her number. Will assumed nothing had come of it. But here she was, all these months later, with Aidan's arm around her waist.

'That was brilliant!' she gushed.

'Thanks . . .'

'As soon as I heard your voice, I recognised it – I've seen you busking at the station.'

'Yeah . . .'

She turned to Aidan, put her hand on his forearm. 'I saw him get arrested.'

The familiarity of that touch, the *intimacy* of it, left him burning all over.

36

Chapter 9

March 2016

Liv

I love waking up in my room at Dad's every other weekend. The best thing is the display of my favourite vinyl album covers on a narrow shelf running around the room. I've got a turntable here too. There's nothing like the crackle of the needle hitting the groove, that rich sound filling the room – you can really feel the music. I've got all the records in the world on my phone, but when I love an album, it gets a special place on the shelf. I need to add Will Bailey's *Fragments*.

I pad downstairs in my dressing gown. Dad has left a note on the kitchen counter: *Gone for a run. I'll make bacon sandwiches when I get back x.*

Dad's place is all glass and dark leather, no wires or handles showing. Mum's house is cosier, homelier, messier. I'd go mad living here all the time – it's way too tidy. Rain hammers on the glass doors, the patio is quickly turning into a swimming pool. I wonder if Dad has the Will Bailey album. Mum doesn't have any records or CDs, she never listens to music. There's a radio in the kitchen but she only puts it on when we go out, so burglars think we're in. I open the cabinet by the TV and run my finger along the spines. He doesn't have a CD player anymore, but he kept limited editions and box sets. They're organised in alphabetical order. One CD

37

has a thinner spine: it must be a single or an EP. I pull it out – it's Will Bailey's *Yellow Feathers*. The cover is a photograph of a beautiful sculpture made from yellow and gold objects. Jewels, beads, flowers, and feathers spiral outwards in a circle. It's mesmerising.

I turn it over and read the track listing, four songs: 'Yellow Feathers', a live version of the same song, 'Innocent' and 'Roo'. The small print at the bottom says: *Cover image: Eos by Emily Lawrence.*

Oh my God – Mum.

I take pictures of the cover and the small print and send them straight to Chloe. She replies in a second: Whaaat?! Your mum MADE that?

Me: Who knew?

A shout from the front of the house makes me jump.

Slipping the CD into the pocket of my dressing gown, I go to the hall. The front door is wide open, and Dad is soaked to his skin holding a quad stretch under the dripping porch.

'Oh, you got wet,' I say sarcastically.

'Ha, ha. Can you get me a towel, please?'

I run upstairs and come back with a towel.

He pats himself down and kicks off his trainers, then stepping inside, he opens his soggy arms out to me. 'Come here, give me a hug.'

'No way.'

'Don't make me come and get you.'

'No Dad, seriously, *do not* hug me!'

I back away, and when he pounces, I'm ready. He's right behind me as I run into the living room, his wet feet squeaking on the hardwood floor. I put the dining table between us, and he mirrors me as I feint left, then right. He makes the deciding move, and I try to run, but it's awkward behind the table and he grabs me with his damp, freezing hands.

He clamps me to his clammy chest and rubs his wet cheek against mine. I squeal, 'Get off!'

I try to drop out of his grasp, but he follows me down, lowering me to the ground. The CD clunks on the floor as he tickles me until I'm gasping for air. He gives me a moment to catch my breath, then renews the attack. The CD clatters again as I kick him off.

'What's that?' he asks, helping me to my feet.

I pull the CD from my pocket, and he recognises it immediately.

'I haven't got a CD player, you know,' he says, walking away, leaving a trail of damp footprints.

I follow. 'Did you know Mum did this artwork? Her name's on the back.'

'Yeah, she made that at college. It was this big.' He spreads his arms out. 'It took ages.'

I knew they studied art together at college, but I assumed she wasn't any good – Dad runs his own design agency, but Mum works in the office at my old primary school.

I place the CD on the counter. 'But this is really good.'

'She was brilliant, so talented, far better than me. She had her own exhibition at a gallery before she'd even finished the course.'

'Why did she stop doing it then?'

He hesitates. 'Well, you showed up and after that, she was busy being a mum.'

'Oh.' My brain is whirring at a hundred miles an hour. My mum was friends with a rock star, *and* she was a talented artist – how did I not know this? I don't know her at all.

He pours a glass of water and drinks it all in one go. 'Listen Liv, don't mention this to Mum.'

'Why not?'

'This whole thing with Will Bailey . . .' He picks up the CD. 'She's sensitive about it. Sometimes you never really get over these things. Curb your curiosity – for her, will you? Promise me?'

'But I just want to know—'

'You're lucky, you've never lost anyone. You don't know what it's like. Grief can be hard, Liv. Don't ask her about this, okay?'

I want to argue with him but he's giving me his puppy-dog eyes and they're his ultimate superpower. 'Okay . . .'

'Thank you.' He kisses my forehead, takes the CD, and puts it back in the cabinet.

Chapter 10

September 1994

Will had been lying in bed for hours but sleep would not come. The events of that night were stuck on repeat in his head: Mitch dropping them in it, Reu throwing up, that final round of applause. But the image of Aidan with Emily was the most persistent. How long had they been seeing each other? What were they doing right now?

He switched on the bedside lamp, reached for his jeans, and felt in the pockets. He panicked for a moment thinking he'd lost it but there it was in the last pocket he checked.

A business card:

Richard Eason
A&R Co-ordinator

Island Records

When the Space Junkies came off stage, Will bought them a drink to thank them for lending their kit. Their set had been great. It was no surprise they had A&R interest. Even though the Space Junkies bought their fair share of drinks, Will still ended up spending a fortune.

When they were packing up their gear, a guy in a leather biker jacket came up to Will and, pressing the card into Will's hand, said, 'Let me know when you're playing again.' He left before Will had a chance to respond.

Matty and Reu had gawped at the card when he'd shown them. The realisation of what it meant sent them into a wild, whooping frenzy until the bouncer recognised Reu from earlier and kicked them out because he was underage.

Will held the card in his hand now, turning it over and over, his thoughts still jumping around as the sun came up. They needed a decent gig in London if they wanted to invite Richard Eason along. And they needed a drummer. Oh, and a van.

He'd spent the last of his Greece savings last night. He was officially skint, so he also needed a job.

At 6:30 a.m., he gave up trying to sleep. He got up and went to the newsagent to pick up the local paper. Walking back up the path to the house, he checked Aidan's bedroom window. The curtains were closed. Was Aidan in there? Was he alone? He'd been staying out a lot lately. Will knew why now.

Inside, he combed the job section while the kettle boiled. By the time he drank his coffee he'd circled three jobs – all involved driving a van. He waited until office hours opened to make the calls. By 10 a.m. he'd secured an interview at a local printing company.

The interview was with a man called Nigel, who took a hands-on approach to every aspect of his printing business. Once Nigel confirmed personal use of the company van was allowed, Will agreed to a three-month trial starting Monday.

*

Will lay soaking in the bath on Monday evening, his muscles complaining about all the lifting he'd done on his first day in the job. He must have nodded off because he awoke with a start to thumping on the bathroom door. He squeaked upright.

'Oi! Stop hogging the bathroom, you selfish git!' came Aidan's voice through the door. 'Some of us have places to go!'

Will sank back into the tepid water. 'Twat.'

He hadn't seen Aidan since the Mean Fiddler gig, so despite not wanting to vacate the bathroom for him, he hauled himself out of the tub. He wanted to talk to him before he disappeared again.

Wrapped in a towel, with what he hoped was a nonchalant air, he leant against Aidan's bedroom doorframe and said, 'Emily seems nice.'

'Yeah, gorgeous, isn't she?' Aidan was forming a pile of dirty clothes on the floor, no doubt to give to their mum.

'Is she that barmaid from the pub?'

Aidan threw a sock onto the pile. 'Yeah, she's a student. She works there two nights a week.'

'How long have you been seeing her?'

'Dunno. A while.'

'So, you called her straight after that night at the pub?'

Aidan picked up a t-shirt, smelt the armpits. 'Pretty much. What's this, twenty questions?'

'Just making conversation.'

'Stop being so bloody nosy,' said Aidan. 'Listen, I just told Mum, I'm moving out.'

'Really? When?' Was he moving in with her?

'Rob and I are renting a flat in Cowley.'

Will breathed a sigh of relief. 'Poor Rob.'

Will remembered Aidan teaching him the alphabet from the top bunk bed in this room. Will thrusting his feet into the mattress above to the rhythm of their chanting, wobbling Aidan with every letter. It was the end of an era.

Chapter 11

March 2016

Emily

I'm dreading Friday afternoon, and it arrives sooner than ever. Florence Harding's dad (as he will forever be known) arrives later than usual to collect his daughter from her guitar lesson. He doesn't say 'hello' when I buzz him in, and he takes the furthest seat from the counter. Kay squirms in her chair. She was only trying to do me a favour, setting me up with a handsome single guy, and I'd thrown it back in her face. The ticking of the clock on the wall is deafening. I should apologise, try to explain. I can't sit through this every Friday. Kay's eyes are on me as I stand and go through to the waiting area.

Mr Harding looks up from his phone as I take the seat next to him. 'Let me explain—' He goes to interrupt, but I continue, 'Please?'

He nods.

'Kay was telling the truth. I *am* single, but I've been single for a long time, so I panicked. Sorry for the mixed messages.'

'It's only coffee.' His tone is kind.

'I know. I don't know why I made a big deal out of it.'

'Does that mean you've changed your mind?'

'Well . . . no, but . . .'

'Look, why don't we swap numbers and if you change your mind, you can drop me a message? No pressure, okay?'

'Okay.'

He brings up a new message on his phone and I tell him my number. He types something, and my phone pings back at my desk.

'Ms Lawrence!' booms Mrs Taylor from behind the counter, making me jump out of my skin. 'Can I see you in my office? Now. Please.'

My cheeks flush. How long has she been standing there? I hate the way she adds 'please' as an afterthought. It's worse than not saying it at all.

Mr Harding whispers, 'God, it's like being at *school*!'

I stifle a chuckle, but Mrs T's eyes are burning holes in me, so I get up saying, 'Well, I hope that explains the process.'

I scurry off to follow Mrs T to her office. She sits behind her desk but doesn't invite me to.

'That's the second time I have caught you *flirting* with that man in school—'

I can't believe what I'm hearing. 'Excuse me?'

'May I remind you school is not a place to organise your social life, neither is it a dating agency.'

'I—'

'I will not have my staff *carrying on* with parents.'

'I was just explaining—'

'You can stop there,' she says in a tone usually reserved for disobedient boys. 'I heard you giving him your personal telephone number.'

I don't know what to say.

'You leave me no option but to issue you with a verbal warning,' she adds.

'A verbal warning? For giving someone my telephone number?'

'It's not just that. Ever since the car accident, your conduct has been questionable.'

'What do you mean "questionable"?'

She counts on her fingers. 'Taking excessive sick days, countless physio appointments, talking to me in a disrespectful tone, flirting with a parent, *at school*, when you're supposed to be working. It's simply unprofessional.'

I stand there, my mouth flapping, and as I go to speak, she's talking over me again.

'If I don't see real improvements in your conduct over the coming weeks, the next step will be a written warning.'

My heartbeat pounds in my ears. 'I've worked with you for ten years and you're giving me a verbal warning?'

'You leave me no choice.'

'Well . . . you leave *me* no choice.'

She raises her spindly drawn-on eyebrows.

'You can stick your verbal warning,' I tell her, my voice trembling. 'And you can stick your job.'

Her mouth falls open.

'You're nothing but a bully, and it's about time someone stood up to you.' I whip around and stride to the door.

'You're fired!' she calls after me.

I hesitate in the doorway, then turn back. 'Too late,' I tell her. 'Weren't you listening? I already quit.'

I slam the door behind me.

*

As soon as I get in the house, I kick off my shoes and head straight for the fridge. The soft glug of wine from bottle to glass soothes my raw nerves, and when the first gulp hits my stomach, my shoulders sag.

'Fuck,' I say aloud, knowing Liv is at Chloe's.

I sit at the kitchen table and cover my face with my hands. I stare into the darkness of my palms, replaying the entire conversation in my mind, wincing at every embarrassing detail.

How the hell am I going to pay the mortgage?

It'll be okay. I'll get another job. People get new jobs all the time.

By the time I've drained the second glass of wine, my thoughts become blurry at the edges. Who stays in the same job for ten years? That's not normal. It's time for a change.

My phone pings.

Kay: **Where did you go? What happened?**

I don't know how to even begin to explain.

Then I spot the unread message Florence Harding's dad left earlier: **Whenever you're ready.**

He signed it with a coffee cup emoji.

I groan.

My neck is killing me. It's been bothering me since the crash, but now it's throbbing, and it keeps locking up. It must be from holding my shoulders tense the whole way home.

I pop the heat pad in the microwave and set the timer. Liv's laptop is charging on the counter. We had an online safety workshop at school the other day; the speaker said to check your child's search history regularly. Now's the time to check it, while she's not around. As I wait for the laptop to fire up, the microwave pings. I retrieve the heat pad, drape it around my shoulders, and settle at the table with the laptop and another glass of wine. I navigate to the browser history and scroll through the list.

All the homework-related searches are interspersed with questions about bands or song lyrics. I knew it – she can't focus on her studies if she's listening to music. She says it helps her concentrate, but clearly, it's a distraction. Scrolling further, I find searches on 'how to do a messy bun' and 'how to use tightliner' – whatever that is. I'm intrigued. Liv's not a girly girl. Is this because Nathan Hall's on the scene?

I'm finishing up when at the bottom of the list I spot 'Will Bailey – Rare Radio Interview 1997'.

Seeing his name sets my heart pounding. Liv asked so many questions after the crash I should have known she wouldn't drop the subject.

My finger hovers over the track pad. I have an overwhelming twisted desire to hear his voice. Even as I click, I'm willing myself not to. An image flashes up on the screen, and it's so loaded with memories I screw my eyes shut to block it out. But it's no good. It hangs in my mind as though burned into my retinas. I know every part of that picture: the relaxed pose, the dark of the room, and the light on his face.

I know because I took that photograph.

I remember that day; I remember the weather; I remember what I was wearing. It seems like yesterday and a lifetime ago all at once. Tears come despite my tightly closed eyes. When I finally open them, blinking, all that's in focus through the tears is the play button. I don't know why, but I *have* to press it. I brace myself as a female voice says, 'Now I'm joined by Will Bailey ahead of his gig at the Roundhouse tonight.' There's a smattering of applause and she continues. 'Hi Will, thanks for joining us.'

He says one word, 'Hello—'

I slam the laptop shut and shatter into a million pieces.

Chapter 12

March 2016

Liv

Mum calls from downstairs, 'Liv! Package for you!'

I race down the stairs and snatch the padded envelope from her.

'What is it?' she asks.

'Flash cards. For revision.'

'I'm popping to Sainsbury's. Lock the door behind me and don't answer the door to anyone.' She always says that when she leaves the house.

'Okay, bye.' I shut the door, turn the lock, and mutter, 'I'm not *five*.'

Through the window in the hall, I watch Mum get into the company car Dad lent us after the crash. As soon as she's gone, I tear open the package. It's the *Yellow Feathers* EP I ordered online. There's a small scratch on the plastic case but otherwise it's in good condition considering it's twenty years old. Dad put his copy back in the cabinet, but the next time I checked, it was gone. Well, I have my own copy now and I can look at it whenever I want. I tuck it back in the envelope.

I've been waiting for Mum to go out so I could look through the old photos. It was Chloe's idea, she thought I might find something that connects Mum to Will Bailey. I go to the cupboard in the lounge and drag the box out. I haven't looked in here for years. The first wallet is filled with photos of me on my second birthday, the next contains pictures of me at the zoo when I was about four. I go through all the packets. All the photos are of me. My grandparents pop up and so does Dad, but there are hardly any photos of Mum. I find one of her with me as a toddler. She's crouched beside me in a pile of autumn leaves, beaming at me in my little red wellies with total adoration.

I lift the flap on the next packet, they're Christmas pictures but they're old. When I slide them out, I don't recognise anyone in the top photo. Digital numerals glow in the bottom right-hand corner: '25/12/94'. I flip to the next picture and there's Mum. She's about the same age as in the Glastonbury video. She's wearing a big fluffy roll neck with a velvet mini skirt; her long legs are clad in thick black tights. She looks elegant, like a fashion model, sitting on a sofa beside a handsome man I don't recognise, bundles of screwed-up wrapping paper at their feet. She extends her arm towards the camera, showing a bracelet. Was it a gift? The man's hand is clamped around her upper arm, pulling her towards him. Who is this guy?

I pull out my phone and play the Glastonbury video again. I find the point where the girl is dancing in tiny denim shorts and a cool waistcoat, long strings of beads swinging at her neck. She looks bohemian, chic. It's obviously the same person but I don't get it. Mum only wears boring black jeans. I was with her the last time she went shopping. She bought the same top in five different colours, so she wouldn't have to decide what to wear to work every day. I've never seen her wear any kind of accessory. Chloe always borrows her mum's clothes – I wouldn't be seen dead in my mum's.

I shuffle to the next photo. The couple are sitting in the same place, but this time they're kissing. This wider shot shows people sitting either side of them. Everyone is smiling at the couple, except one guy. He has longish brown hair. Could that be Will Bailey? He looks like him but it's a profile shot, and I can't be sure.

I hear Mum's key scraping in the lock. She can't be back already. Or maybe I've been so engrossed I didn't realise how long I've been sitting here.

Quickly, I put the pack of Christmas photos to one side and shove the box back in the cupboard. Jumping up, I scan the bookcase for an alibi.

Plastic bags rustle and the front door slams. 'Liv!' she calls from the hallway.

'Yeah?'

She pauses in the doorway with three overflowing shopping bags in each hand. 'Will you help me put this lot away?'

'Can't,' I say, holding up a dictionary. 'Revision.'

She tuts and shuffles off to the kitchen. I tuck the photos inside the envelope with the CD, grab the dictionary and head upstairs.

At my desk, I sneak another peek at the photos. It's weird seeing my mum kissing a stranger – kissing anyone. Then it hits me: Mum has never had a boyfriend. Dad has had loads of girlfriends, but Mum has never been involved with anyone romantically.

My parents aren't divorced or anything. They never split up because they were never together – in a relationship, I mean. I remember when Maisy Morgan's parents got divorced in Year Two it made me wonder if Mum and Dad were divorced too. 'Divorce' seemed such a scary word. I was relieved when Mum said they weren't. She said families come in all shapes and sizes. I didn't think much more of it until I was a little older and Bella Thompson suggested I was a mistake. I didn't really understand what that meant. I don't think Bella did either, but she had older twin brothers, so I guess that word cropped up a lot. When I asked Mum about it, she said there's a difference between 'unplanned' and 'unwanted'. Yes, I was unplanned, but it was a wonderful surprise, like getting a present when it's not even your birthday or Christmas.

And I've never *felt* unwanted. Both my parents' lives revolve around me, and we seem much happier than a lot of families I know. Beyond that, I didn't question it. It's all I've ever known.

But looking at these pictures, I'm curious about the whole thing again. They obviously had sex at least once but why weren't they ever a couple? And why doesn't Mum have relationships? Maybe she does, but keeps it secret? But she never goes out. She never does anything. The only time she does anything, she does it with me. She's so boring . . . so *uninspiring*. Unlike Chloe's mum, with her high-powered solicitor job, the glamorous charity galas she organises, and her excellent taste in shoes. I want an interesting job. I want to travel, go places, *do* things. I don't want to be one of those women whose lives revolve around their kids. I don't want to end up like Mum.

But this woman, the one in the photograph, the one in the video at Glastonbury, the one who had her own art exhibition before she even graduated . . . Now, *she's* interesting and I want to get to know her.

Chapter 13

December 1994

Festive tunes were playing on the radio when Will climbed into Aidan's car on Christmas morning. The whole family usually travelled to Oxfordshire together on Christmas Eve to stay with his uncle, but this year, Will and Aidan had to work. Their parents thought Aidan was being generous when he offered to give Will a lift, but Will knew he only wanted someone to go halves on the petrol.

This year Emily was joining them. Will was excited to spend three days in her company, but the thought of her being anywhere near Aidan turned his stomach. Aidan honked the horn as they pulled up outside her house.

'I bet her parents love it when you do that,' said Will.

'They're not in now. I'm not *that* rude.'

As Emily emerged from the house, Will hopped out to give her the front seat.

She kissed his cheek. 'Merry Christmas.'

He caught a hint of her perfume. 'Merry Christmas.'

He took her Mary Poppins bag to the boot, and as he slammed it shut, he saw them kissing through the rear windscreen. He loitered for a moment before getting into the back of the car.

As they set off, 'Winter Wonderland' came on the radio.

'I love this one!' Emily said and began singing along. She turned to Will. 'Come on – you're the singer around here!' So, he joined in. Aidan didn't sing, he just smiled at her with his hand on her thigh.

Traffic was light, and the journey that seemed endless to him as a kid passed in a flash. When they pulled up, every inch of their uncle's house was covered in coloured lights, as it was every year.

Sixteen guests sat down for Christmas lunch, the dining table extended with a wobbly trestle table usually reserved for DIY. As guest of honour, Emily was given a proper dining chair beside Aidan, while Will sat opposite them on the same low stool he'd sat on as a child. The room was loud and hot, with everyone talking over each other, pulling crackers, and calling out the jokes. He'd always loved their big Irish family Christmases, but this year, he wished he was elsewhere.

After lunch, the family gathered in the sitting room to exchange gifts. Emily opened her present from Aidan – a simple gold bracelet. She was thrilled, kissing him on the lips in front of everyone. Aidan fastened the clasp, and she held out her arm for his aunt to take a photograph.

It didn't suit her style at all.

Will remembered all the times in this very room Aidan had whinged about Will's toys, never satisfied with his own. His parents would make them share, knowing Aidan would soon lose interest once he got his way. Aidan had only got Emily's number because he noticed Will looking at her. How long before he tired of her?

Emily had bought presents for everyone.

When she handed him his gift, he felt terrible. 'I didn't get you anything . . .'

'Don't be silly.' She waved a hand. 'It's only little.'

The parcel was indeed small, wrapped in white tissue paper and tied with red and white striped string. She watched as he opened it, revealing three tortoiseshell plectrums with varying patterns and colours. They were beautiful.

'I think they're vintage,' she said.

Turning them over in his hands, he wondered who might have used them, what music they might have played. He looked up. She was waiting for his response but the thought of her choosing a gift for him and finding something so perfect threw him and all he could manage was a quiet: 'Thank you.'

He held her in his gaze, and she let him. For a beat longer than he expected.

Later, the younger people took the dog for a walk by torchlight in the country lanes. They played parlour games into the evening until the older generation began dozing on the sofa and local family members headed home.

Will played a game of Monopoly with Aidan and Emily that went on long after everyone else had gone to bed. Aidan's speech was slurred by the time he cheated his way to victory. He stood up to celebrate, but stumbled and fell to the floor in a shower of banknotes. They hauled him up from where he was wedged between two dining chairs and had to support him up the stairs.

When they dropped him onto the bed, he fell asleep immediately. Will helped wrestle him out of his jeans, groaning in disgust while Emily giggled at Aidan's ability to sleep through the whole episode.

They stood looking at Aidan lying in his underwear on the bed, snoring.

'Night cap?' Will asked.

Emily sighed. 'Okay. One more.'

She padded silently down the stairs behind him. The kitchen was lit only by the small light over the hob and the fairy lights in the window, giving the room a warm, festive glow. They perused the display of spirits on the counter.

'What do you fancy?' he asked.

She selected a bottle. 'Gin and tonic, please.'

'Coming right up.'

She leant against the counter while he fetched a couple of glasses and filled them with ice. He found the tonic in the fridge. 'Slice of lemon?' he asked.

'Lime if you have it.'

He plucked a lime from the fruit bowl and cut a slice on the chopping board beside her.

'Here.' She took the lime from him. 'Wedges are better.'

'I forgot. You're the expert at this,' he said, relinquishing the knife.

She was as close as you can get without touching. Warmth radiated from her.

'I was hoping to get the night off,' she joked. She sliced a wedge and ran it around the rim of the glass. 'Gives a nice *zing* when you sip.'

'Aidan said you're a student,' he said, passing the gin. 'What are you studying?'

She unscrewed the cap, poured them both a generous shot. 'I just started an art foundation course in London.'

'Oh cool. How's it going?'

'I love it.' She topped the drinks up with tonic.

'You must have been on a different course when I used to see you at the station, then?'

'I was doing A levels back then – art, graphics, and English Lit.'

'You had a lot of yellow feathers.'

'I did! I caused chaos in the station that day, but then so did you . . .' She held a glass out to him, her eyes on his, a little jolt of electricity as her fingers brushed his.

He lifted the glass to his lips, took a sip. Her persistent gaze flustered him for a moment before he realised she was simply waiting for his verdict on the drink.

'And there's the zing!' he noted.

She sipped her drink and ran her tongue over her bottom lip. 'Good, right?'

Will was suddenly hot. 'Very good.' But he hated gin – he only had one because she was. 'So, what were you doing with all those feathers?'

'Oh, they were for a piece inspired by the Greek goddess of dawn. She has these golden wings and a tiara, so I used jewels and feathers. I wanted it to be strong and feminine at the same time – a sort of tribute to my grandmother. God, that sounds pretentious . . .' Even in the dim light, he could see her cheeks flush.

'Not at all. It sounds amazing. I'd love to see your work.'

'Maybe you can? I need to move a sculpture from one campus to another for an exhibition, but it's too big to fit in a car. Aidan said you might help with your van?'

'Of course. Anytime.'

'Thank you.' She touched his shoulder. Her hand was there for half a second, but he could still feel it.

'Shall we sit?'

She nodded and followed him into the sitting room.

The dog was lying on the floor in front of the Christmas tree. He raised his head and thumped his tail on the carpet. Emily sat beside him and scratched his ears. Will joined them on the floor, leaning his back against the sofa, legs outstretched.

'Can you draw something for me?' he asked.

She smiled and frowned at the same time. 'Why?'

'I just want to see how good you are. See what all the fuss is about.'

'What shall I draw?'

'I don't know – something small.'

She chewed the inside of her cheek. 'I'll need a pen and paper.'

He went to the kitchen and came back with a pen and torn-off page of a small notepad he found in a drawer.

She scooted to the coffee table and began to scribble, turning her head this way and that as she worked. She'd been drawing for a few minutes when she said, 'If I'm drawing something for you, you have to sing something for me.'

'You've heard me sing before,' he said. 'I've never seen you draw.'

'No song, no drawing.' She shielded the paper with her hand.

'But you've finished it now – just show me.'

'Sing.'

'Wow. You're bossy.'

'Sing!'

He groaned and grimaced.

'Stop bellyaching – just do it.'

He took a breath. 'Have yourself a merry little Christmas . . .' he crooned in his best Frank Sinatra voice and stopped there.

'That's it? That's all I get?'

'Did you see the size of that bit of paper?' he laughed. 'Come on, a deal's a deal.'

She went to hand him the paper, snatched it back, but let him have it the second time.

It was a delicate line drawing of a snowflake, prongs radiating out from the centre and branching off in all directions, little dots and curlicues filling the spaces.

'Lovely.' He held it out to her. 'Can you sign it, please?'

Smiling, she quickly wrote at the bottom and returned it. 'What are you going to do with it?'

He took out his wallet and tucked it carefully behind the notes.

'I'm going to sell it obviously, it'll be worth a fortune when you're famous.'

She guffawed at that. A big belly laugh, too big for her slender frame. It was infectious.

He kept her talking for an hour, hanging on her every word until their glasses were empty and she said, 'Well, I'd better turn in.'

They cleared away the glasses, and as they crept upstairs, they could hear Aidan's snoring despite the closed door.

'Are you sure you want to go in there?' he asked.

She groaned. 'Not really . . .'

'Have my bed. I can sleep on the couch.'

'No! You can't do that. If he keeps me awake, *I'll* go on the couch.'

He opened the bedroom door a few inches. Light from the landing cast a stripe across the bed. Aidan lay exactly where they'd left him, mouth open, gurgling and snorting.

Will was surprised how close Emily's face was as they peered around the door. Too close to see all of it at once – he had to take in each feature individually. Those dark doe eyes, the freckles on the bridge of her nose, her soft lips, slightly parted.

'Goodnight,' she whispered.

'Night.'

She smiled and slipped inside.

Will was staying in the tiny box room next door. He climbed into the bed he'd shared with Aidan as a kid. They'd slept top to toe until Aidan got too big and Will had to sleep on the floor.

As Will lay there watching the flashing lights around the window, he was acutely aware of them in bed together in the next room. Whenever he heard a thick snort from Aidan, it was a little more bearable. He couldn't have handled the sound of anything else.

Chapter 14

January 1995

Will waited in the reception area of the events company he had been making regular deliveries to. He came here so often he even knew the receptionist's name – Izzy. This job was taking over his life. The other night, he'd even dreamt about it. He felt a wave of panic. Jesus, what if he ended up being a delivery driver his whole life?

It had been almost four months since Richard Eason from Island Records had given him his business card. He was probably expecting contact before now, but a gig was out of the question. They rehearsed every Sunday night, but Reu, talented as he was, still needed practice. What he needed more was a drum kit. They got by with the crappy kit at the rehearsal studio, but they had no kit to practise on or take to gigs. They couldn't invite Richard Eason along without giving him a bloody good show, and that wasn't happening anytime soon.

Will sighed.

'Everything okay?' asked Izzy.

'Just ready for the weekend.'

'They're checking that proof now – shouldn't be long. Take a seat.'

He could put an ad in *NME* for a drummer or ask around, but he was determined to stick with Reu. He was a natural. Imagine how good he would be if he could practise every day.

The phone rang and Izzy answered in a sing-song voice. She was cute: petite, blonde, curvy. He could see quite a lot of her from the low buttoning of her blouse. She smiled at him as she talked. He wished Emily would look at him like that.

He needed to stop pining over his brother's girlfriend. He thought about her every day. His mum invited Aidan and Emily to dinner every few weeks. Whenever Aidan turned up alone, Will was disappointed, but when she came, it was worse. If Aidan put his hand on her leg or even made her laugh, it was torture.

He sighed again.

Izzy chuckled. She was off the phone now. 'Maybe you should get it off your chest?'

'I didn't even realise I did it that time.'

'I'll see how long they'll be.' She swished out of the room, giving him a great view of her arse.

She returned a few moments later with the cardboard tube he had been waiting for. 'All signed. Sorry to keep you waiting.'

Will met her at the reception desk and took the tube. 'Izzy,' he said. 'Do you fancy going out for a drink sometime?'

She seemed less surprised than he was at the words coming out of his mouth. 'I thought you'd never ask,' she said, scribbling her number on a Post-it note.

Chapter 15

March 2016

Emily

I'm drinking tea in the kitchen when Liv comes home from Chloe's.

'Hi honey,' I say. 'Did you have fun last night?'

'Yeah.'

Talkative as ever.

She goes to her laptop where it's charging on the counter, unplugs it, and heads out to the hall.

'Where are you going?' I ask.

'Upstairs, I've got homework.'

'Hang on, can we talk for a bit? I haven't seen you in twenty-four hours.'

She sighs like it's a terrible inconvenience and sits at the table opposite me. She looks tired, the remnants of what I guess is 'tightliner' clinging to her lashes. Perhaps they were putting make-up on each other? She fiddles with the laptop, avoiding my eyes.

'What did you get up to at Chloe's?'

'Actually, we went to a friend's house.'

'Oh? Which friend?'

The fridge clunks and hums to life. 'Jordan.'

'I haven't heard you mention Jordan. Does she go to your school?'

'Yeah, he's more of a friend of a friend.'

'Jordan's a boy?'

'Yes,' she sighs at my stupidity. 'Jordan's a boy.'

'What were you doing at his house?'

'He was having a few friends over for his birthday.'

The fridge falls silent. 'Olivia, why didn't you tell me you were going to a party?'

'It wasn't a party; it was more of a . . . gathering. I didn't tell you because we didn't decide to go till the last minute.'

She's lying. She knew she was going five days ago when she googled hair and make-up tips.

'We've discussed this, Liv. You need to tell me where you're going!' My voice is too loud.

'We told Chloe's mum – she was fine with it. She gave us a lift there and back. We were safe.'

'Liv, I still need to know where you are.'

'Why? You're so controlling!' Her voice is shrill.

'I don't even know this Jordan. I don't know who his parents are. Or what's going on at this party!'

She huffs. 'It wasn't a party . . .'

'Was there alcohol there?'

'Yes but—'

'Jesus, you've been drinking? What was Chloe's mum thinking?'

'Mum, don't say anything to Linda. She'll kill Chloe if she finds out. Besides, Chloe didn't even drink anything.'

'But *you* did?'

She raises her chin. 'A couple.'

'A couple of what?'

'I had two bottles of cider. Small ones,' she says, without the slightest hint of apology.

'Oh my God!'

'Don't worry Mum, I'm not stupid enough to get drunk and pregnant like you!' Her chair scrapes behind her as she stands. 'And have a baby I don't even want!'

She picks up her laptop and storms out of the room.

63

I'm reeling.

'It wasn't like that!' I call after her.

I follow her to the bottom of the stairs.

She stops halfway up and turns to me. 'So, you weren't drunk when you got pregnant?'

'No, of course not!'

'Don't lie! Nobody accidentally gets pregnant when they're sober!'

She turns and continues up the stairs.

I march up after her. 'Actually, it happens all the time. Anyway, don't turn this around – this isn't about me. You're the one who's been lying.'

She stops on the narrow staircase leading to her loft room and whips around. 'I haven't lied.'

'But if I hadn't asked any questions, I wouldn't even know you were at a party. Let alone drinking alcohol. Keeping secrets is the same as lying.'

'And I suppose you never lie?' She has the high ground a few steps above. 'Or keep secrets?'

I grip the banister. 'As I said, this is not about me . . .'

'That's not exactly fair, is it? One rule for you and another for me? You should practise what you preach!'

'What do you mean?'

'You keep secrets from me! You lie to me!'

'I don't know what you are talking about!' But, of course, I do.

'You told me you didn't know Will Bailey!'

I wince. 'That wasn't really a lie. I just didn't know him that well—'

'Ha!' Her laugh is pure ice. 'Even that's a lie!'

'Well, it's hardly important whether I knew—'

'No, you're right. Forget it. It's not important!'

'Liv . . .'

'I want to live with Dad!'

I freeze. 'What?'

64

'I don't want to live here anymore. I want to live with Dad.' The words tumble out of her as though she has been holding them in for too long.

'That's not your decision.' I meant to sound firm, authoritative, but I just sound hurt.

'I can decide when I'm sixteen. I'll wait a month if I have to, but I'll be miserable.'

'Miserable?'

'Yes! You make my life miserable!' With a toss of the head, she stamps up the last few steps to her room.

The door slams.

Teenagers say this to their parents. I probably even said it to mine.

But I am one big bruise, raw and tender, and her words dig into me like pointed fingers.

Chapter 16

January 1995

When Will and Matty pulled up outside the rehearsal studio that Sunday, Reu wasn't waiting outside.

'Where is he?' Matty asked as they got out of the car.

'Maybe he's inside?' But the door was locked.

'The buses are probably running late. Shall we get started?'

They spent half an hour jamming. Will wasn't feeling it, but it was Matty who spoke up. 'Something's not right. Reu's always here first. We should look for him.'

Will agreed. 'Let's follow the bus route back to his place. You know what it's like when a bus breaks down, they kick you out and make you wait for the next one.'

They jumped in Matty's mum's car and checked all the bus stops on the route until they reached Reu's estate.

Will looked up at the concrete high-rise. 'Whenever we've dropped him off before, he goes in that door. Don't suppose you know his flat number?'

'Nope. The one time I picked him up, he was waiting outside.'

Two teenagers loitered nearby. Will got out of the car. 'Hey guys, do you know Reu? Skinny kid. Long black, curly hair.'

'Yeah, what's it to you?' asked the spotty one.

'Do you know his flat number?'

'What's it worth?' asked the taller one.

'You're joking. You want money to tell me where he lives?'

'Either you wanna know or you don't.'

'Fucksake.' Will rummaged in his pockets. 'I've only got a tenner.'

'That'll do.'

'I know it'll do. It will more than bloody do.' Will called over to the car, 'Matty, have you got any change?'

'It's the tenner or nothing, mate,' said the tall one, but Matty was shaking his head, anyway.

Will held out the note but wouldn't let go until the spotty one said 'Forty-four' and they ran off laughing. He could've picked a number at random. Will pressed the buzzer gingerly.

'Yeah?' came a female voice.

'Is Reu there?'

'Who's asking?'

'I'm a friend of his – Will.'

She paused. 'Reu doesn't live here anymore.' Then she hung up with a click.

Will walked towards the car but turned back and buzzed again.

'What?'

'Sorry to bother you again. Do you know where he moved—'

'How should I know? Fuck off!'

As Will got in the car, he hoped it wasn't Reu's mum he'd been talking to.

*

Will had been worried about Reu all week. A night out with Izzy had been the only distraction. Their date began with irresponsible drinking and ended with enthusiastic fucking. When Sunday rolled around again, Will was relieved to see Reu sitting in his usual spot outside the rehearsal unit.

'Sorry about last week, guys,' Reu said as they got out of the car. 'I couldn't make it at the last minute.'

He helped bring the gear inside, and when Will switched on the lights, he was shocked at the state of Reu. He was dirty, his long, curly hair matted at the back, and he was skinnier, if that was even possible.

Matty shot Will a look as Reu assembled the drum kit.

'What's going on, Reu?' asked Will.

'I'm sorry. It won't happen again. I promise.'

'It's not that, mate,' said Will. 'We're worried about you. We went to your flat. They said you moved out.'

Reu's face crumpled. A fat tear ran down his cheek and he swiped it away.

Will put a hand on his shoulder. 'What happened?'

'It's nothing . . . I can still play . . . Let me play.'

'Course you can play, mate.' Matty perched on his amp. 'Just tell us what happened. We're here for you, man.'

Reu took a deep breath and sank onto the drum stool. 'My stepdad kicked me out.'

'Shit, Reu. When was this? Where have you been staying?' asked Will.

'A week ago. I stayed at my friend's house the first night. He lent me some school uniform till I could sneak home and get some stuff when my stepdad was out.'

'Christ, what about the rest of the week?' asked Matty.

'I've been sleeping rough. I even stayed here one night. I told the band that was leaving I was the cleaner.'

'And they didn't find that suspicious? This shithole's never been cleaned,' laughed Matty, bringing a smile to Reu's face.

'Listen, you can stay at mine for a bit. We'll get this sorted,' said Will.

'Nah. I'll be all right. I can manage.'

'Have you been going to school?'

'I went all week except Friday. I stank.' They laughed; the laughing seemed to help.

'We need to keep you in school, otherwise they'll get social services involved, if they haven't already.' Will was thinking out loud. 'When was the last time you ate anything?'

'Yesterday? The day before maybe?'

'Right, that's it,' said Will. 'Come on, let's go to my house. Bloody hell, my mum will love feeding you up!'

'No! I want to play!' Reu whined. 'I've been waiting two weeks to play!' In that moment, he sounded like the child they kept forgetting he was.

'All right,' said Will. 'We'll play for half an hour, then go to mine. We need to get you cleaned up ready for school in the morning.'

*

Refusing the hospitality of the Irish is difficult, but refusing Mary Bailey's hospitality was impossible. She fed Reu to bursting, and he was relaxing in a hot bath while Will explained why there was a strange teenager in her bathroom.

'God love him,' said Mary when she heard what Reu had been through. 'We need to ring his mother, though. Get her number off him.'

'He won't let you do that.'

'Go on!' she shooed.

Will listened as she made the call. Mary made it sound like Reu's mum was doing *her* a favour by letting him stay, not the other way around.

'You've got my number now. Call whenever you want. He can stay here as long as he needs to. Thank you . . . Of course . . . Thanks again.'

But Reu's mum never called. Mary rang her once a week to tell her how he was doing. She could tell when his stepdad was around because the conversations were always much shorter.

Chapter 17

March 2016

Emily

My brain is swollen, it doesn't fit in my head. I turn over in my bed and it thumps against the inside of my skull. My mouth is arid, my eyes raw. I feel like shit. What's wrong with me?

Oh yes, I had some wine. An entire bottle. And some gin.

Then I remember.

Liv is gone.

A stab of anxiety twists in my stomach. I've pushed her away. I have failed at the one thing that was most important to me: being a mother.

Who am I kidding? I've failed at everything else too. Sticking at the same crap job, year after year. No friends (except Kay, but she's more of a colleague). No relationships, no lovers. But I didn't try at any of that. It didn't matter. Motherhood mattered. I tried at that.

Obviously not hard enough.

What was that look on her face when she left?

Pity.

Even my fifteen-year-old daughter feels sorry for me. She shouldn't be looking at me like that. The same way everyone has been looking at me since . . . Will died.

My throat aches, and fresh tears flow.

Scott's words from yesterday ring in my ears. 'She wants me to come and get her,' he'd said on the phone.

'She's not moving in with you, Scott. That's ridiculous.'

'Why is it ridiculous?'

'She can't move house every time she disagrees with one of us.'

'Look, why doesn't she stay with me for a few days until we all calm down, then we can have a rational discussion about it?'

I sighed.

'Emily, this is just the start. Accept it – she's growing up. She loves you, but she needs independence. Cut her some slack.'

'Teenagers need boundaries.'

'She'll be off to university in a couple of years,' he said, sensing victory. 'You need to start letting go. You need to live your own life.'

I haul myself out of bed, head pounding, and get in the shower. When I'm done, I turn the water to cold and let the icy stream cool my head.

Jesus, I hope he can behave himself in his bachelor pad while Liv's there. And the exams, he's got to make sure she's revising, eating properly, and getting enough sleep. I catch myself. Am I being overprotective and controlling? The cold water is hurting, so I turn off the shower and get out.

Wrapped in a towel, shivering, I realise what Scott was trying to tell me.

Get a life, Emily.

Before I head downstairs, I hesitate on the landing. Something draws me to the staircase up to Liv's room. Her room is unusually neat; things must be missing, but I'm not sure what – it doesn't look empty, just strange. Tears well up and threaten to spill over. A flash of yellow catches my eye on her desk. The moment I recognise the CD, my chest tightens. I shouldn't be surprised; I knew she was listening to Will's music. But why buy a CD when she has nothing to play it on? She left it here on purpose, to tell me she knows. I pick it up for a closer look. I'm torn between affection and hatred for it and drop it to the desk with a clatter. Maybe she didn't see my name in the small print. Nobody reads the small print.

Downstairs, everything is tidy. No cereal box left on the side, no Rice Krispies littered across the counter, no schoolbooks on the kitchen table. Just my phone. I usually charge it by my bedside. I must have forgotten last night. The screen shows an unread message.

FHD: Great – can't wait.

What's this?

I click on it and scroll back through the short message history. The first one is '*Whenever you're ready*'. Florence Harding's dad. I must have saved him as 'FHD' in my contacts last night.

Oh shit.

I messaged him after midnight. Drunk.

Me: Do you, by any chance, have a nickname? Perhaps your friends call you Liam or Bill? Maybe your mum calls you William?

Oh my God.

His reply a minute later: You don't want to know what school kids do with a surname like Harding.

Then: I'm only William when I'm in trouble. Why?

Me: Long story . . . Are you free Friday night for a drink (alcohol, not coffee)?

FHD: I would love to but I'm away for the Easter hols (taking Flo to my parents in Devon). Can do Friday the week after, though. How about Hemingways, 8pm?

Me: It's in the diary. Looking forward to it.

Suddenly the word '*online*' appears at the top of the screen, then morphs into the word '*typing* . . .'

Shit. He's messaging me right now.

FHD: BTW you can call me anything ;)

Chapter 18

April 2016

Liv

I pull out my earphones before pushing through the revolving doors. A huge glass atrium rises above me with several walkways crisscrossing the space. I may have said 'woah' out loud. The wall behind the long reception desk is one huge screen playing a video of what looks like the inside of a lava lamp. When no one's looking, I take a picture and send it to Chloe. The reception desk is manned by a team of female clones dressed like cabin crew. I tell the nearest one I'm here to see Dad's friend Tom.

Her long fingernails clack on the phone keypad. 'I've got Olivia Lawrence in reception for you.' Then to me: 'Please take a seat. He's sending someone down.'

My phone buzzes while I'm waiting. Chloe has sent a picture of her dad's office. It's the opposite of this place, all wood panelling and leather-bound books.

Chloe: I'm soooooo booooooooooored!

Tom's office must be on one of the upper floors, because no one comes for ages. My mouth is dry, I have to keep running my tongue over my teeth.

A guy approaches me. 'Are you Olivia?'

I stand. 'Yes.'

'I'm Ben.' He offers his hand. 'Tom's in a meeting. He asked me to meet you and get you a security pass.'

Ben is so cool; he's wearing a smart shirt with dark jeans, but his hair's all flipped up like a Mr Whippy ice cream and a full-sleeve tattoo pokes out from the cuff on his left wrist. We pick up a pass from security and take the lift. As we rise through the floors, Ben asks me what I got up to at the weekend. I'm pretty sure he doesn't want to hear about my sleepover with Chloe, so I say, 'Nothing much.'

We exit on the twelfth floor and cross a walkway spanning the atrium.

I avoid the edge and don't look down. 'Are there any music magazines here?'

'Yep. *Amplify*, they're over there,' he says, pointing to the opposite end of the walkway.

Ben waves his pass at a set of doors which lead into a large open plan office with amazing views across the city. I follow as he points out the various departments: circulation, editorial, advertising, sales and marketing, before showing me to my desk in the art department. There's no sign of Tom, so Ben tells me to familiarise myself with the website and look at back issues while I'm waiting.

Once I have read the entire *Luminaire* website, I switch to the *Amplify* site. Within a few quick minutes, I know who the editor is (Paul Raymond), what he looks like (from his Twitter profile), and what he had for breakfast (Instagram – *pain au chocolat*).

When Tom finally shows up, he's surprised by how tall I've grown. 'I'm sorting out something for you to do. Why don't you pop up to the café on the top floor to get us some coffees?'

I take the order – eight drinks and a few snacks. People make comments like 'coffee is an essential part of the magazine business' and 'good to see they've got you doing the important stuff', which is hilarious. God knows how I'll carry this lot back down in the lift.

I head out onto the floating walkway. The lifts are on the opposite side by the entrance to the *Amplify* magazine office. I call the lift, and while I'm waiting, I peer in. There's a massive blown-up copy of an old *Amplify* cover on the wall featuring Christie Blackmore of The Underdogs. I wave my pass in front of the sensor; it makes a high-pitched beep, flashes red, and remains shut. Behind me the lift makes a less alarming *bing*.

'Can I help you?' comes a voice from behind me. It's Paul Raymond looking exactly like his Twitter profile picture.

'Hi! Yes!' There's no need to shout, he's right there. 'Paul!'

'Yes . . .'

'Raymond. Paul Raymond. Editor of *Amplify* magazine.'

His eyebrows lift. 'And you are?'

'My name's Olivia. I'm on work experience over at *Luminaire*.' I jerk my thumb towards the other end of the walkway. 'But I was hoping I could swap.'

'Swap?'

'You know, do my work experience here instead of there. It's only two weeks. I'll do anything you want. I'll do all the boring stuff no one else wants to do. And I make excellent tea.' I don't. Not according to my mum, anyway.

'Hang on a minute,' he says kindly. 'Let's get in here and talk about this.'

He flashes his pass at the door, and I follow him in. He gestures for me to take a seat under Christie Blackmore.

'How old are you?' asks Paul Raymond, sitting down beside me.

'Almost sixteen.'

He looks mildly surprised at this. 'Why do you want to do your work experience here?'

'I love music.'

'What kind of music?'

'All kinds of music.'

He arches a bushy eyebrow. 'You must have a favourite.'

'Nope.'

'Okay, what are you listening to right now?'

I don't hesitate, 'Will Bailey.'

'There's a blast from the past. What else? What else this month?'

I list a bunch of bands and artists I've been listening to. He tries to catch me out with a series of questions that would stump even the geekiest of music nerds, but I ace them all.

Paul Raymond sighs. 'Okay, I'll talk to the guys at *Luminaire* and we'll give it a go, but if you're any trouble, you can go straight back there.'

Chapter 19

February 1995

When Will pulled up in the car park of Emily's college, she was waiting on the front steps as arranged. He raised his hand in greeting.

'Thanks for doing this, Will,' she said at his window.

'No problem.'

It was a *bit* of a problem, though. Nigel wouldn't let him take a couple of hours off, so he had to pretend he was stuck in traffic.

He parked the van and followed her up the steps through a doorway with the word 'BOYS' carved in the stone above it. This must have been a school once. The vast church-like interior was divided into cubicles with partition screens. The hum of conversations and faint music echoed around the space. Emily led him through the maze of screens, all covered in sketches and paintings. Students were standing around chatting or busy creating, ranging from trendies wearing thick, black-framed glasses to crusties with purple hair and piercings.

Will loved the place.

He got distracted by a sketch of a skull and had to run to catch her up.

'This is me.' She turned a slow circle in her cubicle.

Her artwork covered every inch of the screens enclosing her space.

'Woah.' Will stepped closer to examine a detailed watercolour of a shiny conker in its spiky shell. He traced his way from one gem to the next, murmuring his appreciation.

He stopped at a large charcoal sketch of a naked man and turned to Emily with raised eyebrows. 'Must have been cold in here that day,' he said.

Her giggle echoed in the space.

That's when he noticed the sculpture on a table beside her. 'Is this it?' he asked.

She gave a bashful nod.

'Wow.' Twisted spirals of copper wire formed an organic shape with spikes protruding from it at all angles. He touched one of the points, 'It's beautiful. What is it?'

'Pollen.'

'Huh?'

'It's a pollen particle – here.' She opened her sketchbook and turned to a spread pasted with photocopies from a science book. 'This is what they look like under the microscope.'

'Wow, who knew? Those beautiful little bastards make you sneeze.'

Her laugh rang out again. God, she was lovely. She couldn't get any lovelier, but seeing her here, surrounded by her work – she was perfection.

'Right,' she said, pulling him back from his thoughts, 'how shall we do this?' She set the sketchbook down. 'It's not heavy, it's just awkward.'

The structure had a board beneath it. 'You take that end. Let's lift on three.'

The sculpture slid a little until they levelled it.

'Trust me to take something microscopic and make it massive,' she said. 'I'll go backwards, as I know the way.'

As she turned this way and that to see behind her, Emily's oversized sweater slipped from her shoulder and Will couldn't drag his gaze from that triangle of perfect collarbone.

They tackled the set of steps back down to the car park slowly, and as they neared the van, Emily called out to a guy who was smoking nearby. 'Hey Scott, give us a hand!'

Scott jogged over. He was dressed in a trendy skater brand – the trainers alone must have cost a fortune – but the entire outfit was splattered with paint.

'Can you take Will's end so he can open the van?'

Cigarette still hanging from his lips, Scott gave Will an upward nod before swapping places with him. Will swung the back doors open, and the three of them moved the sculpture inside like an injured animal.

'I'd better stay in the back with it,' said Emily. 'Scott, do you mind coming to show Will the way?'

'Sure.' Scott took a last drag and flicked the cigarette away.

'Will you be okay in there?' asked Will. She nodded, so he shut her in.

As Scott climbed into the van beside him, Will was gutted. He'd been looking forward to riding with Emily. It was the reason he'd come all this way.

'It's not far. Go left out of here,' said Scott. 'So, you're the boyfriend's brother? The songwriter.'

'Yeah.'

'She's always playing that song . . . what's it called? "Fever"?'

'Yeah, "Fever".' Will felt a sudden thrill. Not only that a stranger knew the name of one of his songs, but also that Emily had been listening to his music. Aidan must have given her a demo tape.

'When's your next gig? A few of us want to come along.'

'Nothing planned at the mo, but I'll let Emily know.'

'Get in the right-hand lane here.'

A robotic melody rang from the cup holder – the mobile phone work gave him for sorting deliveries. It made him jump every time it went off. That would be Nigel, wanting to know where the hell he was. He ignored it.

'Up here on the left,' said Scott. 'You can pull in there.'

Emily and the sculpture were both unharmed when Will opened the doors. She scrambled out and stretched.

'Do you need help taking it inside?' asked Will.

'No, we've got it from here.' Unexpectedly, she reached over and hugged him. 'Thank you so much. I owe you one.' He caught the scent of coconut in her hair.

Will cleared his throat. 'No problem.'

He helped them slide the board out of the van and opened the door to the building for them.

'See you soon!' she called, walking backwards, and disappearing into a crowd of students.

He jumped in the van and checked the phone – two missed calls and a text from Nigel: Get back now. Delivery for Canbury.

Canbury Events was Izzy's company. He turned the key and crunched into gear.

This could be awkward.

*

When Will pulled up outside Canbury Events, most of the lights were off. He jumped out of the van and started unloading the boxes he'd picked up from the print shop. He'd never seen Nigel angry before. Canbury needed these leaflets for an event first thing in the morning, so someone would have to wait for him to deliver after hours. As he stacked the boxes onto his trolley, he hoped it wasn't Izzy.

He wheeled the first trolley-load towards the door, peering in to see who was in reception. In the dim light, he could just make out a figure talking on the phone. He pressed the buzzer. The door hummed as it unlocked with no voice from the intercom.

'I'm sorry I couldn't get here sooner – the traffic was murder!' he called to the figure.

Then he recognised Izzy's voice as she spoke on the phone. It sounded like a personal call. She continued her conversation, and raising a finger, pointed out where to put the boxes.

As he shifted the boxes off the trolley, he suspected she was faking the call.

He used a box to prop the door open and went back to the van for the second trolley-load.

On his return, he kicked the box away from the door and it swung shut behind him. She was off the phone and out from behind the reception desk, perched daintily against it, her legs crossed at the ankles, her hands resting on the countertop either side of her hips. He imagined her arranging herself into that pose, and it brought a smile to his lips.

'Hello,' he said.

'Hello.' Her voice was neutral, maybe a touch of frost.

'I'm sorry I'm late.'

She said nothing.

He propped the trolley upright and took off his gloves. 'How are you?'

'I'm fine,' she said, then her expression darkened. 'I'll be honest with you, I expected to hear from you after our date.'

Will did a mental calculation – it had been just over a week. That wasn't long, was it? 'Yeah, sorry about that. I've had some stuff going on that I needed to sort out.' He wasn't lying – Reu moving into his brother's old room had completely distracted him, and he'd forgotten all about her.

'Have you fixed the problem?' she asked.

'Almost. It's a long story, but I was going to call you tonight.'

'Were you?' She sounded sceptical.

'Yeah.'

'And what were you going to say?'

He paused. 'I was going to say . . . I'd like to see you again.' Until then, he'd planned to say the exact opposite.

She raised her chin. 'And what makes you think I want to see *you* again?'

He walked towards her and whispered into her ear, 'Because of the noises you made last time.'

He stepped back. Her cheeks showed the slightest flush in the dim light.

'Well?' he asked.

'Well, what?'

'*Do* you want to see me again?'

She tucked her hair behind her ear. 'That depends. Where are you taking me?'

'Hmm . . . How about a walk along the river, a few drinks, and maybe Thai food?'

She pursed her lips. 'Not bad . . .'

'Is that a "yes"?'

She paused. 'Yes.'

'Good. Are you by yourself? I can wait while you lock up, make sure you get to your car okay?'

'It's the least you can do, seeing as you're the reason I had to stay late.'

Then he leant in and kissed her. First, on her neck by her ear, then pulling the collar of her shirt to one side, along her collarbone. It wasn't Emily's perfect collarbone he'd glimpsed earlier that day, but when he closed his eyes, he imagined it was.

*

His mum was cleaning up the kitchen when he got in. 'You're home late.'

'Yeah, had an urgent delivery to do.' He gave her a kiss on the cheek, grabbed an apple from the fruit bowl, and took a bite.

'I saved you some dinner. Do you want it now?'

'I'll have it later, thanks. Where's Reu?'

She nodded to the garage door. 'In there, bashing on two buckets and my washing basket.'

Will laughed. 'Really?'

'He's been in there since he got in from school.' She swept a cloth over the surfaces, catching invisible crumbs in her hand.

'Mum, are you sure you're okay with this?' He sank his teeth into the apple again.

'Well, I didn't realise quite what we were getting into. I expect he'll be here a while.'

'You think?'

'Sounds like the stepfather's a right bastard. It'd be best for everybody if he's out of their way for the time being. Reuben's at an awkward age. They're probably rubbing each other up the wrong way.'

'If it gets too much, we'll sort something else out.'

She stopped what she was doing and leant against the counter. 'Despite all he's been through, he's a good kid. He's so grateful to be here; it brings a tear to my eye. But he's too thin. He's not leaving my house until he puts weight on.'

'Thanks Mum. You're the best.'

She smiled and went back to her wiping. He dropped the core into the bin and headed for the garage.

'Will?'

'Yeah?'

'Wipe your face – it's covered in lipstick.' Without looking up from what she was doing, she muttered, 'Working late, my arse . . .'

He laughed and rubbed his sleeve across his face.

Rhythmic thumping passed through the garage door in fast, complicated beats. The kid was gifted. Will opened the door to find Reu sitting on the upturned washing basket, hammering away on an array of paint tins and buckets before him. He finished with a flourish, a light sheen of sweat on his face.

'Sounds brilliant, Reu.'

Reu's eyes dropped to his feet. 'Thanks.'

Will picked up one of his guitars and hooked the strap over his head. 'I've got an idea about how to get you a drum kit.'

'What is it?'

'Busking.'

Reu laughed. 'Busking?'

'Yeah, me on the guitar, and you on the, er . . . buckets.'

'You think we can make enough money for a drum kit?'

'I reckon this Saturday we can make enough for a down-payment. Then three, maybe four more Saturdays and we'll have paid it off.'

'No way.'

'Trust me, this will sound great.'

*

Will was wrong about the busking.

They made enough money to pick up a second-hand drum kit that first day, and it only took one more Saturday to pay it off. They had to prise Reu off his new kit to come into the house for meals or to go to school. Will was in awe of Reu's talent and dedication. It inspired him, and the songs kept coming. Matty came over every other night to jam. Playing together was a buzz. Even Matty had to admit – something was happening, something special.

Chapter 20

April 2016

Liv

When I tell Tom I want to move to *Amplify* magazine, he's not annoyed, he looks relieved. I take him to meet Paul Raymond, then he rings Dad, saying, 'To be honest, mate, I didn't know what I was going to do with her.' Then he wishes me luck before hurrying back to his office.

And just like that, I'm working at *Amplify*.

Paul doesn't waste any time. No coffee runs here. He has me listening to a new hip-hop album and tells me to have a go at writing a review.

I panic. What the hell am I going to write? But once I listen to the music, I realise I have a lot to say about it. By home time, I've written 722 words. I email my review to Paul and wish him a good night.

*

The following morning, I arrive early. My new pass lets me into the office with a happy beep. Paul is at his desk, wearing headphones.

I do a dorky wave to get his attention.

'Liv – you're here!' he shouts.

'Hi.'

He slips his headphones onto his shoulders. 'I read your review.'

'Oh.' Suddenly I'm boiling.

'It's not bad. Not bad at all. How old are you again?'

'I'll be sixteen next week.'

'In that case, it's great. Well done. I'm going to send you some suggestions – see if you can make it even better, okay?'

'Okay, yeah.'

'There are a few others you can have a go at as well.'

I spend the first couple of days practising writing reviews, then Paul introduces me to the marketing assistant, and I help her come up with a month's worth of social media posts. She even lets me write a few.

The rest of the week is a mixture of social media and fake writing projects. It's such a buzz whenever I get a like or comment on any of the posts I've been involved with, and my writing must be improving because Paul is sending it back with fewer edits. There – I used the word 'fewer' in my own head. I've learned more in the last week than all the years in Miss Baker's English class.

On the Monday of the second week, Paul asks me to join the features meeting. I recognise the permanent staff members, and he introduces me to the others who are freelancers. I take the furthest seat. Paul goes around the table asking everyone for ideas. He must be getting desperate because when he gets to me, he says, 'What about you, Liv? Do you have any ideas for a feature?'

'Me?' Heat creeps up my neck to my face. 'Uh, I haven't really thought about it.'

'Well, think about it now. What kind of article would you want to read in *Amplify*? We're targeting a younger audience.'

'Er . . .' Everyone looks at me.

'There are no wrong answers, Liv. This is a brainstorm.'

'Okay . . . er, well . . . I like to read reviews, and I like to know what the next big thing is, but you've already covered that . . .'

'Uh-huh.' He's still looking at me.

'But I guess I'm also interested in artists' influences. You know, where they get inspiration from, the bands they listen to.'

He writes something in his notebook, then looks back at me.

'And, er, something that's always coming up on the social media channels, what gets people talking, is the meanings behind songs. You could do a regular feature explaining where the ideas for songs came from, influences, what they're about. Do some research, maybe interview the artist? Readers could get involved on social media and request the songs they want you to cover.'

Everyone looks from me to Paul.

'What would we call it?' he asks the entire table.

'Tracks Decoded?' suggests a girl with a cool sixties-print top and Harry Potter glasses.

'Yes! Love it, Tumi!' says Paul. 'Why don't you come up with guide questions for this feature? Liv, give Tumi a hand with that.'

Tumi smiles at me. Her nose wrinkles, lifting her glasses up on her face.

I like her already.

*

The alarm goes off and when I open my eyes, it's cool blue serenity everywhere. I'm not expecting that. I'm expecting the dusty pink clutter of my room at home – I mean, Mum's.

Then, I remember it's my birthday.

I'm sixteen.

I've waiting ages for this day but now it's here, it already feels like an anti-climax.

My phone buzzes beside my bed.

Chloe: Happy sweet sixteen! May your playlists always be full of hits! Can't wait to celebrate with you. Love you loads x.

She signs off with cupcake and sparkles emojis and it warms my insides.

Dad knocks on the door. 'Morning birthday girl!' he trills. 'Can I come in?'

I sit up. 'Yeah.'

Carrying a tray, he sings 'Happy Birthday' out of tune the whole way across the room. Before I even see it, I know what's on it: pancakes and hot chocolate with squirty cream – my birthday breakfast request since I was five. As he places it on my lap, the cream avalanches over the side of the cup.

'No! I kept that balancing all the way up the stairs!' He rescues a little present from the spillage and hands me the box.

'Now, I know you asked for Beatland tickets, but Mum said *no way* and I didn't know what else to get you . . .'

I knew Beatland tickets were a long shot. 'Can I open it?'

'Go ahead.'

I tear off the paper to find a gold box, and inside is a roll of twenty-pound notes tied with ribbon. 'Ah, thanks, Dad.'

'This way, you can buy whatever you like.'

'Except Beatland tickets, right?'

He pulls a comedy grimace. 'Yeah, sorry.'

*

On the train into London, I check the *Amplify* Twitter account. Yesterday, I tweeted asking for requests for the Tracks Decoded feature. There are 363 replies. Tumi squeals when I tell her at the office. She asks me to come up with a shortlist. As I go through them, I notice there are a few requests for Will Bailey's 'Fever' – probably because of the movie trailer, but I put it at the top of the shortlist when I show her.

'That's not a bad idea,' she says. 'A friend of mine did a special on him a few years ago on the anniversary of his death for *Mojo* magazine. I'll drop him a message.'

She taps on her phone with lightning thumbs and, as we finish the list of potential songs, Tumi's phone lights up.

'My *Mojo* contact has sent through the details for Will Bailey's brother. Apparently, there's an archive of notebooks, letters, and photographs. I'll call him now.'

I listen as Tumi arranges to view the archive that Friday morning. The moment she hangs up, I ask if I can go with her.

'Of course,' she says. 'I'm not trawling through that lot on my own.'

Back at my desk, I try to concentrate on researching the songs on the Tracks Decoded shortlist, but Chloe keeps messaging because she's bored at her dad's office, and I can't stop thinking about Friday and the chance to look through Will Bailey's stuff. I wonder if there will be any trace of Mum there.

The next time my phone buzzes it's not Chloe, it's Dad. He wants to know where I am. We were supposed to meet downstairs twenty minutes ago. I say bye to Tumi and Paul, and dash out.

It takes ages for the lift to come, and when it does, it stops at every floor. I'd forgotten all about my birthday celebrations. When I said no to a party, Dad suggested dinner and a West End show with him and Mum.

Outside, my parents are chatting away and don't see me coming. Things have been weird between Mum and me since I moved out. Dad arranged a couple of dinners, but it's been like making polite conversation with a stranger. We used to be so close, but the last year or so she's been so frustrating. Not letting me do anything. Always wanting to know where I am. It's suffocating. Mum spots me, our eyes meet, and she beams at me. For a split second, she looks like the girl in the old photographs, and I'm reminded of her old life as a cool artist with a rock-star boyfriend and it's so confusing because the woman in front of me couldn't be further from that. I wish she would talk to me.

'Happy birthday!' Mum says in a high-pitched voice.

Her mouth is smiling, but her eyes are sad. She throws her arms around me and squeezes me so tight it hurts my bruised ribs.

Chapter 21

February 1995

Will leapt onto the stage to the loudest applause he'd ever experienced. Reu climbed behind his shiny 'new' kit, eager eyes on Will, like a dog waiting to fetch a ball. With a quick nod from Will, Reu clicked his sticks together, counting them into their opening song.

Matty had wangled a support slot at the University of London Union. It was the biggest venue they'd ever played. It could hold up to 800 people, and it looked full already. Will left messages telling Richard Eason from Island Records about the gig, then missed Eason's return call during a busy delivery shift, but he left a promising voicemail. 'Thanks for letting me know about the ULU gig. I'm gonna try to make it, but if I can't, I'll send someone else along.'

Will scanned the crowd for Eason as he played but couldn't quite remember what he looked like. A few regulars jostled down at the front, but there were a lot of unfamiliar faces, too. The atmosphere was charged.

The first three songs were upbeat, they went down well and got people moving. Next up was their latest song, 'Intertwined'. It was a ballad – it could kill the mood, but it was his favourite song at the moment, and he wanted to see what people thought of it.

By the end of the first verse, a few people had gone to the bar, but he still had everyone else. He gave the chorus his all, hoping people would get goosebumps as he had when they'd first played it together in rehearsal. Lost in the music, he shut his eyes and forgot about the audience – and Richard Eason – only opening them to synchronise the final strum with Reu's last beat.

A cacophony of whoops and cheers erupted behind him, and Reu's face became one huge, toothy grin.

The rest of the gig passed in a blur. There were no mistakes. Hell, they sounded great, and the crowd was feeling it. They even got an encore.

When they headed to the bar afterwards, Izzy was there with friends. She had said she didn't want anyone to know they'd been seeing each other, but as soon as she saw him, she threw her arms around him and squealed, 'Oh my God, you were amazing!' So much for playing it cool.

She introduced him to her friends. He'd always thought of himself as a musician, but to them, he was just a delivery guy with a hobby. Maybe they were right.

A familiar voice interrupted the conversation. 'Great gig, mate. You smashed it!'

Will turned to see his brother. 'Aidan, what are you doing here? I thought you were going to Emily's private view at her college tonight.'

'Nah, I couldn't be bothered with that. I've seen the photos. Besides, I can't stand those art student dudes. They're full of shit.'

'How very supportive of you,' Will muttered.

'What?'

'Nothing.' Will excused himself to get the drinks in.

He lingered at the bar, making himself available for the elusive Richard Eason, but after a while it was pretty obvious he wasn't coming. Will tried to shake off the bleak mood descending on him. He gathered up the drinks and took them back to his bandmates. The guys were on a high, but Will felt flat as they clinked bottles. *All that effort for nothing.* Reu was talking ten to the dozen, delivering his post-gig analysis with Matty nodding intently. Will had never heard Reu say that many words in one go before – his first proper gig had brought him out of his shell. Will didn't join in, just drained his beer.

Will felt weird, like he wasn't really there, like he was falling backwards. He looked around. The headline band's fans were shuffling forward as they came on stage; Izzy was talking into her friend's ear; Aidan and his mates were chatting to some girls at the bar.

A passer-by interrupted him, 'That was amazing! What a voice!'

Comments like that kept coming. One guy even congratulated him at the urinal, which was awkward, but as the evening wore on, Will was slipping into a gloomy hole.

At the end of the night, Izzy came to say goodbye.

'See you soon?' she purred.

Behind her, Aidan was making his way towards the exit, a giggling girl in tow. What the hell?

Izzy stood on tiptoes and whispered something unintelligible in his ear.

'Huh?'

'When will I see you again?' she asked.

'Sorry, excuse me a minute.' He wanted to catch his brother before he left.

Will elbowed his way through the crowd, and out onto the street in time to see Aidan climbing into a black cab.

As the cab trundled past, Will got an excellent view into the back, where Aidan was snogging some random blonde.

'Fucking arsehole,' Will muttered, his fists clenched tight by his sides.

Chapter 22

April 2016

Liv

Aidan Bailey has the same blue eyes as his brother, although his have more wrinkles at the edges. He invites me and Tumi into the house and leads us to the kitchen, where he introduces his mum. *Their* mum. In a strong Irish accent, she offers us tea and as she fills the kettle, Aidan takes us through a door off the kitchen.

'This is the garage where Will used to write,' says Aidan. 'We've bricked up the garage door, but otherwise it's exactly as it was when he worked on his music in here.'

A row of guitars perch on stands, and above them is a shelf filled with notebooks. An old leather sofa covered with a throw sits nearby and Persian rugs line the floor. It's cool in a grungy sort of way.

I get chills. Will Bailey wrote some of my favourite songs in here. I feel his presence.

'It's great you've kept everything as it was,' says Tumi.

'There's more stuff in there.' He points at two huge black trunks with metal trimming, the kind bands use on tour.

'Can we take a look?' Tumi asks.

'Sure.'

He opens the latches and lifts the lid of the closest trunk. It's filled to the top with boxes of all different shapes and sizes. He opens a random shoe box at the top and inside is a pile of letters tied with string.

'There are letters, notebooks, concert flyers, set lists, lyrics,' he says. 'I'm sorry it's not organised. We've all tried to go through it over the years, but . . . it's too painful.'

'It's not a problem, as long as you don't mind us looking through it,' says Tumi.

'All I ask,' says Mrs Bailey, carrying in a tray of tea and biscuits, 'is that you're careful with it.'

She places the tray on a wooden crate beside the sofa.

'Of course,' says Tumi. 'We understand. It's very precious.'

'There's no point in having all this if no one ever looks at it,' says Mrs Bailey. 'You two – you're going to tell his story. And that's what we want, for people to remember our Will and his music.'

When Aidan and Mrs Bailey leave the room, I say, 'Woah. This is cool.'

'I can't believe they're letting us go through all this,' says Tumi. 'Let's start with the notebooks.'

She takes one end of the shelf and I take the other. I grab a notebook and sit on the floor. Most of the scribbles covering the pages make no sense to me, but I find the odd gem as I flick. I spot lyrics I recognise, and as I turn the pages, the words evolve as he honed and perfected them. Some sections are like diary entries, and it feels wrong to read them, but I do. I flip through the pages, consuming his thoughts and ideas.

'You could write a book with all this material,' says Tumi. 'We should speak to someone who worked with him during the songwriting process. Someone who can explain all this.'

My mum could help us now. I expect she knows all about how he wrote songs. Suddenly I'm sad. Sad I can't talk to Mum about this. Sad Will Bailey is dead. Sad his mum has preserved this room almost exactly as it was when he was last here.

Tumi senses my mood. 'It's emotional, isn't it?'

Our eyes meet and all I can manage is a nod.

After an hour, Mrs Bailey pops in, asking if we want more tea. I say no but Tumi says yes and asks to use the loo. Alone in the room, all I can think about is the letters in the trunk. What if there's a mention of my mum in there?

Mrs Bailey is clinking cups in the next room. The trunk's still open, with the letters visible. I pick up the bundle. The surrounding string is loose, and the top envelope slips out easily. I lift the flap and pull out the contents: two sheets of yellowing paper, every centimetre covered in words and sketches. A doodle of a jar of Marmite catches my eye.

I scan the page so fast I can't make sense of the random snippets. But I can tell the letter is intimate. Whoever wrote this knew him well. I turn the pages, rushing to find who has signed it before Tumi gets back.

The letter is so full the last line finishes vertically up the margin:

I miss you so much it hurts. I think about you all the time. I can't wait till New York. I love you. Yours forever, Milly x.

Milly? Could that be Mum? Come to think of it, that looks a little like her handwriting. I don't know why but I want it to be her. I hope she meant something to him, that they had this amazing love affair. That she was his muse or something.

I can hear Tumi talking to Mrs Bailey in the kitchen, so I use the last few moments alone to scan the rest of the letters in the stack. They're addressed to him at various hotels in America, all in the same handwriting. This Milly was important to him. She wrote a lot, and he kept all her letters.

I go to the shelf and pick another notebook. I can't stop thinking Mum could be Milly and I can't concentrate on Will's notes, so it's a while before I realise Tumi hasn't come back.

I open the door to the kitchen. Tumi and Mrs Bailey are sitting at the kitchen table, mugs of tea and a plate of biscuits between them, chatting away like old friends.

'Mrs Bailey was just telling me about "Fever",' says Tumi.

'Call me Mary, please.'

'Will went travelling when he was twenty-one. He got a mysterious illness while island-hopping in Greece. He almost died!' Tumi sounds weirdly pleased about it. '"Fever" is about the mad hallucinations he had while he was recovering in hospital.'

'Ah Jaysus, it was awful!' cries Mrs Bailey. 'I never could listen to that song.'

She pats the seat beside her, so I pull up a chair. Aidan Bailey joins us then and fresh tea is made. We sip the tea and nibble biscuits and listen to a still-grieving mother reminisce about her late son. Aidan Bailey is quiet, staring down at his hands, but the few times he speaks it's clear he misses his little brother.

When Tumi is satisfied we have enough for our article, she says it's time to go and Aidan offers us a lift to the station. But I don't want to leave. There's so much more to see. I panic at the thought of never seeing this stuff again.

As we say goodbye to Mrs Bailey, I have a crazy idea. 'If you like, I can come back and organise the archive for you?' I blurt at the front door. 'I could even scan the important stuff so you can put it on the website.'

'You'd do that?' asks Mrs Bailey.

'We'll need to check with the office on that,' says Tumi.

'I'd be happy to do it in my spare time.'

'We can get back to you on the detail,' says Tumi. 'Thanks again for letting us look. This collection is very special.'

*

Back at the office, as it's the last day of my work experience, I hand out the Krispy Kremes Dad gave me to say thank you. I'm just biting into one when Paul calls me into the meeting room. Tumi is sitting beside him.

'We've been reading the reviews you've written this week and there's one that stands out.'

My heart pounds. 'Which one?'

'The debut album of that four-piece from Wigan. We wanted to tell you we've decided to run it.'

'Run it?'

'Print it in the magazine,' he explains.

'Will it have my name on it?'

'Of course! You wrote it.'

It's only 150 words and will sit among hundreds of other album reviews but I'm made up.

'You'll be a published writer!' gushes Tumi. 'At sixteen.'

'We've been really impressed with your enthusiasm and hard work over the last couple of weeks,' says Paul. 'We've got a proposition for you. How would you like to come back in the summer for an internship?'

My stomach flips.

*

Nathan comes over that night to watch a documentary about legendary recording studios. We sit side by side on the couch, electricity fizzing between us as we watch back-to-back episodes. For almost three hours, we hardly speak or move and I'm almost relieved when his dad messages to say he's coming to get him.

I walk Nathan out to the hall.

'Have you got a ticket for Beatland yet?' he asks, tying his shoelaces.

'No, have you?'

'Yeah, a group of us got some, but Rhianna's parents won't let her go now, so there's a spare ticket if you want it.'

A little buzz of excitement hums through me. 'Really?'

'Yeah, talk to Ella. I'll add you to the group.'

He pulls out his phone and taps away at it. A few seconds later, mine buzzes: Nathan has added you to the group 'Beatland or die!'

More tapping.

Nathan: Ella – Liv might take the spare ticket. Persuade her!

He stands. 'Moon Illusion are playing now, too.'

'Are they?' It would be an absolute dream come true to see Moon Illusion at Beatland with Nathan Hall.

'Yeah.' He's kind of in my personal space.

'Great.' I have to lift my chin to look at him; he's so close.

My phone buzzes in my pocket, and his is buzzing, too.

'I hope you take that ticket.'

Suddenly, his lips are on mine. I panic – what if Dad comes out here? He pushes his tongue into my mouth. I try to relax and kiss him back while our phones buzz in unison.

His phone buzzes on its own and we break apart, breathless.

He checks the message. 'My dad's outside.'

I nod.

'Oh, I almost forgot. I got you a birthday present.' He fumbles in his pockets and hands me a little rectangle of folded blue tissue paper. 'Sorry it's late.'

'Thanks.' I unravel the layers and lift a silver necklace from the wrapping. Two charms dangle at the end of a delicate chain – a tiny 'L' and a miniature set of headphones.

I'm so touched, I don't know what to say.

'If you don't like it, I can change it,' he says.

'No, I love it. Thank you.'

'Well, bye.' He pumps the door handle.

I turn the lock and open the door for him. 'Bye.'

He jogs down the drive and gives a wave before disappearing behind the tree. The Beatland chat has fourteen unread messages. The first is from the most popular girl in Year 11.

Ella: Liv! You HAVE to come. You can share my tent. We'll be roomies!

I feel like pinching myself. Today has been the best day of my entire life.

*

In bed later, I call Chloe. I tell her about working at *Amplify* over the summer, about visiting Will Bailey's house, and about the letters from the mysterious Milly. I don't mention Nathan; I don't know why, but the thought of talking to her about him makes me cringe. At first, it was because I didn't want to jinx it, but now we've been to each other's houses and kissed, it's weird not to say anything. I keep going to tell her, then chickening out. I don't bring up Beatland either – it probably won't happen.

It's gone midnight when we hang up and I'm drifting off to sleep when my phone buzzes.

Chloe: There's one way to find out for sure if your mum is Milly.

Me: How?

Chloe: If there are letters to Will from Milly, then there must be letters to Milly from Will. I bet if you look for them at your mum's, you'll find them.

Chapter 23

December 1995

Christmas Day

Things had changed a lot in a year. Will sat in the back seat behind Aidan so he could steal looks at Emily – that was the same. She was singing 'Santa Claus is Coming to Town' at the top of her voice, looking back at him and laughing as he harmonised in a comically deep voice as he had the year before. But this year, Reu was with them, cracking them up with his mock falsetto.

Will thought back to that first day of busking. As they got to the chorus of 'Stand by Me', Reu burst into song. Will looked down wide-eyed at Reu sitting on his mum's orange bucket, slapping the side of it, and singing his heart out. And what a voice – he sounded like a young Stevie Wonder. Since then, Reu had been singing backing vocals.

Reu was still as skinny as ever, despite his mum's best efforts, but he looked happier now. And, between himself and Reu, was Izzy. She was wearing a Santa hat, the furry white bobble kept hitting him in the face as she bopped her head around to the music.

She had invited herself. They had been seeing each other on and off for almost a year now. He didn't get her present until the day before yesterday because they'd been in an 'off' period, but they'd got back together a week ago. He'd stayed at her place last night and they'd exchanged gifts in her bed this morning. She gave him the jumper he was wearing. It felt soft and expensive, and it brought out the colour of his eyes. She gave him a scarf and a wallet too. He felt bad when she opened the discounted bottle of perfume he hadn't even bothered to smell, but she seemed delighted. She slipped her arms around him, and with her mouth close to his ear, she whispered: 'I love you'.

He wasn't expecting that.

He didn't know what to say.

So, without breaking her embrace, and being sure to avoid eye contact, he lay her back on the bed and distracted her with a line of kisses that began at her throat and inched lower. It did the trick. She didn't mention what she'd said again, or his lack of response.

And here she was beside him in the car, singing.

He'd dodged a bullet there.

*

This year, Izzy and Reu were the guests of honour. Reu acted like he'd never had a Christmas dinner before, hoovering everything up, even the Brussels sprouts. After dinner, when Uncle Brian asked for volunteers to take the dog for a walk, Izzy put herself and Will forward. Reu was too full to move from the sofa, and the dark, wet afternoon meant they couldn't persuade anyone to join them.

They borrowed a huge golf umbrella and stepped out into the drizzle. Izzy linked her arm through his, and the dog steered them up the lane.

'Do they like me?' she asked.

'Who?'

'Your parents. Everyone.'

He kept his eyes on the lane ahead. 'Of course they like you.'

'Your aunt asked me how long we'd been together. Have you never mentioned me?'

'I don't see them all that often . . .'

She stopped walking. 'Will, I can't keep pretending this morning didn't happen.'

'What do you mean?'

'I meant what I said.'

'What?'

'Don't play dumb. I told you I love you.'

'Oh . . . that.' Will kicked at stones on the path.

'I can't pretend it doesn't matter that you didn't say it back. It's not like I'm rushing things. We've been seeing each other for eleven months now. I need to know how you feel about me.'

Rain pattered on the umbrella. 'Well . . . I care about—'

'Oh, come on, Will! Not "I care about you", *please*.'

'I don't know what you want me to say . . .'

'There's a conventional response, and if you can't bring yourself to say it, then I don't know what we're doing here!'

The dog whimpered at his feet. 'I like you; I really do. You're a lovely girl. It's not you, it's—'

She slapped him hard across the face. He sucked air through his teeth at the sting of it.

'Don't give me that one as well! Don't give me all the fucking clichés, Will! It's like you're waiting for someone better to come along.'

He said nothing.

'Oh my God, there's someone else!' Her voice was shrill.

Will stalled, trying to find the right words. 'I have . . . *feelings* . . . for someone else, but I haven't—'

'It's Emily, isn't it?'

'What? No—'

'The way you look at her. You're always looking at her. She's your brother's girlfriend, for God's sake!'

'It's not Emily, Izzy. Look, it doesn't matter who it is. What matters is, if I'm thinking about someone else, it's not fair on you.'

'So we're finished?'

He paused. 'I think that would be best.'

She tips her head skyward to stop tears from falling. 'Right.'

'I'm sorry. I don't want to hurt you, but it's better now than months down the line.'

'Happy fucking Christmas.' She turned on her heel.

'Izzy!' he called as she marched back down the lane towards the house. 'Take the umbrella!'

She kept walking.

'Do you know the way back?'

'I'm not a fucking moron!'

'Do you want me to come with you?'

'No. Walk the fucking dog!'

The dog whined and pulled in the opposite direction, so he carried on up the hill. Shit, he'd handled that terribly.

Fat drops of rain began drumming on the umbrella. Izzy would get soaked. He tipped the umbrella to see how far she'd got, but the darkness had already swallowed her. He hadn't planned to say any of that, but she'd given him no choice. If he said he loved her, then he couldn't break up with her. And he was always trying to break up with her, always keeping her at arm's length. She was pretty, sexy, a good laugh. Why couldn't he be satisfied with that? He hated doing this to her. Here. Today. He'd have to face the music back at the house, but despite that, he was relieved.

*

All eyes were on him as he entered the sitting room half an hour later.

'Jesus Christ, Will, you dumped her on Christmas Day?' You could always rely on Aidan for his tact.

Will sighed. 'Where is she?'

'She's upstairs crying her eyes out, you bastard. Emily's looking after her.' *Oh, great.* 'Couldn't you have waited a few

104

hours? Now you've ruined everyone's Christmas.' Aidan was trying not to smile. This had *made* his day, not ruined it.

'I didn't *plan* it. She put me on the spot . . .'

'I thought you liked Izzy?' asked his mum.

'I don't want to talk about it, Mum.'

'No one can drive her anywhere now. We've all been drinking,' she said. 'I'll take her to the station in the morning, assuming the trains are running on Boxing Day.'

Emily appeared in the doorway and gestured for him to join her. His heart drummed as he followed her to the kitchen and closed the door.

'Is she okay?' he asked.

Emily's expression was pained. 'Just embarrassed and humiliated.'

He groaned.

'Sorry, that was harsh, but you know what I mean. Listen,' Emily's tone went serious, 'I know she's been drinking but . . .'

Emily ran a hand through her hair and that pained expression deepened into a full-blown grimace.

Oh shit. 'What did she say?'

Emily lowered her voice. 'She said you're *in love* with me.'

Will feigned ignorance. 'What?'

'Why would she say that?' Emily studied his face.

Will sighed. 'I told her I'm into someone else and she's jumped to conclusions.'

'Why would she think it's me?'

'I don't know.'

'She was going on about a song you wrote. She said the lyrics were about me. Then she started crying and asked me to get her a drink.'

'Sorry you got dragged into this. She's upset. She's not thinking straight.'

'She's got a bottle of vodka up there.'

'Oh Christ, she's already had a bottle of wine. Don't worry, I'll go up and—'

Emily shook her head. 'That's not a good idea. She doesn't want to see you.'

'Okay, I'll send Mum up.'

Emily stared at him, pinning him to the spot. 'Will, she said "Forbidden" is about me. It's not about me, is it?'

Will scolded himself: he should have realised those lyrics would be obvious to Izzy.

'You can say no,' she prompted. 'Just say it's not about me.'

Will swallowed. 'What if it *was* about you?'

She paused, frowning.

'But I'm with Aidan,' she said at last.

'You don't have to be . . .'

'Will—'

'Emily, I'm mad about you. I have been ever since I saw you get off the train when I was busking at the station.'

'You never even spoke to me . . .'

'I was going to, but I got arrested, remember? Then Aidan asked you out before I got the chance. Look, if you're happy with him, I'll walk away. But if not, maybe you could think about . . . *us*.'

Her eyebrows were drawn up in the middle of her forehead.

'But if it's "no" – that's fine, you can tell me now. I'll get over it.'

Emily opened her mouth to speak, but Aunty Sandra burst into the kitchen. 'Right, everyone out of here! I'm putting the sausage rolls on. Will, can you put this rubbish out?'

Chapter 24

April 2016

Emily

I don't want to be in this bar – everyone here is half my age – but FHD is back from his holiday and this is finally happening. I feel sick.

But why worry about your first date in twenty years when you've jacked in your job and have no way of paying the mortgage? That helps put things into perspective.

If I hadn't quit my job, I'd have agonised for hours about what to wear tonight, but with the help of *perspective*, I chose a low-cut top and a pair of ancient but well-fitting jeans in minutes. With indifference, no less. I even put on my sexiest underwear (only M&S black cotton but with lacy bits). Thank you, perspective.

I've almost finished a large glass of wine – I should slow down, but I take another mouthful. Let's get this over with.

'Hi!'

I jump out of my skin.

FHD has come up behind me as I'm swallowing a great glug of wine. I'm coughing and spluttering and trying to breathe all at the same time. Wine is coming out of my nose, and I have to wipe it along the back of my hand.

'Oh God, I'm sorry,' he says. 'I startled you.'

'It's fine,' I wheeze.

I need a drink to stop the tickle in my throat, but that's the last of my wine. My eyes stream as I embark on a fresh bout of coughing. I hold up a finger and make a face that I hope says, 'excuse me while I nip to the loo'.

In the mirror, my face is dark crimson, and my low-cut top shows a vast expanse of blotchy décolletage. I'm sweaty and my eyes are bloodshot, only adding to the delightful green bruise that remains from the car accident. Then I remember I have no job and my teenage daughter has moved out. I have far more important things to worry about.

I make my way back to FHD who's chatting amiably with the barman. He exudes such confidence. What must that be like? To be at ease wherever you go? I remember my 'get a life' motto – I need to be more like him even if I have to fake it. 'Shall we try that again?' I ask.

He orders our drinks and we find a table in the corner.

I ask about his holiday. He tells me about his trip to Devon and then I draw a blank. I sit facing him, dismissing every question that pops into my head. When was the last time you went on a date? Are you on any dating apps? How long have you been divorced? Who split up with who? Even *I* know that's not what you're supposed to talk about on dates.

'You look like you're trying to solve a riddle,' he says.

I laugh. 'Sorry.' Suddenly I think of a question that's not terrible: 'So, what do you do?'

'I was hoping you'd ask me that,' he says. 'I'm in IT.'

'IT?'

'Yeah. I tell people to switch it off and back on again.'

'Fascinating. Tell me more.'

'Well, people ring up and they say they're having a problem and I say "try switching it off and back on again". And they do and it works and they're all grateful and pay me lots of money.'

'You must be very proud.'

'A friend and I set up the business eight years ago now.'

'Are you still friends?' I ask, cheekily.

'Funnily enough, we are.'

We both take a drink, and the silence is only a little awkward.

'I already know what *you* do,' he says. 'Very important work at the primary school.'

'Not anymore.'

He pauses, his drink halfway to his lips. 'You got a new job? Where are you off to?'

'No, a sane person would find another job first, then hand in their notice. I got angry and quit on the spot.'

'What happened?' He sips his drink.

'Long story.'

His smile is slow and lazy. 'I'm here all night.'

'I lost my temper with the Head and told her to stick her job.'

'Ooh,' he chuckles. 'Sounds juicy! She's got quite a reputation for being a bit of a dragon. What did she do to piss you off?'

I don't want to tell him she accused me of flirting with him. 'It was a catalogue of things, really. Ten years' worth. It all came to a head over nothing in the end.'

'I bet it felt good to quit, though?'

'It's the kind of thing you fantasise about, isn't it? I've always wanted to tell her to stick it, but it didn't quite go how I'd hoped. I've been replaying it in my mind ever since.'

'Still, it took balls. I've seen the way she spoke to you, and others. She had it coming.'

'Yeah. The only thing is, I don't have a job and I'm not sure what I'll do without a reference.'

He pulls a face. 'Ah.'

'Hmm.'

A group of young men at the next table burst into laughter.

'Well, you're better off out of a job you don't enjoy. I know Florence and the other kids will miss you, though.'

It's kind of him to say, but the kids won't even notice I've gone.

We talk about our daughters. He flatters me by saying I don't look old enough to have a fifteen-year-old. When I tell him about Liv moving out, he looks genuinely terrified about what he has in store.

After a while, he changes the subject. 'You know, a friend of mine might have a job for you. He needs someone to help look after his café while he's in Thailand for six months. He doesn't want to sell it until he's sure about the move – new girlfriend and all that. How are your barista skills?'

'Non-existent.'

'Well, it's not brain surgery, is it? He's got one girl who has been working with him for years – she can run the place – she just can't do it full time. They'd show you the ropes, obviously. He's getting desperate; he's been let down twice already, and he should've been in Thailand by now.'

I picture myself running a coffee shop – I like the mental image.

'There's no harm in having a look, I suppose,' I say.

'You'd be doing each other a favour and the good thing is, it's only for six months, so it's not like it's forever.'

'It sounds like fate.'

He raises his glass. 'To new beginnings.'

'I'll drink to that.'

*

We share a cab. His place is closer, but he insists on dropping me first. I'm quiet on the ride home, my mind racing. Is he expecting to come in? Do I want him to come in? I put the underwear on, but I'm not so brave now.

'When would you like to visit my mate's café?' He has the calendar open on his phone. 'How about Monday morning?'

'I have nothing on for the foreseeable future.'

'Pick you up at ten?'

I fix him with a confident smile. 'Sure.'

110

We pull into my road, and I direct the cabbie to my house. I take off my seatbelt, my 'get-a-life' mantra ringing in my ears again, then hear myself say: 'Would you like to come in for coffee?'

He hesitates.

'What am I saying?' I backtrack. 'It's late—'

'Sure, why not?'

Even as I put my key in the front door, I haven't decided whether I mean coffee or 'coffee' in inverted commas. I look to FHD for inspiration. His hands are deep in his pockets as he stares into the distance.

'Come in,' I say, putting my handbag on the sideboard.

He follows me through to the kitchen. I flick on the lights, the dim ones that only light up the counter.

He sits at the little breakfast table.

'Coffee? Tea? Night cap?' I ask.

'Night cap?'

'Let's see . . .' I rummage in a cupboard. 'I've only got gin, Baileys or Pimm's, I'm afraid. Or white wine?'

'Gin's good.' He smiles. His eyes crinkle at the corners, and I get a flash of those lovely teeth.

Am I really doing this?

I cut a lime into wedges and break ice out of the mould. He watches as I run a wedge of lime around the rim of the glass before giving it a squeeze and dropping it into the drink.

'Very professional.'

I hand him his glass and sit down.

We drink.

He has the kind of stubble that's almost a beard. It's flecked with grey and there's a little grey at his temples. His knee is bobbing up and down like he's listening to some internal soundtrack. I drag my eyes away before he catches me staring at him, the phrase 'it's like riding a bike' rolling around in my head.

'I thought about what you said before.' He looks at me intently. 'About it being a long time and I want you to know

111

I'm not in a hurry so . . . you know, when you're ready to . . . I mean, I know what it's like . . . to start seeing people again after . . . whatever . . . and I had a good time tonight. I enjoyed spending time with you so . . . I'm happy to, you know, hang out until you're ready—'

I'm not sure if I want to put him out of his misery or if I just want him to shut up, but I shift forward in my chair and kiss him. I taste the lime on his lips and smell whatever aftershave that is.

I pull away to gauge his reaction.

He grins. 'Or we could rush in.'

Heat flushes my cheeks, and as I look away, something catches my eye on the table.

It's Liv's door key with its 'O' keyring.

She's here.

Chapter 25

December 1995

Christmas Day

When Will went into the sitting room, Reu was spinning around with his mouth wide open.

'*Mary Poppins*!' shouted Aidan.

Reu shook his head.

'*Ghostbusters*!' called Uncle Brian.

Reu shook his head again.

'*The Sound of Music*?' guessed Will.

Reu pointed at him while touching his nose, the universal gesture for a correct guess in charades. Reu had just learned it and was enjoying using it.

Aidan groaned. 'You didn't even see how many words it was!'

Will squeezed onto the sofa next to one of his cousins. Emily was sitting apart from everyone else, staring into space, running her thumb up and down her glass.

He wished they hadn't got interrupted; he could have explained. Oh, who was he kidding? No amount of explaining would help him now. Izzy had set a chain of events in motion this morning and there was no going back. And even though it was likely to end in public humiliation, he was glad. Whatever happened, at least it was out there. He'd finally told her how he felt.

Aidan was shouting his guesses over everyone else's, taking the game too seriously, ever competitive. Will ought to feel guilty about betraying his brother, but he didn't. When Aidan went off in a cab with that girl, everything changed. Aidan didn't care about Emily. Maybe he should have spoken to Aidan first. Told him to tell Emily about his infidelity or *he* would? No. Will knew exactly how Aidan would respond to that ultimatum.

Anyway, it was done now.

Uncle Brian came in with a tray full of warm sausage rolls and everyone swooped on him like a flock of vultures, but the thought of eating made Will feel sick. Emily remained quietly detached from the group, but Aidan was too busy stuffing his face to notice.

Throughout the evening, Will's mum and aunt took turns to check on Izzy. At the last check, she'd been asleep, and he'd started to relax a little. The older generation chatting on the sofa while the younger ones argued about what game to play next. A bossy cousin wrenched Will from the sofa – and his thoughts – for a game of Swear Word Scrabble. Before he could refuse, he found himself teamed up with Emily and squashed at the table, his thigh pressed up against hers. He kept his eyes firmly on her fingers as she picked out their tiles from the box. Just when he thought the moment couldn't get any more awkward, Izzy appeared.

'Hello Izzy!' His uncle was ever the cheerful host. 'Will you join us?'

Izzy stood swaying in the doorway, her eyes ringed with smudged mascara. 'I thought I might.'

'Why don't you join Reu and Aidan's team?'

She staggered around the table and took the empty chair beside Aidan. He inclined his rack of tiles towards her, whispering tactics in her ear. Izzy rearranged the tiles on the rack, then cupping a hand around her mouth, whispered something to Aidan. Aidan's gaze lifted from the rack and landed on Will. Was she talking about him or the game? Aidan placed four tiles on the board.

'*Damn*,' said Aidan. 'With the triple letter score, that's nine.'

Will exhaled, having forgotten to breathe for the entire exchange.

Izzy didn't contribute much more, she sat slumped over the table, propping her chin in her hand. She kept nodding off and jerking herself awake. The game dragged on until Aidan's team finally won, and the group dispersed. Will's mum settled Izzy into an armchair and within moments she was asleep. It was a good job most his family were half-cut too, or this day would have been even more embarrassing. Will went to the kitchen for a glass of water. He was drinking at the sink when he saw someone behind him in the reflection of the window. He turned to see Emily walking away.

'Wait,' he said. 'Do you want something?'

'Just some water.'

He got a glass from the cupboard, filled it, and handed it to her.

He gently touched her arm. 'Are you okay?'

She said nothing; her doe-eyed look of confusion left him guilty and hopeful all at once.

She took a sip of her water, put the glass on the side, and stared at it like it was going to tell her what to say.

He wanted to put his arms around her so badly. 'Emily?'

She didn't look up, so he gently took a hold of her chin and angled her face towards him. Very slowly, she raised her eyes to meet his.

'Look,' he said, 'I'm sorry—'

'What the fuck?' Aidan yelled from behind them.

They jumped apart, which only made them look guilty. Aidan lunged at Will, grabbed a fistful of his jumper, and yanked him closer.

'Izzy told me you're obsessed with Emily, but I thought she was talking shit because she's drunk,' Aidan snarled in his face. 'But here you are, feeling her up in the kitchen!'

'I'm not *feeling her up*!'

Aidan thrust Will backwards, and he clattered against the draining board where a stack of plates was drying.

'And you!' he spat, pointing a vicious finger at Emily. 'I bet you've been encouraging him.'

Emily stepped back, wide-eyed and blinking.

'Don't talk to her like that!' Will steadied himself and straightened up. 'Izzy's stirring – she's trying to get back at me, you idiot!'

'Don't call me a fucking idiot!' Aidan shoved Will again but he was braced for it this time. 'Izzy's right, you *are* always looking at Emily. Did you think you could get away with that? She's my girlfriend!'

'Like you give a shit! You didn't bother to go to her exhibition, you don't show any interest in her art, or her friends!'

'Will . . .' Emily pleaded.

'And I suppose you do, do you?' Aidan stepped closer, squaring up to him.

'You only asked her out because you saw me looking at her!'

'Bullshit!' A fleck of spit flew out of Aidan's mouth and landed on Will's cheek.

'What about the night of Emily's show? You came to our gig at ULU and you left with that—'

Aidan's fist connected with Will's cheekbone with such force it threw him backwards. Everything slid into slow motion on the long journey to the floor. He saw his dad come up behind Aidan and wrap his arms around him. Why was he hugging him? Uncle Brian was there too, shouting silently. And Emily – beautiful Emily – brought her hands to her mouth, her eyes brimming with tears.

Chapter 26

April 2016

Emily

I drag Liv's keys towards me across the table. 'My daughter. She's here.'

'Here?' asks FHD, his eyes reflecting my panic.

I run to my handbag in the hall and rummage for my phone, which I've kept politely zipped up for our entire date. I haven't checked it once.

There are three messages and a missed call from Scott.

The latest reads: Please call or text me when you get this. I'm getting worried.

The previous one: She wants to stay over. I hope that's okay.

And the first one says: Liv needs a book from yours for revision. You should take this opportunity to talk. I'll drop her over shortly.

I kick off my heels and run back to the kitchen.

'I'm sorry, but you have to leave,' I hiss. 'She's upstairs.'

He gapes at me before following me obediently out to the hall.

'I'm sorry,' I whisper. 'Can you get an Uber from up the road?'

'Sure.'

'Thanks for tonight.' I practically shove him out the door. 'Sorry,' I add, before shutting it on him.

I run upstairs to Liv's room in the loft. Hopefully, she didn't hear anything from two floors up. The door to her room is ajar – unusual for her – she likes her privacy. The lights are off. I wait for my eyes to adjust and make out the shape of her body under the duvet. Is she asleep or do I want to believe she is to avoid explaining why a strange man was in the house? She hasn't slept through me coming into her room for years.

I back out and go downstairs. I text Scott to let him know I'm okay and text FHD to apologise.

After I take off my make-up and peel off my best underwear, I lie in bed alone. I'm glad we didn't end up doing anything. It would have been a mistake.

I remember the last time I had sex. Scott and I had taken Liv on a 'family' holiday. We did that when she was younger. Where was it? Majorca? Liv must have been about ten. We always got separate rooms, me in with Liv, and Scott in an adjoining room or on a sofa bed in the lounge area.

It was a hurried, hushed fumble in the dark with Liv fast asleep in the next room. We didn't speak about it afterwards, and just as we had the handful of times it had happened before, we pretended it hadn't. He always obliged, never questioned, and never asked for anything more.

The next day I was embarrassed and guilty and lonelier than ever. I caught him looking at me from the next sun lounger where he and Liv were playing travel chess in the shade. I remember the pity in his eyes. And after that, I insisted we went on separate holidays.

I lie awake for more than an hour thinking about this when floorboards creak overhead. Liv doesn't come down to use the loo as I expect and I can still hear her moving around quietly so I decide to go up and see her, give her a hug, apologise for not being here when she arrived. I could do with a hug.

I pad up the stairs. A sliver of light surrounds her now-closed door.

As I open it, there's a streak of movement I can't work out, and Liv sits on the bed looking shifty. I should have knocked.

'Sorry . . .' I begin.

Then I notice a piece of paper on the bed, and beside it, a pile of envelopes. A box props open the hatch-like door to the eaves. A box with 'personal' scrawled on the side in my handwriting.

A box I never open.

I rush to the bed and gather up the letters. 'What are you doing? These are private!' My voice is high-pitched.

'I'm sorry, I—'

'No, no, you can't look at these!' I can't stand the sight of them, but I can't have them out in the open like this.

She's been here all night, alone. How much has she read?

'How dare you read my private letters!'

She looks defiant. 'I didn't mean to. I was looking for something else and I saw them. I wondered what they were.'

'I thought you came here because you wanted to talk to me. To spend time with me. For the first time in months!'

She drops her eyes and picks at her nails.

'You only came here to snoop around.'

'I didn't plan it. I didn't know you wouldn't be here,' she mutters.

'You knew, even if I was here, you could wait until I was asleep.'

She doesn't deny it and it makes me want to scream.

'They're from Will Bailey, aren't they?' she asks.

'That's none of your business!'

'It *is* my business.' Her voice sounds odd, strangled. 'It's my business because he's my father, isn't he?'

Chapter 27

December 1995

When Will woke on Boxing Day morning, he found himself on the floor next to the Christmas tree, with Reu fast asleep on the sofa beside him. Getting to his feet was painful, his body stiff and his left eye was swollen and half-closed. He groaned at the memory of slamming into the kitchen counter after Aidan punched him. On the way to the bathroom, Will saw Aidan and Emily's room was empty, and when he checked out of the window, Aidan's car was missing.

He was gone.

And so was Emily.

No trains were running, so Will's dad was tasked with driving Izzy home. His mum, mortified by the scandal, banished him along with Izzy, and Reu didn't want to stay without Will. Aidan was supposed to give them all a lift home, but with him gone, they all had to pile into one car. The drive back was silent except for two occasions when Izzy asked his dad to pull over so she could throw up.

When they arrived at her flat, Will got out to fetch her bag from the boot. 'Look, I really am sorry,' he said.

'So you keep saying.' She snatched the bag and marched up the front steps to her flat.

'That was awkward,' said his dad when he got back in the car. 'Shame, I liked that one.'

Will preferred it when no one was speaking.

*

Will and Reu spent the rest of Boxing Day in the garage, unable to hear the neighbours banging on the door to complain about the noise. When hunger eventually drove them into the house, Reu seemed quiet as Will rustled up cheese on toast.

'What's up?' asked Will.

'Nothing.'

'C'mon, talk to me, buddy. Is it because I ruined Christmas?'

'Ha! You *did* ruin Christmas!' joked Reu. 'Until then, it was the best Christmas ever.'

Of course, this was Reu's first Christmas away from his family; it must have been tough. 'Did you speak to your mum yesterday?' Will asked.

'Nah.'

'Sorry Reu, we should have arranged for you to call her.'

'Don't worry. Your mum tried twice. There was no answer.'

'That's crap. I'm sorry, mate.'

'Seriously. It *was* the best Christmas ever. I got presents for once.'

'C'mon. Your mum got you presents, surely?'

'She tried to. My stepdad wouldn't let her spend money on me. He'd get me something off the back of a lorry, usually for the wrong age group. Mum would get me something a few weeks later – once he'd forgotten about it. Something small that he wouldn't notice.'

'What a bastard. What about your little sister?'

'She's his little princess, so she does all right. I don't need to worry about her.' Reu's voice cracked a little.

Will waited for Reu to compose himself.

'I miss her,' Reu whispered. Then he lost it, properly crying.

Will went to his friend and hugged him, but the sobbing only intensified.

121

'Thanks for everything,' Reu sniffed, breaking away. 'I feel more welcome in your family than I do in mine.'

'I'm sorry I ruined your best Christmas ever . . .'

'You didn't. It's still the best Christmas ever.'

'Even though we came home early?'

'*Especially* because we came home early. All day drumming, followed by cheese on toast – I'm in heaven. I'm sorry you fell out with your brother, though.'

'*I'm* not. He's an idiot.'

'Your mum was pretty annoyed about it.'

Mary had wanted to know exactly what they were arguing about. Will tried to explain, but Aidan kept talking over him, telling everyone Will had been coming on to Emily. Will and Emily protested their innocence until Izzy piped up.

'It's true. He's obsessed with her,' she said.

'Oh, for God's sake. I'm not obsessed with Emily!' Will insisted.

Mary had had quite enough by then. 'I don't want to hear another word! It's Christmas – I want no more fighting and arguing. Let's all go to bed and sort this out in the morning when everyone's sobered up.'

They went to bed, Emily with Aidan – why shouldn't she? – and Izzy alone in the room they were supposed to share. Will didn't get to finish what he was saying about Aidan snogging that girl in a taxi.

They never got to sort it out in the morning.

*

Will sat by the window, looking up the road towards the town centre. He picked at the label on his bottle of Bud, his knee bouncing up and down. What the hell was he doing here? Since they'd got back from Oxfordshire, he hadn't been able to get Emily out of his mind. He needed to talk to her, tell her what she needed to know. Then he remembered she might be working during the Christmas break from college. So here he was, sitting in her pub waiting for her shift to start, which – according to the barman – was in ten minutes.

His mum's voice echoed in his mind.

'Jesus, I'm mortified. Fighting in Brian's kitchen on Christmas Day!' she'd scolded, when she rang from Oxfordshire the day after he got home.

'He hit *me*. I didn't touch him.'

'I can't believe you'd carry on with Emily. How could you do that to your own brother? To our family!'

'Why are you taking his word over mine?'

'I'm not taking sides. You're both my boys – I don't want you two falling out over a girl.'

'I didn't do anything. And even if I did, he doesn't care about her. He was cheating on her.'

She tutted. 'That's no excuse. He's your brother, his girlfriend is off-limits. You're to have nothing to do with her – she's trouble. Things like this can break families apart. Promise me you'll leave her alone?'

'Mum—'

'Promise me!'

'We're not getting anywhere here, and I've got to go.'

She gave him instructions to water the plants, put the bins out, and make sure Reu was eating enough. She said goodbye but before she hung up, she said: 'And Will?'

'Yeah?'

'Stay away from Emily.'

But he couldn't stop thinking about her. For all he knew, Emily was living happily ever after with Aidan. He couldn't stand not knowing.

A figure came into view, walking towards the pub. It was her. She didn't notice him as she passed the window and when she came in, she slipped behind the bar, out of sight. Will's mouth was dry. He took a swig of his drink, his heart pounding. She emerged a few moments later, having shed her coat. Halfway through tying her apron, she froze. They locked eyes. It was a full three seconds before she snapped out of it and rushed over.

'What are you doing here?' she hissed.

Good question. 'To be honest,' he said, 'I don't know.'

'I'm supposed to be working. Come and sit at the bar so I can talk to you.'

He grabbed his bottle and pulled up a stool at the bar as she made her way to the other side.

She began emptying the dishwasher, grabbing two wine glasses in each hand, and clinking them onto the shelf above their heads. Will squirmed on his stool.

She placed some pint glasses on the lower shelf and looked up at him.

'Seriously, what are you doing here?' she said at last.

'I'm sorry. I shouldn't have come, but I needed to see you. To see what's going on.'

She exhaled. 'I don't know what's going on. One minute I'm happy with my boyfriend, spending Christmas with his family, then all this happens!'

She looked for a moment like she might cry, but went back to unloading.

The only words on Will's lips were 'are you still with him?' but he didn't dare to ask.

'What happened . . . after . . .?' he ventured.

'After your mum sent us to our rooms?'

'Yeah.'

She stopped what she was doing and looked into his eyes.

'Aidan accused me of cheating on him with you. He was angry and aggressive and wouldn't listen to anything I said.'

A customer came to the bar, and Will had to wait while she served him. Then she picked up from where she'd left off. 'I told him I wouldn't talk if he wasn't prepared to listen, so we left it at that.'

'What happened in the morning?'

'I said I wanted to go home before everyone woke up, so he drove me home.'

'How was *that* journey?'

'Awful. He kept apologising, saying he didn't mean what he said, that he was drunk and jealous. He kept asking me to forgive him.'

'Did you?' *Please say no.*

'I told him I don't like violence, and I can't be with someone who would punch his brother. He said, "Every bloke who *has* a brother has *punched* his brother".' She rolled her eyes at the idea.

'So you dumped him?' Will prompted.

'He begged me to give him another chance. He was . . . *emotional*. He said he loved me. I said I need time to think.'

Will panicked. She didn't need time to think. She deserved better; she deserved the truth.

'He cheated on you,' he blurted.

Her body stiffened. 'What?'

'He cheated on you. The night of your show, he came to our gig, and he left with a girl.' Will's words came out in a rush and hung in the air between them.

Emily knitted her brow. 'What girl?'

'I don't know – some blonde.'

'How do you know she wasn't a friend?'

Will faltered. 'I saw them kissing.'

Emily's eyes narrowed. 'Do you hate each other that much you would use me to get at each other?'

'No—'

'Please go.' Her tone was suddenly ice cold.

'Let me explain—'

'Please, Will. I can't handle it!' She came out from behind the bar and marched around the pub collecting dirty glasses. When she returned, she said, 'What are you still doing here?'

'Look, I didn't mean to upset you. I just wanted you to know the facts before making any decisions.'

'How can I possibly know the facts? Why should I take your word over his? I hardly know you.'

Her words stung. 'I'm telling the truth. Deep down you believe me. You deserve better than him. You deserve better than me too but give me a chance.'

A couple entered the bar. 'I need to get back to work,' she said.

'Please, think about what I've said. You've got my mobile number.' He couldn't keep the whiny desperation from his voice. 'Call me when you're ready.'

'I've got to go,' she said, walking away.

He should never have come here. 'I'm sorry, Emily.'

'Goodbye, Will.'

Chapter 28

April 2016

Emily

I stand at the foot of her bed, clutching the letters to my chest.

'What?' I ask, exasperated.

'Will Bailey's my father, isn't he?' Liv sits cross-legged on her bed, wearing pyjamas with 'do not disturb' printed across the front. 'You slept with him before he died, didn't you? It says so in these letters . . .'

'You read my private letters and now you want explanations? You're the one who owes *me* an explanation.'

'If you slept with him before he died, then he could be my dad.' Her voice is shaky.

'You've put two and two together and got five—'

'Just admit he could be my father!' she roars.

I'm stunned into silence.

Her forehead's all scrunched. This must have been eating her up all night.

'*Scott* is your father,' I say plainly. 'That's all you need to know.'

'But how do you know *for sure*?' she persists.

'I don't know what you think you've read, but I didn't sleep with Will before he died.' The letters tremble in my hands. 'There's absolutely no doubt who your father is. Now, that's the end of it. I don't want to hear any more about it. And I don't want you dragging up the past anymore. I can't handle it.' My throat contracts.

She stares at me then looks away.

'It's too painful. Promise me. Promise me you'll stop all this snooping.' My voice cracks and it's a moment before I can speak again. 'Liv?'

Her eyes meet mine for a fraction of a second and she looks down and mumbles, 'I promise.'

I go to put the letters back in the box, then change my mind. I take the bundle towards the door.

'Why won't you talk to me about him?' Her voice wobbles.

I face her, the weight of the letters heavy in my hands and in my heart.

'Because it's all my fault,' I blurt, a sob catching in my throat. 'I killed him.'

Chapter 29

January 1996

Will's mobile phone rang. Even though it was a work phone, but he'd given the number to Matty for organising gigs. He'd also given it to Emily to organise the day he went to her college to move her sculpture. It was 8 p.m. so it wasn't work, and that wasn't Matty's number on the screen.

He kicked his bedroom door shut and answered before the third ring. 'Emily?'

'Yes. Hi.'

'Happy new year,' he said.

'Same to you.'

Had she thought about what he'd said at the pub? Did she believe him, or had Aidan won her over?

'How did you celebrate in the end?' she asked. They were supposed to see the new year in together with Izzy and Aidan. They'd planned it months ago, but that went out the window after the scandal of Christmas.

'Reu and I drove down to Brighton in the van. We did an impromptu gig at a little bar in the Lanes playing cover songs for free beer.'

'Sounds fun.'

'The fireworks on the beach were pretty cool.' He swapped the phone to the other hand and wiped his palm on his jeans. 'How about you?'

'I worked at the pub in the end.'

She hadn't said much so far but he was getting a sense she was preoccupied, building up to something maybe?

'Not during the biggest celebration of the year?' he joked.

'Afraid so. It wasn't so bad; I got triple time and loads of tips. Listen,' she said, suddenly business-like. 'We should meet. To talk.'

He closed his eyes and breathed deeply. 'Okay. When?'

She suggested they meet on Thursday at a bar in central London. 'See you then,' she said, wrapping up the call before he'd finished scribbling down the address.

'It's good to hear your voice . . .' he ventured, not wanting her to go.

'See you Thursday,' she said and hung up.

He knew then, she only wanted to meet because she was too nice to break bad news over the phone.

Chapter 30

January 1996

On the train into town, Will sipped whiskey from his dad's pewter hip flask as suburbia slid by in the dark. She would let him down gently, face to face. That's why she wanted to meet.

He was early, so he sauntered through town and found the ancient wonky bar she'd chosen with an hour to spare. Hops dangled from heavy beams on the ceiling and shabby antique mirrors advertised stout with faded lettering. He bought a pint and settled at a table next to an old guy wearing a fedora, reading an SAS survival book. Beyond him, by the window, a girl was holding something up to the lamp on the table. Was that Emily? He grabbed his drink, took a few steps in her direction and saw it was her.

'Will! You're early . . .' She stood and kissed him lightly on the cheek. Just as she did when she came to the house for dinner with Aidan.

'So are you.' He smiled – happy to see her, happy she was early too. 'What's that you're looking at?'

'I just picked up these transparencies from a lab around the corner.' She showed him a plastic sleeve filled with photographic images. 'We can only process black and white film at college.'

'Can I see?' He pulled up the chair beside her.

'Sure.'

She held the sleeve up to the lamp and he had to put his face close to hers to see.

Each image was a splash of iridescent colour, a couple of inches square, all the same subject but with slight variations in composition. A small wooden treasure chest sat open in the centre and pouring out of it, in all directions, were butterflies and beetles. The colours ranged from vibrant purples and emeralds in the middle to deep, glittering black at the edges. It was intricate and beautiful.

'Wow. I love it. Where did you get all those creatures?'

'I made them. They're paper sculptures sprayed with metallic paints,' she said, her voice animated.

'That must have taken ages.'

'It did. I found some of the objects – like the peacock feathers. I collect stuff.' Her eyes were bright like they were that day at her college. This was her passion.

'Is this for college, then?'

'No, it's for a competition. The winner gets five grand and their own exhibition at a gallery.'

'You'll win it easily,' he said.

'I doubt it,' she laughed. 'But the runner-up prizes are quite good. Maybe I'll get a year's supply of pencils or something.'

'No, you'll win it. Seriously. That one's the best.' He pointed to his favourite. 'You've got this in the bag.'

'I like that one too. I'll get it printed. Fingers crossed.'

'Is that the dream for you? To have your own exhibition one day?'

Her face flushed. 'I suppose so. It's the one thing I'm good at. But it's not like I have a choice about it. I *have* to do it. It would be amazing if one day someone liked my work enough to pay for it.'

Will knew exactly what she meant. He understood that compulsion completely. 'It'll happen! You're uber-talented.'

'Even if you're "uber-talented" – which I'm not – it's difficult to earn a living. I chose my course because you study design and illustration as well as art, so hopefully I can support myself that way. I couldn't work in an office. It would kill me.'

'Me too.'

The guy in the fedora lit a pipe and the smell wafted over, reminding him of his grandad who died a long time ago.

'So, what's the big dream for you?' she asked.

'Same as you. I just want to earn enough money to carry on with my music. It's about doing what you love. Because you have to.'

She looked at him. Really looked at him, like she was peering into his soul. And something in her expression made him worry she was about to deliver the bad news.

Well, he wouldn't make it easy for her. He wasn't going home yet.

'Same again?' he asked, nodding to her half-empty glass.

'White wine would be great, thanks.'

*

As they drank, she told him about her course. How the rich kids spent so much money on their projects it was hard to compete. He told her about the record company that was interested and the gigs he had lined up. Neither of them mentioned Aidan or his family.

They had a few more drinks which – along with the whiskey he'd had on the train on an empty stomach – were taking effect. He was loosening up, enjoying himself even. He still rushed to fill gaps in the conversation – he didn't want her to say what she'd come to say. She was tipsy, too, leaning in when she spoke and laughing at all his lame jokes. He kept her talking right up to last orders.

'Oh no!' she cried when she heard the bell. 'I didn't realise the time. We've missed the last train.'

133

'We'll have to get the night bus. We can get one from Trafalgar Square.'

They downed the dregs of their drinks, put on their coats, and stepped out into the cold.

'Do you still live with your parents?' His words formed clouds in the chilly night air.

'Yes. Unfortunately.'

'It's not far from mine. I'll see you home.'

'If you're sure . . .'

They chatted as they walked past the theatres on Shaftesbury Avenue, underneath the tunnel of lanterns in Chinatown and on down a narrow lane that opened out onto Trafalgar Square. As they passed the fountains and lions, he fought the urge to take her hand.

The bus stop was across the square and the bus came while Emily was still checking the timetable. He followed her to the top deck. She warned him the journey was long – but it was the shortest hour and a half Will had ever experienced. They talked about everything and nothing. When he thought she might give him the bad news, he distracted her with the book of poetry he'd folded into his coat pocket to read on the journey. He explained how they inspired his lyrics and pointed out his favourites. Then she got out her sketchbook, and he was mesmerised.

As they got closer to home, and he relaxed his hold on the conversation, she hit him with it: 'Will, we need to talk about—'

'Look!' cried Will. 'There's a chip shop! It's still open! If we jump off now, we can get some chips and walk the rest of the way.'

He ushered her off the bus, adding another ten minutes to their walk, but at least he'd diverted the conversation. They bought chips and ate as they strolled, steam rising from the wrappers.

'We still need to talk—'

'Can you hold my chips a sec?'

He dipped into the shadows of an alley to take a leak. His heart raced as he walked back to where she stood waiting under a streetlamp, holding the chips like an illuminated angel.

'Sorry about that.' He took his chips back and they continued walking.

'You can't keep changing the subject, you know. I need to tell you this.'

'I wasn't, I—'

'I saw Aidan last night.'

Will's heart sank.

'I wanted to talk to him before I came to meet you,' she continued. 'I told him it's over between him and me.'

Will's heart jumped back up, hammering hard. Did that mean what he thought it meant?

'That shut you up.' She popped a chip into her mouth, then screwed up the bag before throwing it into a nearby bin. No longer hungry, he did the same.

She shivered and folded her arms across her chest, shoulders high.

'I've got something to warm us up.' He patted his coat pockets and pulled out his dad's hip flask.

'What's in there?'

'Whiskey.' He handed it to her.

She unscrewed the cap and hesitated before taking a swig. As she swallowed, she scrunched her face up and squeezed her eyes shut. 'Oh yeah. It burns all right!' she wheezed, handing it back.

He took a swig himself and struggled not to cough.

'We should play a drinking game,' she suggested.

He raised his eyebrows. 'Okay.'

'I ask you a question and if you don't answer, you take a drink.'

'Challenge accepted.'

135

'Right. My first question is . . .' She looked skywards. 'Have you written any more songs about me?'

Her directness threw him.

'I have an entire album's worth,' he joked, but it wasn't far from the truth.

She went to ask another question, but he cut her off: 'No more, my turn.'

'Okay, fire away.'

Her question emboldened him. 'Have you thought about me at all since we last saw each other?'

She smiled and put her hand out for the flask.

'Ah, avoiding the first question: very revealing.' He handed it over.

She drank and pulled the same pained expression as before. 'My turn. What are you going to do now I'm available?'

He'd been in a daze since she said they'd broken up. Now, these words, so forward and flirtatious, left him reeling. He shook his head to clear it.

She giggled, her voice tinkling in the night air. 'I haven't been able to get a word in all night and now . . . silence.'

He came to a stop, but she didn't notice for a couple of steps and turned back.

'I meant what I said at Christmas.' His voice came out quieter than expected.

She stepped closer. 'Sorry?'

'I meant what I said at Christmas,' he said again.

'You said a lot of things at Christmas.' But she wasn't teasing now.

'I know.' He dragged a palm over his mouth. 'I've messed stuff up, caused trouble for both of us. Hurt people. But I can't stop thinking about you. Haven't been able to stop thinking about you for . . . I don't even know how long.'

She dropped her chin. Was she hiding a smile?

She screwed the cap back on the flask. 'That's why I'm here.'

'Sorry . . .' He squeezed his eyes shut for a moment. 'Why are you here?'

She exhaled a little cloud of steam. 'I'm here because nobody's ever done anything like that for me before.'

He stood there trying to grasp what she was saying. All evening, he'd thought she was telling him one thing and now she was saying the opposite. His head hurt.

'And I like it,' she added.

She slipped the flask into the pocket of his coat and kept her hand there. Half a second later, her other hand hooked into his other pocket, her fingers like ice touching his. She had never been so close. Energy thrummed in the air between them. A break in the traffic left the street silent as her gaze dropped slowly to his lips. She tilted her head slightly and inched her face closer until her nose was alongside his, her breath warm on his cheek. His heart was beating so hard he could feel it reverberating through his entire body. The tiniest brush of her bottom lip against his and his insides melted. Her face was hovering there, and he was paralysed, waiting for her next move. A van rumbled past. He couldn't wait any longer. The slightest dip and his chin and his mouth was on hers, soft as marshmallows. She parted her lips. The tips of their tongues touched. She tasted of whiskey and salt.

It was a brief kiss. There was a lot more almost kissing than actual kissing. Before he knew it, she'd retrieved her hands and was walking away and he had to run to catch her up.

She stopped at a gate two houses up. 'This is me.'

All he could think about was kissing her again, but she had opened the gate and was on the other side.

'Call me,' she said

He composed himself. 'Oh, I will.'

'Goodnight,' she called from the door.

'Night.'

She smiled and closed the door.

He turned and headed for home, a ball of excitement bursting in his stomach and a huge grin on his face.

He paid no attention when the car engine started up behind him. As it pulled up alongside him, he barely noticed. He didn't even look over until the door slammed, but by then it was too late to run.

Chapter 31

April 2016

Liv

I message Dad and ask him to pick me up from Mum's early.

He waits until we've pulled away from the house before asking, 'What happened, Liv?'

He says it in such a kind voice I burst into tears. I don't deserve his kindness. I'm a terrible person.

He lets me sniffle for a while. I look out the window, wiping my eyes, buying time.

When we get in the house, he gives me an enormous hug in the hallway.

He rests his chin on the top of my head. 'Talk to me.'

I don't want to say out loud what I've done, but it's easier if he can't see my face. 'I did something bad,' I confess.

'We all make mistakes. What did you do?'

I hesitate. 'I thought Mum might have letters from Will Bailey, so I looked through the boxes in the loft.'

I brace myself for him to have a go at me, but he just sighs. 'I'm guessing you found some?'

'Yeah.'

'And you read them?'

I start to cry again, and he strokes my hair.

When I try to speak, it sounds like something's stuck in my throat. 'I read . . . *all* of them.'

His ribs contract as he sighs again.

'Come on,' he says. 'Hot chocolate will help.'

I follow him into the kitchen. 'This might be beyond the powers of hot chocolate.'

He fills his fancy coffee machine with milk and clatters around, getting mugs from the cupboards. He's doing that thing where he keeps quiet, waiting for me to talk – he should be a therapist. I lean on the counter, building up to it.

'I read something in the letters . . .' I say eventually, 'That made me think you might not be my dad.'

There's a flicker of shock in his expression before he composes himself and fixes his eyes on me. 'I'm your dad, Liv. There's no doubt about that.'

'How do you know, though?'

'Because I was there Liv, I remember it.'

I don't want to talk to him about sex. 'But you can't be sure she wasn't . . .'

He comes to me, takes my hand, and leads me to the mirror in the lounge. He stands behind me, his head above mine. I study our faces. We are alike. Everyone says it.

'You have brown eyes,' I say.

'I know you're mine.' He stares into space for a moment, then snaps out of it. 'Hot chocolate!'

Back in the kitchen, he pours hot milk into the mugs, swirls cocoa powder in mine and a shot of espresso in his.

'Did you tell Mum about your theory?' he asks.

'Yeah . . .'

'What did she say?'

'She said you're my dad, and that's the end of it. She was more annoyed about me reading the letters.'

He slides my mug towards me. 'You won't let this go, will you? No matter how much we try to convince you?'

'I don't know how you can be so sure.'

'Okay,' he says. 'We do a paternity test.'

'What?'

'You can get them online these days.' He pulls his phone out of his back pocket. 'Will that put an end to all this?'

I'm not sure how I feel about it. 'I guess so.'

My drink is too hot. I blow in it while Dad scrolls and taps away at the screen.

'Right, that's ordered,' he says. 'Now we need to have a talk about respecting people's privacy . . .'

*

'Tell me what happened,' says Chloe as we flop on her bed.

'Remember you said there might be letters from Will at Mum's house?'

She leans forward. 'You found some?'

I get my phone out and call up the photos I took of all the letters. I pick one at random and zoom in.

Chloe reads it: '"Dear Milly" – I told you she was Milly!'

'I know, right?'

She flicks through the photos. 'Jeez, how many are there? What do they say?'

'Loads. Mostly, he's telling her how much he misses her while he's away on tour and they're madly in love, but then there are all these letters where they've broken up. He's apologising for all the things he's done wrong and begging her to talk. Here, read this one, it's the last one.' I hand her my phone and read over her shoulder.

18th July 1999
    Dear Milly,
    I know you don't want me to contact you. This is the last letter, I promise. I don't want to make you cry anymore. I want you to be happy.
    I want you to know how sorry I am. It has been a weird few years and I'm not sure I'm coping with it all that well. Especially now we're not together, but

141

I wanted to say thank you for everything and thank you for last night. I know the circumstances weren't great, but to be with you again and feel your body close to mine and know you cared enough to do that after everything I've put you through. It meant the world to me. You mean the world to me.

I know it's a cliché, but . . .

I'll always love you,

W

x

I can almost see the cogs whirring in her brain.

'You think he's your dad, don't you?' she asks.

She's always been able to tell what I'm thinking.

'It had crossed my mind . . . He died in July 1999, and I was born in April 2000.'

She counts the months on her fingers. 'It's a definite possibility.'

'But the letters say they broke up in June 1999. So he can't be my dad, can he?'

'Ah in that case – no . . .'

'Then *that* letter,' I say, pointing at my phone in her hand, 'dated July 1999, sounds like they . . . well, it sounds like they *did* it. What do you think?'

'Thank you for last night . . . your body close to mine . . . you cared enough to do that . . . sounds like it. But it's not proof.'

'No, it's not proof, but it goes from him *not* being my dad in June to *possibly* being my dad in July.'

'True,' she says. 'But don't forget babies can come early or late. Did your mum ever mention that?'

'She sometimes complains I'm always late – have been since the day I was born.'

'Well, in that case the overlap is even bigger. And you know – no offence to your mum – she could have been sleeping with both of them.' Chloe grimaces when she sees my horrified expression. 'But the details don't matter,' she adds. 'The fact is, it's definitely a possibility. How do you feel about it?'

My stomach twists. 'I don't know . . . sort of . . . muddled up,' I tell her. But that doesn't really explain it. 'I love my dad, it would throw my world upside down if he wasn't my dad, after all. I can't stop thinking about it.'

'It's just biology. It doesn't change anything. He'd still be your dad.'

'But it might change the way he feels about me.' As soon as I say the words out loud, they hit me. My throat is closing.

'Come here.' She gathers me into a hug.

What would I do without Chloe?

'He's been your dad for sixteen years,' she says into my shoulder. 'He couldn't forget that. He wouldn't. It wouldn't change the way you feel about him, would it?'

I sniff. 'No.'

She pushes me to arm's length. 'And your biological dad would be a rock star.'

'Yeah, a *dead* rock star.'

She lets go of my shoulders. 'Have you talked to your mum about it?'

I tell Chloe about Mum catching me reading the letters. Her eyes grow wider with every sentence and when I tell her Mum said she killed Will Bailey, they nearly pop out of her head.

'You don't think she *literally* killed him?'

'No. She's not capable of that. Not on purpose, anyway.'

'So, she feels somehow responsible?'

'That's what I think.'

'But she said Scott's your dad. Don't you believe her?'

'She sounded certain. That's what *she* believes. But it's my life, I need to be sure. When I told Dad, he offered to do a paternity test.'

'Oh my God, it's like a movie!'

'He ordered a test kit yesterday. We'll have to wait and see. I've got to try not to think about it.'

'Good job we've got exams to take your mind off it then, eh?'

'Yeah,' I reply, deadpan. 'Thank God.'

*

My first exam is tomorrow. I'm supposed to be revising, but I'm reading one of Will Bailey's letters on my phone. As I squint at the handwriting, a message pops up on the screen.

Ella: **Hey roomie, do you want this Beatland ticket or what?**

I want to go to Beatland so much it hurts, but Mum would never agree to it – especially now. We've not spoken since the argument about the letters a week ago. She'd kill me if she knew I'd taken photos of every one of them.

The doorbell goes. I wander onto the landing as Dad answers the door.

I hear Mum's voice. 'Is she in?'

'She's upstairs revising. Come in. I'll get her.'

'No, leave her if she's studying.'

'Have a cup of tea, then she can take a break.'

Mum follows Dad into the kitchen.

I creep halfway down the stairs and wait until the kettle stops boiling.

Mum says, 'She's not going out too much or spending too much time with Nathan?'

'She goes to Chloe's to study, but you know Chloe, she's a good influence.'

She's come over to keep tabs on me. Right, that's it. I'm taking that spare Beatland ticket.

I pull out my phone and reply to Ella: **Count me in!**

I'm going now, and there's nothing Mum can do about it.

'How was your date?' Dad asks. *Shit*, when I told him about the man in Mum's kitchen, I didn't think he'd mention it to *her*.

'She told you about that, did she? I knew she was pretending to be asleep!'

'It must have gone well for you to bring the guy home.'

'I only invited him in for coffee! And I wouldn't have done if I'd known Liv was upstairs.'

'Who is he?'

I sit down on the steps and press my head against the banister to hear.

'One of the dads from school,' she says. 'He's been . . . persistent. I thought I'd put him out of his misery.'

'Persistence always pays off. Do you like him?'

Mum hesitates. 'I suppose so.' She changes the subject. 'How's Katya?'

I'd forgotten about Katya. She hasn't been around at all, and Dad hasn't mentioned her.

'That sort of fizzled out.'

'Sorry to hear that. That one lasted a long time – for you. Was the age difference too much for her?'

'It was too much for me, actually.'

'I hope she wasn't too upset.'

'She'll get over me,' he jokes. 'So, will you see that guy again?'

'That's up to him, I suppose.'

'Are you ready for a relationship now, then?'

There's a pause, then she says, 'I don't feel ready, but I doubt I'll ever feel ready.'

'You're ready. It's been long enough,' he says. 'I'll get Liv . . .'

I scamper out of sight as Dad comes out to the hallway.

'Liv!' he calls.

'Yeah?'

145

'Mum's here!'

'I'm revising!'

He lowers his voice. 'Take a break.'

In the kitchen, Mum holds out her arms. I go to her and give her the briefest of hugs with my face turned away. Dad throws me a warning look. I don't know why we have to pretend we're best friends.

'I popped over to wish you good luck for tomorrow,' she says.

'Thanks,' I mumble.

'You'll be great. Just put in all your effort for this last push. It will be over in a few weeks, and you can forget all about it.'

'Yeah, well, I'd better get back to it.'

Dad says, 'Liv, weren't you going to say something to your mum?'

'Was I?'

'About the other night?' He's pulling a weird face.

'Oh yeah,' I say. 'I'm sorry about reading your letters. I shouldn't have done that.'

For a moment, she's not sure what to say. 'Thanks for apologising. I'm sorry I lost my temper.'

'I've got a lot to do, so I'd better . . .' I jerk my thumb towards the stairs.

'We're so proud of you, Liv,' she says.

Now I feel bad.

Chapter 32

January 1996

'You fucking bastard!' spat Aidan, striding towards him, his face twisted in rage.

Aidan shoved him so hard he fell into a garden hedge, twigs puncturing his clothes and skin. He lost his footing, trying to right himself, and slapped onto the pavement.

As he scrambled to get up, Aidan booted him in the stomach, knocking the wind out of him and sending shock waves of pain through his core.

With a guttural wail, Will rolled over and curled up into a protective ball.

Aidan's boot rammed into his exposed lower back once, twice, three times. This new pain was raw and astonishing. Every nerve ending in his body screamed for attention. Will pushed himself onto all fours, gasping for breath. Nausea spiralled up from his gut, filling his mouth with saliva. He spat on to the ground. What was Aidan waiting for? He had him on the ropes. He could finish him. Will grabbed the hedge and dragged himself up to standing.

'What the fuck, Aidan?' he panted.

'I just saw you with Emily!'

'She dumped you, you fuckwit.'

'*Yesterday!* And you're sniffing around her already. Would you jump in my grave as quick?'

Aidan thrust his palms into his chest, but this time, Will was ready and pushed back, his hands tingling with adrenaline.

'You're not together anymore. Get over it!'

Aidan squared up to him, chest puffed, chin jutting forward. 'She's a slut!'

That was it. Something snapped in Will, and he gave in to the overwhelming urge to punch that stupid face. He swung his fist, and it connected with a satisfying thud.

For a split second, Aidan looked surprised, his mouth open in a little 'o' shape. Then he composed himself and was back talking and shoving and getting in his face. 'Go ahead. I couldn't give a shit. You can have her.'

Will swung again and again, not always hitting his target, but mostly.

'Oi!' came a shout from an upper window. 'Clear off or I'll call the police!'

Aidan retreated, wiping the corner of his mouth with the back of his hand.

'You can have my sloppy seconds,' he said.

He got back into his car and sped off, tyres squealing.

Chapter 33

January 1996

Will had left the house early that morning without seeing anyone. Shifting boxes in and out of the van all day had been agony. His entire midsection was aching and the knuckles on his right hand were bruised and swollen. He was glad to be home, but when he entered the kitchen, he wished he could be anywhere else.

His mum was sitting at the kitchen table, her eyes red and puffy, and his dad sitting opposite her, with a furrowed brow.

Will had an inkling but asked anyway: 'What's the matter?'

'You know what's the matter!' snapped his mum. 'How could you?'

Will sat at the table and wiped his palms down his face with a sigh. 'What?'

'The state of Aidan's face.' She was crying now. 'How could you do that to anyone, let alone your own flesh and blood? I never thought you could be capable of something like that.'

'Mum, I don't know what he told you, but he waited for me and jumped me on the street. He pushed me to the ground and kicked me in the stomach and the kidneys.' Will got up and lifted his shirt.

His mother gasped at the sight of his bruises, and her sobbing intensified.

'All I did was defend myself,' he added.

'It's that bloody Emily. She's splitting this family apart. I told you not to see her. I told you!'

'Mum, I know family is everything to you, but Aidan hasn't acted like a brother to me—'

'Enough!' barked his dad, making them both flinch.

Will couldn't remember the last time he'd heard his father raise his voice.

'Neither of you are to see her,' he continued. 'Those are the rules while you are under my roof. If you don't like it, you can clear out.'

'What about Reu?'

'Jesus, don't tell me he's sleeping with her as well?' said his mum sarcastically.

'Of course not.'

'Well, this is his home – he's not going anywhere,' she said.

Will rose from the table. He realised what Aidan was up to. He needed to speak to Emily. Now.

Up in his room, he dialled her number on his work mobile. 'Emily, it's Will,'

She sighed.

He knew then he was too late.

'Has Aidan been to see you?' he asked.

'No, but I bumped into him at the station.'

'Oh, that's convenient.'

'What do you mean?'

'Listen, I don't know what he said but let me tell you my side of the story. Hear me out.'

'I can't keep—'

'Please?'

She exhaled, so he continued.

'After I left you last night, I got halfway down the road when Aidan pulled up. He jumped out of his car and kicked the shit out of me. But – and this is the weird bit – he let me get up and goaded me into hitting him. He didn't defend himself. He literally stuck his chin out, making it look like I'm the bad guy.'

'Will—'

'I don't blame him for giving me a kicking. I deserved it, but he wants you to think I'm violent because he knows that's why you dumped him. And he wants my parents to think it's my fault too. He came over today to show off his bruises.'

'You think he planned it?'

'I doubt he planned it. He must've come to talk to you last night, and when he saw you with me, it wound him up. He wanted to hurt me, but at some point, he must have realised he could hurt me *and* get me in trouble with you and my parents as well.'

'What did your mum say?'

He didn't want to tell Emily his mother blamed her. 'She's upset.'

'This is making everyone miserable. I bet they all hate me.'

'No! Aidan's angry, but he'll get over it.' He hesitated before asking, 'Can I see you?'

'That's not a good idea.'

'Come on, please . . .'

'I've got a deadline.' She was softening.

'I've got a gig tomorrow night,' he said, 'but what about Sunday? Let's go for a walk somewhere.'

She was silent.

'Please . . .' he persisted.

'All right.'

They said their goodbyes.

Now he needed to find somewhere to live.

*

The next day, Will parked the van outside his parents' house and walked up the path to the front door. It felt weird to ring the doorbell instead of using his key. Reu opened the door.

'Hi,' said Will. 'You all set for the gig?'

151

'Yeah.' Reu shuffled from foot to foot, his hands deep in his pockets. 'Do you want to come in?'

'Nah, just open the garage door and we'll load the van.'

'I think your mum wants to speak to you.'

'Is Dad in?'

'No.'

'Okay, why don't you start loading the van?' He gave Reu the keys. 'I'll be out in a minute.'

Will found his mum sitting in the lounge; she looked tired.

'Where did you stay last night?' she asked.

'Matty's.'

There was silence for a moment, then she said, 'I can't believe you would choose *her* over our family.'

'I'm twenty-three. I shouldn't be living with my parents at my age. It's about time I moved out.'

'I want you to know,' she said, her tone serious and solemn, 'if you're ever in trouble, despite what your father says, you always have a home here. And when you're finished with her—'

'Mum—'

'You think that won't happen, but it will. So – when you're finished with her – let's put all this behind us and be a family again.'

'I'm an adult. I get to decide who I want to be with.'

'Well, remember what I said – you can always come to me.'

'Thanks Mum, I love you.'

He kissed the top of her head and went through to the garage to help Reu.

While Reu put his kit in the back, Will went to the passenger side of the van, where Matty was waiting.

Matty wound the window down. 'What's up?'

'I think you're going to have to drive, mate,' said Will.

'You okay?'

'My hand's killing me.' Will raised his right hand, the knuckles were swollen and purple.

152

Matty whistled. 'Jesus. Is that from hitting Aidan?'

Will gave a bitter smile.

'How the hell have you been driving all day?'

'It wasn't too bad this morning, but it's throbbing now.'

'Will you be okay to play?'

'I'll have to be.' Matty had secured a support slot at another legendary venue – the Dublin Castle in Camden.

'Yeah, you'd better be. It's taken me weeks to get this gig.'

*

They'd barely finished sound checking when the venue started to fill up.

'Maybe you should strap it up?' said Matty as showtime approached.

'No, that would be harder to play. I've taken painkillers, it'll be fine.'

It wasn't fine.

The set was short, but every minute was agony. Will inevitably made mistakes. He kept thinking of Aidan: how he'd tried to put Emily off him, how he'd upset their mum, and how this evening was ruined because Will couldn't play properly. What an utter prick. The pub was packed now. The headline band had a decent following. And the crowd were listening too, not just waiting for the main act. More than that, they were jumping around, singing along to the choruses. As Will stomped and shouted his way across the stage, screaming the crescendo parts, people were feeding off his angry performance. During the last song, a photographer was taking pictures, the camera flashing in his face every few seconds – pissing him off even more.

After the last agonising strum, he dropped to his knees in front of his amp, generating an ear-splitting squeal of feedback.

The crowd went wild.

Chapter 34

May 2016

Emily

FHD rings the doorbell at ten o'clock on the dot on Monday morning. We exchange polite, double-cheek kisses.

'I'm sorry about the other week,' I say as we get in his car.

'No worries. Was everything okay with your daughter?'

I don't want to get into the truth of it. 'Yes, she was asleep. She didn't hear you come in.'

'Good.'

'Not that there's any reason I should be ashamed of you,' I try to clarify. 'I haven't ever—'

'No, I get it.'

We pull up outside Boho Café ten minutes later. It's nestled in a row of shops around the corner from the station. Large wooden box planters enclose the outside seating area with colourful flowers. Inside, all the walls are exposed brick apart from the one behind the counter, which is one huge blackboard. The counter is a collection of glass domes displaying pastries, cakes, and muffins. There's a play area for toddlers in the corner where a couple of mums sit nattering over their babies' heads. The place is charming.

The barista looks up from scribbling in her notebook. She recognises FHD and calls out the back to his friend. FHD greets his childhood friend, Dylan, with one of those arm-clasping handshakes before introducing me.

'Are you ready for your taster session?' Dylan asks me.

I give a nervous little nod.

FHD has to get back to work so he says goodbye and startles me with a quick peck on the lips. 'Let me know how it goes.'

'Magda,' says Dylan. 'Why don't you show Emily how to make a decent coffee first?'

I spend the next hour making dozens of cups of terrible coffee. Magda is patient and encouraging, giving gentle instructions in her strong Eastern European accent. By the time I graduate to mediocre coffee, I'm a little wired from all the tasting.

'How long have you worked here?' I ask while waiting for the next espresso to pour.

'Almost four years,' she says. 'I love it, the customers are so friendly.'

I spot the notebook she's left open on the counter; a loose sketch of the two mums sitting in the play area fills the spread. 'Your drawing is lovely,' I tell her.

She blushes and thanks me but closes the notebook.

A little later Dylan samples one of my cappuccinos and manages not to pull a face. Then he talks Magda and me through all the ins and outs of running the café while he's away in Thailand. He makes the whole thing sound easy.

After we've closed, I stack the chairs onto the tables and Magda mops the floor.

'So, what did you think?' asks Dylan.

I've taken in so much information, my head's pounding, but this day was far better than cleaning up vomit and being bossed around by Mrs T. 'It was great,' I tell him truthfully.

'Well, you don't have to decide now,' he says. 'Why don't you sleep on it at least?'

I walk home tired but buzzing. I won't need to sleep on it.

*

155

The first two weeks Dylan was in and out of the café, but this week Magda and I have been running the place on our own. He's at the end of the phone should we need him, but we haven't yet. And despite getting up at six every morning and being exhausted every night, I love it. The regulars have been very friendly, and I'm slowly learning everyone's names.

I'm wiping down a table when Scott's car pulls up across the street. He and Liv jump out and dart across the road with alarming disregard for the traffic.

'What are you two doing here?' I ask, hugging Liv.

Liv shrugs. 'Dad wanted to come.'

Scott rolls his eyes. 'I was giving her a lift to the station, and we thought it would be nice to pop in and see you.'

Liv works at the music magazine on Saturdays until her exams finish in a few weeks when she'll work there over the summer. They sit at the closest table while I go behind the counter to prepare their drinks.

'What are you working on at the magazine today?' I ask.

'Social media planning, I expect,' she says.

She pulls out her phone and starts tapping and scrolling.

I make a face at Scott, and he chuckles.

'You don't have a social media presence at all,' Liv says.

'Me?' I ask.

'No, Boho – the café,' she says like I'm a complete idiot.

'Oh? Should we?'

'Well yeah, if you want to keep in touch with your customers and get new ones.'

'Liv's a social media expert now,' says Scott.

'Oh my God, your website's *hideous*!' she cries.

'Is it?'

Scott takes her phone. 'Ooh yeah, that's bad.'

This is his area of expertise. 'Let me see.'

The website is indeed hideous.

'I can get the intern to knock something better up?' asks Scott.

'I don't know if Dylan would want to pay for that.'

'We won't charge. I need to give this kid something to do, anyway. If you don't like it, he can use it for his portfolio. Liv, take pictures of the cakes and the outside. Use my phone – it's got a better camera.' She comes up to the counter and snaps away.

I ask Magda to pour one of her beautiful flat whites with a leaf pattern on top and Liv takes pictures of it before I bring it over to Scott. I sit in Liv's chair while she's outside.

'How's she doing?' I ask.

'Good,' he says. 'She's knuckling down with her revision.'

'I'm so disconnected from her I don't know what she's into anymore. We were drifting apart before, but now it's accelerating.'

'She just needs time. She'll come round.'

'You think?'

'Of course.'

Once Scott and Liv finish their drinks, they take off, so she doesn't miss her train.

'Was that your daughter?' asks Magda when they're gone.

'Yes, that was Olivia. Sorry, I should have introduced you.'

'She is pretty.'

'Thank you.'

'She doesn't look like you,' she continues, and I try not to be offended. 'She looks like your husband.'

'Oh, he's not my husband.'

'You are divorced?'

'No, we were never married.'

'He is your boyfriend, then?'

'No—'

'Of course, Dylan's friend is your boyfriend.'

'Oh no, he's not my boyfriend.'

'But he kissed you the other day, no?'

'Well yes, but . . . Sorry Magda I just remembered I was supposed to order paper cups.' I nip out the back to the little office and take a deep breath.

'We don't need any cups.' Magda's voice behind me makes me jump. 'We got the delivery yesterday.'

'Ah yes.' I don't have any reason to be in the office now, so I follow her back out to the café, hoping that's the end of all the questions.

I busy myself rearranging the cakes and go round to the other side of the counter to check it but this doesn't deter Magda. 'Your daughter, she was . . . how do you say . . . an accident?'

I lose my rag. 'Look, these questions . . . they're all rather *personal*, don't you think, Magda?'

'Not at all,' she says to my utter exasperation. 'You didn't marry the father. You are young to have a teenager. I am saying what is obvious. It is not personal.'

'But—'

'My son was also an accident.'

With that bombshell, the spotlight shifts from me to her, and I'm much more comfortable with that. Magda tells me about her sixteen-year-old son, the after-school art club she runs at his old primary school, and her art student years back in Krakow.

And I wonder what else we might have in common.

Chapter 35

February 1996

Will's shadow stretched along the path ahead, merging with Emily's in the low winter sun. When she said she'd never been, he couldn't wait to show her around Richmond Park. And so far, it hadn't disappointed. They'd already witnessed a parakeet flypast, a drilling woodpecker, and a majestic stag – all within the first ten minutes.

'You're right,' she said as they strolled, 'bumping into Aidan at the station was weird. He never gets the train, and he was coming *into* the station as I was getting off the train, but when we finished talking, he walked out. He wasn't there for any other reason than to talk to me.'

'It wouldn't surprise me if he'd been hanging around waiting for you to get off the train.' Will knew all about doing that. 'What did he say to you?'

'He acted surprised to see me, and of course he knew I'd ask what happened to his face, and when I did, he said "ask Will".'

'I swear to God, Emily, I was defending myself.'

She changed the subject, 'So, I'm finally moving out of my parents' place. I've found a flat with a group of college friends.'

'You have? Where?'

'Balham. I can't wait to get out of my parents' house.'

'That's great,' he said, but he was gutted. It would take him ages to get to Balham. 'When do you move?'

'Next month.'

'Do you need a hand moving your stuff with the van?'

'Thanks, but my dad said he'd take me. It's furnished, so I won't need much. You'll have to visit, though.'

'I'd like that. I'm looking for somewhere myself. Any spare rooms in your flat?' he joked.

She laughed. 'No. We've even got someone using the lounge as a bedroom.'

'How many of you?'

'Four of us. You met Scott, remember? He helped us move the sculpture that time?'

'Scott – yeah. Expensive trainers, covered in paint.'

She smiled. 'That's the one. He found this cool flat – there's a balcony at the front and one at the back. My friend Miranda is taking the other bedroom and one of Scott's mates will be in the lounge.'

'Sounds cosy.'

'My room's the smallest, too.'

Did she have a double bed? Imagining her room made him lose his train of thought for a moment, then his mobile phone rang.

'Sorry,' he said, rejecting the call. It was only Matty – he'd call him back.

A few seconds later, his phone dinged.

Matty had left a voicemail.

He switched it to silent and put it back in his pocket.

Rust-coloured ferns curled over the edge of the path as it wound its way through a grove, birdsong echoing in the trees above and sweet chestnut cases crunching underfoot.

'Are we lost?' she asked after a while.

'I was following you.'

'How big is this place?'

'Big.'

'Will we ever see our families again?'

'Unlikely.'

160

He took her hand to help her over a fallen tree, and she didn't let go.

'Shall we sit?' He pointed to a bench beside a little pond.

She nodded, her cheeks pink from the cold.

A breeze scattered sparkles across the surface of the water. He stretched his arm along the bench behind her and, as the wind picked up, he gathered her in. When she rested her head on his shoulder, he suddenly forgot how to breathe.

Will's mobile phone buzzed in his pocket.

'It's Matty again,' said Will. 'I better see what he wants.'

'Have you seen the *NME*?' asked Matty, not waiting for a 'hello'.

'No—'

'Buy a copy and ring me back.' Matty hung up.

*

They parked by Richmond station and found a newsagent in the forecourt. He paid for a copy of the music paper and stood outside, flicking through it.

'I don't even know what I'm looking for,' he told Emily as they scoured the pages together.

Then he saw it.

A half-page picture of himself on stage at the Dublin Castle yelling into the microphone, a spotlight flooding him with blue light.

'That's you!' cried Emily.

The headline said: *When the support act steals the show.* Words jumped off the page as Will skimmed the article: 'haunting power', 'voice of a generation', and 'sky-scraping vocals'.

The last line read: *There's no doubt about it; Will Bailey is onto something big.*

Chapter 36

March 1996

Will was sofa surfing while he saved for a deposit to rent a flat, which meant there was no money for nights out. Emily had just paid hers, so she was skint, too. She'd be moving into her new place in Balham soon, but in the meantime, she didn't want to introduce him to her parents. They were just getting used to her split from Aidan and she was reluctant to tell them she was seeing his brother so soon after.

They had nowhere to go.

A friend of a friend was looking for a flatmate, so Will went to view the two-storey flat above a grocery shop. It was filthy, and the bedroom was small and damp, but he was sick of living out of a bag and desperate for somewhere to be alone with Emily, so he took it.

Will spent a week cleaning every night after work to get the place into a state where he could invite her back, and it was a constant battle to keep his flatmate, Alan, from messing the place up again. Once the bedroom smelled less musty, and the toilet bowl was almost white, he took Emily to the local Italian for dinner. He ordered the cheapest thing on the menu, and despite telling her to have whatever she wanted, Emily chose the same, and they shared a bottle of house red. She offered to go halves, but he insisted on paying and they walked the short distance to his place.

He led her down the alley behind the shops, and they climbed the stairs to his new home. He opened the door and quickly dashed in to check the kitchen was still respectable before inviting her in.

'Drink?' he asked.

'No thanks.' She peered in from the hall. 'Good-sized kitchen.'

It was difficult to come up with positives, but neither of them were thinking about the size of the kitchen.

Will was hoping Alan would be out, but he was watching TV in the sitting room.

'Alan, this is Emily, Emily – Alan,' said Will.

Alan turned the volume down, stood up, and said, 'Ah, Emily.'

Like that didn't sound weird.

'Nice to meet you,' said Emily.

'Come on,' said Will, taking her by the hand upstairs to his room. He didn't turn on the main light but went ahead in the dark to switch on the lamp he'd borrowed from the sitting room. It looked out of place and took up valuable floor space but was better than the stark overhead bulb. He shut the door behind her, took her jacket and bag, and placed them on the amp under the window. His single bed looked forlorn pushed up against the wall in his tiny room.

'Nice place you've got here,' she said.

He smiled. 'No, it's not.'

As he leant in to kiss her, he was sure she must be able to hear his heart pounding. All the kissing up to that point had been the long, lingering, teasing kind, but these new kisses had a breathless urgency bordering on impatience. She unbuttoned his shirt, and he tried to help her with her dress until they realised they could do it faster themselves. He'd imagined taking time to explore her body, but that went out the window. In his haste to lead her to the bed, he stumbled, and she fell on top of him with a giggle. She didn't break eye contact as she shifted her position and the sight of her naked astride him made his breath catch in his throat. He needed to be inside her.

As she lowered herself onto him, she let out a tiny 'oh'. That 'oh' nearly killed him. It was almost game over right then. He brought his hands to her hips, feeling her move, but he dared not move himself. Watching her was too much. He had to keep closing his eyes. He felt her breath on his neck, her half kisses teasing his lips, then her hands pushing against his chest. Opening his eyes for the briefest of moments, he glimpsed her, back arched, eyes closed, chin lifted in the dim light. He moved with her then. He couldn't have lasted any longer, anyway. She shuddered as she came and curled over him, breathless, her hair brushing against his chest, and he finally let go.

As she kissed his neck, a lump formed in his throat. Jesus, what was wrong with him? He was still *in* her, for Christ's sake. A tear escaped, slipping down over his temple and pooling in his ear.

She lifted her head, smiling until she saw his face.

'What's wrong?' she asked.

'Nothing,' he whispered. 'I'm just happy.'

She lay down beside him, gathering him into her arms.

And he felt his soul spill into her.

*

Emily woke in a tangle of limbs, her face close to the wall. She felt Will's rhythmic breathing as he slept close behind her. She turned to face him, their noses almost touching.

'Hi,' he said, a sleepy grin spreading across his face.

She felt as though a balloon was inflating inside her. 'Hi.'

He swept a lock of hair from her face and tucked it behind her ear. 'Did you sleep okay?'

She nodded. 'You?'

'Mm-hmm.' Their bodies were so close the sound vibrated through her.

She fought the sudden urge to take his bottom lip between her teeth, but bit into her own instead. His gaze dropped to her mouth, watched as she released her lip slowly through her teeth.

That time, it was different. He was more relaxed, more playful, and very eager to please. He took his time caressing and tasting every inch of her body and by the time he slipped inside her, she was half-crazy with the need for him.

Afterwards, she lay in the crook of his arm.

He murmured into her hair so softly she almost missed it, 'I love you.'

She lifted her head to search his eyes. He looked weary, sort of defeated.

'I love you,' she said. It wasn't a reply, more of a statement.

She had said it before.

She meant it every time she'd ever said it, but this was different.

This was so intense, it kind of hurt.

Chapter 37

May 2016

Emily

'So, you will come to dinner one evening?' asks Magda as she puts on her jacket. I'll finish cashing up then head home, too.

'That's very kind. I'd love to.'

'Tonight?'

'Er, let me think, I'm sure I was—'

'You already told me you are not doing anything this evening.'

'Ah yes, in that case, that would be lovely.'

Magda writes on the notepad, tears off the page, and hands it to me. In neat forward-slanting letters is her address and telephone number.

'See you at seven,' she says and heads to the door.

'Looking forward to it.'

*

Magda's flat is small, but tidy and clean. A little kitchenette sits behind the sofa where I've been invited to sit.

'In my home, we drink vodka,' Magda says, handing me a glass of red liquid. 'You'll like it.'

I can't taste vodka, but I detect cranberry juice and something else, maybe pineapple. 'It's delicious.'

A teenage boy wanders into the room, his eyes fixed on his phone. He doesn't know I'm there.

'Say hello to Emily,' says Magda.

His eyes don't leave his phone. 'Hello, Emily.'

'Emily, this is Alfie. He is very rude.'

'Hello, Alfie.'

He nods at me and goes straight back to his phone. 'What's for dinner?'

She says something in Polish. He tuts and leaves the room.

'Are you still dating Dylan's friend?' she asks.

Jesus, straight in with the personal questions.

'Sort of. How about you?' I deflect. 'Are you seeing anyone?'

'I have a date on Friday night with someone I met on Tinder.'

'You're on Tinder?'

'You're not?'

I shake my head.

'What app do you use?'

'I've never used a dating app.'

Magda blows out her cheeks. 'How do you meet people?'

'I don't.'

She frowns. 'How did you meet Dylan's friend?'

'I used to work at a primary school. His daughter goes there.'

'You should go on Tinder.'

'Ooh no!'

'Why not?'

'I'm not sure. I've never even considered it.'

'We will set up your profile after dinner.'

*

I've had three red vodka drinks before the food's ready. Magda has cooked Thai green curry. She lets Alfie eat in his room.

'Did you consider an abortion?' she says, as I fork a mouthful of curry in. I almost choke.

As I chew, she leans in and whispers, '*I did.*'

'You did?'

She nods. 'That's the reason I came to the UK. I went to the clinic. I sat in the waiting room.'

'What happened?'

'I had paid for it. I was sure it was the right choice. Then, suddenly, I was not sure. I walked out. I walked for hours. And when I got back to the place where I was staying, I knew I would have a different life. Not the life I had planned but it was the right decision for me.'

'What about Alfie's dad? Is he involved?'

She shakes her head. 'I never told him I was pregnant.'

'Why not?'

'Because he was married.'

'Did he have kids?'

She takes a big glug of her drink. 'Two.'

'Did you love him?'

'I still do.'

It's only when I stand up to go to the loo after dinner that I realise my legs aren't working and all the furniture is trying to stop me reaching the bathroom.

'This is the man I'm meeting on Friday,' she says when I return.

She hands me her phone: he's very hairy and built like a rugby player.

'Ooh. What's his name?'

'Irvine.'

'He looks . . . nice.'

I flick through the screenshots she's taken of his profile while she gets us another drink. When she sits down, I hand back her phone.

'I saw Dylan's friend on Tinder yesterday,' she says.

'FHD?'

'What?'

I'm not surprised he's on Tinder but I'm curious to see his profile. 'Show me.'

She takes a few minutes to find the screenshots. I drink almost the entire cocktail while I'm waiting. Damn, these things are easy to drink.

'Will Harding, thirty-seven. That's him, no?'

'Yes, that's him.' I scoot closer.

FHD is tanned and happy eating seafood with palm trees behind him. In the next picture, he's standing on a paddle board out in the middle of a flat, glassy ocean wearing low-slung board shorts.

'He has a six-pack,' observes Magda.

The next shows him paddle boarding along a tree-lined river wearing a wetsuit.

'Too many clothes,' she says and swipes to the last photo.

FHD is among a group of friends. They all have their glasses raised, and he's cracking up about something.

He's normal; he has friends; he has a six-pack.

But he's on a dating app. He could be on a date right now. And I'm not sure how I feel about that.

*

My tongue's made of leather. Not smooth leather, but more like suede. It's like the tongue of a shoe.

My eyelids are stuck together. I go to rub my eyes, but my arms are tied to my body. *Shit*. Where am I? Who tied me up? I squirm and writhe around until I free my arms from their bonds. I rub my eyes, creating just enough moisture for lids to slide over my arid eyeballs.

It's bright. I sit up – I'm on a sofa. There's a blanket over me. Whose sofa is this? I need water.

Behind me is a kitchenette. I go to the sink, turn on the tap, and scoop handfuls of water into my mouth. The moisture doesn't penetrate the rough suede of my tongue. I open the cupboard above my head and find a mug. I fill it with water, drain it in long gulps, and gasp to catch my breath.

This is Magda's flat.

I drank a lot of vodka.

But I'm okay, no headache – just thirsty and tired. My watch says 9:13 a.m. Shit. I was supposed to open the café at 7:30 a.m.

I bolt back to the sofa. On the coffee table tucked under my phone is a note.

Gone to open café – could not wake you. Make sure the door is shut when you leave. M x

I gather my stuff and leave. The moment I shut the door, I regret not checking a mirror – Christ knows what I look like. My car is waiting on the street outside, but with my head still fuzzy, I leave it there and walk instead.

I've got Madonna's 'Holiday' playing in my head. Why 'Holiday'? I haven't heard that song in years. Oh God. Was I singing 'Holiday' in Magda's kitchen? Shit, yes. Into a fucking *spoon*. I have a mental image of us not only singing at the top of our voices, but doing the dance routine, too. Jesus. That would have been my idea. That choreography has been taking up space in my brain since I was a kid.

At what point in the evening, did I lose my inhibitions – and my dignity? Ah yes, that would be right after we created my Tinder profile. Holy fuck. I stop in the middle of the street, pull out my phone, and scroll frantically through my apps until I find it hiding at the bottom of the last screen. I delete it immediately and continue walking. Was I crying at one point? Oh my *God*. I was properly wailing. I told her about Will. I never talk about him. That red vodka drink must have been some kind of truth serum. She's so bloody nosy she probably interrogated me with a lamp shining in my face.

As I walk on, events from the previous evening come back to me in disjointed little bursts. She had heard of Will. She had been a fan. She had the album and even travelled to some

170

European city – Berlin? – to see him play. I was there that night, watching from the side of the stage.

As I turn the corner, the café comes into view. Inside, Magda's busy serving a regular group of NCT mums. When I go behind the counter, she stops what she's doing and envelopes me in a hug. Like we're old friends. She might even know more about me than anyone.

'How do you feel?' she asks.

'Not too bad,' I say. 'Why did you let me drink so much, Magda?'

'You needed to let down your hairs.'

Chapter 38

March 1996

Will was dazzled by the blue stage lights. The same blue lights that flooded the photograph in the *NME*. Thanks to the review last month, they were back at the Dublin Castle. But this time they were headlining. And on a Saturday night, too.

He checked the tuning on his guitar one last time and stepped on the reverb pedal. He turned to Reu, whose mass of ringlets were glowing like a blue halo, and gave him a nod. Reu bashed his sticks together, and they launched into 'Random Anthem'. To Will's surprise, a few people sang along to the chorus. A group of lads – maybe Reu's friends? – were jumping up and down at the front.

The lights dipped and changed to red, illuminating the twelve A&R dudes lined up at the back behind the crowd. Will didn't know for sure they were A&R, but that was Matty's theory. In his words, they 'stood out like turds in a fruit bowl'. They weren't wearing suits, but they looked different somehow from the average gig-goer.

The blue lights came on again, and he could go back to pretending no one was watching.

He propelled the song to its final crescendo, and the crowd erupted into enthusiastic applause.

As he stepped up to the microphone, the lights dipped again, showing several of the A&R suspects staring at the stage. None of them were talking and at least three of them had their arms folded across their chests. Talk about negative body language. Will swallowed. 'This one's called "Forbidden".'

As he played the opening chords, he searched the crowd for Emily. He found her right in the middle, beaming at him. For a moment it was just the two of them, her eyes holding onto his. Then the lights changed, and she was gone.

She was there with her friends Miranda and Scott. He'd met Miranda before the show. She wore a Stones t-shirt knotted at the waist with the sleeves cut off, revealing her extensive tattoos. When Emily went off to the loo, Miranda had said something about 'treating her right or answering to her'. She made out she was joking, but she meant what she said.

He recalled the angry performance he gave the last time he was on this stage. Matty offered to smash his hand with a hammer, to get him in the mood tonight, but he didn't need to be angry. He needed to focus on that glowing review, the sold-out tickets and the record company dudes at the back of the room. He had every reason to believe in himself.

He got caught up in the song and the crowd came along with him. And when it finished, the applause was long and loud. Matty's face said it all – eyes gleaming, beaming smile. It didn't get better than this.

The rest of the set was exhilarating, and they left the stage to thunderous, drunken applause. Another advantage of playing the headline slot was people were more up for a good time and too pissed to notice any mistakes. Backstage, Will drew Matty and Reu in and they jumped up and down, whooping as the applause continued. They were hoping for an encore, and they got two, squeezing in four more songs before the landlord pulled the plug.

Matty ushered them out to the bar. 'Richard Eason's here. He wants to buy us all a drink – let's order doubles.'

Eason was waiting at the bar in his signature biker jacket, even though it was a hundred degrees in the pub. 'That was awesome!' He took Will's hand and pumped it up and down. 'There were some flashes of brilliance there and things we can work on. Listen, I want to sign you.'

Will's heart stopped beating. 'You do?'

'Yes,' Eason leant in and bellowed in his ear over the chatter of the bar. 'But it's not only up to me. I want to get this over the line. Let me take you for lunch next week. I'll bring the big boss, and we'll make this happen.'

'Okay. Great.' He would have to chuck a sickie at work.

'Let me tell you something. You see these guys behind me?' Eason jerked his head towards a group of men hovering nearby.

'Yeah . . .'

Eason grabbed his elbow and steered him away. 'They're from XL Recordings but they won't have the budgets we have at Island. They won't give you the support you need to launch a career with a future.'

'Uh-huh.'

'You need to think long term, Will.' Eason sounded serious. 'You understand?'

Will nodded. 'Yeah.'

Eason kept him talking for ages, Matty jigging around in his peripheral vision for most of the conversation. As soon as he could, Will excused himself to go to the gents' and Matty followed.

'Jesus, that guy can talk,' said Matty, taking the space beside him at the urinal. 'XL Recordings want a meeting next week.'

Will nearly pissed on his jeans. 'What?' He would have to chuck two sickies. Nigel would go ballistic.

'And there are people here from Virgin, Black Dog Music, and Flux Records!'

'Richard Eason wants to sign us.'

Matty's voice was high. 'So do these guys!'

'Eason said they won't have big enough budgets.'

174

'He would say that. Anyway, he doesn't know what their budgets are. We should talk to everyone. Play them off each other. We're in the perfect position to negotiate. Let's not rush into anything.'

Will buttoned his fly and went to the sink.

'Holy shit,' he told his reflection.

*

That night they drank with Richard Eason until they got ejected from the Dublin Castle. Matty invited everyone back to his place and went ahead with some mates on the tube. Emily, Scott, and Miranda jumped in the back of the van with the gear, and Reu rode up front with Will. They stopped at a petrol station and spent a small fortune on alcohol and snacks.

As they turned onto Matty's road, bass boomed from his flat. The party had spilled out onto the street even though his flat was on the second floor. Some of the people hadn't even been at the gig – Matty must have picked them up along the way.

They carried the booze up the stairs, and as they entered the flat, everyone cheered. There was a lot of backslapping and congratulating as he crossed the room.

He played it down, saying, *Let's see what comes of it . . . It never rains, it pours, right? . . . Hope they don't forget about us when they sober up.*

Having been the designated driver, Will was distinctly sober, so he went straight in with whiskey. Taking a swig, he watched his friends laughing and drinking, and tried to let go of the nagging worry about what the next week would bring.

Reu was sitting on the floor in front of the stereo, surrounded by piles of CDs, creating a decent party soundtrack while simultaneously rolling a joint. That kid was always surprising him. Pretty soon everyone was dancing and singing – or more accurately, jumping up and down and shouting lyrics at the top of their lungs.

Being on the brink of all your dreams coming true was a thrill. It reminded Will of being a kid at Christmas with a pile of unopened presents under the tree. That was his favourite part, when you didn't know what was underneath all that wrapping paper. Whatever it was, could never live up to that moment of not knowing, even if it was exactly what you wanted. That was how he felt now. Tomorrow was full of possibility. It might hold more than he could wish for.

Will felt slightly separate from everyone else but it was probably because he was just drunk, and they were all completely wasted. Reu played 'Paradise City' and Will joined the circle of bodies in the centre of the room, everyone linked with arms over shoulders: Matty spilling his drink as he pogoed, Reu moshing his ringlets around, Miranda dropping her cool to belt out the chorus, Scott breaking off to play air guitar, and Emily bent double with laughter.

He took a swig of whiskey and gave in to the excitement in his gut, allowed warm elation to spread through his body. It was happening. It was finally happening. The beat of the music reverberated through his body – booming in his chest.

And he wondered if he would ever feel this good again.

Chapter 39

April 1996

It all happened so fast.

First, Will met Richard Eason for lunch near his King's Cross offices with Matty and Reu. It was only pizza, but it was fancy pizza. And beer, lots of beer. Eason gave them the hard sell, and it gave Will indigestion. Matty said he wasn't offering enough. Two days later, Will and Matty met with XL Recordings at their offices in Notting Hill. Reu didn't bother with that one. There was no food or drink on offer, and he found business talk boring. When Will and Matty left that meeting, Richard Eason was waiting in a car outside the XL building. He told them to get in. By the end of the twenty-minute drive, he agreed to beat the offer they'd just received.

Meetings with three more labels and two weeks of negotiations followed. As he lay awake at night, Will swung between fearing it would never happen and worrying about the consequences if it did.

Three weeks after the Dublin Castle gig, Will got the tube back from a meeting in central London to Emily's new place in Balham.

She buzzed him up on the intercom and when she opened the door, she didn't say hello, just: 'Well?'

'We're taking it,' he said.

She squealed and jumped onto him, wrapping her legs around him. He spun her around in the cramped hallway and they clung to each other, laughing and kissing.

'Oh my God. Oh my God,' she whispered.

Miranda came out of the kitchen clutching a Pot Noodle. 'Ugh, get a room.'

They took her advice.

Emily's room was much nicer than his, cleaner and brighter, but her bed was only a single like his.

They lay on her bed and she made him recount the whole thing from the beginning. He explained how Eason had finally met all Matty's demands and they signed a six-album deal with Island Records that afternoon.

'I'm so happy for you,' she said. 'You're finally getting the recognition you deserve. You must be excited.'

'Yeah.' His stomach hurt. He still had to tell her the rest.

'Let's go to the off-licence and get champagne – or sparkling wine on our budget, but we should celebrate,' she said. 'Get a takeaway.'

He should tell her now. It would be harder once they left the flat. 'They want us to support Paradigm.'

She pushed herself up onto her elbows. 'That's amazing! You get to meet Brett Lewis. When?'

'In four weeks.'

'Oh my God – so soon? See? That shows how much they value you.' Her voice was high-pitched. 'They know you're good enough to support Paradigm.'

'They want us to support them on their entire US tour.' His voice was flat.

'That's great!' She was on her knees on the bed beside him now, making everything wobble. 'Why aren't you happy? What's the problem?'

'There's no problem, it's just . . . it's a long time.'

'How long is it?'

'Five months.'

She didn't hesitate. 'Oh, that'll fly by! You'll be having the time of your life.'

He was hurt. She wasn't anywhere near as devastated as he was at the prospect of being apart for that long.

'This is what you wanted your whole life!' She shook his shoulders against the mattress. 'Surely you knew this would happen?'

'I dunno. I s'pose I didn't believe it ever would or else it never really mattered until we got together.'

'Ah, that's sweet,' she said. 'But pull yourself together. Now's not the time to be all romantic and pathetic!'

'I'll miss you,' he whined.

'That's your brain trying to cope with all the excitement. It's looking for negatives. That's normal. Ignore it.'

'Won't you miss *me*?'

'No. I'll be able to get some work done.'

'You don't mean that . . .'

'You're such a terrible . . . *distraction*.' Her stony expression morphed into a smile. 'It'll be worse for me. I'll be stuck here, bored out of my mind. You'll forget all about me.'

'No . . .'

'You'll be surrounded by groupies, going "Emily who?"'

He pulled her into a hug to shut her up.

*

Even Nigel at work, who was pushing sixty, had heard of Paradigm.

'I can't hold your job open for you,' he said, 'but get in touch when you're back and I'll see what I can do.'

Nigel obviously had high hopes for the longevity of his music career.

Will wouldn't miss the delivery job, but he was sad to hand back the keys to his van.

He asked his mum if he could pop over. When he arrived, she had arranged a rather formal lunch and Will felt like a guest sitting at the dining table with his parents. Reu wasn't there. He'd been working as a plumber's apprentice since he left school in the summer. He rarely worked weekends, but he used it as his excuse to make himself scarce today.

The first thing Will's dad said was: 'Are you still . . . *seeing* your brother's girlfriend?'

He had hesitated at the word 'seeing', as though toying with a different verb.

Will sighed. 'Actually, she's *my* girlfriend.'

In hindsight, that might not have been the best way to get him onside. His dad sat there glaring at him, his jaw clenched as his mum handed around a plate of assorted sandwiches cut into neat little triangles.

'She's not bloody pregnant, is she?' he asked.

'No!'

Dad narrowed his eyes. 'What have you come to tell us, then?'

'I wanted to let you know I've got a recording contract.'

'Will! That's fantastic!' said his mum.

'So, you're jacking in your job?'

'Well, I wouldn't, but they want us to go on tour for five months.'

'What will you do after that?'

'Hopefully, record an album. Tour some more.'

Dad shook his head, lips pursed. 'How will you pay your rent?'

'I'm thinking of moving out of my flat as I'll be away for so long. I was hoping to leave my stuff here until I get back – there's not much.'

'The garage is still full of your stuff, anyway. It won't make much difference.'

He knew his dad wouldn't object to this. He hated anyone wasting money.

His mum offered him a slice of pork pie, but he shook his head. 'Reuben's not going with you, is he?' she asked.

'Well, yeah. He's the drummer.'

'He can't go away for five months!' cried Dad. 'What about his apprenticeship?'

Will closed his eyes and took a deep breath. 'He'll have to take a break from it.'

'You can't take a five-month break from a plumbing apprenticeship! Do you know how many strings I had to pull to get him that job? He has a real chance to make something of his life. He'll be able to charge a fortune when he's qualified. You shouldn't be filling his head with this nonsense.'

It stung that they didn't have any expectations of him, but it would be a tragedy if a gifted musician like Reu spent his life installing toilets. Will didn't have the same belief in his own talent, but championing Reu was easy.

'Reu's seventeen. Plumbing will still be there when he gets back. If he doesn't do this now, he'll regret it for the rest of his life.'

By now his dad's face had turned deep red. 'Well, on your head be it!'

Chapter 40

May 2016

Emily

It's seven-thirty in the evening, but it's still balmy, adding to the nervous damp patches in the armpits of my dress. I open the gate, take a deep breath, and walk up the path to FHD's modest Victorian end-of-terrace. I could turn around, text some excuse, go back home to my safe little life.

But now I'm here, I'm curious to see what's behind that teal door. I reach for the doorbell, then hesitate. We had plans to go for dinner, but his ex asked him to have Florence at the last minute, so I agreed to come here instead. Not wanting to wake her, I text him to say I'm outside.

FHD opens the door in shorts and a tasteful Hawaiian shirt with a tea towel over his shoulder. 'Hi,' he whispers, 'come in.'

I follow him to the kitchen where French doors open out onto a little patio. Bob Marley is crooning softly in the background. I hand him a bottle of rosé and he kisses my cheek.

'I thought we could have a barbecue.' Everything's prepared in covered dishes. I'm impressed. 'Mojito,' he says, handing me a glass full of mint leaves and ice and leads me outside.

We sit at a small round table surrounded by pots of flowers. I keep my arms clamped to my sides as I sip the mojito, praying my deodorant holds out.

'How's it going at the café?' he asks.

'I'm loving it. I look forward to going to work now.'

'I'm glad it's working out.'

'Have you heard from Dylan?'

'He texted last night to say he's having a blast. Water sports all day and running the bar at night. I'm hoping to get a free holiday out of him at some point.'

'I guess they must do paddle boarding over there. You'll be in your element.'

As soon as I've said it, I realise my mistake.

'How do you know I do paddle boarding?' He looks at me, his face serious.

I can't believe I've been here five minutes and I've already put my foot in it. Heat flashes at my cheeks.

'Have you been googling me, Emily?'

Sweat trickles down the middle of my chest. 'No . . .'

'No?'

I clear my throat. 'I swear, I haven't googled you.'

'Then how do you know about my hobby?' There's a glint in his eye now.

'I saw your profile on a dating app.'

He lifts an eyebrow.

'I mean, I'm not on any dating apps. My friend is. She showed me.'

'And what did you think?' He's playing with me now.

'You sound interesting. Had many takers?'

'A few.' His face is a little red, but perhaps it's from the sun. 'Hungry?'

'Starving.'

While he goes inside, I guzzle the rest of the mojito. I'm not at all hungry. If anything, I feel sick. Why is this so difficult? A moment later, he's back with a bowl of olives. He tops up our drinks from a jug and lights the barbecue.

'Do you fancy giving it a go?' he asks as he sits back down.

'What?'

'Paddle boarding.' He smiles, one eye screwed up against the sun.

'Oh.' I laugh. 'I don't know. How likely am I to fall in?'

'I guarantee it.'

'Hmm.'

He chuckles. 'I can tell you're tempted.'

'I like the idea of the standing up part, not the falling in part.'

'You should try it,' he says. 'It's a lot of fun once you get the hang of it.'

I think about my new 'get a life' motto. 'Maybe I will.'

'I'll get the food going.' He gets up and heads inside.

'Can I help?' I call after him.

'No, relax.'

I need to take his advice. I lift my chin to the sun and exhale. We chat while he cooks. He's easy to talk to. Insects buzz around us, parakeets chatter in a neighbour's tree. The mojitos are dissolving the tension in my shoulders and the smell of honey and garlic chicken grilling revives my appetite. By the time he's done, the little table is overflowing with chicken skewers, garlic prawns, flat bread, couscous, and salad.

'This is delicious,' I say.

'I love cooking, but I can't be bothered when it's just me. Flo's too fussy, there's no point cooking when she's here; it's all chicken nuggets and macaroni cheese.'

'Well, you won't be getting an invitation to my place now.'

'Why not?' He's mock-exasperated.

'I can't compete with all this.' I wave a speared prawn. 'Besides, my specialities are chicken nuggets and macaroni cheese.'

After we've eaten, I excuse myself and follow his directions to the bathroom. The first door at the top of the stairs is open, the bedside lamps on, although it's not yet dark. He knew I would see this room, decorated in shades of grey with an abstract painting in copper colours hanging over the bed.

I find the bathroom at the end of the landing. After washing my hands, I can't stop myself from peeking inside the mirrored cabinet above the sink. It contains all the things you'd expect: a razor, shaving foam, moisturiser, floss. My reflection swings back in front of me as I close the cabinet. He's too good to be true. He cooks, he flosses, and he *moisturises*, for God's sake. There's probably a dead body in his wardrobe.

On the landing, I take a final glance at his bedroom.

'What are *you* doing here, Miss Lawrence?'

I spin around to see Florence in unicorn pyjamas and plaster on my friendliest smile. 'Hello Florence. I'm here because . . . Daddy needs to sign a form for school.'

'Oh, okay.' She goes into the bathroom.

'I'll tell Daddy to come up and tuck you back into bed.' I run downstairs.

FHD's in the kitchen pouring wine.

'She's awake!' I hiss. 'I said you'd tuck her in.' He looks only a little concerned as he passes me in the narrow kitchen. 'I told her you had to sign a form for school. That's why I'm here.'

'Okay, wait here.'

A few minutes later he calls down: 'Miss Lawrence?'

I clear my throat and step out into the hall. 'Yes?'

'Florence wants to say goodbye.'

FHD comes down the stairs, little Florence in his arms. She clings to his neck, her head resting on his shoulder. He hands me an envelope from the table by the door. 'There's the form – all signed.'

'Great, thank you.' I force a smile.

He opens the door for me.

'Well, goodbye,' I say brightly.

'Goodbye,' they say together.

Halfway down the path, I turn and wave.

Framed in the doorway, they wave back, then he shuts the door.

185

Now what? My phone, purse, keys are all in there. I go out of the gate and loiter behind a bush, clutching his gas bill. I want the ground to swallow me up.

A few minutes later, he's leaning out of his gate beckoning me back to the house. I follow him cautiously.

'It's okay,' he says, 'her room's on the other side.'

Back inside, I pick up my bag.

'You're not leaving, are you?'

'It's not fair on Florence. What if she wakes up again? How will you explain that?'

'She won't. She never wakes up . . . usually.'

I smile, eyebrows high.

'Please?' he says.

'I wasn't going to stay late, anyway.'

We wait for my cab. I'm poised to duck around the side of the house should Florence make another appearance.

'I think the universe is conspiring against us.' He laughs. 'Or our daughters are.'

He might be right.

Chapter 41

May 1996

Will met Emily for lunch at a little sandwich shop in Covent Garden. He'd been shopping with Matty and Reu, spending his clothing allowance. Emily made a face when she saw what he'd bought.

'What?' he asked.

'Nothing.'

'That face isn't saying "nothing". It's saying "you've spent two hundred quid on a load of crap". What's wrong with it?' he asked, folding a checked flannel shirt, and dropping it back in the bag.

'I thought the money was for "stage clothes".' She put the last of her sandwich in her mouth.

'It was. This is what I wear on stage.'

'But you're a signed artist now, supporting Paradigm on their tour with the opportunity to expand your fan base.'

He blew out an exaggerated huff. 'I don't care about all that.'

'What *do* you care about?'

'I care about the music.'

'And you don't want to catch the eye of a Paradigm fan who might not bother to listen to your set? Before you even open your mouth, they'll decide if they want to listen to you or go to the bar.'

He shrugged. 'True.'

'How much have you got left?'

'Seventy-five.'

'Give it to me.' She held out her hand. 'Do you want to come with me, or do you want to look at guitars?'

'I want to look at guitars.'

She kissed him and disappeared with the money.

*

A few hours later, they met at her place, Will lugging a guitar case, and Emily carrying a scrappy shopping bag. He opened the case, revealing his brand-new Butterscotch Blonde Fender Telecaster. He was desperate to play it, but sensed she didn't want to spend one of their last evenings together watching him tinker with it. She made the right noises, and he tucked it back in the case like a sleeping child.

'I went to a couple of charity shops near college.' She dipped into her bag. 'They've always got original sixties stuff.'

She pulled out a tuxedo jacket, her eyebrows raised. The lapels were black, but the rest of it was a dark rust colour shot through with gold thread. The jacket was cool, but he couldn't see himself wearing anything like that.

'What do you think?' she asked.

Matty and Reu would take the piss out of him if he wore it.

'Try it on,' she said.

'What, over this?' He was wearing a black t-shirt.

'Yes.'

He got a musty whiff as he wafted it around to slip his arm in. 'It stinks.'

'We'll get it dry cleaned.'

She ruffled his hair and stood back to get the full view. She was pleased with her purchase.

'Hold on, I'll get Scott's Polaroid camera.' While she was out of the room, he checked himself out in the mirror on the back of her door. Surprisingly, he didn't look like a complete knob. He looked like a musician.

When she came back with the camera, she adjusted the way he stood and barked 'chin down!' before taking the shot. They lay on the bed watching the bleached-out, ghostly image appear. When it did, it looked like an album cover.

'See?' she said. 'You look like a rock star.'

She pulled him in for a kiss.

'You don't smell like one, though,' she said. 'Take it off!'

He didn't need to be told twice.

*

This wasn't how he imagined spending the last few days before leaving to go on tour. He'd imagined spending them with Emily. Specifically, *in bed* with Emily, but he was spending every waking hour – and some he should be sleeping – in a deconsecrated church in Islington. The record company decided at the last minute to cut an EP before they left for America. Apparently, it was possible to record four songs in five days but, having never set foot in a proper recording studio before, Will was sceptical. Thank God he'd moved out of the flat with Alan and stored his stuff in his parents' garage. He was already packed and living out of a suitcase at Emily's. The sooner he got the tracks down, the sooner he could get back to her, but the sessions didn't go well. He could barely stay awake at the end of each long day. The producer was a condescending wanker who didn't hide his frustration with their inexperience. His attitude only improved when they recorded Will's vocals, and he realised it wasn't a complete waste of time. The last day was the longest – they finished the last track at 1 a.m.

*

Emily had turned out the light to go to sleep but lay awake in the dark. She'd left her key in the usual spot under a rock in the flower bed by the front door. At last, she heard it turning in the lock and Will closing the door behind himself.

Opening her bedroom door, he whispered, 'Milly?'

'I'm awake.' She switched on the bedside light.

He gave her a kiss and sat on the bed beside her.

'How does it sound?' she asked.

'Brilliant. I'd play it to you, but if I hear it one more time, I'll scream. I'll leave a tape for you to listen to . . . tomorrow.' He didn't say *after I've gone*. 'I need a shower.'

When he got back from the bathroom, he slipped into the bed, his body still a little wet.

That last time was slow, how she liked it. Damp and a little sad, the occasional icy drip from his hair surprisingly pleasurable.

She expected him to fall straight to sleep afterwards – he must have been exhausted, but she could tell he was awake from his breathing.

'You could fly out and meet us at some point,' he suggested after a while.

'Maybe at the end of term.' She was reluctant to make plans. He might change his mind once he was on tour.

'When's that?'

'End of June. Where will you be then?'

'I don't know. I'll find out and get tickets organised.'

They lay in silence.

'I don't want you to be sad about leaving,' she said. 'I want you to be excited about this adventure.'

'I am.'

'Good. Let's get some sleep.'

She turned on her side and it was a little while before he curled his body behind hers as he usually did.

Would this be the last time they shared a bed? Would she ever see him again? She wasn't being dramatic – it was a distinct possibility. His life was changing, and she wasn't sure there would be a place for her in it. And he would be different – she might not like the person he became.

She didn't want him to make promises he couldn't keep. Over the last few weeks, every time she thought he might say something he would later regret, she changed the subject. She knew it was pissing him off. He thought she was indifferent to him leaving, but she couldn't help it. It was a kind of survival mechanism.

She was still awake when the birds started singing and she knew he was, too.

A car came for him early. A 'car' being a cab you didn't have to call or pay for. Something he was already getting used to. They had agreed she wouldn't go to the airport. He took his suitcase down to the car and she sat on the bed, waiting for him to come back up to say goodbye.

He was gone for ages. She thought maybe he'd left without saying goodbye because it was too hard or because he thought she didn't care, but at last he came back in.

She went to him. He pulled her in close and wrapped his arms around her. She buried her face in his neck and squeezed him. She tried to commit the feel of him to memory, the smell of him, how it felt to be held by him. Her throat ached.

They stood like that for a long time.

She felt him swallow. There was a weird tension in his body, like he was holding his breath. When she pulled away, his eyes were wet.

'Don't . . .' She kissed his tears, sobbing herself now.

'I've waited longer than five months for you before,' he whispered.

She laughed. 'You did. And this time I'll be waiting for you, too.'

He wiped his nose on his sleeve. 'I know.'

'Have a wonderful adventure. Then come home and tell me all about it.'

'I will. I'll call you.'

'Wait,' she said. 'I've got something for you.'

She went to the bedside table and took a Polaroid out of the drawer and handed it to him. It was a picture he took of her the other night. She was wearing the tuxedo jacket she'd bought him. And nothing else. It was sexy, but tasteful.

'So you don't forget me,' she added.

'No fear of that.' He scooped up the t-shirt she had worn in bed the night before. 'Can I take this, too?'

'Sure – I hope it smells okay.'

He buried his face in it. 'It smells of you.'

'I already stole one of yours.'

A horn sounded.

'You'd better go. I'll come down with you.'

He picked up his guitar case, and they went down to the street.

'I love you,' she said into his neck when they hugged.

'I love you, too.'

He got in the car and raised a hand at the window as it pulled away.

She raised hers back and watched the car travel down the street until the brake lights flared and it turned out of sight.

Chapter 42

May 2016

Liv

Today I brought Chloe with me to the Baileys' house to help me with the archive. I made her wear smart clothes, and when I introduced her to Mrs Bailey as my 'colleague', Chloe had a coughing fit. She's not helping much, though. I haven't done nearly as much as I usually do. She keeps picking up the guitars and pretending to play them like a heavy metal guitarist. We're cracking up every five minutes, then shushing each other in case Mrs Bailey realises she has two schoolgirls rummaging through her son's precious belongings.

I've been here every Saturday for the last three weeks. Mum and Dad think I'm working at *Amplify*, but that doesn't start until the summer holidays. Tumi didn't think we needed to bother Paul with it, but she insisted on getting my parents' permission so I suggested we print a permission slip like they do at school. I forged Dad's signature and sent it back to her the next day.

Before I started, I googled what equipment I'd need and Mary got everything on my list, from fireproof and waterproof boxes to acid-free plastic sleeves for storing paper documents and photographs. I'm not sure if what I'm doing is right, but it's got to be better than leaving this stuff in flight cases to rot.

I show Chloe my system of adding stuff to a spreadsheet and how to use the scanner I borrowed from the *Amplify* office. She's humming an annoying tune as she unpacks a box onto the trestle table we have set up for sorting.

'Is this your mum?' she says after a while, examining something under the light.

She hands me a photograph. It's a girl laughing at the camera, wearing nothing but a man's blazer. There's a lot of leg on show and a little cleavage, but all the important bits are covered.

'Oh God,' I say, embarrassed. 'Yeah, that's her.'

Neat handwriting curls along the bottom border of the Polaroid: Don't forget me. Milly x 20/05/96.

'That's around the same time as the first letter he sent her.' I grab my phone and scroll through the photographs of all the letters I found in the loft. It takes a while to find the one I'm looking for. I need to put these on the laptop in date order so I can follow the conversation.

Dear Milly,

I miss you already, and it's only been two weeks. What will I be like in five months? A quivering, miserable, horny wreck. I can't stop thinking about you. We're always waiting around, but have no time to actually do anything, no time to make a call, no time to see the sights. No days off.

The ink changes – he must have written this later.

It was so good to hear your voice yesterday and I was gutted I couldn't talk for longer. I didn't know it would be this hard to get to talk to you. Anyway, you want me to be more positive and I said I'd write about everything, so here goes . . .

We were shitting ourselves before the first gig – we kept peeking through to the auditorium as it filled up. You know what Reu's like – he threw up twice before

194

the show. And when we went out on stage, the noise from the crowd was deafening. They didn't even know who we were and hadn't heard anything yet, but it was the most amazing feeling. I can't wait for the day when that noise is for us, not Paradigm. American crowds are much noisier than British ones. The venue last night had a capacity of two thousand, tonight it's five thousand. I can't wait to hear it.

I have someone to look after my guitars – his name's Kev, he's my guitar slave. He hands them to me when I'm on stage and replaces broken strings. He loves my guitars more than I do. He polishes them and if I play them too hard, he tuts and sulks.

The tour bus is a disgusting can of stale farts. Mostly supplied by Matty. Paradigm travel separately but we have a bunch of their surplus entourage travelling with us. I think they're responsible for some of the farts, too.

Brett Lewis is an absolute arsehole, by the way. You think he's sexy, but he's a twat. Even though we got introduced when we arrived, he keeps forgetting my name. The rest of Paradigm are good fun though.

I have the worst hangover today. Matty and Reu want to party all the time. Reu went missing for four hours the other night. We found him passed out in an alleyway. Matty's always getting kicked out of bars. I swear to God – it's like I'm their babysitter.

If we're lucky we get two hotel rooms between the three of us. Which means I'm stuck with Matty who snores like a foghorn. You'd never guess, but Reu's a big hit with the ladies! Reu has a room to himself so he can bring his 'friends' back. There were two girls in his room last night. They love his ringlets and his accent. He's a god!

I saw the proofs of the EP today – your artwork is stunning, especially the twelve-inch vinyl version. Your name is on the back. I'll get them to send you some copies. Thanks for letting us use it. It's perfect.

We have a tour manager – Ed. He's actually Paradigm's tour manager, but we share him. Ed gives us a schedule in the morning. Every second of the entire day is planned out. If it's not on the schedule, it's not happening. You practically need permission to take a shit. Ed has tagged us onto all the promotion that Paradigm are doing. We have nothing to promote – the EP's not even released yet – but apparently, we have to promote 'ourselves'. If Paradigm are doing an interview with a local radio station, we are too. But shorter and with more boring questions. If I get asked how we met one more time, I'll scream.

Matty has invented a game where we need to insert a specific word into our interview answers. Yesterday, I got the word 'haemorrhoids' into the conversation. The journalist didn't even bat an eyelid.

Please come over at the end of term. I need to see you. We'll still be on the east coast then. I can get Ed to organise flights for you and we'll get you picked up from the airport.

I can't wait to see you. I miss you so much.

Love,

W

x

Mrs Bailey pops in from the kitchen. 'Girls, will you have a toasted cheese sandwich?'

'Yes, please,' I say. Her toasties are the best.

'No thanks,' says Chloe.

Mrs Bailey's eyes narrow. 'What will you have then? Ham, tuna, chicken?'

'Oh, nothing thanks. I'm not hungry.'

Mrs Bailey retreats into the kitchen, offended.

When she returns with my sandwich, I ask her about Matty and Reu.

'They were Will's bandmates,' she says, putting my plate on the wooden crate. 'Matty played bass guitar, and Reuben played the drums. Will and Matty were friends since they were little.'

'Would he talk to us? About Will and his music?'

'I'm sure he'd love to.'

After lunch, Chloe and I go through more boxes. At the bottom of the first box I look in, I find a cassette. Handwritten on the label, it says *28/07/99* in marker pen.

'How do we listen to it?' asks Chloe.

'Will must have had something to play it on. Maybe it's around here somewhere.'

I bag up the tape, make a note of it on the spreadsheet, and carry on.

A while later, Chloe says, 'Can we play that tape on this?'

She pulls a machine out of a box and places it on the trestle table. It has a cassette-shaped compartment at the top.

'Maybe, if it still works.'

We find a power socket and plug it in. I put the tape into the compartment and when I press the play button, it almost swallows my finger. The tape whirs and the circles in the centre turn.

'It works!' I say, delighted.

The machine emits the muffled, tinny sound of faraway music.

'Where's the volume?' asks Chloe.

I fiddle with all the dials, but nothing happens.

Then I notice a cable dangling out of the back of the machine.

'There must be separate speakers,' I say.

Chloe and I empty the entire box and find two small speakers at the bottom. We connect them to the cables, and when I press play this time, the music plays at the perfect volume. We crouch over the speakers and rewind the tape back to the beginning.

'I'll record it,' I say, setting my phone close to the speakers.

The music is haunting. It begins with a simple melody on an acoustic guitar and builds in layers. After a long, winding intro, Will Bailey sings and the sound of his voice gives me chills. Our eyes meet – Chloe feels it, too.

I've looked up every Will Bailey song there is, but I've never heard this one.

'Does his family know about this song? Should we tell Mrs Bailey?' asks Chloe.

'Not yet,' I say. I want to keep it to ourselves for now.

If I can't hear
your voice in my ear
Your laughter and your tears
Your secret hopes and fears

If I can't hear
you talk about your goals,
Your thoughts and your ideas
Little pieces of your soul

Then I can't go on
Although I'm afraid
This pain will stop
When the music fades

'Wait,' I say. 'What was the date on the cassette?'

Chloe ejects it and reads: 'The 28th of July 1999.'

'Are you sure?' I reach for the tape. 'That's the day before he died.'

Chapter 43

June 2016

Liv

I can't get Will Bailey's last song out of my head. I've listened to it so many times I know the lyrics off by heart, but I still don't understand them. I'm humming it under my breath as Chloe and I queue up outside the exam hall. I spot Nathan approaching and I start to sweat. As he walks past us to join the end of the queue, he throws me a 'hey'. It's the perfect blend of acknowledging me and playing it cool until I see Chloe's face. She looks like a cartoon character, her mouth open and her eyes on stalks.

'Oh my God, Nathan Hall *likes* you!' she whisper-shouts.

'Don't be silly . . .'

'Did you see the way he looked at you? He *spoke* to you!'

'He just said "hey", he was probably talking to Harry.' Harry's ahead of us in the queue.

'Harry's gone!'

She's right: Harry's gone into the hall. This is the perfect moment to tell her. I might not get another chance without it being weird, but I say, 'Come on, everyone's going in.'

'He definitely likes you,' says Chloe as we shuffle towards the entrance. 'I can tell. Do *you* like *him*? What am I saying – who doesn't? He's fit. I mean, he's way too tall for me, but you, you'd only have to tiptoe to kiss him. That's perfect. I'd need a chair. I would literally have to get a chair to stand on.

But I wouldn't mind. I'd carry a fold-up chair around with me, on the off chance . . .'

Normally I'd be rolling around on the floor laughing at her going off on one like this, but this is making me squirm. Luckily, when we go through the doors, we're not allowed to talk anymore.

After the exam, Chloe waits outside for me. We walk to the gates together, comparing answers to the exam questions. Chloe's dad is parked across the street, waiting to take her to her tennis lesson. We're saying goodbye when Nathan appears out of nowhere.

'Hey Liv, I listened to that playlist you sent me last night – it's awesome,' he says. 'That Underdogs track's amazing – awesome drum solo. I'll send you that Liars song, the drums on that are cool. See you later.' Then he's gone.

He has never said that many words to me in one go. This is the one time I'd rather he'd kept his mouth shut.

Chloe's eyebrows pull together. 'You've been sharing playlists with Nathan? And you didn't tell me.'

'There's nothing to tell—'

Chloe storms off to the crossing and I run to catch her up.

'I tell you everything!' she says. 'Every stupid bloody detail of my boring life and you didn't even mention swapping numbers with him, let alone sharing bloody playlists! How long has this been going on?' She jabs at the button for the crossing.

'There's nothing going on, I—'

'You know what I mean!'

'He started talking to me at the bus stop a few weeks ago. Really, it's nothing.'

'Don't worry about it. I understand. You don't want to tell me stuff.'

'I don't know why I didn't tell you. I was embarrassed . . .'

'Liv . . .' She turns to face me. 'That's a pathetic excuse.'

'I know. I *do* want to tell you stuff . . .'

'Well, start talking. What else don't I know?' She folds her arms in front of her chest, her eyebrows high.

'I . . . I went to his house . . . once and—'

'For God's sake, Liv!' The lights change and she runs across the road, her shiny black ponytail, the envy of my entire childhood, bouncing as she runs.

'Chloe!' I yell.

But she doesn't look back. She hops in the car, and a moment later, they drive off.

Chapter 44

May 1996

Emily tried for the fourth time that day to get through to Will.

The ring tone sounded alien, far away.

'Hello?' Just two syllables but un-mistakably Will.

'Will, you're there!'

'Hang on, I'll call you back.'

She put the phone down, and a moment later it rang. This was the arrangement, so there were no arguments with her flatmates about the phone bill.

She snatched it up. 'Hi.'

'Hello gorgeous. Are you okay?'

'I'm fine.'

'You don't sound fine.'

There was nowhere to sit by the phone in the hall, so she slid down the wall to the floor. 'No. I'm sort of mixed up.'

'About what?'

She let out a breath. 'Do you want the good news or the bad news?'

'The good news.'

She could hear the hum of the shower down the hall. 'I won the competition.'

'The competition, that's brilliant! You won the competition! Wow!' He paused. 'What competition?'

'Remember, on our first date, I showed you the photographs? You said I'd win it.'

'Oh yeah! The treasure chest with the butterflies and the beetles. You see? I told you! What do you win again?'

'Five thousand pounds and my own exhibition at Marshalls, this cool gallery in Covent Garden.'

'Wow, Milly that's fantastic! So, what's the bad news?'

'The exhibition is in two months.'

'Okay, it's not long, but you'll work hard and get it done. You can do this.'

Emily took a breath. 'It means I can't fly out to visit you next month.'

A siren wailed on the street outside.

'Why not? It's only a week.' His voice was small.

'I need every minute, Will. There's a big room to fill. At the moment, I only have three pieces.'

'You can't cancel – I need to see you. I've been counting the days. I miss you.'

She grimaced. 'I miss you too, but what am I supposed to do?'

'We can work something out . . .'

'Like what?'

'I dunno. You could work on it here.'

She rubbed at her forehead. 'In hotel rooms?'

'Yeah?'

'I need all my stuff and I need space. Besides, I make a mess when I'm working. And how would I get it back in one piece?'

The shower shut off down the hall. Silence.

'I'm sorry. I want to be there . . .'

He sighed, and she heard a muffled sound, like he was collapsing onto a bed. 'I know. I'm just feeling sorry for myself.'

The bathroom door opened and Scott padded across the hall to his room wrapped in a towel.

'Don't cancel,' he said. 'Why don't we see how you get on? Maybe you'll get it all done super-fast?'

'Will, this is important to me.'

'I know . . .'

'If you had an extra week to work on a song, would you leave it or use the time to make it better?'

He breathes out, long and slow. 'Fair point.'

'Anyway, we're over halfway now; the second half will fly by.'

'I'm sorry. We should be celebrating. You've got your own exhibition! That's big, that's massive. You're so talented, it'll be great.'

The forced brightness in his voice made her ache.

*

Emily bought an extension lead for the phone so she could sleep with it by the bed, the wire trailing in from the hall. It rang once, and she picked it up before it woke everyone.

'Will?'

'Babe.' His voice, one word, filling her up.

'Hi.'

'I miss you.'

'I miss you, too.'

'Are you lonely?' he purred.

'Yes.'

'*I'm* lonely.'

He started singing 'Are You Lonesome Tonight' and, even though he was drunk and he messed up the words, it was beautiful.

'Talk to me,' he said.

She lay on her back. A streetlight cast the shadow of a tree across the ceiling, leaves trembling in the breeze. 'What do you want me to say?'

'Talk to me about your work. Describe it to me.'

'Okay . . . So, today I worked on a wooden piece. I'm pleased with how it's turning out. I've collected driftwood and twigs and they all fit together. They tell me where they should go, and I fasten them with wire. It's getting big now. I never know when to stop. I have these twisty curly twigs. I'm not sure what sort of tree or bush they're from, but they're lovely—'

'Like you.'

'Ha, like a *twig*?'

'You know what I mean . . . carry on.'

'I painted the tips of the twigs gold, and they catch the light. Maybe I'll wire in some gems. I'm not sure. I'll try it tomorrow, maybe green ones . . .'

When she paused, she heard gentle snoring down the line. She curled up on her side with the phone to her ear and gathered in the t-shirt he'd left behind. It didn't smell of him anymore. It hadn't since day two. She lay there for a while, listening to his breathing. Ed had been on at him about the phone bills, so she counted ten more of his breaths, then hung up.

*

'You've got a message on the answer machine,' said Scott, when she got in from college later that day.

'Okay, thanks.' She dropped her keys on the table in the hall and pressed the play button.

'Hi Emily, it's Will,' his formal, other-people-are-going-to-hear-this voice. 'I need to talk to you, so if you can stay near the phone later, I'll try to call you before the show . . . or after. I'm not sure what time it is there, but anyway . . . Speak later.'

'Sounds ominous,' said Scott.

She chewed her lip. 'Yeah.'

They were supposed to be going for a drink with Miranda, but Emily had to stay in and wait for Will's call. Scott said he'd stay in too and they watched *The Godfather* on video in his room in the absence of a proper living room. Scott's friend Ryan had the living room as his bedroom, but he was hardly ever there. They needed his share of the rent, so it meant watching TV in Scott's room, but he didn't mind.

The horse's head scene had just finished when the phone rang.

'Don't pause it.' She jumped up from his bed and dashed out to the hall.

'Hello?'

'Milly, it's me.' She could hear the frown in his voice.

'Hi.' She took the phone into her room and shut the door. 'Is everything all right?'

'Not really . . . They want us to stay on in New York to record the album.'

Her heart sank. She didn't know what to say. If she tried to look on the bright side, he'd be hurt, and if she didn't, she'd bring them both down.

'I get it now,' he said.

'Get what?'

'What it was like for you when you won the competition. I'm excited about getting in the studio, but I'm gutted I can't come home and see you. I'm sorry.'

'Don't worry.' She swallowed away the thickness in her throat. 'Wow, recording in New York!'

'Yeah.'

'How long will it take?'

'They've booked six weeks for the basic tracks, but we might add string arrangements and stuff, so it depends.'

She forced a smile, hoping he'd hear it in her voice. 'String arrangements! You always wanted to do that!'

'I know. I hope they go for it.'

'They will.' The smile was fading, folding in on itself.

'Listen, I can't talk long – we've got to get on the road. I'll try to call you later, okay?'

She cleared her throat. 'Okay.'

'Milly, could you come over for a week or something?'

'I could try.' But she couldn't. She was already behind on her coursework because of the exhibition. They'd kick her off the course if she didn't get back on track.

'But it's only six weeks,' she added. 'We've done the hard part.'

Chapter 45

June 2016

Liv

I've never pitched a tent before, but I manage it all by myself following the instructions that fall out of the bag of Ella's brand-new purple three-man. She can't help because she'll ruin her nails. There are twelve of us sharing five tents. We arrange them in a circle, leaving space in the middle for us to hang out. I told Dad I'm staying at Chloe's. It's the only alibi that raises no questions. But she's still not returning my calls.

Nathan and I pore over the festival programme, planning who we want to see. All the others are interested in is food and drink, so we head to the food area and stuff ourselves with chips. Everyone puts money in, and Nathan and Ella go to the bar because they look older. They return with two trays full of plastic pints of cider, and we sit on the grass drinking as the sun sinks.

I check my watch. 'Moon Illusion are on the main stage soon. Shall we head over?'

'What's Moon Illusion?' asks Ella.

'Tonight's headliner! Come on, you didn't come all this way to sit in a field!'

Charlie smirks. 'I did.'

'Anyone?' I ask.

Lottie pulls a face.

'I'll come,' says Nathan.

The two of us make our way to the main stage under zigzags of rainbow bunting fluttering in the breeze. Literally everyone we pass is laughing or smiling. A couple of stilt walkers lope past. I love this place.

The closer we get to the stage, the more tightly packed the crowd becomes, so Nathan takes my hand and drags me through. There's a loud but muffled announcement and all I can make out is: 'Moon Illusion'. Applause ripples towards us from the stage, and when it hits us, it sends tingles down my spine. We stop where we are and clap and whoop, grinning at each other like idiots.

As the band starts to play, another wave of applause washes over us. The sun is setting to the left of the stage; the sky streaked with pink and gold. I have never felt a buzz like this.

Every Moon Illusion song is an anthem that gets people singing along and jumping up and down and we're so squashed in, it's impossible to stand still. The warm fuzzy feeling from the cider is helping. My cheeks hurt from smiling, and whenever Nathan and I exchange glances, his eyes are gleaming. This is the best thing ever. I just want to go to music festivals for the rest of my life. I don't want the set to end but after two encores it's clear Moon Illusion aren't coming back on stage no matter how much we chant 'More!' The stage goes dark, the compère says something about looking out for each other and everyone shuffles towards the tent field. Nathan takes my hand even though there's no danger of us getting separated now and I feel like I'm floating.

The sun is long gone and there's a chill in the air. Our friends are not where we left them at the falafel stall and neither of us have phone signal, so we head back to camp.

'I wish I'd paid more attention to what our tents looked like now,' says Nathan.

'The people next to us had a big Italian flag.'

It takes half an hour to find the flag using the torches on our phones. Two strange tents have been squeezed into the space we left in the middle of our circle, but there's nobody around.

'Do you want to wait in our tent?' asks Nathan. 'Charlie's got beer.'

'Okay.' I'd prefer water, but beer would have to do.

We take off our boots and crawl into his tent. A lamp dangling from the top of the dome lights up the mess as he switches it on.

'Sorry, Charlie's a slob.' Nathan sweeps aside a pile of clothes, straightens his sleeping bag, and gestures for me to sit. He pulls two cans of beer from a rucksack and hands me one.

'That was epic,' I say, cracking the pull and guzzling down warm beer. It does nothing to quench my thirst – if anything, it makes me thirstier. He puts his can into a nearby trainer to keep it upright, so I do the same.

There's an awkward silence. I go to say something, but suddenly his mouth is on mine. I was hoping he'd kiss me, but I wasn't expecting it right at that moment, so it takes a minute to recover. He's not pushing me exactly, but definitely encouraging me to get horizontal. I lie back and he's on top of me, his hands working their way under my top and over my bra. Rowdy voices belt out the chorus of the last Moon Illusion song. Stones dig in my back. Fabric rustles as people bush past the tent.

Suddenly I don't want to be here.

I thought I was ready.

I'm not.

What's wrong with me? I like Nathan. I want to lose my virginity, to get it over with, but it doesn't feel right with only a thin piece of fabric separating us from the outside world.

Without warning, the dome of the tent caves in.

Nathan's body weighs even heavier on me. Outside, people laugh. Someone shouts, 'Sorry!'

I can't breathe. The dome pings back into shape and I push Nathan off.

'Are you okay?' he asks.

'Yeah, you?'

'Just about. Idiots.' He rubs his shoulder, then moves to pick up where we left off.

'I'm sorry. I can't . . .'

'Why not?'

'It's weird with all these people around . . .'

'They've gone now.'

'Charlie could come in . . .'

'I can put the padlock on the zip.'

'It's his tent!'

'He won't mind.'

My cheeks burn at the thought of them arranging this. Was he confident I'd end up in his tent or that someone would? I hear our friends' voices outside. I grab my can of beer and clamber out.

They're all completely wasted. They take turns recounting jokes they heard in the comedy tent and they're all falling about laughing, but you really had to be there. We sit outside drinking and chatting until it gets too chilly, and we go into our tents. I try to catch Nathan's eye as we all say goodnight, but he doesn't even look my way.

Ella is so drunk I have to take off her boots. My necklace dangles in her face, as I help her into her sleeping bag.

'Did Nathan give you that?' she asks. 'Jade's got one, too. His mum makes them. Hers has a cat on it.'

Then she's snoring.

I lie awake. My fingers find my necklace, the little 'L' and the miniature headphones. How many other girls has he given his mum's jewellery to? I wish Chloe was here or that she would pick up the phone at least. I've been looking forward to this for months, risked so much to be here, and now all I want to do is go home.

211

Chapter 46

November 1996

Mixing a track was like a visit to the opticians. Tony the audio engineer would fiddle with knobs and faders and Will had to decide 'better or worse?', 'more or less?' They'd listened to 'Intertwined' a thousand times, and it was making him pine for Emily.

'Hello!' came a voice from behind them.

Standing there in thigh-high boots looking unbelievably glamorous was Christie Blackmore – *the* Christie Blackmore.

She held out her hand. 'Christie Blackmore from The Underdogs.'

He knew who she was; everybody knew who she was.

'Hi.' He shook her hand. She looked great. She must have been, what, forty? Forty-five?

'We're label-mates,' she said. 'I thought I'd introduce myself. We're recording down the hall.'

'It's great to meet you!' The high-pitched excitement in his voice was mortifying.

'I was hoping I'd run into you at some point. I've been playing "Fever" on repeat for two weeks now, haven't I, Joe?'

There were two minions behind her. The one called Joe nodded enthusiastically.

'Sorry about that, Joe,' said Will.

'How's it going?' she asked.

'Uh . . . it's going great. Just working on the last few tracks – we've got ten days left.'

'You're in expert hands with Tony here. He's a genius.' Christie exchanged air kisses with Tony. 'Are you staying at the Four Seasons?'

'Yeah.'

'Island puts everyone up there. We should all grab a drink and hang out before you go back,' she said.

'That would be amazing.' He was buzzing – Christie Blackmore had written some of his favourite songs.

'How about tonight? Say, ten? In the bar?'

'Sure,' he squeaked.

'The Library Bar, not the lobby bar.'

'Library Bar. Ten.' Matty and Reu wouldn't believe this.

'See you later.' When she smiled, it lit up the whole room.

'Yeah. See ya.'

Will stood gaping at the door as it closed behind her.

'I had posters of her on my wall when I was a kid,' he told Tony.

'Jesus,' said Tony. 'Don't tell *her* that!'

*

Christie Blackmore knew how to party. She took over the Library Bar, dispensed with the pianist, and played the piano into the small hours. Everyone sang along, and she would hear no excuses when she asked Will to sing a duet. She ordered so many shots Ed had to help Reu to his room before midnight. Her entourage was about thirty strong, all friendly, but very loud. By 4 a.m. most had left and even Matty was calling it a night. Will stood up to leave with him when Christie said, 'Do you want to hear our new song? It's not finished yet, but it's nearly there.'

213

Will was getting a headache. He should go to bed, but how often did you get the chance to hear an Underdogs record before its release?

'That'd be brilliant.'

He was having trouble walking straight as the three of them headed to the lifts. Matty was even worse, stumbling over nothing and landing on his arse in the corridor. Christie appeared completely unaffected by all the tequila slammers she'd knocked back.

Matty stumbled out of the lift at the tenth floor. He couldn't be persuaded to join them, and zigzagged off down the corridor. Christie pressed the button for the penthouse, and at the top floor, they walked the length of the corridor to the double door entrance to her suite.

She swung them open to reveal a wood-panelled living room with leather sofas and bookshelves reaching up to the high ceiling. A grand piano stood gleaming before a twinkling slice of the New York skyline.

'Wow!' He went to the window. The first glimmer of sunrise glowed pink behind the Chrysler to his left, and the Empire State rose to a point on the right.

'Drink?' She handed him a glass of something amber coloured on ice.

'Thanks.' He shouldn't drink any more – his head was killing him.

An ivory key made a bright *tink* when he pressed down on it.

'Do you play?' she asked.

'Only "Chopsticks".'

'You should learn. I started playing piano around your age.' She fiddled with the stereo. 'This is that song I was telling you about.'

He settled on a sofa as music filled the room. Her song was fantastic. It pissed all over what he had been working on that week. He'd always loved her voice. He felt like pinching himself: he was in a penthouse suite overlooking Manhattan, listening to the latest Underdogs song before anyone else. With Christie Blackmore.

He splayed his arms along the back of the sofa. His eyelids were heavy, he closed his eyes and let the music wash over him.

The jerk of his head woke him with a start.

He blinked. Christie Blackmore was kneeling before him. Jesus, he must be dreaming. He squeezed his eyes shut and opened them again, but she was still there, sliding her hands up his thighs.

'What are you doing?' His speech was slurred.

'Worshipping you, like everybody else,' she said. 'Isn't that why we do it? For adoration?'

The feel of her fingers on his fly was enough to get things stirring.

'Wait . . .'

All communication from his brain stalled.

'Relax, enjoy it.'

Oh God, what was she doing with her tongue?

She looked up at him through her thick eyelashes, the same look that had followed him around his room when he was a teenager. He remembered listening to her husky vocals alone in his room with her poster on the wall watching him, whatever he was doing.

No, no, no.

He struggled to find the words to refuse politely.

Christ, why did he need to be polite?

'I'm sorry . . . I can't . . . I'm with someone . . .'

She pulled back and laughed. 'So am I. So what? I don't want to fucking *marry* you.'

With each bob of her head, she was blowing his mind.

He'd stop her in a second, but – oh God – she was insanely good at this. All he needed to do was ask her to stop. He should do it now before it was too late. He should do it right now. Oh God, he'd reached the point of no return. He may as well get it over with.

As he came, pain detonated in his skull.

*

Daylight flooded the room, the baby grand piano a silhouette against the bright window. He needed to piss. He stood up but collapsed back onto the sofa, his head throbbing. He tried again, this time not fully straightening up, gathering his undone jeans at the waist. Using the sofa to support himself, he shuffled towards the hallway. He paused, leaning on a table with an enormous display of flowers. The smell of lilies turned his stomach. Across the hall he found the bathroom in all its honey marble splendour with another slice of the city reflecting in the mirrors. He pissed, then lay down, resting his forehead on the cool marble floor. He must have dozed off again because he woke to the sound of Christie talking on the phone across the hall.

He needed to get out of there.

He hauled himself up on the toilet bowl and staggered to the sitting room. Where the fuck were his shoes? He crawled around the sofa on his hands and knees, searching for them. He'd have to go barefoot. It took all his effort to make it down the corridor to the lifts. Where the hell was he? He got in the lift and pressed the ground floor button. Jesus, this was the worst hangover he'd ever had. His head was on fire, but his body was freezing, and his throat felt raw when he swallowed. He allowed his body to slide down the mirrored wall of the lift and sat shivering on the floor, praying no one would get in. The bell dinged, and he made it out of the lift just before the doors shut. Ed always made sure they each had a hotel business card, so no matter how hard they partied, they could get a cab back to the hotel. He rummaged in his pockets: no card, no wallet, nothing. Sweat was collecting in his eyebrows. He couldn't think straight. He'd stayed at so many hotels over the last few months, he couldn't remember where he was staying.

A front desk clerk was approaching – no doubt she wanted to kick him out. He was out of place, bedraggled and barefoot in the smart lobby. At least he'd done up his fly in the lift.

'May I help you, sir?' She took him by the elbow and led him to a discreet desk behind a pillar, where he sank into a seat.

He went to speak, but his throat was coated in broken glass. All he could manage was a hoarse grunt. He tried again, but it was no use – he'd lost his voice. *Fuck.*

'I'll get some water,' she said.

She was back in a moment. He took a gulp of the iced water, but swallowing was agony.

'Do you need a doctor, sir?'

He shook his head.

She sighed. 'You're with the record company, aren't you?'

He nodded. She got a pen and notepad out of the desk drawer. 'What's your name?' she asked, sliding them towards him.

He scrawled his name on the paper.

Her frown melted as she read his name. '*You're* Will Bailey?' She looked at him with wide, round eyes. 'I love "Fever"! I bought it yesterday.'

He wrote: I can't remember where I'm staying.

'You're staying here!' she gushed.

Relief washed over him.

'Have you lost your key?'

He nodded.

'I'll get you another. I'll be right back.'

His head was so heavy he rested it on his forearms while he waited.

'Here's your new card, Mr Bailey. When you use it, the old one will be deactivated automatically.' She spoke with a sing-song voice. 'You're in room 1046. Take this elevator to the tenth floor and follow the signs.'

He took the key card and mouthed 'thank you'.

As he walked the few steps towards the lift, it was as though someone was turning down the volume on the world. The edges of his vision became bleached, closing in around him.

Everything went white.

Chapter 47

November 1996

When Emily arrived, Ed, the tour manager, was waiting for her in the hotel lobby.

'How is he?' she asked.

'He's sleeping at the moment.'

'Did the doctors say what's wrong with him?'

'He's suffering from exhaustion.'

'Exhaustion?'

'Well, it's a virus, but when you're burned out, you pick up bugs more easily. He's been working hard. We all have.'

Emily wasn't going to argue, but it was obvious to her who was to blame for Will's condition – it was the tour manager in charge of his schedule.

'I've got you a separate room for now,' said Ed. 'So you can freshen up and have something to eat without disturbing him. The doctors want him to rest his voice, so whatever you do, don't let him speak.'

'Okay.'

'Not that he could speak even if he wanted to.'

Ed showed her to her room and told her he'd call her when Will was awake. It was frustrating, after all these months, to be this close to Will but not allowed to see him. She waited hours, but Ed didn't call. She put on the hotel slippers, marched down the corridor to Ed's room, and knocked on his door.

'Look, this is ridiculous,' she said when he answered. 'Let me see him.'

Ed sighed, disappeared into his room, and returned a moment later with the key card to Will's room. 'If you need me, dial six, then my room number – 1047. Remember, don't let him speak.'

'I won't,' she promised, taking the card.

At Will's door, she swiped and pushed on the beep.

Across the room, Will's body was concealed under the covers. She kicked off the slippers, crept over and climbed onto the bed. The movement caused him to stir, but he didn't wake. She lay down beside him. The bedside lamp lit his face, his long lashes casting shadows down his cheeks. Girl's eyelashes – completely wasted on him. A few days' stubble darkened his chin. She took in every millimetre of his face – a luxury after all these months. Her throat tightened and tears stung her eyes. She stroked his cheek, ran her fingers through his hair and across his jawline. Those pretty eyelashes fluttered and lifted. He went to say something, but she put a finger to his lips.

'Shh,' she said. 'Don't speak.'

He gestured for her to come under the covers, so she got in the bed and pulled him close; his head was hot against her neck.

'I've missed you so much.' She breathed in the smell of him.

He whispered something, but it came out as a strangled rasp.

'Shh!' she said. 'Ed will kill me!'

He mimed writing and pointed to the bedside table behind her.

She propped him up on pillows and handed him the pen and notepad.

'How do you feel?' she asked. He was pale.

He wrote: like shit and gave a wry smile.

She felt his forehead. He had a fever. 'Have you had any drugs recently?'

He shrugged.

Emily reached for the bedside phone and dialled Ed. He told her where to find the medicine and how much to give. Will took the tablets, and as she settled beside him on the bed, he handed her a torn-off page from the notepad.

I'm sorry I couldn't meet you at the airport. I wanted to run towards you in slow motion with my arms open.

She smiled. 'This isn't quite how I imagined it would be after all this time.'

He mouthed 'sorry' and started scribbling again.

Thank you for coming. I hope Ed didn't freak you out when he called and told you I was ill.

'He told me they'd signed you off work for two weeks and you'd kill him if he didn't arrange a visit. But I think he just wants a babysitter.'

You're probably right. Sorry about that. Where's your nurse's outfit? He wiggled his eyebrows.

'Ed wouldn't allow any funny business, even if you were up for it.'

I'm up for it.

'No you're not. Look at you, you can't even hold your head up. You should sleep.'

It's not fair. I hadn't planned on sleeping much once you got here.

But he didn't resist when she took the notepad and pen from him.

As she slipped under the covers, she realised this was the first time they had ever been in a double bed together. The

221

space was a luxury she didn't want. She preferred it when they were closer. Everything was strange.

'Goodnight.' She kissed him on the forehead.

'Love you,' he squeaked. He sounded like Micky Mouse on helium.

*

Emily had six days in New York, and Will was in bed for all but the last two. Whenever Will was sleeping or had doctor visits, she would go out and explore the city, documenting her days with her camera or in her sketchbook.

She took most of her meals in the room with him, but occasionally he would insist she went to a restaurant with Matty and Reu while Ed stayed behind to babysit.

It was a relief when he showed signs of improvement, but even when he was allowed to talk, he was told to use his voice sparingly.

On her penultimate day, Will had a long scribbling argument with Ed about going out for the day with Emily. Ed eventually agreed to a short walk in Central Park. It was only two blocks away, but Will was tired by the time they got there, so they found a bench by a pond and watched the world go by.

He wanted to take her to the Museum of Modern Art before Ed called out a search party, so they hailed a cab, though it wasn't far. When they got there, he was running on fumes.

'What do you want to see the most?' his voice was husky. He didn't sound like Will.

'Van Gogh's *Starry Night*,' she said without hesitation, so they headed straight for it. The painting was popular. They had to sit on a nearby bench until the crowd thinned out. They got the painting to themselves for maybe two whole minutes, but those two minutes were magical.

'Have you ever been anywhere where you've seen stars like that?' she asked him.

'Uncle Brian's,' he croaked.

'I saw the most amazing stars on holiday in Malta when I was a kid. It felt like they were right there, not millions of miles away. And if you tiptoed, you could touch them.'

'I love the swirls,' he whispered, threading his fingers through hers.

'The paint looks like icing on a cake. You can almost taste it.'

Will cleared his throat. 'He only sold one painting, right?'

'That's the legend – that he only sold one painting in his lifetime. The truth is, they don't know exactly how many, but he did sell a few and some he exchanged for food. But that was only a tiny portion of his almost one thousand finished works. So yeah, he never got the recognition he deserved. Wasn't around to see his success.'

Will eyed the painting, solemnly. 'Imagine creating something so beautiful and no one wanting it,' he rasped. 'How could you keep painting?' Since he'd started to recover, he hadn't spoken so many words at once. It seemed to take it out of him.

'Come on,' she said. 'Let's get you back.'

*

Ed allowed them to go out for dinner on her last night. They waited ages in the lobby for a cab, then three pulled up at once. A woman in shiny thigh-high boots stepped from the first cab, shrieking with laughter. The passengers from all the cabs seemed to know each other.

'Is that Christie Blackmore?' Emily whispered to Will.

He gave a little shrug.

The woman headed straight for them. 'Will!' she cried. 'How *are* you? Ed told me you've been laid up.'

Will went to speak, but his voice cracked and set him off coughing.

'He lost his voice,' Emily explained.

'Oh, no!' said Christie. 'Rest that gorgeous voice of yours. Drink honey and lemon. But make sure the water's warm. Not hot or cold – *warm*.'

Christie turned to Emily. 'You must be . . .?'

'Emily,' she said, offering her hand.

'Yes, Emily. Will's told me all about you.' Christie gave her hand a squeeze.

'He has?' Emily glanced sideways at Will. He was smiling, but not with his eyes.

'Yes. So lovely to put a face to a name. And what a beautiful face it is. No wonder he's so enamoured with you.'

Emily felt her cheeks bloom. 'Oh, thank you.'

'Where are you off to?' Christie seemed genuinely interested.

'We have reservations at Mildred's in Greenwich Village,'

'Oh, I *love* Mildred's! Tell Paolo I sent you – he'll look after you. Have a wonderful evening.' As she walked away, she called back over her shoulder. 'And Will, remember . . .'

Will raised his eyebrows and swallowed.

'*Warm* water.'

He nodded, and she strode off to join her waiting entourage.

'Oh my God!' said Emily as they climbed into the cab. 'You never told me you met Christie Blackmore!'

'I forgot,' he wheezed. He was sweaty and grey.

'Are you okay? We don't have to go if you don't feel good.'

He shook his head, avoiding her gaze. 'I'm okay.'

*

It was awkward eating in a fancy restaurant with Will unable to talk much. She asked about the recording sessions, but the brief answers were becoming tedious for them both.

224

'So, how did you meet Christie Blackmore?' she asked.

'Studio. Same label.'

'She's naturally beautiful, isn't she? Wasn't her sister a supermodel? Imagine looking like that and being talented as well. That's hardly fair, is it? And so *nice*—'

'I feel rough,' he blurted.

'Do you want to go?'

He drew his knife and fork together and pushed his plate away. 'Finish your food first.'

*

They stood side by side at the sink in the tiny hotel bathroom, brushing their teeth. Emily looked at Will in the mirror. This was the first time he'd been able to brush his teeth standing up. He caught her eye and smiled, mouth foaming. He leant over to spit and rinse, then moved out of the way so she could do the same.

When she straightened up, he was standing behind her, eyeing her reflection. He put his hands on her hips and began kissing her neck. She watched in the mirror as he slipped the straps of her nightdress from her shoulders and let it fall to her waist. He ran his fingertips over her breasts, sending tingles down her spine.

'Feeling better?' she asked his reflection.

'Mm-hmm.'

'About time.' She turned around and kissed him hard on the mouth.

'I need to lie down, though,' he said, leading her to the bed.

Chapter 48

June 2016

Emily

It's a beautiful sunny day, and the café is quiet. My phone vibrates on the counter – Chloe's mum is calling.

'Hi Linda.'

'Emily, I wanted to let you know Chloe's in hospital.'

'Oh my God, what's happened?'

'She'd been complaining of stomach pains for a couple of days – turns out she had appendicitis. She's just had emergency surgery.' Her voice cracks and she sobs.

'Oh, Linda, that must have been terrifying. How's she doing?'

Linda sniffs. 'She's doing okay. They're keeping her in for the time being.'

'Is Liv with you at the hospital or back at the house? I'll come and get her.'

'Sorry?'

'Liv stayed with you last night, didn't she?'

'No, I haven't seen Liv for weeks,' said Linda. 'That's why I'm calling. I thought it would be nice for Liv to visit Chloe. Cheer her up.'

My heart rate quickens.

'Oh right. In that case, absolutely. I'll get hold of her then call you back to make arrangements. Keep me posted. And if there's anything I can do, don't hesitate, okay?'

'Thanks, Emily.'

I hang up and ring Liv.

It goes to voicemail.

I ring Scott.

'Hi Em.'

'Did you say Liv was staying at Chloe's last night?'

'Yeah. She's staying again tonight. Apparently, they didn't finish the film they were watching. She texted earlier to ask if she could. Why?'

'Linda rang. Chloe's in hospital. She says she hasn't seen Liv in weeks!'

'She didn't stay there last night?' I hear the worry in his voice.

My hands are shaking. 'No!'

'Okay. Don't worry. We know she's all right because she texted earlier.'

'Where the hell is she?'

Scott sighs. 'I'm guessing somewhere we don't want her to be . . .'

'I'll try Nathan.'

'Do you have his number?'

'No, but I know where he lives. I'll call you back.'

Magda finishes serving a customer. 'Is everything okay?' she asks, but she knows it's not.

'Do you mind holding the fort? I need to find Liv.'

'Of course, go.'

I'm going to kill Liv.

*

Nathan's mum answers the door. She's exactly the sort of woman who would have tidy little lollipop trees on her front step.

'I'm Liv's mum. Is she here?'

'No, I'm afraid not. Nathan's away for the weekend. He's gone to a music festival in Gloucestershire.'

227

Of course that's where she is. 'Ah . . .'

'There was a group of them going. Might she be with them?'

'No, she wouldn't go to a music festival without telling me,' I lie. 'Have you spoken to Nathan at all?'

'He rang us to say they'd arrived, and we've had a couple of texts, but the signal's not great.'

I ask her to call me if she hears from him, and we swap numbers. She gives me a sympathetic smile. I'm mortified.

*

'There's no point in driving all the way to Gloucestershire,' says Scott when I turn up at his door ten minutes later.

'She's missing, Scott; we have to look for her.'

'How will we find her among a hundred thousand people?'

'Maybe we should call the police?'

'She's old enough to look after herself and she's with friends. They're not stupid.'

'She's with a boy, Scott! Sleeping in a tent! Drinking alcohol . . .'

His expression changes. He doesn't like the picture I've painted in his head.

'I'll get my keys.'

According to the sat nav, it'll take two-and-a-half hours to get to Beatland. As the countryside whips by, my mind is flooded with images of Liv: getting drunk, getting sick, doing drugs, having sex, getting an STD, getting pregnant. I can't believe she went behind our backs, didn't tell either of us. And she's still got one more exam – she's supposed to be revising.

Scott must sense I need distracting. 'How's what's-his-name?'

'Who?' He means FHD, but I'm still having trouble with his name myself.

'That guy you're seeing – the dad from school.'

'Oh, Billy.' I've never called him Billy. 'He's fine. He got me the job at the café.'

'So, are you an item now?'

My cheeks grow hot. 'Of course not.'

I try Liv's phone, but it goes straight to voicemail again. Scott says nothing for a while and when I look over, he's frowning.

'What's the matter?' I ask.

He keeps his eyes fixed on the road. 'Nothing.'

Twelve minutes pass. I know because I count them on the clock. Then he lets out a long sigh. I'm expecting him to say something about Liv, but out of nowhere he says, 'What's this Billy like, then?'

Why is it so difficult to think of something to say about him? 'He's nice.'

'Nice?' Scott pulls a face. 'What does he do?'

'Do?'

'For work. What's his job?'

'He's in IT.' I've made him sound boring. I don't know why, but now I feel the need to big him up. 'He's interesting . . . you know, easy to talk to, funny . . . he's a brilliant cook . . . oh, and he's into paddle boarding.'

Scott sets his mouth in a tight little line and nods. It must be enough to satisfy his curiosity because he says nothing for the next hour, keeping his eyes firmly on the road ahead.

At last, I spot a sign for Beatland. 'Look, there's the entrance.'

'That's for deliveries.'

'It doesn't matter. We'll explain.'

We spend ten minutes explaining, but the security guard says we need to get a ticket like everybody else. Leaving the car there, we follow his directions around the edge of the site until we come to a gate and Scott buys a couple of day passes.

In the late afternoon sunshine, there's a lot of red flesh on display. The girls are all in bikini tops and the boys are all shirtless. Distant music pounds.

'Where shall we start?' he asks.

I leave him studying a map while I join the queue for the Portaloos. The stench hits me as I open the door. Outside, I wash my hands in the long water trough and scan the posters pinned above it for any bands I might recognise. Liv has mentioned The Liars. They're on the main stage in an hour. I take a picture of the poster and go back to Scott.

'We're not here to party!' I scold, as he hands me a plastic pint of beer.

'It's only shandy. We need to stay hydrated.'

I take a sip as we trace a route on the map and head off into the next field. As we emerge through an archway of brightly coloured bunting and ribbons, I gasp. Between us and the stage at the far end of the field are thousands upon thousands of people. My heart sinks. I scan the heads, straining to find Liv, but it's impossible. I feel like dropping to the ground, kicking and screaming. I want my daughter.

Scott takes my hand. He doesn't say 'I told you so', he simply pulls me into a hug. Over his shoulder, a girl not much older than Liv is slumped in a heap under a hedge. I sob.

'Don't worry, she's fine,' he whispers. 'She's with friends and they'll look after each other.'

I pull myself together, wiping my eyes. A friend goes to the girl in the hedge and helps her sit up. For a moment, I think everything will be okay; then the 'friend' hands her a pint of beer.

Scott follows my gaze.

'You can't be mum to everyone here, you know,' he says.

'I know.'

'Come on. We're here now. We might as well look around.'

We weave through the thickening crowd and, as we near the stage, the music is so loud my ears might bleed. Every third girl is Liv's doppelgänger.

The next field is full of circus tents. It takes an hour to go through them all and it's exhausting, more-so because it's so futile. Right now, she could be entering the tent we left ten minutes ago.

I sink to the ground by a totem pole and drain the last of my warm shandy. Scott sits down beside me. The sky is a riot of pink and lilac. The crowd in the next field erupts into applause. If the circumstances were different, this would be a magical moment. There's a buzz in the air. Scott is pulling little tufts out of the grass. He lifts his eyes to mine. It's as though he's trying to tell me something with those dark, doleful eyes. Then the moment is gone.

'There's Nathan!' he says.

'Where?'

'There.' He points to a tall, blond boy being swallowed by the crowd. We jump to our feet.

'If we get separated,' says Scott, 'meet back here at the totem pole.'

He has such a tight hold of my hand, I doubt that will happen.

He drags me through the crowd back to the field with the main stage. It's more tightly packed with people now.

'He's with Liv!' he calls over his shoulder.

Our hands get pulled apart, and he comes back for me twice.

As we reach the edge of the field, Scott says, 'Shit, I lost them.'

I scour the row of food stalls and spot Nathan's blond head in the distance. 'There!'

We bob and weave through people carrying trays of food and drink and leave the field under another decorated archway. The hillside before us is an ocean of multicoloured domes. We follow the most obvious path through the tents, swivelling our heads left and right. In the distance, Nathan and Liv make their way up the hill, then turn off the path to the left. As we reach the turning point, they dip down and out of sight.

'They disappeared by that Italian flag,' says Scott.

I follow him as he picks his way over guy ropes, leaning over each dome to listen.

He stops beside a blue tent. There's movement inside and noises.

Scott recognises the sound at the same time as me and dives at the zip.

Within seconds, he's pulling Nathan's gangly, wriggling form out by the waistband.

'What the fuck?' says Nathan, holding onto his unzipped shorts as he rises to his full height. He recognises Scott and has the sense to shut his mouth.

Liv is fastening her bikini top as she pokes her head out of the tent, her hair hanging in her face. As she straightens up, she tucks it behind her ears.

And that's when I see – she's not Liv.

'Where's Olivia?' Scott grabs Nathan by the front of his t-shirt, but I pull him back.

Nathan shrugs. 'How should I know?'

I let Scott go, and he dives at Nathan, grabbing two fistfuls this time. Despite being an inch taller, Nathan is suitably terrified.

'You'd better start talking,' Scott warns.

'I haven't seen her all day!'

'But she's here?' I ask.

'Yeah.'

Scott gives Nathan a firm shake. 'When did you see her last?'

'I don't know. This morning?'

'You'd better stop answering questions with questions.'

The girl tiptoes off, carrying her Doc Martens. Scott interrogates Nathan. He asks who they came with, which is her tent, what they've been drinking, whether anyone has taken drugs. He co-operates.

'She didn't seem all that happy today. She went off by herself,' he says.

232

Scott shoots Nathan a dirty look. 'Anything to do with you hanging around with other girls?'

'She wanted to see The Liars and Twisted Sphinx! It was nothing to do with me.'

'Come on,' says Scott. 'You're going to help us find her.'

Chapter 49

June 2016

Liv

The entrance to the VIP area is simply a gap in the hoarding manned by a single security guard. I would never have found it if it wasn't for the tiny map on the back of the press pass in my pocket. Tumi gave it to me weeks ago when I told her I was coming to Beatland. I almost didn't bring it as it only admits one and I didn't plan on being separated from my friends. But things haven't worked out as I'd planned. Nathan ignored me during breakfast, then went off somewhere with Charlie. Ella and the other girls went to the market area to spend money on outfits that'll look ridiculous anywhere but here. I went off by myself determined to watch the bands I'd come here to see but it's been no fun alone, standing self-consciously at the edge of the crowd, too embarrassed to dance and sing along and too scared to plunge closer to the stage. I'd been waiting months to see Twisted Sphinx, but I couldn't face watching another band on my own, so here I am, deciding if I have the guts to go into the VIP area. Pulling the pass from my pocket, I unravel the rainbow ribbon and loop it over my head. I take a deep breath and approach the security guard.

It had seemed like a mistake to let Ella do my make-up this morning – especially when Nathan didn't even look my way – but as the guard waves me through, I'm glad I did. I follow a passageway as it winds around four or five bends, then opens out onto an area about the size of a football pitch.

Glamorous people wearing sunglasses and insanely cool outfits lounge around on Bali beds like the ones you find by the pool at luxury holiday resorts. A long marquee stretches along the entire back fence, filled with stalls serving food and drink. A huge grill gives off delicious barbecue smells. Picnic tables painted all the colours of the rainbow are dotted around the sun-scorched grass and the whole place is draped in strings of retro lightbulbs – it's magical in the twilight. I wander around listening in on conversations and trying to spot celebrities. I nip in the marquee for a bottle of water and when I step back outside, there's a commotion as a noisy group of people make their way across the enclosure. Leading them is a man in a purple suit. He must be a celebrity; no normal person would dress like that at a festival. As they cross in front of me, I recognise the man despite the compulsory sunglasses.

It's Brett Lewis.

From Paradigm.

I don't know what comes over me. All I can think is *this man knew Will Bailey* and I have to speak to him.

'Brett!' I call, speed-walking alongside him.

A large man steps forward, palms up as a barrier, but Brett Lewis lowers them with a hand. The entire group is looking at me – at least I think they are, it's hard to tell with all the dark glasses.

'Brett,' I say breathlessly, 'can you spare a few minutes for *Amplify* magazine?'

There's a moment of silence. Brett looks me up and down. '*Amplify* magazine?'

I wave my press pass. 'Yes.'

'Okay. This way.'

The next thing I know, I'm climbing a staircase following Brett Lewis onto a balcony overlooking the festival site.

Brett invites me to sit on a red velvet sofa.

'Wow,' I mutter, as I take in the view.

Lights are coming on all over Beatland, twinkling in the half light as the sun disappears into the horizon in a soft pink glow. Music carries on the breeze as thousands of people mill around the fields below. A helter-skelter rises out of the crowd – how have I not seen that this whole time?

'Awesome, isn't it?' Brett pops the cork on a bottle of champagne that has appeared out of nowhere and pours us both a glass. 'So, what did you want to ask me?'

What would Tumi do in this situation? Suddenly, I remember the dictation app she made me download during work experience. 'Is it okay if I record this?'

Brett nods.

My hands are shaking as I unzip my phone from my tiny cross-body bag. There's plenty of battery thanks to the power pack Ella brought along. I set the app to record our conversation.

I start with questions about the new Paradigm album – thank God I've listened to it – and follow up with more about their upcoming tour. Brett doesn't seem in a hurry to get rid of me, but I don't know how long I've got, so as soon as I dare, I skip to the questions I really want to ask.

'Will Bailey supported Paradigm in 1996, didn't he?'

'Was it 1996?' A shadow passes over his expression. 'Yeah, must have been.'

'Did you get to know him?'

A flicker of a frown. 'Why do you ask?'

Silence stretches between us while I think of a sensible answer. At last, something pops into my head. 'We're doing a feature on Will Bailey for the twentieth anniversary of the *Fragments* album.'

Brett removes his sunglasses, his eyes blaze. 'I love that album! Has it really been twenty years?'

Brett gushes about Will's songwriting genius, quoting his favourite lyrics and raving about song structure, melodies, riffs, and hooks until they bring another bottle of champagne.

'It's so sad what happened. Such a waste.' Brett pauses for the first time in half an hour. 'I wish I'd done more to help his career. I could have promoted him more, got the word out. He never got the recognition he deserved in his lifetime. He probably never knew how good he was.' Brett shakes his head. 'You know, I was an absolute arsehole to him that whole tour. I was jealous. That voice – I'd kill for a voice like that.' He trails off, scans the view. It's dark enough now to see a smattering of stars in the sky.

There's a commotion behind us. A woman in tight leather trousers with legs that go on forever arrives on the balcony. A noisy group spill over the top of the stairs after her, laughing and talking at maximum volume.

'Brett, there you are!' she calls.

'Christie!' Brett gets up to greet her. 'What are you doing here? Aren't you supposed to be on stage?'

'In a minute.' She waves a hand. 'George said you were here, and I wanted to say hi. It's been forever.'

I pause the recording on my phone and fidget in my seat while they hug. As they break apart, I see her face.

Oh my God – it's Christie Blackmore! Rock royalty.

And the people she's with – they're The Underdogs.

'I'm finishing up here then I'll be over to watch,' says Brett.

Christie Blackmore arches an eyebrow at me. Thank God I closed my mouth in time.

'This is – sorry, what's your name again?' asks Brett.

'Olivia Lawrence.' I shake Christie's outstretched hand. 'Liv.'

'Liv's from *Amplify*,' explains Brett. 'They're doing a feature on Will Bailey.'

'Will Bailey?' Christie touches my arm. 'Oh, how wonderful. Is it for the *Fragments* anniversary? I'd love to contribute. I've got a few stories to tell about Will. Listen Liv, I'm supposed to be on stage now, but my people will be in touch. We'll set something up, okay?'

It takes all my willpower not to squeal. 'That would be amazing. Thank you so much.'

'Now, do you mind if I borrow Brett?' she asks.

'No, go ahead.'

Brett gives me a telephone number to call if I have any more questions. He wishes me luck with the feature and heads off with Christie Blackmore. They pile downstairs with their combined entourages, and I'm left standing on the balcony trying to take in what just happened.

I jump as my phone buzzes in my hand. It must be better reception up here at the top of the festival site. Two missed calls from Mum and a message from Nathan: Hey Liv, where are you? I need to talk to you. Can you meet me at the totem pole?

My heart jumps in my chest. What does he want to talk to me about? Maybe he feels bad about blanking me this morning. Maybe it was all a misunderstanding. Maybe he still likes me.

Me: Okay. I can be there in ten minutes.

Downstairs, the VIP area is now packed. I weave my way through the crowd and back along the winding walkway. The security guard gives me a nod as I leave.

The last twenty-four hours have been a rollercoaster ride. I can't wait to tell Nathan all about it. The festival site is different in the dark, and it takes a moment to get my bearings. I walk for a while, then turn under one of the ribbon archways. I'm expecting to see the field with the circus tents, but it's a car park full of lorries. I don't know where I am. I head back towards the VIP area to ask the security guard the way to the totem pole.

Suddenly, someone grabs my hair from behind and yanks. My head jerks back sharply and the force of it drags me to the ground. I land in a heap, one leg folded under me, my torso twisted. I cry out in pain, but a sweaty palm smothers my mouth and a voice close to my ear hisses, 'Shut your fucking mouth!'

Chapter 50

June 2016

Emily

Scott frogmarches Nathan away from the tents, back down to the main festival site.

'You said she wanted to see Twisted Sphinx. When are they playing?' I ask as we walk.

'Now, on the main stage,' says Nathan. 'They'll be finished soon.'

'Where would you agree to meet?' asks Scott.

'Probably at the totem pole.'

Scott halts. 'Text her now. Tell her to meet you there after Twisted Sphinx.'

Nathan pulls out his phone and does as he's told with Scott supervising at his shoulder.

We trudge on down the hill and a moment later Nathan's phone beeps.

'Is that her?' I ask him. 'What does it say?'

'She says she'll be there in ten minutes.'

He leads us to the totem pole, and we wait in the space between two food stalls out of sight. Applause and cheering mark the end of the Twisted Sphinx set and a steady stream of people file past us towards the tents. We wait twenty minutes, but there's no sign of Liv. After another twenty, I'm getting worried. Scott and I exchange looks. Nathan says he needs the toilet, so Scott drags him off to the Portaloos, but it's not long before he's back. Alone.

'Where's Nathan?' I ask.

'Little shit gave me the slip.' Scott runs both hands through his hair. I was worried before but seeing him riled ramps my anxiety up even further. 'He was no help anyway.' Scott pulls out his phone, dials and holds it to his ear. 'Fucking voicemail again.' He stabs at it and shoves it back in his pocket. 'Okay, I'm going to look for her. You wait here in case she shows. Stay where it's well lit. I'll come back and check in with you in half an hour.'

I pace the area, examining every face I pass, my stomach churning. On my third lap, I see a figure coming up the dark path from behind the food stalls. I recognise the silhouette, but the gait is wrong – she's limping.

'Liv!' I run to her.

As she steps into the light, I see she is crying. Her legs are streaked with mud. *Oh my God* – there's blood down the side of her neck.

'Liv?' I call, my voice shrill.

She sees me. Her whole body sags and I think she's going to run off, but she runs towards me, sobbing. 'Mum!'

She slams into my arms, her body quivering.

'Honey, are you hurt?' I grab her shoulders and hold her at arm's length. 'You're bleeding.'

Her fingers flutter to her right ear and come away bloody. She stares at it blankly.

'What happened?' I move her hand out of the way to see her earlobe is torn.

'A man . . .' she says between sobs. 'He took my bag . . . it was across my chest . . .'

'Slow down. Breathe.'

She draws in a ragged breath. 'He pulled it over my head. The strap caught on my ear, but he kept pulling it.'

Her right cheek is red raw. He must have scraped it with the strap as well. Rage boils in my blood. How dare this man hurt my daughter? I'm afraid to ask, but I force myself. 'Then what happened?'

'Once he got my bag, he ran off. He's got my phone, my money, everything,' she wails. 'I'm sorry.'

'That doesn't matter, so long as you're okay.' I pull her close.

'What are you doing here?' she asks. 'Did Chloe tell on me?'

'No. Linda rang – Chloe's in hospital.'

Liv pulls away. 'Chloe's in hospital? What happened?'

'She had to have emergency surgery for appendicitis.'

Her eyes grow wide with concern. 'Is she okay?'

'I think so. She's recovering in hospital. Come on, let's get into the light.'

She's limping as we walk to the totem pole. 'What's hurting?' I ask.

'My knee, it got twisted.'

As I help her to sit, I notice what she's wearing: denim shorts, a burgundy vest, and a brown corduroy waistcoat with a long string of beads and a lanyard dangling from her neck. I've never seen her in an outfit like that before.

She looks like me.

I wore an outfit almost exactly like it, for the entire summer of 1997, when I was festival hopping around Europe on a tour bus with Will, living out of a backpack.

I sit beside her. She's trembling as I gather her in. I try Scott, but the call doesn't connect.

'Did you talk to Nathan?' she asks.

'We asked him to help us find you,' I admit.

'Nathan didn't want to meet me, did he? He only messaged because you made him.'

I draw my mouth into a line and nod gently.

She buries her face in her hands.

242

'You're better off,' I say. 'He's an idiot. I don't know what he sees in that other girl.'

Liv drags her fingers down her face and fixes me with a glare. 'What other girl?'

Just then, I spot Scott on the far side of the enclosure. I give him a wide, sweeping wave and he heads towards us.

'We thought he was with you, so we followed him,' I explain. 'He went into his tent with this girl—'

'He was in his tent with a girl?'

'I thought you knew. I thought that's why you went off by yourself—'

She fixes me with an icy stare. 'Why would you tell me like that? How could you be so mean?'

I wince. 'I'm sorry, I didn't—'

'Whatever,' she snaps. 'It doesn't matter.'

But of course, nothing matters more to her. Her eyes shine with tears and resentment.

She heaves herself up and hobbles towards Scott. He envelops her in his arms; they stand there for a long time hugging and talking. I can't hear what they're saying. Over her head, Scott glares at me.

Clearly, he's disappointed in me, too.

Chapter 51

February 1997

Emily heard Will coming into the flat. That meant Miranda and Scott would have heard him too. The alarm clock said 3:15 a.m. The floorboards creaked as he passed her room to the bathroom.

Since he returned from the States, he had been renting a flat with Matty and Reu on a short-term lease, but it was a dump, so he stayed at hers most of the time. When they weren't playing gigs, they were rehearsing, so he often got home in the early hours.

She must have fallen asleep because the bed rocking woke her, his lips on her neck, his hands running up her thighs.

She turned to face him. 'I've got to be up in three hours.'

'It won't take *three* hours,' he joked, the minty smell not quite disguising the alcohol on his breath.

'Seriously, I've got a critique tomorrow . . .' He silenced her with a kiss and lingered until she kissed him back.

'I'm not sleepy,' he murmured.

'Well, I am.'

He rolled onto his back. 'We got the tour dates,' he told the ceiling.

Her stomach lurched. They had been expecting this news. 'And?'

'It starts in May and goes all the way through to the end of September.'

'Just Europe?'

'And America. They're talking about Japan and Australia at the end of the year.' He was talking about it like it was a prison sentence.

'Any festivals? You were hoping for Glastonbury?'

'Yep, we got Glastonbury, Reading, Roskilde, and one in Ireland.'

She slipped her hand into his. 'That's fantastic!'

'You could join us for the summer. When do you break up?'

'End of June. I can't though, I've got to get a summer job, otherwise I won't be able to pay the rent.'

They lay in silence for a minute.

'We need a photographer!' he blurted, too loud.

'Shh!'

'They're talking about hiring a photographer for the tour,' he whispered. 'It could be you.'

She didn't fancy tagging along as his girlfriend, but as the photographer, she'd be *doing* something. Something she was good at. 'Would they agree to that?'

'It's what I want, so they have to.'

'You're such a diva.'

'So, you'll come?'

'If it pays what I would make waitressing . . .'

*

Will had been away for six weeks by the time college broke up. She flew straight out to join them at a festival in Ireland. Ed met her at the VIP entrance. He gave the first of many wristbands she would wear that summer and told her where to find Will.

The Irish countryside glowed vibrant green in the late spring sunshine as though the grass was artificial. She wandered the site, following the faint strumming of an acoustic guitar towards a circular marquee in a small field. Inside, Will sat alone onstage playing to a small crowd with a film crew recording the scene.

It took all her effort not to run over and fling herself at him. She skirted the edge of the audience and, lifting her camera from where it hung at her neck, began clicking away. She didn't recognise the song; it sounded like an Irish folk song. It sparked the hairs on the back of her neck as the audience sang along. Scanning the faces through the viewfinder, she settled on a girl with tears in her eyes and clicked. He could make you ache with that voice.

As she neared the stage, she zoomed in on Will, concentration etched on his face. When she lowered the camera, their eyes met, and he gave a discreet nod that made her heart skip.

She could hardly contain herself as she waited by the stage while they filmed an interview. Will fidgeted on his stool, giving monosyllabic answers – either he was impatient to get to her, or all the questions about his Irish heritage were pissing him off. Emily wondered if he'd spoken to his mother lately.

The moment they were done, Will gave a wave to the audience and leapt from the stage. Without a word, he grabbed her hand and whisked her backstage.

Cupping her face in his hands, he breathed, 'God, I've missed you—'

A voice in a fake Irish accent made Emily jump. 'Top of the morning to ya!' Behind them, Matty stood holding a tray of Guinness, with Reu trailing behind. 'Are you ready to enjoy the *craic*?'

Before they'd even finished their pints, Ed whisked them off to sound check. Then it was showtime, leaving only two hours to enjoy the festival before they had to hit the road.

The atmosphere on the bus was raucous. Will introduced Emily to all the crew, and they drank and sang into the small hours until Ed finally convinced them all to call it a night.

The bus was moving when Emily woke the next morning, a sweatshirt wedged between her head and the window. Will was sitting opposite her, a bottle-strewn table between them as the bus trundled through the countryside.

He smiled when he saw she was awake. 'Good morning.' He looked tired.

'Didn't you sleep?'

'Nah, I can't sleep on the bus.'

They still hadn't had a moment alone together since she'd arrived, so when they got to the ferry port half an hour later, she dragged him into the disabled toilets when no one was looking.

*

If she thought she was going to see Europe, she was mistaken. Endless motorways, shabby service stations, and budget hotel rooms were all she saw. She might as well have been doing laps of the M25. It didn't matter that every day brought a new city because every day was the same. To fight boredom, the band and crew played pranks on each other. Lots and lots of pranks. Cling film on toilet seats, chilli sauce in snacks, fake turds in beds – Emily was soon immune to the sound of shrieking.

She became nocturnal, snatching sleep whenever Will was busy, so she could stay awake when he wasn't. It was a running joke she could sleep anywhere. They'd find her curled up in a corner, the hood of a sweatshirt pulled over her head, drawstring pulled tight, revealing only the tip of her nose. It was a wonder she never got left behind.

Every night brought a stellar performance, rapturous applause, oceans of swaying lighters and bellowed sing-a-longs, the boys so pumped when they came off stage, they would need a few hours – and a few beers – to wind down.

Emily was secretly happy that Will had trouble sleeping,

because those quiet hours before dawn were when she could have him all to herself.

'Are you having fun?' he would ask, curled around her as the sun came up on another city.

She assured him she was, and it wasn't always a lie.

She was getting through a ton of film and had filled three sketchbooks. She would draw people napping on the bus, make collages out of ticket stubs and empty sugar sachets, and doodle over set lists and napkins.

There were other girls around, but they changed with the cities until Naomi joined the bus after Glastonbury as a favourite of Matty's. Emily expected her to disappear once they got to France, but she was still with them when they went through Germany. Once it was clear Naomi wasn't going anywhere, they gravitated towards each other, enjoying the distinct lack of testosterone.

If it wasn't for the festivals, she would hardly see daylight. The pressure was off at festivals – not being the headline act meant shorter performances, leaving more time for fun. Watching other bands, sitting around campfires, shaking hands with idols.

They were somewhere near Prague the first time their single came on the radio. A massive cheer went up on the bus. Emily was about as far away from Will as she could be as they shared a look from opposite ends of the vehicle, his wide eyes gleaming with delight as the crew ruffled his hair and slapped him on the back. Her stomach fluttered with the thrill of him seeking her out in that moment, and she glowed with pride for him. Someone turned the radio to full volume and the whole bus sang along. A champagne cork popped, and the bottle was passed around. The lukewarm fizz tickled the back of her nose and she spilled it down her chin as she laughed.

The album was out, sales were good, venues were filled to capacity, extra dates got added and nights off got fewer and farther between. More fans were waiting at the back of the venue each night. Beautiful girls asking for an autograph, or a photograph, or a hug, or a kiss.

Rare days off became even more precious. One was spent on an Austrian lake, messing about on boats, somersaulting off a floating dock, seeing who could jump the furthest and dive the deepest. Emily laughed until her cheeks ached. That night they lay in bed, sun kissed and merry, laughing at the memory of Matty splitting his shorts trying to impress Naomi with a headstand.

When Will asked her that night if she was having fun, she realised she was having the time of her life.

Chapter 52

August 1997

The bus pulled up outside the venue in the heart of Vienna. Lashed across the front of the ornate Victorian building was a huge banner advertising that night's show. Emily looked up at the enormous photo of Will, wearing the gold lamé jacket she got from the charity shop back in London.

'Oh God.' Will groaned and ducked inside.

Reu came up beside her, reading the wording. 'Is it the 10th today?'

'Must be.'

Reu stared at the banner, his eyes glassy.

'What is it?' she asked.

He shook his head as though trying to snap himself out of it. 'It's my sister's birthday today.'

'How old is she?'

His voice was a whisper, 'Eight.'

She stepped closer, touched his arm. 'Why don't you call her?'

He shook his head again.

'Why not?'

'My stepdad wouldn't let her speak to me.'

'If we ring now, won't he be at work? I rang my parents last night – they're an hour behind.'

'My mum would hang up . . .'

'Maybe your sister will answer. Do you want me to try? I'll pretend I've got the wrong number if your mum answers.'

Reu hesitated.

'There's a pay phone over there,' she said.

'We're supposed to be sound checking—'

'It'll only take a minute. We're early anyway.'

She grabbed his hand and dragged him across the street to the pay phone.

'What's your sister's name?' she asked as they squeezed into the booth.

'Tiffany.'

She fed coins into the slot and punched in the number as Reu dictated it. He pressed his ear up to the back of the handset as it rang.

'Hello?' The voice was female – childlike.

'Is that Tiffany?' Emily asked.

'Yeah . . .'

'I have a special birthday surprise for you, Tiffany. Would you like to speak to Reu?'

'Yes!' exclaimed the little girl.

A voice in the background was asking, 'Who is it?'

'Say it's Nanny,' whispered Reu. 'Mum won't want to speak to her mother-in-law.'

Emily relayed the message and handed him the receiver.

'Happy birthday, Tiffy!' cried Reu, and launched into 'Happy Birthday' – the squashed tomatoes and stew version. 'How are you? . . . What did you get for your birthday? . . . You're so lucky! You must've been really good.'

Emily sorted through the coins in her purse, thumbing the European ones into the phone.

Reu was talking like a children's TV presenter. 'McDonald's? Good choice . . . No, I can't . . . I'm sorry, Tiff . . . I'm in Austria . . . No, kangaroos live in Australia . . . I'll come and see you soon, though, I promise . . .'

Emily slotted her last few cents into the phone.

'I miss you, too,' he was saying as she slipped out of the booth.

She waited outside. When Reu emerged, blinking in the sunlight, his eyes were swimming.

Emily opened her arms, and he fell into her.

She felt him quaking as they stood on the street, people bustling past. Had she made a terrible mistake suggesting he call Tiffany? When at last he pulled away, wiping his nose on his sleeve, he managed two words: 'Thank you.'

*

What better place for the final show of the US leg of the tour than the legendary Red Rocks Amphitheatre? Will followed the sound engineer up the corridor to the stage, and as they rounded the corner, the amphitheatre opened out before them. Two colossal sandstone rocks jutted out either side of them, soaring upwards to a point and wrapping the stage in its sculpted wings. Hundreds of steps, seemingly carved out of the rock, rose sharply to the azure sky. He'd seen pictures, but they didn't do it justice.

As he wheeled slowly around taking in the view, his chest felt like it would burst. Reu was practically bouncing with excitement; Matty's mouth hung open and Emily let out an awestruck giggle that bounced off the rock. She slipped her arm around his waist, her camera bumping into his ribs as she leant in and whispered, 'We made it.'

The corridors backstage were lined with photographs of iconic acts that had performed here over the years: The Beatles, Jimi Hendrix, Bruce Springsteen, Bob Dylan, the list went on. And they were about to join that list. Become part of history.

They had time to kill after the sound check, so they hung out in the dressing room, its craggy walls reminding them this was no ordinary venue. Reu relieved the boredom the same way he always did, by slapping rhythms on a nearby table. The beat reminded Will of 'Under Pressure' and he found himself humming the melody. Reu caught his eye, and they both started singing the lyrics at the same time. Each line was more rousing than the last, and soon they had the whole room singing. Roadies, technicians, venue staff – even the guys that brought the catering – were crooning along, the unique acoustics making everyone sound half decent. Reu's delivery of Freddie Mercury's nonsense-word scatting had everyone in hysterics. Reu met Will's gaze, a feverish spark in his eyes as he grinned back at him. A flurry of applause echoed in the space when they finished, and in the silence that followed, Will suddenly felt the enormity of the occasion. It loomed over him like the monoliths outside. His excitement see-sawing into anxiety. What if no one turned up? What if they bombed here, in this stunning location, on this historic stage? What a spectacular failure that would be.

He felt a hand on his. Emily breaking through his thoughts, pulling him out of his seat, a wild look in her eyes. What was that look? It took a moment for him to recognise it, but as soon as he did, he was up and following. She led him down a corridor to a storeroom. She shut the door behind him and stood with her back against it, her eyes locked on his. He loved it when she got like this.

He took her hard and fast up against a speaker, the perfect height for her to wriggle her short denim skirt up and wrap her legs around him. The warm soft wetness of her, the tangle of her fingers in his hair, the soft moan in his ear when she came – she made him feel invincible.

*

That night, when they rounded the corner onto the stage, they were met with a wall of people stretching up as far as you could see. Their cheers bounced off the rocks, lit up in red and gold against the night sky.

Will waded through the smoky haze to pick up his guitar and stepped up to the microphone.

'Hello Red Rocks!' he yelled, and the applause was like thunder.

They played their set; the same one they'd played every night for weeks, but it seemed different. Elevated. Will's voice was strong, reaching all the highs and lows he asked of it. Reu's drumming rang out sharp and clear. Even Matty's bass lines thrummed along harmoniously.

Spotlights swept over the crowd, illuminating thousands of bodies bouncing in unison, arms aloft. Picking out a line of trees high on the rock, dancing in the warm breeze. Despite his earlier wobble, this was the easiest show he'd ever played. He didn't even need to think. Every moment was utterly effortless. This must be what athletes meant when they said they were 'in the zone'. This setting, this crowd, this moment – it felt spiritual somehow.

The applause for their final song was so loud it reverberated in his chest. He felt like a god. Euphoria filled his body, tingling in his fingers and threatening to lift him into the air. He'd tried speed once, but all it did was make him talk too much. This natural high was unbeatable. Addictive.

This place had been sacred to the Native American tribes who'd lived here. It was sacred to him too now.

When the lights went out, the sky was black velvet studded with diamonds.

Backstage, Reu was a jittery ball of energy. 'That was fucking awesome!'

Will chuckled. 'Yes, it was.'

Suddenly, Reu threw his arms around him, squeezing tightly. 'Love you, man,' he croaked.

'Love you, too.'

Reu released him as suddenly as he'd grasped him and bounced off, turning at the door to flash the rock 'n roll salute and yelling, 'Let's party!'

Will followed Reu through to the next room where the catering was laid out. He spotted Emily talking to someone on the other side of the room. He grabbed a bottle of beer from an ice bucket, high-fived a passing roadie, and was on his way over when the person turned.

It was Christie Blackmore.

Shit. What were they talking about?

'Fantastic show!' cried Christie when she saw him.

Will gave her a chaste peck on the cheek. 'What are you doing here?'

'I've always wanted to see a show here, so when Ed said you were playing, I had to come out.'

'You remember Emily?' he asked.

'How could I forget? We've been having a lovely chat.'

Will's armpits prickled. 'Oh, yeah?'

Emily smiled. 'I was just telling Christie we've got a few days off before I have to go back to college, and you head off to Australia.'

'Yeah, I can't wait to have a break,' said Will. 'We're all knackered.'

'Why don't the two of you stay at my pad in Malibu?' said Christie. 'I'm heading to New York tomorrow. You'll have the place to yourselves.'

Emily's jaw dropped. 'Really? That would be brilliant!'

'That's really kind of you, Christie,' said Will. 'But we're going to LA with the guys—'

'You've spent the last four months with them, Will,' said Christie. 'LA's only an hour away. You can still see the boys, but this way you get time to yourselves, too.' Christie swigged her drink and gave him a discreet wink. Why was she being so nice?

Emily pleaded with her eyes.

In his mind, he cycled through every possible excuse. No sane person would refuse an offer like this. But he felt sick with guilt whenever he thought about that night in Christie's penthouse suite. Two weeks of constant reminders of what he'd done would be torture. Just standing near her made his bones itch.

*

The house in Malibu was fabulous, but there were photographs of Christie Blackmore everywhere. Her presence hung over him like a shadow, that night in her penthouse suite playing over and over in his mind. He wished he'd never gone up in that lift with her. He should have got out on his floor with Matty. He hated himself for what he'd done.

But playing house with Emily was bliss. Waking beside her, without Ed knocking on the door, telling them to be in the lobby in thirty minutes, making breakfast side-by-side, barefoot in the kitchen, with nowhere to be – living like normal people. Though Christie's house was anything but normal with its pool, gym, and home cinema. They even had the use of her Mercedes 300SE convertible. Not quite normal life, but more normal than living on a bus with twenty dudes.

They lay side by side on loungers by Christie's pool. Emily held her book up to shade her eyes from the sun as she read. He felt a pang. The summer was almost over. She'd be heading home soon, and he was going to miss her. He wanted to ask her to come to Australia, but he knew she wouldn't.

'Are you looking forward to going back to college?' he asked instead.

She rolled on her side to face him. 'I'd rather stay here with you.'

'You're missing your work, though.' Her bikini was distracting. Just three small triangles.

'Hmm. A bit. I enjoyed taking the photographs, though. I can't wait to see how they turned out.' She paused. 'Have you spoken to your parents yet?'

256

He reached across and played with the string tied at her hip. 'No.'

'It's been over a year; isn't it time?'

He sighed. 'I'm fed up with Mum giving me grief. Reu speaks to her. He tells her how I'm doing. It's better this way, talking through him.'

'I'm sorry.'

'It's not your fault.'

She let out a long exhale. 'It kind of is.'

'Milly,' he said, his tone serious. 'It absolutely is not.'

She gave a tiny shrug and went back to her book.

He closed his eyes and tried to visualise their future. Try as he might, he couldn't shoehorn this Malibu mansion life into their life back in London. His schedule was relentless. It was like being on a rollercoaster with no way of getting off. And she had her course to get back to. Red Rocks had been the single best experience of his life and this past week with Emily had been idyllic, but now he was crashing down from that high and she hadn't even left yet. Soon she'd be on the other side of the world. Literally as far away as it was possible to get.

He opened his eyes and squinted in her direction. She lay stretched out along the lounger with the pool throwing watery reflections on her tanned skin. He wished he could pause this moment and stay here forever.

Chapter 53

June 2016

Liv

I'm worried Chloe will look ill, but when I go into her hospital room, she looks the same as always – if you ignore the dark circles under her eyes, the ugly gown, and the grumpy expression on her face. She's still angry with me.

'Hey,' I say.

'What are you doing here?'

'Your mum asked if I would visit. I'm sorry, I thought you knew.'

'So you're not here because *you* wanted to visit?'

'Of course I am. I got here as soon as I could. I've been worried about you.'

She says nothing. A bag of clear liquid dangles above her, connected to her arm by a tube.

'How are you?' I ask.

'What do you care?'

'Chloe, I care—'

'How was Beatland?' She says it in a nasty sarcastic voice that doesn't sound like Chloe.

'You heard about that?'

'I heard you told your parents you were staying at mine when you went off for the weekend with your boyfriend.' She gives me an intense, cold stare, then looks away.

'He's not my boyfriend, and it wasn't just Nathan – it was a group of us.'

She shakes her head slowly. 'You *used* me.'

'No, I—'

'Why didn't you invite me?'

'To Beatland?' I ask, buying time to think of an answer. 'A spare ticket came up at the last minute – there was only one, otherwise I would have.'

She picks up the book resting on her lap and starts reading, so I sit on the chair by her bed.

'I'm sorry I didn't tell you about Nathan . . . and Beatland,' I say, but she carries on reading. 'I'm sorry I wasn't there for you when you got ill.'

She lifts her eyes, they sweep over my raw cheek and pause on my patched-up ear, but she says nothing.

'Chloe, please let—'

'Liv, just go.'

*

On the drive home, Mum asks, 'How did she seem?'

'She didn't want to talk to me. She told me to leave.'

'What happened between you two?'

'I didn't ask her to come to Beatland. She didn't know I'd been texting Nathan,' I admit. 'I've been a terrible friend.'

Mum sighs. 'Well, we all make mistakes. All you can do is apologise and try to make it up to her.'

'It's not as simple as that, Mum.'

'No, it's not, but good friends are worth fighting for and if she's a good friend, she'll forgive you eventually.'

Mum pulls up outside Dad's house. I'm still having trouble thinking of it as home.

'You know what would be cool?' she says, brightly. 'If you made a photo book for her. You could fill it with pictures of the two of you growing up together. A record of your friendship. There are loads of companies that do it online. You upload the photos and sort them into the template.'

I consider pulling a face, my default reaction to anything she says lately. But I'm sick of being horrible to her. I'm sick of failing to be the sort of person I want to be.

'That's actually not a bad idea,' I tell her, and she looks at me like I gave her the best compliment, which makes me feel even worse than if I'd been mean.

Chapter 54

September 1998

Tyres crunched on the gravel in the courtyard. Will went to the window and saw Emily pulling up in her mum's old Mini.

He jogged out to the car and as she stepped out, he gathered her up, nuzzled her neck and squeezed her so tight she squealed to be let free.

'Come on, I'll show you around.'

'Don't let me stop you working.'

'Nah, it's fine. We're taking a break.'

He led her through the gate, across the field of cows, towards the pond.

The record company had booked a residential recording studio on a farm in South Wales, away from the distractions of everyday life, to focus on writing the Difficult Second Album. The original booking had been for two weeks, but they had been there three weeks already with nothing to show for it. They'd spent a lot of time climbing trees, shooting arrows, and building rafts. So much for no distractions.

'How's it going?' she asked, as they lay down under a willow tree.

He sighed. 'Everything I've written so far is crap.'

'I'm sure it's not.'

'Believe me, it's crap.'

'You've got to start somewhere.'

'The last album was easy. I'd been writing songs my whole life and now I'm supposed to magic this out of nowhere.'

'I had to do the same with my exhibition. Start, and once you have something, you can make it better.'

He wanted to believe her.

They lay on their backs, gazing at the sky through the branches of the willow. He closed his eyes to the sun as it came out from behind a cloud and watched the dappled red on the inside of his eyelids. Everything went dark, and her lips were on his. She was here now. Everything would be okay.

*

Matty and Reu were playing frisbee on the grass in front of the studio when he got back.

'What kept you?' called Reu.

'We all know what he's been up to,' cried Matty. 'Look at the smile on his face.'

'He's much more relaxed, isn't he?' said Reu.

'Yeah, really *relaxed*.'

'Shut up, you two.'

When Emily came into the studio later, he was far from relaxed. The song they were working on was terrible. He didn't want her to hear it. So, as she sat in the corner writing her dissertation, he got the guys to work on something else. She looked up, caught his eye, smiled, and went back to it. It helped she wasn't watching, but it kind of annoyed him she could get on with her work when he was stuck with his.

*

That night, Emily woke to find Will's side of the bed empty. Her watch said 2:45 a.m. She pulled on a jumper and boots and went to look for him. The coach house was dark and deserted, but dim lights shone in the building across the courtyard.

She jogged over and followed the sound of music down the corridor. In a rehearsal room at the end, she found Will strumming an acoustic guitar and singing softly. She paused in the doorway and watched him scribble in his notebook. Just as she was about to speak, he ripped out the page, screwed it up, and threw it across the room.

'Hey . . .' she said gently.

He whipped around in his seat. 'Jesus!'

'Sorry.'

She went to him. He moved the guitar out of the way and pulled her onto his lap.

'Oh God, it's such a cliché,' he whispered as she wrapped her arms around him.

'It's a cliché because it happens a lot. Everyone who's ever been lucky enough to be in this situation finds it difficult. It's hard, but it's not impossible. Why not go back to what made you want to make music in the first place? Listen to your old favourites. Or listen to what other people are doing. For inspiration. It will trickle down through your filter and come out as yours.'

'Hmm . . .' She felt the vibration of the non-committal sound in his throat.

'If it's not happening tonight, try again tomorrow. Come back to bed.'

*

It was six weeks before Emily could make it back to Wales for another weekend. When she arrived, Will was alone in the rehearsal room. He was tanned but looked tired and a little thin. He said he was finishing up and sent her off to join Matty and Reu at the pub in the village, promising to follow shortly.

At the pub, Reu was busy thrashing the locals at pool while Matty looked on, bored.

Emily bought a round of drinks and sat with Matty.

'How's Will doing?' she asked.

'He's pretty stressed out. I think he's lost his mojo.'

'What do you mean?'

'We've been here months and we've got nothing to show for it. *I* like what he's writing, but you know what he's like; he's a perfectionist, and he's being hard on himself.'

'How can we help him?'

Matty thought for a minute. 'You should split up with him, then he'll be all heartbroken and write more brilliant songs.'

Emily bristled. 'What?'

'I'm only messing with you.'

'No, you're not.'

'I am!' He sipped his beer. 'But it's not a bad idea, is it? You split up with him for a few weeks, he gets his mojo back, and none of us have to get a proper job.'

She shook her head. 'Matty, you're an arsehole.'

'What?' He sounded wounded. 'You'd be doing him a favour. What's the alternative? He goes back to being a delivery driver. You get married, have kids, and live happily ever after? You think he'd be happy with that? And all the people who bought the first album and loved it – they'll all be saying: "whatever happened to Will Bailey?"'

His speech sounded rehearsed.

'He just needs time,' she explained calmly.

'Time's running out, Emily. The record company won't keep paying for us to play frisbee in the countryside forever. They're sending the suits down next week. They want to hear what we've got. And we've got nothing.'

That was why Will was still in the studio.

'Think about it,' he continued. 'He wrote most of *Fragments* while pining for you when you were with Aidan. He needs more of that love-sick angst.'

'Don't be ridiculous. I'm not splitting up with him, Matty.'

'Ah, I'm sorry,' he said. 'I don't know what to do. At this rate, we're gonna get dropped . . .'

Her stomach tightened. 'Is that likely?'

'If we've got nothing to sell, of course. It's a business like any other.'

'But *Fragments* is still selling . . .'

'That's why they want us to strike while the iron's hot. Apparently, it's all about timing.'

'What's all about timing?' came Will's voice from behind them. He took off his jacket and hung it on the back of a chair.

'Pool,' said Matty. 'You've got to get your timing right when you take a shot.'

'I thought it was all about your stance?' said Will.

'Yeah, and that.'

Emily joined them in the studio the following morning. She'd brought newspapers from the farmhouse and was sitting on the floor cutting them up and putting the tiny pieces into a bowl. No one batted an eyelid. They were all used to her crazy art projects by now.

When the band took a break, she pulled Will to one side. 'I thought we could try something,' she said.

She took the bowl of newspaper clippings to the table, and Will sat down beside her.

'I watched an old David Bowie documentary; this is how he comes up with ideas for lyrics.'

'With newspapers?'

'It doesn't have to be newspapers, it can be books, or magazines, or stuff you've written yourself. You cut out words and jumble them up. Bowie reckons when you see unrelated words together like this, the subconscious mind tries to make sense of it, and it sparks ideas you wouldn't have had otherwise. Shall we try it?'

'Okay . . .'

Emily picked out random words: 'Choice, forgive, testament, legends, confession, perfect strangers, polite.'

She arranged the words on the table in front of them.

'What now?'

'Well, you see if it sparks any ideas for a song or a line or something.'

Will glanced at the words on the table. 'I don't get it.'

'I'll show you. So, I like the phrase "perfect strangers", it's intriguing. Then I'd choose "confession" and "forgive" and explore how these words might connect. This song, or poem, or piece of art, or whatever, could be about strangers meeting. And maybe they have been thrown together because of a bad thing they've done that needs *confessing* and *forgiveness*. Now I have a theme and if I like it, I keep going or start again with different words. There are no rules. It's better than starting with a blank page.'

He grabbed his notebook and started scribbling. She was pleased he was responding positively to the idea.

'It doesn't make sense,' he said after a while. 'It's all nonsense.'

'Does it matter if it doesn't make sense? Lots of Bowie lyrics don't make sense.'

'But what's the *point* if it doesn't make sense?'

'Well, it's art, isn't it? It provokes thought, and combined with music, it moves people. It gives them an experience and an opinion about that experience.'

His brow creased.

'Try it by yourself for a bit. I'll tell the boys to give you an hour.'

But when she went back later, he wasn't at the table with the clippings. He was on the far side of the room, tinkering with his guitar.

'How did you get on?' she asked.

'It was all gobbledegook.'

'Shall I look? Fresh pair of eyes?'

'Nah. It wasn't working for me. Thank you, though.'

'Do you want to try with some books? I can copy stuff out and cut it up—'

'I can't do it that way!' His voice rang out in the silence that followed. He'd never raised his voice to her before. It stung.

'You can't fix this,' he mumbled. '*I* have to.'

Chapter 55

June 1999

By Emily's last visit, the band had been in Wales for nine long months. Horizontal driving rain hammered into the windscreen the whole journey, littering the route with accidents and leaving her stationary for long periods. With her mind free to wander, it kept returning to the same thing – the letter she'd received that morning. The one that left her stomach in knots.

By the time she reached the farm, she was exhausted and her temples throbbed. The dash from the car to the coach house left her drenched. She dumped her dripping coat and bag in the hall and found Matty in the sitting room nursing a bottle of whiskey.

'Where is everyone?' she asked.

'Will's on a call with the producer and Reu's gone into the village. Again. He spends half his life in that dive of a pub. Here, have a drink.' He poured whiskey into a coffee mug and shoved it in her direction.

She sank onto the sofa opposite him. It was the first time they'd been alone together since he suggested she split with Will.

'How's the recording going?' she asked.

He raised the bottle as if making toast. 'Great!' She detected more than a hint of sarcasm. He took a long drink straight from the bottle and smacked his lips. 'How's the art going?'

'Fine.' She ought to leave him to it.

'How many pictures did you sell at your exhibition, again?'

Emily lifted an eyebrow. Matty had never shown any interest in her work before. 'Quite a few of the smaller pieces sold. There were four big ones; I think the gallery overpriced them, but one of them still sold.'

'Was that the one Will bought? The cover art for *Yellow Feathers*?'

She stared at him. 'What?'

Matty waved a hand. 'Nothing. Ignore me. I'm thinking of something else.'

'Matty, did Will buy the *Yellow Feathers* artwork?'

'No!' He shifted forward, eyes wide. 'Jesus, I don't know why I said that.'

Her mind whirled. 'How would you know about it otherwise?'

'Oh shit.' He scratched at his stubble. 'Don't tell him I told you.'

If Will had bought it, why hadn't he told her and where the hell was it? He didn't even have anywhere to live. From the moment she won the competition, she'd thought there must have been a mistake. At every stage of the process, she'd been convinced they'd change their minds. The fact her boyfriend had bought the biggest piece only reinforced the imposter syndrome.

'Emily, you won't tell him, will you?'

She realised then what Matty was trying to do. He was stirring to get her to break up with Will. He was clearly sticking to this absurd idea that relationship turmoil would inspire his songwriting.

There was no point in calling Matty out on this. He was in no state to have a sensible conversation. 'How much longer will he be?' she snapped.

Matty shrugged. 'Last time he was on a call with Phil, it lasted an hour.'

Her inner critic began whispering at her shoulder, but she shook it off, remembering the letter in her bag. She was talented. The letter said so.

Just then, a gust of wind howled lashing rain against the windows of the old building. 'We're a long way from the California sunshine now!' he slurred. 'I bet you wish you were staying at Christie Blackmore's place in Malibu, not this shithole.'

'Yeah.' She was tiring of this conversation. She'd wait for Will up in his room.

'I'm surprised Christie let *you* stay there, though,' he said, before she could get up.

She sighed, 'Why?'

'I expect she wanted Will all to herself. She wouldn't leave him alone in New York.' He adopted a high-pitched voice: '*Ooh Will, sing this duet with me! Ooh Will, come up to my suite and listen to the latest Underdogs song!* She wanted him to be her toy boy.'

'Sounds like you're jealous.'

'You're right – I wouldn't say no.' His lecherous smile was almost a sneer. 'Not sure how Will managed to control himself when he spent the night in her suite that time.'

Her chest tightened. 'What are you talking about?'

'Didn't he tell you?'

'Tell me what, exactly?'

'I'm sure it was quite innocent. Obviously, he's with you and we all know how obsessed he is with you.'

'Matty, do you think I'm stupid? I know what you're trying to do.'

'What?' His voice was high, overly defensive.

'Oh, fuck off, Matty!' She stormed out of the room.

She ran up the stairs to Will's room, and slamming the door behind her, she dropped onto the bed and buried her face in the pillow. Matty was drunk, he was trying to split them up, but was there any truth in what he said? Did Will spend the night in Christie Blackmore's suite? And if he did, was there any scenario where that could be innocent?

She turned on her side and drew in a ragged breath.

Emily had always thought it odd that he hadn't mentioned meeting Christie on any of their calls and he'd acted strangely around her in New York and at Red Rocks.

And what had Matty said about Will buying the biggest piece in her exhibition? How could Will have kept that from her? When it sold, she had been so proud, so *validated*. Now that was all stripped away. She felt raw.

Angry voices drifted from below, then hurried footsteps pounded on the stairs. The door flung open and Will stood at the foot of the bed, eyes wide with panic. 'What did Matty say?'

Emily sat up on the bed. 'You know, because I heard you shouting at him.'

'He's hammered—'

'He said you spent the night with Christie Blackmore.'

Will tensed, his gaze darting around.

Emily's stomach dropped. 'So, it's true.'

He paced around the side of the bed, running a hand through his hair. 'I can explain.'

Emily's laugh was hollow.

'It was nothing. We didn't even kiss.'

'What does that mean? What *did* you do then?'

'I was drunk. She came on to me. I tried to stop her . . .'

White heat shot through her. 'But what? She overpowered you? All eight stone of her?'

'I didn't touch her.'

'But *she* touched *you*?'

Will blinked and swallowed.

'I see.' Emily felt sick.

'I didn't know what was happening until it was happening.'

271

'Oh, come on! Don't be so naïve.'

'I didn't even enjoy—' He stopped himself too late.

'So it doesn't count?'

'Ah, I'm not explaining this properly . . .' He dropped to his knees, elbows on the bed. 'I made a mistake. I'm so, so, so sorry. It meant absolutely nothing, and I promise it will never happen again.'

Her eyes burned. 'This isn't . . . this isn't what I want . . . this isn't the kind of relationship I want to be in.'

'Emily, please . . .' He reached for her hand, but she pulled it away. 'It was nothing. It was a mistake. A misunderstanding. I mean, it was Christie Blackmore . . .'

'What the fuck does that mean?'

'Up till then, I'd been one hundred percent faithful to you while Reu and Matty have been . . .'

'What? What have they been doing?'

His voice was small. 'You know what.'

'I knew you'd end up resenting me.'

'I don't resent you. This situation, this lifestyle – it's not like real life, that's all I'm saying. If I wanted to play around, I could have. But I didn't. That's the difference between Matty and Reu, and me. I didn't want to because I have you.'

She leapt from the bed. 'You don't get brownie points for only being unfaithful once, Will.'

'That's not what—'

'And you don't have me,' she said. 'Not anymore.'

He scrambled to his feet. 'No. No. No.'

She marched out.

'Don't go. Please, let's talk about this.'

She stopped on the landing and turned to him. 'You don't need to say anything else – I think I've got it. I should be grateful you weren't screwing around the whole time you were on tour. And I should let you off because it was Christie Blackmore. And you didn't even enjoy it. You've said enough.'

His footsteps drummed down the stairs behind her, and as she fumbled with her coat, he shuffled in her peripheral vision.

'I'm so sorry.' His voice was so serious and laced with regret she couldn't look at him.

As she moved for the door, he grabbed her wrist.

She whirled around, wrenching it free. 'Why didn't you tell me you bought the biggest piece in my collection?'

Will's mouth fell open.

'I feel like an idiot,' she continued, 'thinking how great I am – people want to buy my work. They want to pay money for these little pieces of my soul. They even want to buy the big pieces. But they don't do they, Will?'

His eyes were wide and unblinking. 'I'm sorry,' he said at last. 'I didn't buy it because I thought no one else would. I bought it because I love it and I wanted to have it. I couldn't bear for it to hang in some city trader arsehole's apartment and it not mean anything to them. Because it means so much to me.'

'Where is it then, if it means so much to you?'

He paused. 'I don't have anywhere to put it yet—'

'Where is it, Will?'

He was silent.

'Where is it?!' she yelled, making him flinch.

'It's in Matty's mum's loft,' he muttered.

'Oh, *thank* you!' her voice was bitter. 'Thank you for saving it from hanging in some city trader arsehole's apartment!'

'You know I don't have anywhere to live right now . . . Look, I'm sorry I didn't tell you. I just wanted you to feel good. What do you want me to do? How can I make this right?'

'You can't make it right.' She strode to the door and yanked it open.

Rain was still coming down in sheets.

'You're not leaving? You can't drive back now, you just got here.'

She made a dash for the car.

He followed despite the rain. 'Please don't go now,' he said as she struggled with the key in the lock. 'Wait till the morning. I'll sleep on the couch.'

She threw her bag onto the passenger seat, climbed in, and slammed the door. He stood by the window as she started the engine. The windscreen was already steaming up, so she fired up the blowers. While she waited for the fog to clear, she glanced at Will, his body hunched against the rain, arms folded, a hand over his mouth, wet hair hanging in his eyes. He said nothing, but that bedraggled look was pure anguish.

She reversed, turned, and with tears spilling onto her cheeks, drove off, not daring to look in the rear-view mirror.

Chapter 56

June 2016

Emily

I ring Scott's doorbell. We haven't spoken since the trip to Beatland. The drive back from Gloucestershire was excruciating. Scott stared straight ahead at the road and Liv sat in the back in silence.

He texted me this morning: **We need to talk about Liv.**

So here I am.

But he's not answering. I'm about to press the bell again when he opens the door, his phone pressed to his ear. He gestures for me to come in. The conversation sounds heated. He finishes up his call and goes straight to the fridge.

'Sorry about that,' he says. 'Wine?'

'Just a small one.'

He pours two glasses and hands me one.

'What's up?' I ask.

'Ah, it's work. I've got a big Christmas campaign that's giving me grief.'

'Christmas? It's June.'

'We do Christmas campaigns in the summer – we're so behind this year.'

'What happened?'

'We were partnering with an artist – Guy Arnaud. Have you heard of him?'

'No.'

'He's been a nightmare throughout the entire process, a real prima donna, and now he's not returning my calls. I've got a meeting with the client on Wednesday and nothing to show. I'm glad you're here; maybe you can help?'

'Me?'

'This is right up your street, Em. I don't know why I didn't ask you before.'

'Scott, I'm not an artist. I'm a barista, and a poor one at that.'

'I just need an idea. Tell me what you would do.'

He grabs his iPad, and we take our drinks to the dining table. He pulls up a website.

'This client is a luxury hotel group with three hotels: one in London, Paris, and Amsterdam. You know how luxury hotels have big Christmas displays in their reception areas? Well, this year we suggested partnering with an artist. Someone on the client team recommended Guy Arnaud, but he's useless.'

He shows me photographs. 'This is the Amsterdam hotel. We need to put a display in this area.'

He points to the space next to a sweeping staircase.

'It used to be a music school in the 1800s, so it has a music theme. This one is in London. It has a writing theme because Oscar Wilde and Rudyard Kipling stayed there. And this one's in Paris. It's an Art Nouveau palace, so it has an art theme.'

I take the iPad and scroll through the photos. 'Remember those vintage baubles I have? You could have a huge bauble hanging from the ceiling. Do you have a pen?'

He grabs a pen from a drawer and hands me an unopened letter.

I sketch the shape of a fifties-style bauble with a point at the top and the bottom.

'They've got that concave circle with a starburst in the middle,' I say, adding one to my drawing. 'This could be a window; when you peer in, there's a display of violins and saxophones or something. And in the London one you could have quills and books. And the Paris one, maybe paint brushes and palettes.'

'I love it!' says Scott.

'I have no idea how you'd make it, though.'

'Don't worry about that. We have a production company to work that out.'

'You could have three in each hotel, a big central one representing the hotel and two smaller ones hanging either side representing the sister hotels.'

'Can you sketch it for me properly? Show me how you imagine it would look.'

'What, *now*?'

'Do you mind? Have you got to be anywhere?'

'No.' I say. 'Listen, I'll do you a sketch, but you'll have to get your team to do it properly for the client.'

'Okay. I'll get some paper.'

He comes back with a pile of paper, coloured pencils, and fine liner pens. He spreads them out on the table in front of me.

'I'll make us some dinner. Is pasta all right?'

'Great, thanks.'

He tops up my wine and I realise he didn't get me around here to talk about Liv after all.

He cooks, I scribble, and by the time the food is ready, I've finished two of the three sketches.

'So, what shall we do about Liv?' he says, sitting opposite me with two bowls of pasta.

'Well, there ought to be consequences for what she did. She can't go off without telling us where she is.'

'Hasn't she's suffered enough – what with getting mugged and us catching her boyfriend with his pants down?'

'It's not about making her suffer, it's about making her think twice before doing anything stupid like that again.' I shovel in a forkful of pasta; it doesn't taste too bad.

'I thought maybe we should ground her or take her phone away but she and Chloe still aren't talking and I don't want to get in the way of them making up. Their friendship is on the line. It's more important than punishing her.'

'I hadn't thought of that . . .' Jesus, when did he become so good at this parenting lark? 'What should we do then?'

'We should have a conversation about trust and remind her she can talk to us. She doesn't need to keep secrets from us. I'd rather know what she's doing than go traipsing round the countryside looking for her again.'

'So, no punishment?'

'No punishment.'

We eat in silence for a bit.

'*You* should have the trust conversation with her though,' I say. 'It'll sound better coming from you.'

'Fine.'

I hear the front door close and the sound of keys clanking on a table.

'What are you doing here?' Liv says when she sees me.

'Dad needed my help with work stuff.' I go to her and put my arms around her, but she stands rigid, so I let go. 'How was it at *Amplify* today?'

'Good.' She goes to Scott, threads her arms around his middle, and gives him a squeeze. I drop my gaze.

'There's pasta in the saucepan. Help yourself,' he says.

'I've already eaten, thanks.' She grabs a caramel wafer from the cupboard. 'I'll leave you two to it.' And off she goes.

'That's it?' I ask Scott. 'That's all I get?'

He shrugs. 'It's better than nothing.'

Neither of us eats much more, and he clears away the dishes while I work on the last sketch.

His phone rings, and he goes out to the garden to take the call. Whenever I look up, he's pacing and gesticulating, and by the time he comes back in, I've finished the sketches.

'Wow, Em, they look great. You're a lifesaver. This'll look fantastic.'

I'm pleased with how they came out. 'Anytime.'

'Do you want a coffee?'

'No thanks, I'd better get going.'

He follows me out to the hall.

I call up to Liv. She shouts 'bye' but doesn't come down the stairs.

'I hope the meeting goes well,' I say.

'Thanks, I'll let you know.'

He opens the door for me. I step out, then turn back. 'Scott?'

'Yeah?'

'You're great with her. She loves you.'

He gives me a lopsided smile. 'She loves you too, you know.'

'Yeah, I know,' I lie.

Chapter 57

June 1999

Emily opened the door to the flat as quietly as she could, but before she'd even taken off her coat, Scott was in the hall wearing just his boxers.

'Shit, you scared me!' he said. 'What are you doing back? I thought you were away until Monday.'

'I was. It just . . . it didn't go very well . . .' Her voice splintered.

'Hey.' He was there in an instant, arms around her even though she was soaking wet, and he was half naked. 'What happened?'

It was hard to get the words out. 'We broke up.'

He pulled away, his hands on her shoulders. 'Oh shit,' he said simply.

She sniffed. 'Yeah.'

'Come on, let's get you out of this wet coat.' He helped her shrug it off and looked at his watch. 'It's 3:30 a.m., do we want alcohol or tea?'

Behind him, a scantily clad girl dashed across the hall from Scott's room to the bathroom.

'Oh no,' Emily waved a hand. 'You have a guest. I'll be all right. Just need to pull myself together.'

Scott glanced over his shoulder. 'Flatmate in crisis trumps that.' He flicked on the kitchen lights and ushered her to a seat at the table.

Miranda appeared bleary-eyed in the doorway. 'What's going on?'

Emily went to speak but her voice failed her.

'They broke up,' said Scott and passed her in the doorway as if they were a tag team. Miranda rushed over, gave her an awkward standing hug, then pulled up a chair. 'What happened?'

The concern in Miranda's eyes brought tears to her own and Emily couldn't speak. Patiently, Miranda waited for her to compose herself, gently rubbing her arm. Then Scott returned – fully dressed now – and began filling the kettle.

'Scott, you knob,' said Miranda, 'what are you doing? Can't you see she needs a proper drink?'

God, Emily was glad she had these two.

Scott poured them all shots of vodka, but there were no mixers in the flat, so he diluted them with water. It tasted foul, but the burn as it went down was strangely soothing.

Emily filled them in on the events of that day – the drive to Wales, the conversation with Matty, the row with Will, and driving all the way back again. Miranda kept butting in with foul-mouthed insults for Matty and Will. Scott listened quietly.

'Did I do the right thing?' Emily looked from Miranda to Scott. 'I don't know if I did the right thing.'

'Of course you did the right bloody thing,' said Scott.

'Look,' said Miranda, 'What do you want? From your life, I mean?'

Emily lifted her eyes to Miranda's.

'You're always sacrificing yourself for Will,' Miranda continued. 'Travelling to wherever he is. He didn't come to your exhibition.' She stabbed a finger into the table. 'That was your Glastonbury – where was he then? You've got to think of yourself from now on and what you want.'

Scott pursed his lips and nodded his agreement.

'Wait, I have something to show you both.' Emily fetched the letter from her bag and they moved their glasses so she could lay it on the table.

'You got it!' cried Miranda almost immediately, as though she had been expecting it.

Scott tilted his head to read from his position at the table. 'We are delighted to inform you that your application has been successful . . .' He looked up briefly, a question in his eyes. 'We look forward to welcoming you, on the conclusion of your studies, to our two-year residency programme . . . You will have twenty-four-hour access to your own light, spacious studio in the heart of Amsterdam . . . Amsterdam?'

Emily nodded, a weak smile breaking through her misery for a moment.

'Two years?' he asked, eyes wide.

Miranda elbowed him in the ribs. 'We're going to have some wild weekends in the Dam!'

'You knew about this?' he asked.

'I helped her with the application.'

'Wow.' Scott took a swig of vodka.

'I didn't want to tell anyone in case I didn't get it,' Emily explained. 'And when I got the letter this morning, I wasn't even sure I'd accept. I thought it might mean the end of me and Will . . .' Oh God, she was crying again.

'Imagine if you'd turned it down for that fucker.' Miranda poured them all another shot, not bothering with the water this time.

'Imagine choosing Christie Blackmore over you,' added Scott.

They sat drinking until the pale morning light streamed in through the window and Miranda held back Emily's hair as she brought up the meagre contents of her stomach.

*

She didn't want to go out the following weekend, but Miranda and Scott insisted. They dragged her to their old haunt, an indie disco at a basement club on Wardour Street. They drank and danced and yelled in each other's ears and everything was fine until the DJ played 'Fever' and Scott caused a scene at the DJ booth. Before they knew it, a burly bouncer was ejecting them onto the street, so they called it a night and picked up kebabs on the way home. When they got in, the answering machine was flashing.

'Don't listen to it,' warned Miranda. 'Just delete it.'

There were four messages altogether – all from Will. Miranda and Scott stood by, nodding their encouragement as Emily deleted each one without listening beyond the first word. They ate in the kitchen and drank the rest of the vodka – this time diluting it with a can of Coke from the kebab shop split three ways.

'How long does it take to get over someone?' asked Emily.

'Five minutes when they've spent the night with Christie Blackmore.' Miranda bit into her kebab.

'Fair point,' said Emily. It still stung, but she was getting used to the idea now. Whenever she wanted to call Will, she thought about the two of them together, and it strengthened her resolve. 'What do you think they did?' she asked, poking the wound. 'He said he didn't touch her, and they didn't kiss.'

'Hand job?' suggested Miranda.

'Nah, blow job,' said Scott.

Emily dropped her kebab onto its paper wrapper. No, she wasn't ready to hear that. 'How long did it take you to get over Gemma?' she asked Miranda.

'I dunno, couple of months? But we hadn't been together as long as you.'

'How long were you together?' Scott asked Emily.

'Three and a half years.'

They ate in silence for a minute.

'I tell you what helped,' said Miranda. 'Shagging someone else.'

Emily laughed. Scott lifted his eyebrows.

'Seriously, it helps! Especially if you've been cheated on. It's like revenge or levelling the score or whatever. That night with – jeez I don't even remember her name – was like therapy.'

'You had a one-night stand after Gemma? You never told me!'

'A girl doesn't kiss and tell.'

'Never stopped you before,' said Scott.

Emily picked a slice of cucumber from her kebab. 'I don't think I could do that.'

'You need to be more like Scott,' Miranda joked. 'Just don't get emotionally attached.'

'Hey!' Scott pretended to be offended.

'He doesn't understand heartbreak,' Miranda told Emily as if he wasn't there. 'I bet he's never even been in love.'

Emily and Miranda looked to Scott for confirmation. 'What?!' he cried. 'I've been in love. Of course I've been in love. I'm twenty-four.'

'Oh yeah?' teased Miranda. 'With who?'

Scott's ears went pink. 'I . . .'

'Name one person.' Miranda gave Emily a knowing look and drummed her fingers on the table as Scott floundered.

'Okay, okay.' Scott raised his palms in defeat. 'I have a heart of ice.'

They stayed up for one more drink before heading off to bed. Emily's mind wandered to Will, as it often did when she had nothing else to think about. What had he said in those now-deleted messages? She longed to hear his voice but was ashamed to admit it in front of her flatmates. She missed Will now more than she ever had when he was away on tour. All evening, she had been trying to get a minute alone, maybe have a little cry, but Miranda was there whenever she went to the loo, banging on the cubicle door, yelling for her to hurry up. Maybe it was the vodka muddling her thoughts, but she wasn't sure she'd made the right decision at all. It hurt too much.

The more she thought about the whole Christie Blackmore thing, the more she thought she could understand what happened. It was true – their situation was unique; most normal relationships didn't have to survive the temptation of groupies every night. And he had shown restraint holding out as long as he did. Could she have done the same? Lonely, far from home, with it being offered on a plate, no strings attached? Maybe not.

But the thing that made her feel worse. The thing that kept her awake every night since the split was the decision she had made on the drive to Wales. With the windscreen wipers swiping back and forth, she'd planned what she would say. She practised saying it aloud over and over throughout the journey. Those words echoed in her mind now. 'I'm sorry, but I can't do this anymore. It's time I followed my dreams, not yours. If I don't do this now, I'll regret it forever.' But she hadn't needed those words after all, because Will had made it easy for her. And she couldn't sleep knowing how he must be suffering, thinking it was all his fault. She was plagued by that last image of him as she drove away, the pained look, the way his arms dropped to his sides.

But what's done is done. Emily needed to draw a line under it once and for all. She took a deep breath, threw off the covers, and jumped out of bed.

Chapter 58

July 1999

Scott had given up trying to sleep – when he drank too much alcohol, it always kept him awake. He was reading when he heard a gentle knock on his bedroom door.

'Yeah?' he called.

The door opened and there, lit by the soft glow of his bedside lamp, stood Emily. On anyone else, that nightdress would be ordinary, but on her it was beyond sexy.

He tried to keep his eyes on her face. 'You okay?'

Without a word, she turned and quietly closed the door behind her.

'Em?'

She lifted his duvet and slid into the bed beside him. He placed the book on his bedside table and turned back to find her with her head on the pillow facing him. His heart skittered as he lay down beside her. It must be a dream – Emily Lawrence was in his bed, an intense look in her eyes. She scooted closer and brushed her parted lips against his. His whole body thrummed. He closed his eyes as her tongue slipped into his mouth.

What the fuck was happening? He must have fallen asleep. Her hands were on his body, travelling downwards, finding the erection that had sprung up the moment he glimpsed her in that clingy, strappy nightdress. A groan escaped him as her hand closed around it. She kissed him deeply, and he was getting carried away with it all, but a nagging doubt lingered. It was so hard to break away, so difficult to put a hand over hers to still it for a moment.

'Em?'

She ignored him and kissed his neck.

'Em, you have to say something, otherwise I'll think you're sleepwalking.'

She breathed in his ear, 'I'm not sleepwalking.' And it was the hottest thing he'd ever heard.

He let go of her hand, and she began moving it again in slow, rhythmic strokes. He kissed her mouth, her neck, her shoulder. Her soft sighs and shallow breaths became too much for him. She gasped as he flipped her onto her back but her hands were in his hair, caressing his neck, clasping him by the shoulders and pulling him close.

'Em?'

'Shh,' she whispered.

'Em, are you sure you want this?' *Oh God, please say yes.*

She broke away and locked eyes with him. 'I want this.'

And it was as if she'd said something really dirty.

*

He didn't sleep at all. He lay there all night, Emily curled beside him, breathing softly. Even when her hair tickled his nose, he kept very still. In the weak morning light, he watched her eyelids flutter as she dreamt. He couldn't believe this was finally happening.

She woke early as the sun came in through a gap in the curtains of the balcony doors. Silently, he cursed himself for not closing them properly. She rubbed her eyes, yawned, and smiled. She was adorable.

'Morning,' he said.

She covered her face and peeked through her fingers. 'Oh God,' she whispered. 'We totally did it.'

He laughed. 'Yeah, we totally did it.'

Her cheeks were flushed when she slid her hands down to her chin. 'You're good,' she said, arching an eyebrow.

'Good?'

She groaned, covered her face again, and through her fingers said, 'I mean, I can see where you get your reputation.'

'What reputation?'

She laughed like he'd said something funny. 'Right, I'm getting out of here before Miranda finds out and we never hear the end of it.'

She wriggled around under the covers, putting her arms back in the straps of her nightdress. Leaning in, she kissed his cheek chastely. 'Heart of ice, right?'

He set his mouth into a smile. 'The only way to be.'

Then she was up and out of the bed, smoothing the nightdress. At the door, she checked the coast was clear and gave him a little wave before slipping out.

The handle moved down and up as she closed the door silently.

He curled his arms over his head, and muttered, 'Ah fuck.'

And that cold little rock in the middle of his chest cracked.

Chapter 59

July 2016

Emily

FHD is already sitting at the bar as I descend the spiral staircase into the basement gin bar he suggested. I take the steps carefully to stop my heels from catching in my hem. I'm wearing the green dress I bought for Scott's parents' barbecue last summer. It's simple but elegant – everyone said it was lovely, and I remember Scott's eyes roaming over it, giving it the male seal of approval. Maybe I'm a tad overdressed tonight though.

I make it to the bottom of the stairs without tripping and FHD says, 'Wow, great dress.'

We sample different gins with their corresponding mixers and garnishes and taste each other's drinks; we declare our favourites. I don't finish my third cocktail. I'm at the perfect stage of merry.

'How do you feel about Billy?' I ask.

He frowns. 'Who's Billy?'

I laugh. 'You.'

'Oh, me. You mean how do I feel about you *calling* me Billy?'

'Yes.'

He thinks about it, draws his mouth into a line, then nods his head. 'I like it,' he says, 'makes me sound like a cowboy.' He raises his glass. 'Yee haw!'

289

I tap my glass to his with a chuckle. 'Yee haw.'
'Shall we talk about why you want to call me Billy?'
'No.'
That straight-line mouth and nod combo again.
I lean in. 'Billy?'
He inclines his head towards mine. 'Yeah?'
I whisper into his ear, 'Let's go.'

*

The dress is in a green puddle around my feet. I didn't know it would slip off like that. FHD/Billy is behind me, scooping my hair to one side and kissing my neck. The copper artwork above his bed is abstract, but it looks like an aerial view of waves breaking on a beach. I'm having trouble staying in the moment. I drag myself back into my body and concentrate on the sensations. Stepping out of the dress, I turn to face him. Billy's gaze sweeps over my body and suddenly I'm self-conscious standing there in my best underwear. According to the magazine I read in the hairdressers, I have way too much pubic hair. The confident woman whispering in his ear half an hour ago is long gone. I pull at the buttons on his shirt and tug at his belt. It's as though I'm eager to get to it, but I just need him to be as undressed as me.

It's normal, right? To think of the last time you had sex, even if it was a long time ago? Even if it means Scott's on my mind as Billy circles my nipple with his tongue? I tense up as these thoughts intrude on the moment. I tell myself to let go. It takes all my concentration, but I relax. The sex is good, but I don't come, and I don't pretend to.

We lie side by side in his bed, catching our breath. He turns on his side, his face close to mine on the pillow, eyes glinting in the lamplight. 'I'm sorry you didn't . . . did you?'

'It's fine really, it's been a while and I . . . it's different with . . .' This is excruciating.

'Would you like me to—'

'No, honestly. I'm good. It was great.'

I stay the night. Falling asleep is easy with a warm body curled around mine and soft breath on my neck.

*

I wake with the birds. Billy still has his arm around me, and it makes me smile. I need to go home to shower and change before work. The green dress and last night's make-up will not pass Magda's scrutiny. I check my watch: there's still time for at least another hour of sleep, but I'm wide awake. Billy removes his arm and turns onto his back in his sleep. I prop myself up on my elbow gently, so I don't wake him. Studying his face unobserved, I take in his strong, square jaw and defined cheekbones. It's the kind of face you want to draw.

I lay back on the pillow. When was the last time I sketched? That drawing for Scott. I've drawn *his* face once before. Back in college, we did portraits of each other in class. We only had ten minutes. Mine came out well, but I remember he disliked my interpretation of his nose. His sketch of me was flattering, but it didn't really look like me.

I run my fingertips across Billy's cheek and down to his chin. The long stubble is soft. His eyes flicker open.

He smiles. 'What time is it?'

'Early,' I say and lean in to kiss him.

The morning sex is much better. I could get the hang of this.

*

We eat a breakfast of toast and coffee. Billy offers me every conceivable spread for the toast but I plump for Marmite. We eat at his kitchen table chatting, me overdressed in the green frock.

291

He's looking at me like an eager puppy and it makes me laugh.

'What?' he asks.

'Stop looking at me like that.'

He raises a playful eyebrow. 'Like what?'

'Like that.'

He bites a semi-circle out of his toast, chews and swallows. 'I was thinking it might be nice to go away together.'

'Away?'

'Just for a weekend, somewhere in the UK or maybe a bit further: Paris or Barcelona or something.'

Barriers go up inside me. The toast in my mouth takes a long time to chew. He's waiting for a reply, so I say, 'That would be nice.' But my voice is flat.

'Have you ever been to Paris?'

The Arc de Triomphe framed by the window of a tour bus flashes into my mind. 'Once.' Inside, mild panic is rising. Which is very confusing. He's gorgeous. I was – am – very flattered to be his flavour of the week. I thought he was a bit of a player, on dating apps, seeing lots of people.

'Too soon?' he asks, making light of his faux pas.

I smile. 'A bit.'

He leans in, kisses my neck, and whispers, 'You get me all carried away.'

Chapter 60

July 1999

Will pressed the buzzer and waited. There was no answer, so he buzzed again. Still no answer. He stepped back from the door to check the windows. Emily's room was dark, the whole flat was dark. Perhaps she was out, or perhaps she was avoiding him. He made his way around the back of the building. It was difficult to work out which flat was hers on this side until he spotted a red chair on a balcony and recognised it as Scott's. The windows were unlit on this side too. He stood underneath the balcony. If he got up there, he could see in. He spotted a wheelie bin a few yards away and dragged it closer. For the briefest of moments, he thought about what he was doing, how it might look, whether it was a terrible idea. But he needed to talk to her. He was desperate, and there was no room for logic in his brain at that moment. The whiskey wasn't helping.

He wedged the bin against the wall, climbed on, and wobbled his way up to standing. Using the railings to steady himself, he lunged a foot up, stuffed it between them, and hauled himself up. He took a moment to catch his breath before swinging his leg over and landing on the balcony with a thud.

Hands cupping his eyes, he pressed his face to the glass. Scott's room was dark except for a single red light on something electrical, a TV or stereo maybe. The balcony door was locked, so he sank onto the red chair and checked his watch. It was 10:45 p.m. If they were at the pub, they'd be back soon. From the inner pocket of his jacket, he pulled out his dad's old hip flask and took a swig. The cool pewter in his palm reminded him of his first date with Emily, when they shared sips from that flask. Before everything. Before any of this. They'd had their first kiss that night. It was also the night Aidan gave him a good kicking. Will guzzled more whiskey at the memory of that. He hadn't spoken to him since.

Will had been sitting on the balcony a while before he noticed the brick. It was there on the floor by the balcony door like an unexpected gift. Why would there be a brick on Scott's balcony other than as an invitation to smash the glass? Will puzzled over it for a few minutes. The whiskey was making it hard to keep his thoughts straight, but eventually he worked it out. It was a doorstop. It was there to hold the door open. Of course, that made sense. When he checked his watch, it was 11:04 p.m. He'd give them until eleven-thirty, then he'd use the brick.

If he smashed the door, there would be a lot of glass, and someone might hear. There was a little window beside the door. If he smashed the smaller pane, that would make less noise and he could reach around and open the door.

Will's watch said 11:27 p.m. – it was time.

He picked up the brick. It was heavy and rough in his hands. He took a couple of practice swings at the window. Shit, what was he doing? They would be angry about the window. But it was only a little window. He'd sweep up the mess, pay for it to be replaced. He had to talk to her. Just five minutes. He needed to explain, to tell her he'd do anything, he'd change, he'd be . . . better. He had to fight for her. The first step in that fight was to smash the window. He swung his arm back and hurled.

The smash was quieter than he expected. Only a few shards fell on the balcony floor. The rest fell inside the flat and whatever was there muffled the sound. He reached through the window for the keys dangling from the keyhole in the door. Stretching his arm until his shoulder butted up to the window frame, he could reach the keys. It took several attempts to turn the key using only the fingertips of his left hand. He retracted his arm, went to the door, and this time it opened.

It was dark inside and he bumped into a chair on his way out of Scott's room. He ran his hand along the wall until he found the light switch. As light flooded the room, Will checked the damage. The smashed window looked awful, so he went over and lowered the blind. Much better. He turned back into the room and froze. The wall around the light switch was smeared with wide, red arcs. He checked his body – a long gash on his forearm was dripping with blood. You could trace his route across the room with the red splatters he'd left on the floor. The carpet was like a Jackson Pollock. How the hell would he clean that up?

Cradling his arm, he hurried to the bathroom. Even as he ran it under the tap, it kept gushing. What were you supposed to do? Apply pressure and raise it above your heart? He grabbed a towel and wound it around his arm. The towel would need replacing as well. Jesus, this was getting expensive.

He'd have to sweep up the glass and wipe the wall, but he needed to rest for a minute. With his elbow raised, he stumbled down the hall to Emily's room, turned on the light, and closed the door behind him. Her room was messy; she must have been busy working on something. Wooden letterpress blocks, in all different sizes and styles of lettering, were strewn across the desk. Her sketchbook lay open at the end of the long table, plump with the stuff she had stuck in it. For the first time since he broke into the flat, he felt guilty about invading her privacy. He hesitated, then took the sketchbook with him to the bed.

He lay awkwardly on his left side, his elbow propped up on the pillow with the back of his hand resting against the headboard to keep it elevated. Flicking through her sketchbook was like looking inside her mind. She had filled it with scraps from her life. A ripped strip of wrapping paper with an intricate floral pattern. The ticket stub from an exhibition at the Victoria and Albert Museum, postcards of paintings. Sketches of people and places, some washed with colour and outlined in ink, others in scratchy blue biro.

He didn't have the energy to keep turning the pages, so he left it open on a page covered with scribbled words. It was getting hard to focus, but a few words stood out: *lonely, odyssey, wish*. What did it mean? His limbs were heavy. He'd close his eyes for a minute.

Chapter 61

July 2016

Liv

I pull out my new phone. Actually, it's Dad's old phone, but it's better than the one that was stolen from me. Thank God he could download everything from the cloud. Well, almost everything. The interview with Brett Lewis was gone – it was too recent to get backed up – but the number Mary gave me was still there in my contacts.

I dial and a male voice answers on the third ring. 'Hello?'

'Is that David Matteson?' I ask.

'Who's asking?'

'My name's Olivia Lawrence. I'm a journalist at *Amplify* magazine,' I say, mimicking Tumi. 'I was hoping to talk to David Matteson for a Will Bailey feature we're working on. Is he available?'

'I'm David Matteson, but everyone calls me Matty.'

'Matty, would you be willing to do an interview? We wouldn't take up much of your time and we could come to you – wherever's convenient . . .'

'I work in Southwark. I could meet you in a café one lunchtime?'

'Perfect. How's tomorrow for you?'

'Er . . . okay.'

We arrange to meet at one o'clock, around the corner from

his office. I message him to confirm the moment I hang up, just like Tumi does.

I'm absolutely shitting myself.

*

Interview transcript – David 'Matty' Matteson

OL: Thanks for doing this, Matty.

DM: It's good to talk about Will. I still think about him every day, even after all these years.

OL: I'll dive straight in, if that's okay? What was the band's songwriting process?

DM: Will would come up with a riff. The three of us would jam along. He was always scribbling ideas for lyrics in a notebook. He'd have a new song every week. Songs came easily to him because he had girl trouble. He was in love with his brother's girlfriend.

OL: His *brother's* girlfriend?

DM: Yeah – Emily. She went out with Aidan for a couple of years. Will always maintained he saw her first, but Aidan got in there before him. He won her over eventually, though.

OL: How did he do that?

DM: Will caught Aidan cheating on Emily. There was a big family hoo-hah one Christmas, and it all came out. Emily chose Will, and when they got together, his family kicked him out. He stayed at mine for a while until he got his own place. After that, we got signed and were living out of suitcases, anyway, so it didn't matter.

OL: So, he wasn't talking to his family?

DM: No, not for a long time. Not till they split up . . . Anyway, back to the music. *Fragments* was all about wanting someone you can't have. He spent years writing it. I'm so proud to have been a part of it. It did so well, the record company wanted to get the second album out as soon as possible. Will was under pressure.

OL: The songs didn't come as easily?

DM: He had all these years to write the first album, his whole life to pick the best songs and, two years later, they want another twelve songs of the same quality, and he wasn't happy with what he was coming up with. Now he was loved-up with Emily, he had nothing to write about. I was convinced that was the problem. I'm ashamed to say I panicked. My livelihood depended on him writing more songs. I was shitting myself. I'd never done an honest day's work in my life, so I did something I'm not proud of . . .

OL: What did you do?

DM: [Sighs] I told Emily she should break up with Will so he could get his mojo back.

OL: And did she?

DM: No. She told me to piss off, which is exactly what she should have said.

OL: But you said they broke up. What happened?

DM: Well, I'd tried *asking* her to split with him, but she wouldn't, so I made her *want* to split with him for real.

OL: How?

DM: Will bought a picture from her art exhibition. He didn't want her to know. It was a secret. He got someone at the record company to buy it for him so she wouldn't find out. Come to think of it, that thing's probably still in my parents' attic.

OL: What's it doing there?

DM: Will didn't have anywhere to live – we were touring at the time – and he still wasn't talking to his parents, so I offered to store it at my mum's. I need to check if it's still there – I hope it is.

OL: If you find it, will you let me know? I'd love to see it.

DM: I'm going there this weekend. I'll check.

OL: So, he bought it, and he didn't want her to know? Why?

DM: Well firstly, he bought it because he loved it – it was the artwork for the *Yellow Feathers* EP – but he didn't tell her because he wanted her to think someone other than him would want to buy it. I knew it would piss her off if she found out that he'd lied.

OL: That's why they split up?

DM: No. I mean, I had to have a few drinks to pluck up the courage to tell her, so all I remember is that she didn't really react. Not in the way I was expecting, anyway. So, I pushed her even more.

OL: How?

DM: I broke the bro code. I told her he spent the night with Christie Blackmore.

OL: He cheated on her? With Christie Blackmore?

DM: I don't know. I doubt it. Christie was coming on pretty strong, but Will wasn't interested in anyone other than Emily. He went to her suite to listen to her new track, and he didn't come back to our room that night. And I told Emily; what sort of friend does that?

They probably didn't even do anything. When he finally showed up the next day, he was really ill. Turned out he had a virus and was suffering from exhaustion. He was probably just knackered and fell asleep in her suite.

I put him through all that for nothing.

OL: He didn't start writing again?

DM: No. My plan couldn't have backfired more spectacularly. Before, at least he'd been writing, it just wasn't up to his standard. After the split, he wrote nothing. We stayed on in Wales for a couple of weeks, then the record company came to hear what we'd been doing all the months we'd been there. We only had four songs, but we played them anyway. They were shit, and we knew it. The suits said we should go home and come back once Will had more ideas to work on. One suit suggested we work with this songwriter he knew. He thought it would be a great collaboration like Bernie and Elton. Will wasn't having any of it. He wrote his own songs. He didn't want to play anyone else's.

OL: What happened when you left Wales?

DM: The record company put us up in a house in Notting Hill. There was a small studio in a fancy shed at the bottom of the garden. Will was down there all the time. I don't know what he was doing in there, though. One time I went down there, he was asleep on the sofa with Nick Cave blaring out. Reu and I had nothing to do. We played video games all day. I had to feed the record company a pack of lies to keep them off his back.

If I hadn't told Emily that stuff, she wouldn't have broken up with him. And if she hadn't dumped him, he'd still be here. I'm sure of that.

OL: I'm sure that's not true . . .

DM: I didn't think he would do anything like . . . what he did. I wish he'd come to me. We could have talked and maybe . . . [pauses] I wish he'd come to me, you know?

Chapter 62

July 1999

Sleeping with Scott hadn't had the transformative effect Emily hoped it would. She felt as miserable as ever. Fortunately, he hadn't mentioned it and they both carried on as if it never happened. But her sombre mood didn't go unnoticed. Miranda suggested they go to the student union bar after college, and Scott rallied a group of their friends to join them. Emily said little and although she had a few drinks, she remained in control and waited until a respectable hour before saying she was heading home.

Miranda persuaded her to stay for one more and Scott got another round in before they'd finished that one, so they didn't get home any earlier.

'Who wants toast?' Miranda asked as she opened the door to their flat. They hadn't eaten all night. Miranda flipped the light switch and headed to the kitchen.

'Me,' said Scott, following her.

'Please.' Emily sat at the little table while Miranda examined the bread slices for mould before slotting them into the toaster and Scott made tea. They chatted about their evening and their course as they ate.

Emily stood up and poured herself a glass of water. 'Right, I'm off to bed. Night.'

'Me too,' said Miranda, following her to the hall. 'Jesus, what's that on the carpet? Scott, have you spilt Bolognese again?'

'I haven't had any Bolognese.'

'What's that then?'

Scott went to look. 'I dunno – it wasn't me.'

'There's a trail of it coming from your room.'

Emily was staying out of it. She nudged her bedroom door open. That was odd – the light was on. As the door opened wider, she saw a figure lying on her bed with its back to her. She let out a shrill yelp and the glass of water dropped to the carpet with a thud. She stumbled backwards, bumping into Scott as he came up behind her.

'What the fuck?' Scott put himself between Emily and the stranger. 'Get the torch from my bedside,' he whispered.

The intruder remained motionless despite the sound of their voices.

'What is it?' asked Miranda as Emily pushed past her in the hall.

In Scott's room, there was blood all over the carpet. Emily's heart thudded, her brain unable to compute what she was seeing. She was expecting to find a torch on the bedside table, but there was only a magazine and an alarm clock. She rifled through the drawers, but there was no torch. What did he want a torch for, anyway? What was he going to do, dazzle the intruder to death? Then she spotted a torch on the floor by the bed. It was a foot long and when she picked it up, it weighed a tonne. It was a huge metal truncheon.

Miranda was whispering into the phone as Emily passed her on the way back.

She handed Scott the torch, and he gestured for her to stay back. He entered her room cautiously, creeping around her bed, holding the torch two-handed like a baseball bat. The figure was lying on its side, perfectly still.

Scott prodded it with the torch. It rocked and returned to its original position.

'Shit!' cried Scott. 'Call an ambulance!'

'What—'

'Call an ambulance!' he barked. 'Now!'

Emily relayed the message to Miranda who was already on the phone to the emergency services.

Scott rolled the figure onto its back.

'Will? Will, can you hear me? Oh, mate . . .'

Emily rushed to Scott's side. Will lay motionless on her bed. Her heart stalled and she dropped to her knees. His eyes were closed, his skin pale, a blood-soaked towel wrapped around his arm. 'Will, wake up!'

His cheek was cold and clammy.

'Is he breathing?' asked Scott.

Emily put her ear to Will's mouth, but all she could hear was her own heartbeat thumping in her head. 'I don't know! I can't hear anything!'

Miranda was in the doorway holding the phone. 'They want to know what's wrong.'

'He's unconscious, uh . . . lost a lot of blood. A wound on his arm,' said Scott. 'Here, let me try.' Scott bent over Will's face and listened. 'Watch his chest.'

After a few agonising seconds, they noticed a subtle swell in Will's ribcage. 'He's breathing. Just,' said Scott. 'Tell them to hurry!'

'Will, wake up! It's Emily.' Tears were streaming down her face now.

'The ambulance is coming.' Miranda handed Scott a scarf. 'They said to tie something around it and put him in the recovery position.'

Scott wound the scarf around the towel and tied it in a tight knot.

Emily pulled Will onto his side with his good arm and arranged his knee so he wouldn't roll. 'Is that right?'

'Yeah, that's it,' said Scott.

'Will? Can you hear me? It's Emily, wake up . . . *please.*'

She pulled at the neck of his t-shirt, stretching it even though it wasn't tight. 'What should we do now?' she asked Miranda.

'I don't know, that's all they said. They'll be here in a minute.'

'I'll look out for them,' said Scott.

Miranda took Scott's place by the bedside. Emily was on her knees, shaking uncontrollably.

'I'm sorry,' she whispered. 'I love you. Hang on. Just a few more minutes.'

It felt like hours before they heard the siren.

Suddenly, paramedics were in the flat, barking orders, shouting, 'Will? Will? Can you hear me?'

Emily and Miranda moved out of the way into the kitchen and a moment later, they carried Will past on a stretcher. Emily felt Miranda's arm around her shoulders.

'Where are you taking him?' asked Emily.

'St George's,' replied the paramedic.

'Can I go with him?'

'Only one of you.'

On the landing, two police officers were talking to Scott. She followed the paramedics as they manoeuvred Will's stretcher down the stairs.

She waited on the pavement while they put him in the back of the ambulance. Miranda brought her a jacket and her bag. 'We'll meet you there, okay?'

The paramedics wouldn't allow Emily in the back with Will. She had to ride in the front wearing a seatbelt, the late-night London traffic parting in front of her, her head full of questions and her heart heavy with guilt. *Oh God, please let him be okay.*

*

Emily was still waiting in the A&E department when Miranda arrived with two police officers. Miranda held her hand, while the officers asked her an endless stream of confusing questions.

'You okay?' Miranda asked once they had gone.

She nodded. 'Where's Scott?'

'He had to stay at the flat, his bedroom window's smashed. What was Will doing?'

Emily sighed. 'I don't know.'

The sliding doors at the entrance *swooshed* open.

Emily recognised the family that came in. 'Oh, shit . . .'

'Who's that?' asked Miranda.

'Will's parents.' Emily had not seen them since that Christmas Day years ago. She stood up and walked towards them.

'You!' cried Will's mother, stopping Emily in her tracks. 'What have you done?'

'I—'

'What happened?' Mary Bailey's voice shook with anger.

'I . . . I don't know.'

'What do you mean you don't know? You're his girlfriend, aren't you?'

'Not anymore . . .'

'Ha!' Mary's laugh was bitter. 'I knew it wouldn't last! What are you doing here, then?'

'He broke into my flat. He cut himself on the glass. We found him unconscious and bleeding.'

'Well, I hope you're happy with yourself. I hope you can sleep at night. Breaking that boy away from his family and driving him to . . . this.'

'Mum,' said Aidan, taking her by the shoulders. 'Leave it.' Aidan's eyes met Emily's for the briefest of moments before he steered his mother away.

Mary allowed him to usher her towards the reception desk before turning back. 'You're not wanted here. Leave him alone. Leave us all alone!'

Emily stepped forward. 'But—'

'No! Get out of here!'

'I'll wait over—'

'Get *out!*' roared Mary.

Emily stood paralysed as Aidan coaxed the woman away. Will's father's glare was bright with hatred.

Miranda came up beside her. 'Come on, let's wait outside.'

Chapter 63

July 2016

Liv

When I arrive at *Amplify* on Tuesday morning, there's raised voices coming from the meeting room. I can see Paul pacing around above the frosted section of the glass wall. Everyone in the office is engrossed in their work, pretending it's not happening.

I sit at my desk and carry on researching a Tracks Decoded article. Ten minutes later, the meeting room door opens. Paul strides towards me, shoots me a black look as he passes and carries on out the main door. I let out the breath I've been holding.

There's a murmur around the office.

'Liv,' Tumi calls from the meeting room doorway. 'Can I have a word?'

I scurry over.

'Shut the door,' she snaps. 'Sit down.'

I do as I'm told, hiding my shaking hands under the table.

'Paul had a call from Christie Blackmore last night,' she says. 'She wants to contribute to the Will Bailey feature we're doing.'

My mind's racing. I don't know what to say, so I keep my mouth shut.

'Paul felt like a fool, not knowing about a feature in his own magazine. Do you know anything about this?'

'No . . .'

'Funny that, because Christie described the "journalist" she spoke to.' Tumi doesn't need to use fingers for the air quotes; her voice does the job all by itself. 'And she sounds a lot like you.'

'Me?'

'Come on, Liv, just tell me what happened.'

The words tumble out of my mouth in a rush. 'I met her at Beatland. Brett Lewis introduced me to her.'

Her eyes widen. 'And you were with Brett Lewis because . . .?'

I grimace. 'I interviewed him.'

'Hang on,' Tumi gives a quick shake of her head. 'Back up, start from the beginning.'

'You gave me that press pass for Beatland . . .'

Her eyebrows squish together. 'Yeah, to have a bit of fun in the VIP area, lounge around on a Bali bed, nab a free drink and a goodie bag, not to interview rock stars!'

'I know. I got carried away with the whole pretending to be an *Amplify* journalist thing.'

'What exactly did you say to him?'

I tell Tumi about the balcony and the champagne and everything I remember about my conversation with him.

When I'm done, she says, 'Please tell me you recorded the interview?'

'I got the whole thing on my phone . . .'

She slumps back in her chair.

'But it got stolen.'

Tumi sits forward again, her head in her hands. 'No!'

'What is it?'

'Paul's a massive Paradigm fan. He's been trying to get an interview with him for years.'

'Oh.'

She shakes her head as though trying to clear it. 'Where does Christie Blackmore come into this?'

'She turned up, and when she heard about the *Fragments* twentieth anniversary feature, she wanted to contribute.'

'Hence the call to Paul. But how did you get her to agree to it? She's notoriously private – never does interviews.'

'She said she'd get in touch – I didn't think she actually would.'

Tumi chews her lip.

'But this is good, right?' I ask. 'We've got Christie Blackmore interested in doing an interview. If she doesn't normally do interviews, Paul should be pleased.'

Tumi sighs and shakes her head. 'He's angry, Liv. And when he finds out you lost the interview with Brett Lewis, he'll blow a fuse.' She pushes her glasses up her nose. 'So, what's your obsession with Will Bailey, anyway?'

I pause, deciding whether to tell her the truth.

'Come on, Liv. Spit it out.'

'I wanted to find out about my mum.'

She tilts her head to one side. 'What's your mum got to do with this?'

'She was Will Bailey's girlfriend.'

Tumi forgets to be angry for a moment. 'So, why not ask her instead of impersonating a journalist and interviewing strangers?'

'She doesn't talk about it.'

'Why not?'

'I don't know.'

'Did you speak to any other musicians at Beatland?'

'Not at Beatland . . .'

'Oh God,' she exhales. 'Tell me everything.'

Tumi interrogates me for half an hour, sighing and shaking her head the whole time.

She gets up. 'Wait here.'

I sit fidgeting in the meeting room, feeling sick until she finally comes back. 'I found Paul upstairs in the café. I tried to explain but . . .'

'But what?' My voice is shaky.

'He wants you to go, Liv.'

'Go where?'

'He said he told you if there was any trouble, you were to go back to *Luminaire* – whatever that means.'

'But that was before . . . when I was doing work experience with school. I'm working here for the summer now . . . to help with Tracks Decoded.' My throat's tight, my voice sounds strangled. Oh God, I'm going to cry.

'I'm sorry Liv, but I'm in a lot of trouble over this. He's gone out to a meeting. He wants you gone by the time he gets back.'

'I'm sorry, Tumi. I didn't mean to get you in trouble.'

She stands, a pained expression on her face. 'I'll see you out.'

I follow her to my desk, and she hovers nearby while I gather up my stuff.

We ride the lift in silence. My mind is bursting with things I want to say but my voice won't work. I want to tell her about all the articles I've been writing in my spare time. All the work I've put in to pitch the *Fragments* twentieth anniversary feature idea to her. That's all been for nothing. She follows me through the barriers.

'He wants me to take your pass,' she says softly.

I hand her my lanyard.

'Keep writing, Liv. You're good at it.'

'Bye,' I squeak, then turn and run through the doors onto the busy street. I let out the sob that's been jamming up my throat and run all the way to the station with tears pouring down my face.

*

On Saturday, Mrs Bailey greets me as usual, cheerfully offering tea and biscuits. I wasn't sure if Tumi would have been in touch to tell her I'd been fired, but everything seems normal. I don't suppose it matters to *Amplify* if I carry on with the archive. We agreed Mrs Bailey would give me cash for 'expenses' but she usually presses two twenty-pound notes into my hand as I'm leaving each week.

I'm so glad I still have this job to do. Now I'll no longer be researching Tracks Decoded stories or trying my hand at reviews, it's all I care about. I'm almost done though. I will be sad when I finish up these last few boxes.

No matter how hard I try to keep busy today, my mind keeps wandering back to getting fired. Things I wish I'd said to Tumi and Paul keep popping into my head. I want to call Chloe, tell her all about it, but she's still not taking my calls and I have to fight back the tears. I go to put music on to distract me, but when I get my phone out, there are four missed calls and a message from Mum. I've had it on silent all day.

Mum: **Don't forget it's Grandad's birthday. I need you home by 5pm so we can pick up the cake on the way. Let me know you've got this message x.**

If I leave in an hour, I should get back in time. I message Mum to let her know, then I go back to choosing music, but all the recent playlists are ones that Nathan sent me.

And that's it – I'm ugly-crying, cross-legged on the floor of the Bailey's garage.

Only a few weeks ago, we were kissing; he gave me that necklace. I thought he liked me. I had an awesome summer job I was good at, and a best friend to laugh and joke and share stuff with. But all of that's gone. I sit there bawling until I remember I need to head back, or Mum will kill me.

The trestle table is a mess of notebooks, boxes, photos, and letters. I pull myself together, wipe my nose on my sleeve, and start tidying up. The tape machine is taking up space. I go to put it away, but as I pull the box out from under the table, a flash of colour catches my eye. Tucked into the flap at the bottom of the box is a folded piece of orange paper. I pluck it free.

It's a hospital patient leaflet for a condition called oto-sclerosis. What's otosclerosis? I sit on the floor and lift the concertina flap to read:

> Otosclerosis is a disease of the bone surrounding the inner ear. It can cause hearing loss when abnormal bone forms around the stapes, reducing the sound that reaches the inner ear. It's a common cause of hearing loss in young adults.

Did Will Bailey have otosclerosis? Why else would he have a leaflet about it? I read the leaflet from front to back twice. I learn that although surgery sometimes helps, it's risky and doesn't always work. In some cases, it can cause further damage to the inner ear, making things worse. Hearing aids work for some people, but there are no guarantees.

The lyrics to Will's last song pop into my head. Didn't he sing about not being able to hear? I find the recording on my phone and listen to the lyrics.

If I can't hear
your voice in my ear
Your laughter and your tears
Your secret hopes and fears.

If I can't hear
you talk about your goals,
Your thoughts and your ideas
Little pieces of your soul

Then I can't go on
Although I'm afraid
This pain will stop

Since I first heard them weeks ago, these lyrics have puzzled me, but now, with the help of this leaflet, they make perfect sense.

Will Bailey had otosclerosis.

He was losing his hearing.

What could be worse than losing your hearing when you're a musician? This must have been why he killed himself – he couldn't face life without music. Does Mum know about this? Surely if she did, she wouldn't blame herself for his death.

Without thinking, I pick up my phone and call Chloe. All along, she's been as obsessed as I am about finding out what happened to Will. It rings four times, then goes to voicemail and my heart sinks.

Chapter 64

July 1999

Will woke up in a strange bed in a room that smelled of disinfectant, with a bandage wrapped neatly around his left arm and a red bag dangling above him. He felt the cool sensation of someone else's blood entering his system.

Had he dreamt it, or had Emily been there earlier? He thought she had lain on the bed beside him, the coconut smell of her hair. Soft kisses, tears dripping onto his face, her arms gently encircling him.

After breakfast, the police came asking questions, but he couldn't remember much of what had happened. The last thing he recalled was climbing up the balcony, but he didn't tell them that. They said they wouldn't press charges, but Emily's parents were asking about a restraining order. They advised him to steer clear of her, otherwise he'd be in serious trouble.

When he was discharged later that afternoon, his mum barely gave him a choice – she insisted he stay with them, fussing over him as though he were a child. He tried to be patient, grateful even, but after two days of her mollycoddling and his dad's silent, steely glares, the walls of his childhood home began to close in on him. He had to get out of there.

Back at the record company house in Notting Hill, Matty and Reu tiptoed around him at first. They took turns to babysit him until he went back down to the studio at the end of the garden, and they returned to their video games as though nothing had happened.

Will didn't even notice Reu had been gone for a couple of days until Matty mentioned it. They went looking for him and asked around, but no one had seen him. By then, they were worried enough to call around the hospitals.

They found him at St George's, the same hospital where Will had been treated less than two weeks before. The taxi ride was the most agonising forty-five minutes of Will's life. When they arrived, the nurse told them Reu had been found in a squat in Tooting, overdosed on heroin. Luckily, someone had called an ambulance, but by the time it arrived, he was all alone. That was four days ago, and he'd been in a coma since then. The nurse only allowed them in the room one at a time, so Matty waited outside.

Dread settled like a cold stone in the pit of Will's stomach as he entered the room. The slender figure lying in the bed didn't look like Reu at all. If it weren't for the black ringlets fanned across the pillow, he wouldn't have believed it was him. He looked like a frail old man and a helpless child all at once.

The nurse said Reu might be able to hear him. She said to talk to him normally, but he couldn't think of anything normal to say.

'Reu, it's Will.'

He sat in the chair beside the bed. He picked up Reu's hand and cradled it in his own. The wrist was so thin he thought it might snap.

You fucking idiot! he screamed silently. *What were you doing? For Christ's sake, Reu, heroin? What were you thinking?*

But he didn't say any of that out loud; instead he said, 'We'll get you better. The doctors and nurses are all looking after you. You're not in trouble. It wasn't your fault. We love you and we need you to come back now.'

317

Reu lay motionless.

'I'm sorry I wasn't there for you, man. I messed up. I was too wrapped up in my own problems to realise . . .' Will exhaled. 'To realise you needed me.'

The machines beeped to a steady rhythm.

'Let's get you home. We'll jam in Mum's garage. And we'll go busking again with the buckets. You loved that . . . *I* loved that.'

His voice failed him then, so he sat in silence for a while. It was hard to look at Reu's face with that tube in his nose, so he looked at his hand instead. He studied the rivers of greenish veins on the back of it and the pale half-moons on his nails.

By the time he left, he knew every detail of that hand, the hand that could tap the most intricate rhythm on any inanimate object.

Chapter 65

July 2016

Emily

I drum my fingernails on the kitchen table. Where is Liv? The bakery shuts in twenty minutes. If she doesn't get here soon, we won't get there in time to pick up Dad's birthday cake.

My phone vibrates, I snatch it up thinking it's a message from Liv. But it's not.

FHD: Hey. How are you?

Just then, the front door opens. 'I'm back!' Liv calls from the hall. 'Shall we go?'

I pocket my phone, scoop up my father's gift, and follow her out to the car. She scrolls through her phone as I pull away and I simmer with anger the whole way to the bakery. I dash inside, pick up the cake and they turn the closed sign over as they see me out. Liv barely looks up from her phone as I open the passenger door and put the cake box on her lap. 'Don't drop it.'

Back in the driver's seat, I swivel in my seat and come right out with it. 'I rang *Amplify* today.'

She lifts her eyes from her phone. 'What?'

I glare directly at her. 'I rang *Amplify* today.'

'Why?'

'I needed to get hold of you. You weren't answering your phone.'

'I messaged you.' She looks away. 'I told you I'd leave early so we could pick up Grandad's cake.'

'You messaged *eventually,* but before that I tried the *Amplify* office. So, where do you go?'

Her eyes dart in every direction except mine.

'What do you mean "where do I go"?'

'Where do you go on Saturdays?'

'You know where I go on Saturdays.' Her voice is calm.

'Come on, Olivia, I told you I rang *Amplify.*'

She won't meet my eyes. 'So?'

'You're making me say it?'

'Say what?'

'The *Amplify* office is closed on Saturdays.'

The spark of an idea lights up her face. 'It's social media, Mum. It's twenty-four-seven.'

'So, they're open on Saturdays, but no one's there to answer the phones and they let sixteen-year-old *interns* into the office by themselves?'

'Obviously you don't believe me . . .'

I *don't* believe her.

'You don't need to be in the office to post on social media,' she adds.

'Which brings me back to my original question. Where do you go on Saturdays?'

She sighs. 'Look, I didn't tell you because you wouldn't approve.'

Now I'm worried. 'Wouldn't approve of what?'

She mutters something incoherent, but I catch the words 'Will Bailey'.

'What?'

'I said I've been creating an archive for Will Bailey.'

I shake my head in confusion. 'What does that even *mean*?'

'It means I go to his parents' house, to their garage, and I sort through all his stuff, I log it on a spreadsheet.' She speaks slowly. Gently. 'I photograph it and put it on his website and store the stuff properly and "archive" it.'

'What sort of stuff?'

Liv eyes me, concern etched on her brow. 'His notebooks, lyrics, and photographs. I go through it, find the stuff fans would be interested in and I put it on the website.'

'He has a website?'

'Yes, but I'm working on a new one. It's not ready yet, but it will be soon.'

I have no words. I can't compute this. Will's stuff is there in his parents' garage. His family has let a stranger, a sixteen-year-old girl, rifle through his things, and they're putting it on the fucking internet.

How I wish I had more of his things. I kept his t-shirt from the day he left to go on tour with Paradigm, the letters he sent from America, a small box of Christmas and birthday gifts, but it wasn't enough. How I clung to those few objects. 'They wouldn't let me have any of his things. They wouldn't even let me go to his funeral. Do they know who you are?'

'What do you mean?'

'Do they know you're my daughter?'

'No. There's been no reason to mention who my mum is.'

'They wouldn't let you in there if they knew.' My mind's spinning. 'I asked you to stop snooping. You said you would drop it. You *promised* me.' I'm shaking. 'You didn't stop – all the while you were going through his private things behind my back . . .'

'I'm sorry I didn't tell you.' She rests her hand on my forearm. 'I *was* working for *Amplify*, just not at the office. We met Will's family when we were researching an article. They had all his stuff in flight cases and none of them could bring themselves to go through it. I offered to help. I knew you wouldn't approve, but I didn't want someone else to do it. *I* wanted to do it.'

I'm too tired to argue. 'We need to know where you are, Liv. We've talked about this.'

'Mum, I'm working hard on this.' She shifts forward, the cake wobbling on her lap. 'I'm doing it as a fan. I love his work, the words he wrote, the music. So do thousands of others. People will find this stuff fascinating. There won't be any more songs. This gives his fans a bit more . . . of him.'

People want more of Will, of course they do. They did, even when he was alive. They couldn't get enough of him.

Even when he had nothing left to give.

The clock on the dashboard says 5:40 p.m.

'We don't have time for this,' I say and turn the key in the ignition.

*

We are silent on the drive home. I'm exhausted from pretending to be happy for the last few hours, from trying not to ruin my father's birthday, from pretending everything's normal with Liv. As I drive, all I can think of is her in Will's garage going through his things. What has she seen there? And what is she putting on the internet for the world to see? My own daughter.

I pull up outside the house and march up the path. Liv follows me to the kitchen. I go straight to the fridge, but there's no wine. Aware of Liv hovering in my peripheral vision, I go through the cupboards until I find some gin. As I put the bottle on the counter, I glance over. Her face is all screwed up.

'Liv?'

She bursts into tears, and it takes me completely by surprise. She's never been one to turn on the waterworks. Being an only child meant she never had to cry to get her way.

'What's the matter?' I go to her and touch her arm.

'I've messed everything up. *Amplify* fired me and now I'm going to lose the archive too.'

I put my arm around her. 'You got fired? What happened?'

Between sobs, she tells me she got Brett Lewis to agree to an interview at Beatland and how she wrote a series of articles hoping to persuade *Amplify* to run a special for the twentieth anniversary of *Fragments*. I'm furious and proud in equal measure.

322

'I didn't realise it meant that much to you.'

'It means *everything*.'

Her big blue eyes are wet with tears, reminding me of that little girl I miss, the one who relied on me to fix her scraped knee or chase away a nightmare.

Motherly instinct is fighting with the anger that's been simmering inside me all day.

I sigh. 'Get the articles – I want to read them.'

Chapter 66

July 1999

Scott wandered up and down outside the art block smoking a cigarette, kicking at stones while coming up with ideas for a project. Out of the corner of his eye, he spotted a figure coming towards the building from the far end of the car park. Was he being paranoid, or did that guy look like Will? As he got closer, he looked *a lot* like Will.

For fuck's sake, why wouldn't he leave her alone? Even before Will broke into the flat, he'd turned up several times – pressing the buzzer and loitering outside. Scott had to go downstairs and tell him to get lost. Emily was a wreck after every visit. She flinched whenever the buzzer went, and lately, she avoided being alone in the flat.

Now Will was bothering her here. He'd have to confront him again. Adrenaline tingled in Scott's hands as he took one last drag on the cigarette and mashed it into the ashtray on the wall. When he turned back, Will wasn't heading to the entrance but heading towards him.

Scott sized Will up as he approached. They were around the same height, the same build, even. It wasn't obvious who would win in a fight.

'What are you doing here?' Scott straightened his posture.

'Can I have a quick word with you?' Close up, Will had dark circles under his eyes and his long hair was dirty and lank.

'With me? What about?'

'There's something Emily needs to know—'

'I've told you before, she doesn't want to speak to you.'

Will closed his eyes briefly. 'I know—'

'Listen, you broke into our flat. You're lucky she didn't press charges. You're scaring her. Her parents want her to get a restraining order.'

'I know,' said Will, 'but this is about something else.'

'Leave her alone, Will. There are plenty more fish in the sea. Especially for someone like you.'

'Look, I know she doesn't want to talk to me, but this is important. One of our friends is in hospital. He . . . he might not make it. She would want to know. She'd want to visit him.'

'What's this got to do with me?'

'I was hoping you'd give her this note. She doesn't need to speak to me, but she needs to know about this.' Will was clutching an envelope. 'Please, give her this note. It explains everything.'

'If I take this, you'll go?'

'Yes, but there might not be much time. You need to give it to her today.'

'Okay.' Scott took the envelope, but Will stayed put. 'You said you were leaving.'

'I wanted to say sorry about the other night. The mess I made of your room and—'

'You gave us the money. It's all fixed now.'

'Good. Well, thanks for getting me to the hospital and thanks for . . . this.'

Scott nodded, then glared at Will until he got the message and left.

Scott folded the letter and put it in his back pocket. He lit another cigarette and watched until Will was out of sight.

*

325

Scott left college early and got back to the flat before the others. He put the kettle on and while he waited for it to boil, he told himself this was the right thing to do. What if Will was making shit up to get her to read a note from him? It was his responsibility, as Emily's friend, to make sure there was nothing suspicious about this note, that it was safe to give to her. The guy was unhinged.

As steam billowed from the spout, he took the envelope from his pocket and waved it around in the cloud, trying not to scald his fingertips. After a few moments in the steam, the moist seal opened easily. He pulled out and unfolded the single sheet.

Milly,

Please read this. It's not about us – it's about Reu. I know you don't want to speak to me, but you would never forgive me if I didn't tell you this.

Reu's in hospital, he's in a coma. They found him in a filthy squat overdosed on heroin. On heroin, Milly – can you believe it? I know he liked the odd spliff – okay, a regular spliff – but I didn't see this coming. I should have realised. All those times we were partying, he'd be drenched in sweat and his pupils were tiny pinpricks. I should have realised he was on a slippery slope. I should have protected him. He's not been himself. The warning signs were all there, but I've been too preoccupied with my own problems to notice. Money had been going missing, but I didn't suspect Reu for one moment. I should have checked in on him more. I can't believe I let this happen. He would have been better off if he never met me, and that's saying something because his old life was bad enough.

Anyway, they say it's touch and go.

I thought you should know and maybe if you visited him, you might get through to him. You two always got along. He's in the intensive care unit at St George's

Hospital. I'm there most of the time. I'd love to see you. I miss you, Milly. So much. I wish you'd let me explain properly, but I promise I won't hassle you. I just want him to wake up.

Visiting hours are midday till 9 p.m. Could you come tomorrow? I could meet you by the entrance at midday.

I know he'd want to hear your voice.

Love,

Will x

Scott read the letter again. Was Will telling the truth? All the times he'd shouted at Will over the intercom, the times he'd spoken to him outside the flat, it was obvious Will was desperate. The poor lovesick bastard would do anything to speak to Emily. But would he lie about a friend being in hospital? Scott doubted that. But Will might be capable of exaggerating. He was making out Reu was on death's door, but was he really?

Scott paced up and down the kitchen.

And what if he *was* telling the truth? Emily would go to that hospital, and Will would be back in her life. If Reu pulled through, they could get back together and if he didn't, Will was already teetering. It could send him over the edge.

Could Will be on drugs too? They were friends, weren't they? The state of him at college today, he looked like a junkie. Did she really want to get mixed up with drug addicts? She had a bright future ahead of her. She was supposed to be going to Amsterdam next year – this could derail that.

Scott checked his watch – the girls would be back soon

He made a decision.

One he would wrestle with for the rest of his life.

He took his lighter, flipped the lid, thumbed the flint, and dangled the letter in the flame. It licked at the bottom corner for a moment before catching light. He turned the sheet this way and that, as it blackened and curled, and fell in flaming pieces into the sink.

Chapter 67

July 2016

Emily

When I worked at the school, we had our fair share of pushy parents coming into the office. Why isn't my child the star of the play? Why isn't my child on the advanced band of reading books? I've never been that sort of parent, but today I feel like one. Someone buzzes me into the office telling me to take a seat. I gasp at the sight of a huge *Amplify* cover hanging at the entrance. A young Christie Blackmore at the height of her fame pouting suggestively on a cover so big it forms a screen for the waiting area. It completely throws me. I turn my back on her and try to collect myself ready to give this Paul Raymond a piece of my mind.

My phone pings and it takes ages to find it at the bottom of my bag.

FHD: When can I see you?

'Mrs Lawrence?' A man with a kind face peers around Christie Blackmore.

'It's Miss actually, but yes.'

'Ah, sorry, Paul Raymond. Good to meet you.' He offers me his hand.

I stand, take his hand, and give it a single firm pump. He asks me to follow him to a glass meeting room and offers me water. I accept, and we sit opposite each other.

'You wanted to talk to me about Olivia,' he says, placing his hands into a patronising steeple.

'It was unfair of you to fire her,' I begin. 'She's worked hard here. Your social media engagement has *quadrupled* thanks to her. She's written excellent album reviews, which you've deemed good enough to publish, at a fraction of the cost of one of your freelancers, I might add. You don't approve of her posing as an *Amplify* reporter, but I believe this shows initiative and creativity, and – for want of a better word – *balls*. Have you even read the pieces she wrote about Will Bailey? I emailed them to you two days ago. You've not bothered to reply, so I assume you haven't. Well, *I've* read them and they're brilliant. Now, I know you'll say any mother would say that, but I'm talking as someone who knew Will Bailey. She's told his story accurately with . . . emotion . . . and passion . . . as though she'd met him. And, frankly, if you won't publish this feature, then perhaps we should take it elsewhere . . .' I pause because I need to catch my breath, but also because I've lost my train of thought. I take a sip of water.

Paul Raymond chews the inside of his cheek. 'Does Liv know you're here?'

'I told her I was coming, but she didn't want me to.'

'Are you aware she's also been posing as an *Amplify* reporter to go through Will Bailey's personal possessions at his parents' house?'

My phone rings and I'm flustered because leaving it on makes me look unprofessional. I pull it from my bag. It's Liv calling. I reject her call and switch it to silent.

'I just found out about that myself but—'

A muscle at his jaw twitches. 'Do you know we have strict safety measures in place to make sure our journalists are safe when out in the field?'

'I don't doubt—'

'We don't allow our journalists to meet strangers without us knowing where they are. Did she tell you where she was going?'

My face is on fire. 'Well, no . . .'

'I have a reputation to uphold,' he continues. 'If an artist thinks they're being interviewed by an *Amplify* journalist and in reality, they're being interviewed by a fifteen-year-old schoolgirl, how does that make me look?'

'She's sixteen actually . . . Look, I understand where you're coming from, but she got carried away. She didn't think through the consequences. All she needs is another chance and some direction. She's a talented writer and it would be a waste—'

'I agree—'

'Mr Raymond, I'm not leaving here until you promise to give her a decent reference.'

'Mrs Lawrence, you're not listening—'

'It's Miss!' I snap.

'Miss Lawrence, I'm agreeing with you.'

'You are?' My phone vibrates.

'Yes, I agree. Your daughter's writing is extraordinary for her age. She has an obvious love of music, and it shines through her work. She's not restricted by the rules – she writes what she thinks, and although it needs a bit of polish, her voice is fresh and compelling. In answer to your question, yes – I *have* read her feature. I didn't reply because you and I were speaking today. The feature shows promise, but it needs a lot of work before it's publishable. I've emailed her my suggestions and if she's willing to put in the work, we'll see if we can get it into shape.'

I'm relieved to come out of confrontation mode, and that, mingled with my pride for Liv, almost brings me to tears. 'You emailed her?' That might be why Liv was calling.

'Just this morning. I wanted her to sweat a bit.'

'She has been.'

'The only way I can publish a special on Will Bailey is if it coincides with an anniversary, and this twenty-year *Fragments* anniversary could work, otherwise I can't run it.'

'I'm sure she'll do whatever it takes to get it ready in time.'

'I've told her we need an interview with you.'

I freeze. 'With me?'

'Yes. We need the personal relationship angle to give a more rounded portrait of the man himself.'

'I . . . I don't talk about that . . .'

'You could give the piece the edge it needs – so it appeals to everyone, not just his fans.'

If her feature got printed, Liv would be thrilled. All her hard work, her heartfelt words out there in the world, but I can't do an interview.

Paul Raymond checks his watch. 'Now if you'll excuse me, Miss Lawrence, I've got a meeting to prepare for.'

'Of course. Thank you for your time.'

'Liv could go far, but she needs to listen and do as she's told.'

I stand, hitch my bag onto my shoulder and nod. 'Yes, yes she does.'

*

As I walk to the station, I listen to the message Liv left telling me not to 'go mental' at Paul because he'd emailed, and everything would be okay.

There's also a text from Scott: **Hey Em. Can Liv stay at yours tonight?**

I reply: **Sure – everything ok?**

Scott: **Katya wants to talk.**

I don't understand why they need to talk overnight. Is 'talk' a euphemism for something else? Now I have a picture in my mind of them 'talking' and it makes me uncomfortable. I should reply, but what do I say?

In the end I plump for: **Good luck!**

After I've sent it, I wish I could take it back.

331

Chapter 68

July 2016

Liv

I hurry down the stairs at the sound of Mum coming in. I've been a bundle of nerves waiting for her to get back from *Amplify*.

'Hi,' she says, surprised to see me. 'You're here already.'

'Dad dropped me about half an hour ago.'

'Was Katya there when you left?'

'No, she's coming later. Dad's tidying the house.'

She nods. I follow her to the kitchen and watch as she fills the kettle.

'How did it go with Paul?' I ask.

'He's letting you go back for the rest of the summer.'

I'm so relieved, I run over and hug her. 'Oh Mum, that's brilliant! That's amazing! Thank you so much. Thanks for talking to him.' I quickly let go and step out of her personal space.

'But . . .' she says, a warning in her voice. 'He wants you to listen and do as you're told. Don't mess this up, Liv.'

'I won't.'

'What did his email say?' she asks.

'There was no message, just the file with loads of comments on it.'

'He said it needs work, and he'll only run it if it's ready in time for the *Fragments* anniversary. Can you do it?'

There's a strange fluttering in my stomach. 'I've already started.'

The kettle bubbles noisily, so I wait for her to make her drink.

'Mum?' I ask as she takes her drink and sits at the table.

'Yes?'

'Paul wants me to interview you.'

She sighs. 'He mentioned that.'

'Are you okay with it?'

She pauses. 'I'm not promising anything, Liv. Get everything else done and we'll see.'

'Okay.' I fiddle with the handle of the cutlery drawer, plucking up the courage to ask about the archive. 'Mum, it's Saturday tomorrow . . .'

'And?'

'I go to the Baileys' house to work on the archive on Saturdays . . .'

'You know how I feel about that—'

'Please, Mum. The Baileys don't know who I am. There's no need for them to know. And if I don't do it, then someone else will, but they won't care about it like I do.'

'Liv, I can't deal with this now!' she snaps. 'I'm still coming to terms with the fact you've been going through his private things. Behind my back. For months. I've just read all the articles you wrote. About the person I loved . . .' Her voice wobbles. 'And it's been hard . . . really hard . . . to think about him again after all these years of desperately trying not to.'

She's right. I'm being selfish. That must have been difficult. 'Okay, I won't go.'

As I go to leave the room, I think of all she has done for me. Reading my articles, talking to Paul, getting my job back. That must have been difficult for her. She deserves to know it wasn't her fault.

I turn back. 'You didn't kill him, Mum. He killed himself.'

Her eyes meet mine. '*Because* of me,' she says.

'You think he did it because you split up with him?'

'He kept calling, turning up at my flat. I couldn't talk to him. I was a coward. It was easier to avoid him.'

'It wasn't because of you,' I tell her.

'What do you mean?'

'He didn't do it because of you. I'm not saying he wasn't upset about the break-up; he was, but . . . there was another reason.'

She pulls back slightly, her face slackens. 'What other reason?'

Chapter 69

July 1999

Stan had an hour left on his shift. He was looking forward to going home. His wife was cooking lamb chops tonight. He loved living by the sea. He could afford to retire, but he hated sitting at home, so he took a few shifts at the pub by the local beauty spot. It kept him busy, and he enjoyed chatting with the tourists.

The pub had been empty all day; it wasn't the weather for coastal clifftop walks. The clouds were so dark and heavy it was as if night would never relinquish the sky to the day. The first customer came in from the rain, bedraggled, his longish hair stuck to his face. He ordered whiskey and took it to a seat by the fireplace.

Stan tried to remember his training. All the staff had been taught to recognise the signs. Perhaps this young fella had simply got caught out by the rain and was drying off before heading home. A couple came in, laughing as they shook off the rain. They ordered a G&T and a pint of Fosters. He asked where they were from, even though he recognised their Newcastle accent. They wanted recommendations for things to do on a rainy day so he told them about the local theatre and the little gallery in the next village. He gave them a leaflet and served the G&T, but the Fosters ran out with the glass half full. Stan glanced at the fella in the corner. He was slumped in his chair, his forehead resting on his wrists. But his whiskey was still untouched; he wasn't going anywhere. Stan went down to the cellar and changed the barrel quicker than he'd ever done before.

But when he returned, the fella was gone.

His glass was empty, the cardboard coaster ripped to pieces and scattered across the table. Stan cursed himself. He should have talked to him first, the Fosters could have waited.

'Did you see which way he went?' he asked the Geordie couple. 'That bloke, when he left, did he go left or right?'

'He went left,' said the man.

Left was the wrong direction. There was nothing that way but cliffs and sea. And a stunning view, invisible on a day like today.

Outside, the driving rain obscured the view in all directions.

Stan darted back inside, making straight for the telephone. He dialled the number they kept pinned on the wall.

'Didn't he pay?' asked the lady.

But the call connected before he could answer. 'It's Stan from the Queen's Head . . . Yes, a few minutes ago . . . Male, twenties . . . Sorry, I was keeping an eye on him, but I missed him leaving . . . See you in a minute.'

Blue lights flashed around the pub, glinting on the glasses and the polished brass of the pumps. Melanie, the local bobby, came in.

Stan looked at her expectantly, but she shook her head. 'He left his stuff by the edge.'

Stan brought a trembling hand to his mouth.

This was the third time he'd called that number, but the first time he'd been too late.

Chapter 70

July 1999

Emily walked down the street. As she got closer to the flat, she saw a figure sitting on the wall outside their building. It was Scott. He didn't acknowledge her or wave, instead he stood up, ground his cigarette into the pavement and ran inside. What was he up to? You'd expect that kind of behaviour from someone organising a surprise party. But it wasn't her birthday. Maybe he hadn't seen her.

She climbed the stairs and braced herself as she opened the door, but no one shouted 'surprise'. As she hung her jacket on the peg in the hall, Miranda came out of the kitchen. Her eyebrows were pinched together. 'Em, Matty's here to see you.'

'Matty?' Emily whispered as if to say *why did you let him in*? But Miranda's expression was so dark and serious she said no more and followed her to the kitchen.

Matty and Scott stood up from where they were sitting at the table. Matty looked awful. He was unshaven, and his eyes were bloodshot – he was probably hungover. 'Hello, Emily.'

'What are you doing here?'

'Why don't you sit down?' It was odd that Matty was offering her a seat in her own home. A home he'd never visited before.

'What is it? What's the matter?' She looked at Miranda, then Scott.

'If you just sit—' said Matty.

'I don't want to sit down, Matty! I want to know what you're doing here.'

Matty's eyes dropped to the floor. 'It's Will . . .'

'What? What about Will? Where is he?' But she knew it was something bad, really bad.

'He's . . . he died.'

Emily's heart stopped. 'What?'

'He took his own life. Yesterday.'

She felt dizzy. He wasn't making any sense. 'Why would you say that? Why are you saying that?'

'I'm sorry.'

Her breaths were coming in short little gasps. 'What do you mean he took his own life?'

'He went to the coast . . . a beauty spot in Sussex. Someone saw him go to the edge of the cliff . . . They found his body this morning. In the water.'

'It must be someone else . . . It can't be Will . . .'

'His dad identified him—'

'No!' she yelled. 'They've made a mistake. He wouldn't . . .'

A long, low wail filled the room. Emily had no idea where it was coming from, but then it hit her – she was the source of the appalling sound.

'I'm sorry, Emily.'

'Sorry. Why are you sorry?' She stepped towards Matty. 'Did you push him?'

Emily shoved him in the chest, and he stumbled backwards, the chair squeaking against the lino.

'No—'

'Were you there?'

'No, I wasn't—'

'Why weren't you there?' She pounded her fists into his chest. 'Why didn't you stop him?'

338

Matty stood firm against the force of her blows, his arms rigid against his body. Miranda came up behind her, gently taking her by the shoulders. Emily shrugged her off.

'Did he leave a note?'

'Nobody's found one yet.'

Her blood roared in her ears. 'I want to see him.'

'That's not a good idea . . .'

'Why not?' Her voice trembled.

'Mary and Michael . . . they're upset . . . it would make things worse.'

'They think it's my fault! They think I drove him to it.'

'It's nobody's fault . . .'

'I need to see him!'

Everything tilted, shifted, and slid and her knees slammed into the floor.

A colossal crack opened up inside her and spread across everything, tiny fissures shooting from it in all directions, breaking and snapping as it separated this moment from everything that had gone before.

Chapter 71

July 2016

Emily

'I found something,' Liv's eyes are shining. 'In the Baileys' garage.'

'What?' My heart's beating double time.

'I found a cassette; it had a date written on it – the 28th of July 1999. It was his last ever song.'

Her words knock the wind out of me.

'Do you want to hear it?' she asks.

'I can't . . .'

'If it's difficult for you to listen to his music, I could send it to your phone – you can listen by yourself, when you're ready.'

'I don't know.'

'If it's easier, I wrote the lyrics down. You could read them?'

'I don't think I can, Liv—'

'You need to see this, Mum.'

Liv goes to the hall and comes back with a notebook. She flicks through the pages, finds the one she's looking for, and tears it out. She folds it in half and places it on the table.

'You can keep this. Read it when you're ready,' she says. 'And there was something else. It was with the tape. It explains things.'

She takes an envelope from the back of her notebook.

'It's in here. I'll leave it with the lyrics. You can wait till I go back to Dad's or read it while I'm here. It's up to you. Mum, promise me you'll read it?'

'I can't promise—'

'Mum, trust me! You need to read this. Promise me you will?' Her eyes are sincere.

'All right.'

Liv leaves me alone in the room with these pieces of paper. I'm torn between wanting to devour their contents and wanting to destroy them unread before they can hurt me.

Tentatively, I reach for the sheet of notepaper and unfold it.

If I can't hear
your ideas as they spark
The twinkle in your laugh
Your whispers in the dark

Then I can't go on ...

Is he talking to me? Tears sting my eyes. What is Liv talking about? This only confirms I'm to blame. I can't read this!

Choking back a sob, I stand up and pace the room. I open the fridge, slam it shut, and go back to pacing. The paper on the table is screaming at me. I snatch it up, hands trembling, and I force myself to read on.

Even after I've read the whole page three times, the words make no sense. Liv thinks this is significant, but I have no idea why. With my heart pumping, I sit down, reach for the envelope. Inside there's a leaflet entitled: *Patient Information – Otosclerosis*.

I've never heard of otosclerosis.

I read the entire leaflet but it's a confusing jumble of words that make my head ache: *ossicles, malleus, incus, stapedotomy, otolaryngologist*. Liv said she found this with the song, that it would explain things, but it doesn't. I place the notepaper alongside the leaflet, willing them to connect. *If I can't hear . . . If I can't hear . . . Otosclerosis . . . a common cause of hearing loss in young adults.*

The penny slowly drops.

Will had otosclerosis.

A young man whose life revolved around his love – and talent – for music was losing his hearing. Hot tears pour down my face. Poor Will.

But I don't remember him ever showing signs of having difficulty hearing. Perhaps it started after we split? Or could he have kept it a secret while we were together?

And how does this help me?

My stomach is tangled at the thought of Will being tormented by this cruel disease. If we had still been together, I could have been there for him. I could have helped him through it. We could have found a way to make life bearable.

I don't remember standing up, but I'm pacing again. This time when I open the fridge, I pull out a bottle of wine and pour a glass, but before I even take a sip, I tip it into the sink. I need a clear head.

I don't hear Liv come in, but there she is, standing in the kitchen doorway.

Our eyes meet.

'You read them, didn't you?' she asks.

I nod.

'You see – it wasn't your fault.'

'It's not that black and white, Liv.'

'Think about it.' She comes in and sits at the table. 'People break up all the time, but they get over it. This . . .' She taps a finger on the leaflet. 'This is much bigger than that. You don't just get over something like this . . .'

She's right.

How conceited of me to think I was that important.

'I spoke to Mary about it,' she continues. 'She said both

his ears were affected. He had surgery on the worst one, but it didn't work. Surgery on the other ear was too risky after that.'

I pick up the leaflet. 'It says in here you can use a hearing aid.'

'Yeah, apparently he wasn't keen on that idea.'

My mind is spinning. How could he have kept this from me? When did he have surgery without me knowing? He was in Wales for nine months, and I couldn't get there as often as I wanted. Maybe it could have happened then, but why didn't he tell me? Knowing him, he wouldn't have wanted to worry anyone, especially if there was a chance the surgery could be a success. But there were so many people relying on him. The pressure must have been unbearable. 'He kept trying to talk to me. Perhaps that's what he wanted to tell me. I should have been there for him.' My voice wavers and fresh tears come. I bury my face in my hands. I'm angry with Liv but when her arms slip around me, all that melts away.

That night as I climb exhausted into bed, I know in my bones I'm still to blame. I played my part in Will's death. But I fall asleep almost as soon as my head hits the pillow, and it's the best night's sleep I've had in years.

Chapter 72

July 2016

Liv

I've almost finished the photo book for Chloe, but there's space for a couple more pictures. I've used all the ones Mum gave me and the few Dad had on his phone, but I wonder if he has any older photographs in a box somewhere? He's out, but I could have a look around.

Downstairs, I go through all the cupboards in the open-plan living area. I check the cupboards above the washing machine in the utility room before heading out to the garage. I can't remember the last time I came out here. There's a punch bag hanging from the ceiling and a couple of bikes mounted on wall brackets. It's super tidy, with one entire wall dedicated to storage. This is promising. I search through the drawers and cupboards. If I need a screwdriver or hammer, I know where to come, but there's nothing personal in here at all.

The furthest bank on the storage wall contains the wide, shallow drawers you find in the art department at school. I open the top drawer and inside are large sheets of yellowing paper. I pull out the top one and it's covered in sketches of a naked woman sitting and standing in different positions. Oh my God, what have I found? The drawings are rough, the marks angular. The figure has no face, but I can tell it's an older woman with plump folds of flesh. I'm hoping there isn't anything I don't want to see in here. Digging down through

344

the papers, there are sketches of all sorts of everyday items: a pair of well-worn converse high-tops, a cigarette mashed into an ashtray, the tangle of spaghetti around a fork. Is this Dad's work?

I try the next drawer down. Pulling it out a few centimetres, I spot something inside and jump back with a yelp. Was that a creature? I stand well back, waiting for it to crawl out of the open drawer. Nothing happens, so I step forward gingerly, craning my neck to see inside. I wait a moment, and when there's still no movement, I pull the drawer out a little further. It's filled with butterflies and beetles, their iridescent colours shimmering in the harsh fluorescent light of the garage. But they're not alive, they're not even real – they've been lovingly crafted from paper. I pull the drawer out as far as it will go to see they're attached to a dark backboard. But the backboard has a huge crack in it like it's been folded in half. This artwork reminds me of the *Yellow Feathers* cover. It has a similar style – carefully arranged objects spiralling outwards from the centre.

This is Mum's work. I know it.

But why does Dad have it in his garage?

I search the remaining drawers, and each contains another delicate masterpiece.

As soon as Dad gets home, I'll ask him about all this. I close the bottom drawer, flick off the lights, and as I head into the house, I change my mind. When Dad caught me with his copy of the *Yellow Feathers* CD, he put it in the cabinet, but when I checked later, it was gone. If I talk to him about the stuff in these drawers, it might disappear as well. No, I can't risk it. I'm certain it's Mum's art. I don't need him to confirm it. At least this way I can come and look at it whenever I want.

Back in my room, I put the finishing touches to the photo book, filling the last page with a recent picture I hadn't yet used. I click through the virtual pages to make sure everything's perfect, then order two copies. I fill out the form for the gift message: I'm sorry. I miss you.

I don't sign my name – she'll know it's from me and at the last moment I add:

P.S. I found out why WB did it x.

I hope this will tempt her to get in touch.

*

Three days later, my copy of the photo book arrives. I track the delivery of Chloe's copy and see exactly when she signs for it. I keep my phone beside me on the bed in case she gets in touch. Slipping my earphones in, I listen to the *Fragments* album while flicking through the pages, and even though I've seen them all before, reliving the memories brings a lump to my throat. Chloe by my side as I blow out the candles on my eighth birthday cake, bouncing alongside me during my trampoline park party, then tucked in bed with me at Dad's. He brought us a midnight feast – though it was probably only about 9 p.m. We were so excited and full of sugar we hardly slept that night. Looking closer, I see the familiar dimple that always appears on her left cheek when she smiles.

I feel a hand on my shoulder.

Dad looks serious, so I remove my earphones. 'What's up?'

He's holding a letter.

Panic rises in my chest. 'Are those the results of the paternity test?'

'Yes.'

'What does it say?'

'Read it yourself – you're the one who wanted this.'

I practically snatch it from him. The page is a confusing jumble of numbers that means nothing to me. My eyes latch onto the word 'Summary' at the bottom of the page and I read the paragraph below it:

The alleged father is not excluded as the biological father of the tested child.

What the hell does that mean?

Based on the analysis of the STR loci listed above,
the probability of paternity is 99.9998%.

Tears fill my eyes as I look at Dad.
He smiles. 'Told you.'
But something in his expression tells me he's as relieved
as I am.

Chapter 73

August 1999

'Promise me you'll look after her,' said Miranda.

'I told you I will,' said Scott.

'Don't leave her on her own.'

'I won't.'

'Don't let her drink too much.'

'Okay.'

'Encourage her to get some fresh air. Go for a walk or something.'

'Stop worrying. I've got this. It's less than twenty-four hours. You'll be back before you know it. Go be an aunt.'

'Oh my God, I can't believe I'm an aunty! You've got my parents' number. Call if you need to – any time. Right, I'm off.'

'Bye, Aunt Miranda.'

He closed the door, wandered down the hall and hovered by Emily's doorway. It was still ajar, as per Miranda's instructions.

'You okay, Em?'

'No.'

'Can I get you anything?'

'Has she gone?'

'Yeah.'

'Get me some wine.'

Scott sighed, 'If you come to the off licence with me, we'll get your wine.'

No answer.

'Come on. I'll run you a bath. Get dressed and we'll walk down the road. We'll be back in no time with that wine.'

She didn't refuse, so he went to the bathroom, put the plug in the bath, and turned on the taps. He was going through all the bottles on the ledge, trying to find something that would make bubbles.

'The pink one.' Her voice behind him made him jump. She'd hardly been out of bed the last few days. He grabbed the pink bottle and poured a glug into the stream of water, and a mass of bubbles began multiplying.

'I need the loo,' she said. Her voice was hoarse.

She was only wearing an oversized t-shirt, and he saw how much weight she had lost in a few days.

'I'll get out of your way.'

They swapped places in the doorway, and he closed the door behind him. Miranda had deliberately broken the lock a couple of days ago. Neither of them liked the idea of Emily being alone and unreachable.

He loitered in the hallway until he heard a flush.

She opened the door and went to head back to her room. He didn't fancy his chances of getting her out of bed again.

'Look, why don't you get in the bath now – it's half full?'

Before she could argue, he took her by her shoulders and turned her around.

He was glad she was facing the other way when she pulled her t-shirt over her head. He got a brief glimpse of her protruding ribs before dashing off to find a clean towel.

'Here's a towel and some clean clothes.' He dropped them inside the bathroom door.

'Thanks.'

He smoked two cigarettes on his balcony while she soaked, then returned to encourage her to wash and dress through the door. When she finally emerged, exhausted and bedraggled, he sat her on his bed and gently combed the knots from her hair. Outside, the sunlight made her wince. She stood there blinking as if it was hurting her eyes and skin until he took her elbow and ushered her along. He pointed out a sycamore seed spiralling to the ground, but her gaze remained unfocused, her expression blank. The only time she showed any reaction was when he came out of the off licence carrying a single bottle of wine. She scolded him and sent him back for another.

He suggested they watch a film and got her settled on his bed with a glass of wine. They watched four films in a row. Sometimes she slept, sometimes she stared at the screen, expressionless. She drank quite a lot of wine, but he got her to eat three mouthfuls of scrambled eggs. He was making good progress today. Miranda would be pleased.

When he was nodding off himself, he suggested they go to bed. She got up and stretched, and he followed her out to the hallway to go and brush his teeth, but he almost bumped into her when she stopped and turned.

'I don't want to be alone,' she said. 'Is it okay if I sleep in your room?'

'Of course.'

She hesitated before asking, 'Will you hold me?'

'Okay.'

He stepped towards her, and she threw her arms around his neck, clinging to him. He brought his arms around her, returning the pressure. She felt like a bag of bones.

They stood in the hall like that for a long time.

She nuzzled her face into his neck, and he could feel moisture. Was she crying? He went to pull away, but she squeezed tighter. Her lips brushed his neck, soft, damp kisses sending tingles down his spine.

'Em—'

'Shh,' she whispered, her breath hot in his ear.

He untangled her arms from around his neck. 'Emily, you're drunk. You don't know what you're doing.'

'I'm not drunk.' She looked him in the eye. 'And I know exactly what I'm doing.'

She stepped towards him. Her lips were on his neck again and her fingers on his belt.

'We shouldn't . . .' he said gently.

'Don't you want to?'

He groaned. 'You don't want this, you're just—'

'I do. I want this,' she said. 'Please.'

It hurt so much to see her this way.

But it was far worse knowing it was all his fault she was so sad and broken.

*

Scott woke to the sound of the front door opening.

Emily didn't stir beside him. She lay motionless in a deep sleep, in his bed. What time was it? 11 a.m. It must be Miranda back from her sister's. He jumped out of bed and pulled on his jeans. *Fuck*.

In the hallway, Miranda was standing by the door to Emily's empty room.

'Where is she?' she hissed.

'She's in my room.'

'What's she doing in your room?'

'She didn't want to be alone so—'

'What the fuck, Scott?' she whisper-shouted.

'Shh – you'll wake her!'

'Oh my God – you fucking arsehole!' She spoke through gritted teeth. 'You were supposed to look after her. Not take advantage of her.'

'We just—'

'Have you got any idea what she's going through? You couldn't keep your dick in your pants for one night?'

'It's not what it looks like. Honestly—'

Her laugh was bitter. 'I can't wait to hear this!'

351

'I *did* look after her. I got her out of bed, got her to take a bath. And we went for a walk. That's more than you've got her to do.'

'What else did you get her to do? Eh?'

'Miranda—'

'Her boyfriend just *died*, Scott. She's not thinking straight, you fucking moron.'

'We didn't do anything!'

'Yeah, right.'

'I swear. We didn't do anything. I'm not a *complete* scumbag – I love her!' he blurted.

She laughed. 'Don't give me that shit!'

'I do! I have for years! She's the reason I took this course. The reason I organised this flat share.'

Miranda's smirk disappeared. 'Oh, my God. You do, don't you?'

He rubbed a hand down his face. 'Yeah.'

She shook her head. 'You delusional bastard. You know she'll never love you back, don't you?'

'Why not?' he asked, but he knew the answer.

'I want to go home,' Emily's voice came from behind him.

She was standing in his doorway wearing one of his t-shirts, more beautiful than ever despite the tousled hair and hollow cheeks.

And in that moment he knew Miranda was right.

Chapter 74

July 2016

Emily

Scott is building up to something. I can tell by the way he's rotating the paper coffee cup around on my kitchen table. He's invited himself over and brought lattes with him, a sure sign he's buttering me up. Maybe things have progressed with Katya; maybe he's here to tell me they're getting married.

I can't wait any longer. 'Okay, spit it out.'

'I have a favour to ask.' He lifts his eyes from the cup. 'I wouldn't ask you this if I wasn't desperate.'

Shit, this sounds serious. 'What is it?'

'I need you to come to Amsterdam.'

I can't hide how that last word makes me flinch and his eyes flash with concern.

'The general manager of the hotel wants to meet you.'

'Why on earth do they want to meet me?'

'He wants to meet the artist I've been raving about. He's really into his art, Em. He's much more involved with this project than anything else we've done for him. It's only three nights.' He bites his lip, eyebrows high.

'I can't go to Amsterdam for three nights, Scott. I have to work.'

'Can't Magda cover for you? We've got the meeting the first day, then it's the installation, then the photoshoot. He's paying for an artist. He'll be pissed off if the artist isn't there for the installation.'

I sigh. 'What about Liv?'

'She's old enough to look after herself now.' He sees the worry in my face. 'Or she could stay with your parents?'

I've always wanted to return to Amsterdam since visiting briefly with Will on tour. I'd been disappointed there wasn't time to explore the museums and galleries, which was partly why I chose the city for my residency. But I abandoned that dream long ago. Going there now could dredge up past regrets. I'm not sure I can handle it.

Scott's tone is gentle. 'I understand if it's too much . . .'

*

Europe flashes by as we travel business class to Amsterdam on the train. I look the part in an elegant navy dress with a berry red cross-body bag. We read magazines; we chat. They serve wine with lunch, and coffee with our pistachio and apricot tartlets. And, just for the journey, I pretend I'm an artist travelling to Amsterdam for a meeting with a client about a commission. And it's not so bad.

Our taxi drops us at the hotel in the heart of the museum quarter on a street bustling with bicycles and trams. The grand, imposing nineteenth-century exterior hides a sleek modern interior of glass and black steel. The guy at the check-in desk says, 'Welcome, Mr King. Mr Allemand is expecting you. Please take a seat while I locate him for you.'

Our luggage is whisked away, and we're deposited at a table in a huge glass atrium with fresh coffee.

'Who's Mr Allemand?' I whisper.

'The general manager.' Scott is at home in the luxury surroundings. I'm a fish out of water.

An impeccably dressed man with silver hair approaches.

'Ah, Emily! It's a pleasure to meet you. Pierre Allemand.'
As I stand, he clasps my hand in both of his. 'I'm a huge fan of
your work. I'm looking forward to working with you on this
project. It will be a *vrolijk kerstfeest,* indeed.'

I have no idea what he's talking about. I stand dumbstruck
as he greets Scott like an old friend.

'I'm sure you would like to freshen up after your journey.
Let's meet at four o'clock. Ask any of the hosts and they will
direct you to the Blue Room. You will join me for dinner this
evening as well, I hope?'

He's looking at me.

'That would be lovely. Thank you,' I say.

'Splendid.' Pierre gives a slight bow and strides off.

I glare at Scott. 'How the hell is he "a huge fan" of my
work?'

He smiles as we sit down. 'I showed him your portfolio.'

'I don't have a portfolio.'

'I made you one.'

'Using what?'

'Photographs from your exhibition.'

'Where did you get photographs of my exhibition?'

'I took loads of pictures on the opening night. Don't you
remember?'

'No . . .'

'Here, I got you something.' He reaches down into his
laptop bag, pulls out a paper bag, and slides it across the table
towards me. 'To say thank you for coming with me.'

'I should thank *you*.' I peek inside and pull out a leather-
bound notebook. It's been dip-dyed. The top is pale turquoise,
and the colour gets richer and deeper towards the bottom.
The leather is smooth as I run my palm over it. I unravel the
leather tie and flip the pages. There are no lines on the paper –
it's a sketchbook.

'Do you like it?' His eyes glint with expectation.

'It's lovely.' I close it and refasten the tie. 'Thank you.'

'Maybe you could start keeping a sketchbook again . . .'

'Maybe.' But I can't go there, not even in my head.

*

At four o'clock, we go to the meeting room as planned. I'm sick with nerves. Pierre is waiting beside a stack of huge cardboard boxes.

'Shall we?' he asks.

We unpack the boxes. Inside, encased in bubble wrap, are the giant baubles I designed. When we visited the workshop last week, I made some last-minute adjustments to the design and came up with the idea of a set of steps, disguised as a pile of Christmas presents, for smaller children to reach the viewing hole.

'These will look spectacular hanging in the lobby,' gushes Pierre.

Scott and I hold up the larger bauble for Pierre to peer into the viewing hole where the miniature violins and saxophones dangle inside.

'Magical!' he says.

Scott can't stop grinning as we pack everything away until the installers arrive in the morning.

'Come with me,' says Pierre, 'there are some things I want to show you.'

He takes us back to the atrium and stops in front of a bronze sculpture of a giant bunny.

'What do you think?' he asks me.

'Is it Miffy? My daughter loved those books when she was small.'

Pierre laughs. 'Yes, some guests call it "Scary Miffy". Its proper name is *Under My Skin* by Dutch artist Raphael Hermans. Are you familiar with his work?'

'No,' I say. 'I must look him up.'

Pierre takes us on a tour of the entire hotel, stopping at all the various artworks around the building. He asks for my thoughts on each of them and by the end, I'm struggling to come up with anything intelligent to say.

Finally, he leads us back to the atrium, past Scary Miffy, and pauses by a staircase leading down to the spa in the basement. We stand before a bare brick wall. Scott and I exchange glances.

'We need something here, no?' Pierre looks at me like I'm the font of all art knowledge.

'There's certainly space here,' I say.

'Something like your feathery piece would look fabulous here. Do you have time to take on a new commission?' asks Pierre.

My brain appears to be malfunctioning. I have no words.

'You're tied up with commissions until September, aren't you, Emily?' says Scott. 'But perhaps after that?'

'We only have a small budget for this,' says Pierre. 'Around ten thousand euros.' He reads my hesitation as reluctance. 'I could push it to twelve if I take some budget from next year?'

'That could work, couldn't it, Emily?' Scott nudges.

'I—'

'You don't need to commit now. Think about it and let me know if it's something you would consider.'

As I stand in that glorious atrium, counting the eight storeys of brickwork up to the glass ceiling, I feel woozy. But gradually shapes and colours appear in my mind, snaking up the wall like a tree sprouting branches and leaves.

And the fear is tinged with excitement.

Chapter 75

September 1999

Scott waited on the balcony; he'd have had another cigarette, but he felt sick. It had been six weeks since he last saw Emily, almost seven. Why did she want to see him? Why did Miranda have to be out?

The buzz of the intercom startled him; he'd expected her to use her key. His hands were shaking as he lifted the handset and buzzed her up.

He ran to the bathroom and checked his reflection in the mirror. He squeezed a blob of toothpaste onto his finger and rubbed it over his teeth.

She knocked and he opened the door.

'Hi,' she said brightly, but she looked awful. Dark rings circled her eyes, and she was even thinner than before.

'Hi.' He pecked her on the cheek. 'Do you want a cup of tea?'

'Please.' She followed him to the kitchen.

He put the kettle on as she sat at the little table.

'Thanks for seeing me.'

'No worries. It's good to see you. Did your parents tell you I called? Quite a few times, actually.'

'Yeah, sorry. It's been . . .' She didn't elaborate, but he nodded as though he understood.

The obvious thing to say would be 'how are you?' but he couldn't bring himself to ask. He didn't want to hear the answer, so he made the tea in silence. He put the two mugs on the table and sat opposite her.

She took a deep breath and said, 'I'm pregnant.'

It was like a slap across the face.

She must have seen the question in his eyes. 'It's yours,' she said sincerely. 'I want you to know that there's no doubt about that.'

He'd always dreaded hearing those words and now they'd come out of her mouth, they were as terrible as he'd feared. 'I assumed you were . . .' he began, his heart thundering.

'I was on the pill,' she said. 'But I was drinking a lot, I threw up a couple of times that week. It was stupid of me. I should have known it might not work.'

Sweat sprang up on his palms and top lip. His mouth went dry.

'I'm keeping it,' she said. Another slap in his face.

'What about Amsterdam?'

'I turned it down before I found out I was pregnant.' Her voice was flat. 'You don't need to be involved,' she continued, business-like. 'I want nothing from you. No one needs to know it's yours. I thought you should know.'

Her words stung. Actually, they pissed him off. 'Hang on a minute,' he said. 'What about what *I* want?'

'It's my body, Scott. I don't want an abortion.' She started to cry, great big tears, her gaunt face pulled into a grimace.

'No . . .' He went to her and pulled her up into his arms. 'That's not what I meant. I meant we could do this together.'

She drew back to look at him. She wiped her face with her hands, and that determined look was back.

'That wouldn't be fair on you.'

'It's mine, isn't it?'

'Yes, but . . .'

'But what?'

'I'd only make you unhappy.'

'What makes you think that?'

'Because I make people unhappy. Because *I'm* unhappy. Because you're twenty-four and this isn't what you want.'

'I'll be the judge of what I want.'

'You don't want a baby, Scott.'

'I don't want a baby, but I want you.' He let the words hang there for a moment, exposing his soul. 'And if you want a baby, then . . . we can do this.'

She sat down, shaking her head.

'What?' he asked.

'There is no "we",' she muttered. 'I can't be with anyone. It wouldn't work. I can't be in a relationship.'

'You can't be in a relationship, but you're ready to be a mother?'

She didn't hesitate. 'Yes!'

'That doesn't make sense.'

'It does to me. It's the only thing that makes sense to me.'

'Can we at least try?'

She wrapped both hands around her mug and stared into it like she'd find the answers in there. 'I don't want to hurt you.'

'You won't hurt me. If it doesn't work out, it doesn't work out. We should at least try.'

'No . . .'

'For the baby. Doesn't the baby deserve a mum *and* a dad?'

'I can't . . .'

'What about later? When you're ready? You've been through so much; you need time . . .'

She raised her eyes to his. 'I can't promise you I'll ever be ready.'

He sat down, his mind racing. He covered his face with his hands. Jesus, he would do anything.

He let his hands slip down.

'Well, it's my kid too,' he sighed. 'I want to be involved. It's my job to provide for it . . . and its mum.'

'You don't have to do that. This is my fault and my decision.'

'I could have used a condom—'

'Listen, you can't be part of this child's life, then walk out years later when you meet someone or want to have a family. If you're in it, you need to be in it forever or not at all.'

'I agree. I want to be a good dad.'

'Take some time to think about it properly and we'll talk again.' She stood up to go. She hadn't even touched her tea.

'I won't change my mind.' He followed her to the hall.

Her hand was on the door handle, but she turned back to say, 'It's okay to change your mind.' Her eyes were kind. 'Forever is a long time, Scott.'

*

Scott wanted to call Emily that night, but she'd only say he hadn't thought about it properly. He waited two days. Her dad answered the phone and this time he was allowed to talk to her.

'Do they know?' he asked when she came to the phone.

'What?'

'Do your parents know you're pregnant?'

'Yes.'

'Do they know it's mine?'

'No. But they have their suspicions.'

'Are they angry?'

'Worse – disappointed.'

'Ah.'

'In me, not you. Seriously, pregnant is an improvement on my condition over the last few weeks. And my mum's secretly excited about being a grannie.'

There was a pause.

361

'It's okay,' she said. 'My mum and dad want to help me. I'll be fine.'

'I haven't said anything yet.'

'You don't have to. It's the sensible decision. The right one.'

'I want you,' he blurted, 'why don't you want me?'

Silence.

'We could be together,' he continued. 'Have this baby together. Give him a proper family. A mum and dad who love each other and love him.'

'Oh, Scott . . .'

'Why? Why can't we try?'

She drew a breath in. 'Because I love someone else. You know that.'

'He's dead!' he snapped. He hated himself. What a horrible thing to say. 'I'm sorry,' he backtracked. 'I didn't mean that.'

'Scott—'

'It's my baby, too! I want to be involved as much as any normal dad.'

'Why don't you take some more time? You don't need to decide now.'

'I don't need more time. I'm sure about this.'

'It has to be about the baby, not about me.'

'I'm its father and I can't forget about it and get on with my life as if this never happened.'

*

A couple of weeks later, she came to the flat with her dad to clear out her room. Scott made himself scarce, but as soon as they left, he went down to the bin store and rescued her artwork from the wheelie bins. When she didn't return to college, he took a couple of the bigger pieces she left there and stashed them in his parents' loft.

He was charming and respectful when he met Emily's parents, and they were impressed by his attendance at almost all the appointments and antenatal classes. He was by Emily's side at the birth and chose his daughter's name. Once their course was over, he blagged his way into web design, saying he could do things he couldn't, but taught himself how. His dad lent him the money to set up his own business, and he paid it all back before his daughter was two. He worked hard but always found time to spend with her.

But he couldn't win Emily over. He could never compete with a dead rock star who – in Emily's rose-tinted memories – was perfect. No one could compete with him because he wasn't real. He would never fuck up: forget a birthday, look at another girl, buy a shit present. He would always be a perfect ghost, haunting their lives forever.

Chapter 76

July 2016

Emily

The hotel shampoo smells expensive, with its citrus notes and spicy undertones. It lathers luxuriously, and as the suds slide down my body, I think of the beautiful leather-bound sketchbook lying on the bed in the next room. It was a thoughtful gift. I wish I had sounded more grateful. I recall the passionate way Scott spoke to Pierre about my work, the effort he went to, twenty years ago, to photograph every piece in my exhibition. It's touching that he believes in me. Has always believed in me.

Scott is still on my mind as I squeeze water from my hair and apply the creamy conditioner. Him being thoughtful, saying nice things, it reminds me of that day a hundred years ago when I told him I was pregnant. He'd said he wanted me. Wanted me. Remembering that now gives me a stab of guilt.

Could he have meant what he said? Or was he simply in shock after the bombshell I'd just dropped? I lose my train of thought for a moment, caught up with the fizzing in my stomach at the thought of Scott wanting me. That's what he said back then. *I want you. Why don't you want me?*

Ever since Liv told me about Will's otosclerosis, I've been thinking about things differently. But thinking differently about Scott is unnerving and a little scary.

364

I like the idea of him wanting me.

Maybe I want him, too.

I realise with sudden clarity, as if the shower is washing away all the lies I've told myself over the years, that I've been all alone, punishing myself when I could have been with Scott.

All at once I'm sobbing, tears mingling with the shower water. I need to talk to him. I can't wait a minute more – I've wasted too much time already.

I'm not even sure if I rinsed the conditioner out of my hair, but I shut off the water, step out and dry myself hurriedly. Wrapped in the fluffy hotel bathrobe, I grab my key card and reach for the door handle. I glimpse myself in the mirror on the back of the door. My hair is tangled and dripping. What am I doing? If I turn up at his room like this, he's going to think it's about sex. He'll think I'm there for the same old desperate shag we won't talk about afterwards.

'At least put some bloody clothes on,' I tell my reflection.

I run around the room like a madwoman, grabbing clothes, brushing hair, drying it with the pathetic hotel hairdryer. I pull on a black dress and apply a lick of mascara.

This time I make it out of the door and halfway down the corridor to his room before I realise it's totally the wrong time. We're meeting Pierre and the photographer and God knows who else for dinner in less than half an hour. There's no way we can sort out two decades of misunderstanding in that time. And we can't skip dinner. I turn on my heel.

A door opens behind me. Scott's voice echoes down the hall, 'Em?'

I pivot. He's dressed smartly in a navy suit, no tie, the top button of his white shirt undone.

'Hi!' I squeak.

'What're you doing?'

'Er . . . I was coming to knock for you, but I forgot my handbag.'

'You look lovely.' He walks alongside me. The barest touch of his hand at my lower back sends a shiver through me.

'Thanks.' I'm bursting with nervous energy, like a teenager with a crush.

He hovers by the door while I dart around my room, grabbing lip gloss, phone, and clutch.

Thank goodness there are people in the lift, otherwise I might pour my heart out on the way down. I'm not sure how I'll contain myself through dinner.

The table is set for nine. Pierre has me sitting on his left-hand side with Scott opposite us. The table is too wide to talk across, but Scott keeps giving me reassuring looks. He knows I'm out of my depth at this table. Pierre introduces me to the photographer on my left and various members of his team. I can't pronounce most of their names, let alone remember them all. Course after course of food arrives. I don't know what I'm eating, but it all tastes heavenly. Pierre entertains us with stories of demanding wealthy guests and badly behaved celebrities over his forty-year career in hospitality. He doesn't mention names but gives us enough clues to guess. The fine wine goes down easily, the warm buzz of it relieving my anxiety. I'm like a shaken-up snow globe finally settling.

They bring coffee and handmade chocolates. Scott knows I'm watching as he bites into one. His eyes widen and his face melts into exaggerated ecstasy as he chews. I giggle. He composes himself and gives me a wink.

The marketing manager says something to him, and he inclines his head to hear her. His gaze is on me while she talks. Everything slows down. The chatter in the room, the clinking of glass and the scraping of cutlery all fade out.

It's just Scott and me holding eye contact.

And his expression is so serious and steady, and in such stark contrast to the playful face he pulled only a moment ago, it sends a thrill through me. It reminds me of being a kid, sticking your head out of a moving car window and gulping for breath. I try to convey with my eyes what I haven't yet been able to put into words and I'm overwhelmed by the urge to go to him. To kiss him.

'Did you try the truffles?' Pierre holds a little plate before me.

All the sounds are back. I smile, select a chocolate, and take a bite. Across the table, Scott is showing the marketing manager something on his phone. I can tell from his expression, it's a photo of Liv.

After dinner, we ride the lift to our floor. My head's spinning. Every step I take as we walk down the corridor, I go to speak, but words escape me. What the hell am I going to say? *I fancy you?*

We reach his room first. I should say something now but, as I open my mouth to speak, his pocket starts buzzing.

He apologises, pulls out his phone and says, 'Kat, can I call you back in two minutes? Thanks. Bye.' Then he gives me all his attention, and it's like basking in the sun. 'Sorry, were you going to say something?'

'No . . .' *Nothing I can say in two minutes.*

'So, you'll take the commission, right?'

'I don't know. The thought terrifies me.'

'Why don't you see what you come up with? You can always duck out of it later.'

'Well, I *do* have ideas . . .'

'You see!' His grin is wide and infectious. 'Well, better get some sleep, busy day tomorrow.'

'Yes.'

'Goodnight.'

'Night.'

*

I lie in my enormous bed, unable to sleep. Just because the man showed the slightest bit of interest almost twenty years ago, doesn't mean he'd be interested now. He didn't mean what he

367

said when we were young. About getting together. He couldn't have done – he was in shock. I'd just told him I was pregnant, after all. He's never shown any sign of having feelings for me since. Those few times we slept together, they were always instigated by me. He felt sorry for me. It didn't mean anything; it was just sex. Besides, his girlfriend is gorgeous. Half my age. What was I thinking? Thank God I didn't make a fool of myself.

I lie there, willing him to come to my room but knowing he won't. He never once came to my bed in the past. It was always me going to him.

I fall asleep a moment before the alarm goes off at 6 a.m.

Chapter 77

July 2016

Emily

The larger bauble glitters under the lobby lights with the two smaller ones hanging at varying heights behind it. A garland of beads dangles in swooping loops, tying the whole piece together. I climb the Christmas present steps and peer into the viewing hole. The musical instrument models hang inside, rotating around, moving up and down like a carousel.

I skip down the steps and join Scott, who's admiring the display from afar.

'Pleased?' he asks.

'Very.'

We work through lunch to set up the photoshoot. The hotel staff bring us exquisite canapés, the kind you get at fancy functions, but also make an excellent working lunch if you eat enough of them.

Scott has booked a model 'family' for the photoshoot. The adorable little girl he's cast reminds me of Liv when she was small. She climbs the steps and peers into the hole. Her eyes light up and she exclaims something in Dutch and the photographer captures the magical moment with a well-timed click.

After the photoshoot, Scott suggests we go for a celebratory drink and the two of us wander the banks of the canal until we find a quaint bar overlooking a flower-festooned bridge.

'Pierre seemed happy, didn't he?' I say as we sit at a table outside.

'He loved it and we're back on track with the Christmas campaign, thanks to you.'

A waiter comes over. I go to order a glass of wine but Scott interrupts, 'No, we're celebrating. Let's get a bottle of champagne. We'll have the Veuve Clicquot. And some fries, please.'

I laugh. 'Classy.'

Our order arrives. The champagne and fries combo is pretty good.

He raises his glass. 'Congratulations on the commission.'

'Thanks.' I clink my glass to his and can't help smiling despite my terror at the prospect.

We chat about the installation, the photoshoot and Amsterdam. We go quiet and people-watch for a while. He sits back in his chair, legs stretched out in front of him. He flashes me a killer smile and it almost floors me.

My phone buzzes on the table. I lean over it to check if it's Liv. My face automatically unlocks the screen, revealing the message.

FHD: I miss you x

I don't think Scott sees it, but I swipe my phone from the table and tuck it into my bag. FHD is great. He's handsome, he's a nice guy, he's fun to be with.

But he's not Scott.

Maybe that's why I've been avoiding him. Ever since Liv told me about Will, everything has changed.

'I need to tell you something,' I blurt.

His relaxed expression dissolves. 'You're moving in with him, aren't you?' he says, his tone sharp.

'What?'

'I don't understand how you can start seeing this guy and you didn't even think about us.'

'Us?' Is he saying what I think he's saying?

'I can't believe I encouraged you,' he says. 'But it seemed like you were finally coming out from the cloud you'd been under for years. I thought it would be good for you to go on a few dates. I didn't expect . . .'

'Scott—'

'You were upset after Will died. I get that. I knew it would take time. A long time. And I was prepared to wait, but to be honest, it hurts that now you're ready to be in a relationship, you didn't even consider . . . me.'

'You were interested in me back then?'

'Of course I was.' His eyes blaze. 'I only took that course because you were doing it. I only organised that flat share in Balham because you were looking for a place. Every decision I've made in my adult life has been because of you.'

I'm stunned. 'Why didn't you say anything?'

'I did. I told you exactly how I felt when you said you were pregnant.'

'You weren't thinking straight that day. *I* wasn't thinking straight that day. Besides, that was more than sixteen years ago. Are you telling me you've felt that way all this time?'

'Yes,' he says without hesitation.

'Why didn't you say anything?' I ask again.

'Because you weren't ready!'

'But what about Katya?'

'What about Katya?'

'I can't compete with a girl half my age, with smooth skin and pert . . . everything!'

'She can't compete with you at all.'

'Oh, come on.'

'I mean it. You're my best friend, the mother of my child, but I always wanted more than that.'

'But . . . that night . . . you felt sorry for me. You were being kind.'

'Is that what you thought? That I felt sorry for you?'

'What else would I think?'

371

He pauses, then asks, 'That night, could it have been anyone? I mean, was I just in the right place at the right time?'

I consider this for a minute. 'Honestly? I don't know.'

He crosses his arms and looks away. 'Great.'

'I didn't think of you in that way, but I wouldn't have slept with just anyone. I felt safe with you, but beyond that, I didn't plan it. It was an impulsive decision, an attempt to move on. I thought you didn't get emotionally attached. I thought it was just sex for you . . . with anyone.'

'You didn't think of me that way?' He holds my gaze a moment, then looks away.

'I didn't think you thought of *me* that way! All those girls you were seeing . . .'

'I never said I was a *monk*. But I've never been serious with anyone. You know that. You and Miranda took the piss out of me saying I'd never been in love – heart of ice and all that. But I wasn't interested in anyone else. It was always you.'

A torrent of emotion washes over me. Relief that my suspicions were correct, guilt over how lonely he must have been in those empty relationships, and a desperate longing for what could have been. 'If we'd got together then, it wouldn't have worked out.'

A flicker of his eyebrows tells me he doesn't disagree.

'You're right,' I add. 'I wasn't ready. For a long time. But that's what I'm trying to tell you . . . I really believe I'm ready now.'

'But you've only known this guy for five minutes—'

'I'm not talking about him! Listen to me!'

He rubs his brow.

'After Will,' I say, 'I was too sad to contemplate being with anyone else. I didn't think I could be happy, so how could I make anyone else happy? But now, I think . . . I could make you happy.'

He stares at me. 'Me?'

'I think so. I think we could be happy now.'

'Don't play with me, Emily.' He looks so vulnerable, like a little boy. How could I ever have thought he was emotionally detached?

I shake my head. 'I'm not.'

He leans across the table; I meet him in the middle, and our lips touch. We've kissed before, but not like this. He stands up and pulls me close; his arms encircle me. All the turmoil of the last twenty-four hours ebbs away, and it's being replaced by . . . relief? Joy? My chest is full.

He breaks away, a deep frown creases his forehead, and my anxiety is back in a flash.

'What is it?' I ask.

'I need to tell *you* something,' he says. 'I can't have this hanging over us.' He looks like he's taking a run-up to a hurdle.

'What?'

He exhales. 'Will came to see me a few days before he died.'

My heart stops beating.

'He gave me a note to give to you because you weren't taking his calls. Em, I'm so sorry, I didn't give you the note.'

This hits me like a freight train. 'Why not? What did it say?'

'Jesus,' he says, pinching the bridge of his nose. 'I'm sorry, Em, I burned it. I didn't know he would . . .'

'Scott,' I say, trying to keep my voice level, 'tell me what the note said.'

'I can tell you exactly what it said because I think about it every single day.'

I glare at him. If he doesn't tell me, I'll scream.

'Will wanted to tell you your friend was in hospital – the drummer, Reu. He had an overdose and was in a coma.' He's talking so fast I can hardly keep up. 'I didn't believe him. I thought he was exaggerating or making it up to get you to

373

talk to him. He was being weird, hanging around outside, and then he broke into the flat. I thought they were junkies. I was trying to protect you. I shouldn't have made that decision for you, but I did, and I'm sorry. Truly sorry—'

'Stop talking.'

He eyes me like I'm a bomb about to go off.

Tears blur my vision, and the streetlights become crazy starbursts.

'I fucked up . . .' he says.

I can't look at him. I stare into the distance.

'You can't forgive me, can you?'

I drag my gaze back to his face. His eyes are glassy, but my heart is a stone, cold and heavy in my chest.

'Why should you when I can't forgive myself?' he continues.

I can only whisper this time, 'Stop talking.'

He closes his mouth, but his eyes keep pleading with me.

'Did he die?' My voice is barely audible.

'Sorry?'

'Did Reu die?'

'I don't know, I'm sorry.' He hangs his head.

'I'm going for a walk.'

He steps towards me but stops short of touching me. 'You can't walk around a strange city on your own at night. It's not safe . . .' He fumbles in his pocket, pulls out his wallet, and throws some notes on the table.

'I want to be alone.' My voice sounds alien, distant.

I walk away.

Scott follows. 'Em, please . . .'

I whip around to face him. 'What? What do you want from me?' My voice echoes off the quirky architecture and I feel the eyes of the hundreds of people along the waterside.

'I know you want to be alone, but please let me follow. I'll give you space. I just need to know you're okay.'

'Do what you want. I don't care.'

I walk.

374

I weave through the tourists on the canal side, my mind racing. What happened to Reu? I stop, pull out my phone and google 'Will Bailey's drummer'. I'm blocking the path, so I step to one side. The signal is terrible. Scott loiters in my peripheral vision. As the page loads, a blue line crawls across the top of the screen.

Chapter 78

July 2016

Liv

As soon as I knew Mum and Dad were going away, I arranged to visit the Baileys' house. I've missed working on the archive, but once I get stuck in, it's as if I haven't been away. I find a box of CDs in one of the flight cases and I'm photographing them, and creating a Spotify playlist, when I hear voices coming from Mary's kitchen.

He must be here.

Then I hear a baby crying – it's someone else. I go back to my work, but a few minutes later, the door from the kitchen opens.

Mary is holding a fat little baby. She's like a doll, a halo of shiny black curls. She's adorable.

'Shall we have some yoghurt while Daddy chats with Liv?' says Mary, holding the door open.

A man steps into view, kisses his daughter on the forehead. 'Bye-bye, sweetie.'

He turns to me and says, 'You must be Liv.'

I smile. 'Yes, hi. And you must be Reu.'

*

Interview transcript – Reuben 'Reu' Brody

OL: Matty told me Will split with his girlfriend around the time he was writing the second album in Wales.

RB: Yeah. That's when Will was having trouble writing, and it got worse after the split, and we all came back to London. That's when things get a little hazy for me.

OL: You don't remember?

RB: *[Sighs]* I hung out with the Paradigm roadies back when we were touring with them in the US. I started smoking a lot of weed and after that I tried a few other things. I enjoyed feeling out of it. I was young and stupid, and one thing led to another, and I ended up . . . no, I won't make excuses. I was an idiot.

OL: What happened?

RB: All my dreams had come true. All three of us were having the time of our lives then when we got to Wales – it seemed like it could all be over. I was anxious *all* the time – except when I was high. When I was high, I didn't worry. I was happy living in cloud cuckoo land. Nothing mattered. I had to borrow money. Then when people stopped lending me money, I started stealing it. There was a dodgy dealer at the pub in the village. He was always trying to get me to try heroin. I tried it once, and that was it. When we got back to London, I needed to get hold of more.

[Whispers] I stole from Mary's purse. I feel so bad about that. All that woman did for me. She took me in and was a mother to me when my own mother didn't know if I was alive or dead.

[Laughs] I had issues.

I don't remember much of what happened, but it was only the second time I took it, and I overdosed. I was with this bunch of so-called 'friends' at this squat. Matty and Will didn't know where I was. They'd have killed me if they'd known. I guess I was lucky I wasn't on my own – someone called an ambulance. I was in a coma for almost two weeks.

All I know is it was an accident – I didn't mean to do it. I just wanted to feel that rush again. But it was touch and go there for a bit and . . .

[Pauses] I think Will blamed himself.

He treated me like a little brother, you know? *[Tearful]* He made me believe in myself. If he hadn't taken me in, God knows where I'd be now.

[Sniffs] He thought I was going to die, and he couldn't handle it. If I hadn't been so stupid . . . so selfish . . . he'd still be here. But when I woke up, he was gone.

Chapter 79

July 2016

Emily

A boat passes on the canal, 'Dancing Queen' blaring and disco lights flashing. How can anyone be having fun when my world has turned upside down? I check my phone and the page has finally loaded:

Reu Brody is a British drummer who played in the band of Will Bailey, appearing and co-writing one song on his album, *Fragments*, as well as several live releases and EPs.

Born: 3rd November 1978.

I'm bawling now. Spluttering, gasping sobs shake my entire body. At first, I'm crying because I'm relieved Reu made it. He was – *is* – such a sweet soul. So positive, full of energy and talented. But then, I'm crying because I feel sorry for myself.

I will never be happy. Because I don't deserve happiness.

The same old feelings resurface. The pain is not raw. It's a dull, yet excruciating, chronic ache.

A couple loiter nearby. The girl speaks to me in a language I don't understand.

'It's okay,' Scott calls from behind me. 'I'm with her. She's okay.' The couple glance at each other and move on.

But I'm not okay. I will never be okay.

I walk until I can't walk any further, so I turn and retrace my steps. Scott stops in his tracks as I pass him.

How could he have kept this from me for all these years? Will must have thought me heartless when I didn't get in touch. Or did he suspect I didn't get the note?

After a while, I hear Scott's voice behind me. 'The hotel's this way.' His face is lit by the glow of his phone. He must be following our route on a map. I'm too tired to argue, so I follow him.

The smiling doorman wishes us a good evening as he holds the door for us.

When the lift arrives, Scott offers to take the next one.

I ride the lift alone, walk the corridor to my room, and collapse, fully clothed, onto the bed. He knocks at the door. 'Em?'

'Please go away.'

'Call if you need anything.' There's a long pause. 'I'm so sorry, Emily.'

*

I sleep for about an hour. When I wake, my feet are throbbing and my head aches. I need to talk to someone. I need a friend.

I pick up my phone and dial.

'Emily, are you okay?' Magda sounds sleepy and worried at the same time.

'No,' I say, and the tears come again. Magda says soothing things I can't decipher over my noisy crying. When at last I can, I tell her everything. I talk non-stop, for I don't know how long, and when I'm done, there's silence.

Did we get cut off? Have I been talking to myself the whole time? 'Hello?'

'I'm here,' she says. There's a pause, then she adds, 'So, he made a mistake?'

'It was a big mistake, Magda—'

380

'Are you so perfect? You have never made a big mistake?'

'Of course I have—'

'You love him?'

That word shocks me a little. I didn't use that word, but – yes – I had thought I loved Scott.

She doesn't wait for a response.

'He made a mistake twenty years ago and you can't forgive him? No, you don't love him.'

'It's not that simple, Magda.'

'Yes, it is!' she snaps. 'It is simple – you love him, you forgive him. You don't love him, forget about it. Life is too short. You, of all people, should know that.'

I thought she was my friend. I phoned her because I wanted sympathy. Someone to take my side, to wallow in my sorrow with me. But she's no help at all.

I hang up without even saying goodbye.

Chapter 80

July 2016

Emily

I alternate between pacing the room and lying on the bed, staring up at the ceiling until the sun comes up. My second night without sleep.

I need air.

I grab my room key and head down in the lift. I exit through the main doors and bump straight into Pierre.

'Good morning, Emily. You are awake early. No Scott?'

'Er, no. I wanted to get out and, you know . . . see Amsterdam.'

'I can recommend a great place for coffee?'

The café is easy to find, following Pierre's directions. I sit outside despite the early morning chill. When my coffee arrives, it has a thin syrupy waffle covering it like a lid. I take a bite. It's gooey and sweet but as I swallow it sticks in my throat and I feel sick.

My thoughts turn to Magda. I don't know if it's her accent or whether she's really that blunt. She didn't sugar-coat things, but maybe that's exactly what I needed. I've never hung up on anyone before. I feel terrible. She was only trying to be a good friend. What was I thinking? It must have been 3 a.m. The only friend I could call in the middle of the night like that was Miranda.

After Liv was born, we drifted apart. No, that's not true – I pushed her away. She was starting out as a designer, and I was a mum. We had nothing in common anymore, and I made no attempt to maintain our friendship. She put a lot of effort in, but I think I *wanted* us to lose touch. It hurt to see her pursue a life that was lost to me. After she graduated, she moved to America. We sent each other messages on birthdays and Christmases, but after a while I didn't even bother with that. Where is she now? What would she say about all this?

Her voice in my head says, *What do you want from life, Emily?'*

The answer to that question comes quickly – I want Scott. But the note – the betrayal of it. Do I even know him?

I get up and go inside to pay my bill. As I'm leaving the café, I see Scott approaching. He stops and holds up his hands like I'm a wild animal he doesn't want to startle.

'I know you want space,' he calls. 'I was worried when you didn't answer your door. Pierre said you might be here. I'll leave you alone now.'

Please don't leave me alone. 'No, come and sit down.'

He walks towards me, and we sit. He spreads his hands on the table and looks at them as though they will tell him what to say.

'I knew I'd have to tell you one day, and I knew you would hate me for it. I expected it, but it still hurts.' He delivers most of this to his hands but drags his gaze up to meet mine for the last word.

'I don't hate you.'

He drops his eyes again.

'I hope you can forgive me one day.'

'You made a mistake. I know all about making mistakes.'

'I think about it every day. Will wanted to talk to you. I didn't know how desperate he was, or I would've given you the note. What if I'd given it to you? He might still be here.'

'I've wasted so much of my life on what-ifs. What if I hadn't split up with him? What if I'd been in the night he broke into the flat? What if writing the second album had been as easy as the first? But it's all pointless. I know that now. When he ended his pain, he gave it to me to carry for the rest of my life.'

My cheeks are wet with tears.

'But it's not only me,' I continue. 'He gave it to Reu, and Matty, and his parents, and the person who found him. You carry some of it because of that note. We all carry it. And he wouldn't want us to. The pain was too much for him to bear. He wouldn't wish it on us.'

Fatigue is seeping into my bones. I'm heavy.

'I'm just so *tired*,' I say. 'I'm tired of feeling guilty.'

'You need to get some sleep. Let's get you back to the hotel.'

He takes my hand as we walk. I haven't walked down the street holding hands with anyone since Liv was small.

He walks me to my room.

'Do you want to be alone?' he asks, lingering by the door.

'No.'

He follows me inside and looks uncomfortable as I kick off my shoes and unbutton my jeans. He busies himself drawing the curtains and getting a bottle of water from the mini fridge. I'm under the covers when he puts it by my bedside. He says nothing but climbs onto the bed and lies alongside me on top of the duvet, fully clothed. I expect he still has his shoes on.

He strokes my hair like he used to for Liv when she was poorly.

Then he lies down with his arm over me, and I drift into a dreamless sleep.

*

I wake to the sound of my phone ringing. Scott is gone. I rummage through my bag but get there too late. FHD missed call.

I feel a pang of guilt, but I can't deal with that now.

I text Scott: **Where did you go?**

A moment later, my phone rings. 'You're up?' he asks.

'Yes.'

'Feel better?'

'Much. Where are you?'

'In my room. I had to make a few calls. Can I come over?' His voice is husky down the line.

'Give me five.'

I brush my teeth, splash my face, and pull my jeans back on before he knocks.

I let him in and close the door behind him. We stand facing each other.

The sound of suitcases trundling past echoes in the hallway outside.

He goes to say something but changes his mind.

I open my mouth to speak but the words die in my throat.

'Give me a chance,' he says at last. 'Please. Let me make it up to you—'

'I don't want you to feel guilty anymore.'

He closes his eyes for a moment. 'I wish I'd given you that note.'

A door slams down the corridor. Distant voices.

'Neither of us is to blame for what happened,' I whisper. Seeing someone else's guilt so plainly, helps me see my own more objectively. Everything has changed. I couldn't have said these words before. And I know, even before I speak, that this time I believe what I'm saying. 'We both made mistakes, but we've more than paid for them.'

He steps closer, cups my face in his hands, searching my eyes for answers.

Then he's kissing me. Gently, carefully like I might break. As I close my eyes, I sense an energy vibrating beneath his skin, like he's holding back. But I want him to let go.

I want to let go.

I get wrapped up in his kiss, but a ball of panic forms in my gut, and I pull away.

'What is it?' he asks.

'I'm afraid,' I whisper.

'Afraid of what?'

'I'm afraid I'll make you miserable.'

'The only way you'll make me miserable is if you leave me hanging for another twenty years.'

'I'm serious.'

'I'm afraid too. It's different, it's a change, but it's what we both want, so we owe it to ourselves to give it a go. You said yourself, you're sick of what-ifs. Let's see how it goes. No pressure. Okay?'

'Okay.'

'Fancy checking out Amsterdam?'

'Now?'

'Why not? We're leaving in the morning. The concierge told me all the best things to do in half a day.'

'We have an itinerary?'

'And dinner reservations. Are you ready for this?'

'I'm ready.'

*

We grab a bite to eat at a street food market before heading off on a gallery tour. We chat, we laugh, we video call Liv. I thought it would be difficult visiting the city where I was supposed to pursue my dreams, but it isn't. Not now I'm so full of hope for the future. Not now there's an art commission if I'm brave enough to take it and not with Scott by my side. Spending time with him is easy, but there's something else now. We're more tactile than before. There's a flirtatious edge to our conversations, but it's not forced. I suppose, if anything, it was forced before. I would keep my distance, make sure I didn't get too close or look too long. This is more natural. It feels right.

Scott says we don't need to change for dinner. The restaurant isn't fancy, but it's packed with people and the food is amazing.

'Oh, I've been meaning to tell you . . .' he says while we wait for dessert. 'Guess who I got in touch with?' He smiles as he pulls out his phone.

'Who?' I take his phone and there on the screen is a photo of my old friend Miranda, our long-lost flatmate. Happy tears spring to my eyes at the sight of her laughing with a redhead by her side as they tickle the small boy between them.

'That's her wife and son.'

'She's married?'

'Yep, living in Santa Barbara. She asked about you.'

'How did you find her?'

'She popped up on LinkedIn, so I sent her a message. She said she'd love to hear from you.'

I hand back his phone. 'Oh, wow . . . well, I'll definitely contact her when we get back.'

*

On the walk back to the hotel I ask, 'Why did we need three nights in Amsterdam, again? We've done no work today.'

'I wasn't sure how long everything would take. It was just a contingency.'

I smile. 'Contingency?'

'You can't come all the way to Amsterdam and not explore the city.'

As we ride the lift to our floor, there's a fizzing in my stomach. As usual, we reach his room first.

He says, 'I'll walk you to your room.'

When we reach my door, he kisses me. It's a long, slow, delicious kiss.

Then he says, 'Goodnight.'

I'm a little surprised because I sensed an urgency in his kiss that I hoped would lead to more, but perhaps I was mistaken.

387

We shouldn't rush things, anyway.

'Night,' I say.

In my room, I take a few deep breaths to steady my heartbeat. I change into my nightdress, brush my teeth, and climb into bed when there's a knock at the door.

'Hello?' I call through the door.

'It's me.'

I open the door a little. Scott stands there looking apologetic. 'Can I come in?'

This time when we kiss, he tastes of toothpaste.

I undo each button on his shirt with trembling fingers, my breaths coming fast and shallow. He steps out of his jeans and shorts, and lifts my nightdress up and over my head. I haven't seen him naked for years. Never had the chance to look, anyway. He's lean and tanned. I take his hand and lead him to the bed. He lies down beside me, his eyes exploring my body, but I'm not self-conscious.

He brushes my hair from my shoulder. He runs his fingertips along the length of my collarbone, touches the curve of my breast and traces a line down to my navel. I hold my breath as he runs his thumb along the line of my caesarean scar. I know he doesn't see it as ugly, what it means to us both.

I lean in and kiss him, the tips of our tongues dancing around each other.

He takes hold of my hip and rolls me onto my back.

He trails his fingertips slowly up my inner thigh and by the time I feel his tongue on me, I'm desperate for it. I wind my fingers into his hair. With every stroke of his tongue, I open my legs wider, arch my back a little more, until my muscles tremble with the effort.

And just when I'm about to come, he stops.

A little whimper escapes from my lips.

He scoots up the bed, presses his body against mine. My breath catches in my throat as he pushes into me. The slow back and forth of him takes me to the edge of everything.

When I come, the sensation ripples through me; he moves his hips in slow circles, making it last forever. He's not far behind me. He closes his eyes and makes a quiet noise, like a sigh. I've never felt this close to him. He's lost inside himself and me.

He rolls onto his back, spreadeagled. His chest rising and falling. He looks at me, a smile pulling at the corners of his mouth. I must be wearing a similar expression.

'That was nice,' he says.

'Better than nice.'

He lays his arm out in invitation, and I move into the space he's created, my head on his chest. He folds his arm over me. I listen to his breathing and heartbeat slowing. I lie there, knowing I don't have to rush away. This is my room, my bed. He came to me. He wanted me as much as I wanted him. We don't have to pretend it never happened.

We share a bed, just the two of us, the whole night, for the first time in more than sixteen years.

And I dare to hope it won't be the last.

Chapter 81

July 2016

Liv

I have been sending Chloe a funny cat video every day. I gave up on sending messages pleading for forgiveness weeks ago. Lately, it's kittens: being cute, falling over, thinking they can jump further than they can, discovering they have a tail. One every single day. And I'm making progress because Chloe didn't even open my previous messages, but the cat videos get two blue ticks every time. I'm aiming straight for the heart – kittens are irresistible.

But she never replies, and it's been three days since she received the photo book.

I miss her.

Before I head off to *Amplify*, I send my usual cat video. Today's is a kitten climbing up its owner to steal food from the kitchen counter. Two minutes later, my phone pings. She's replied! There, at the bottom of a long string of videos, sits a single emoji – the crying-laughing face. I'm so happy I practically skip to the station. As I wait on the platform, I send another message: How are you?

She doesn't reply, so by the time I get to the *Amplify* office, I'm convinced the emoji she sent earlier must have been a mistake.

But when I check my phone at lunchtime, there's a message. Chloe: We should talk.

Me: OK.

Chloe: Tonight?

Me: I'm staying at my grandparents, but I can come to yours?

*

When Chloe answers the door, her expression isn't exactly friendly. We say *hi* and she leads me through to the living room. She invites me to sit and asks me if I want a drink. It's weird her talking to me like I'm a guest. I usually make myself right at home.

I sit across from her on the L-shaped sofa.

'How's your stomach?' I ask.

'Still sore, but I'm not taking so many painkillers now.'

'That's good.'

'Thanks for the book,' she says.

'No problem. Thank *you* for all the fun memories.'

We go to speak at the same time.

'You go,' she says.

'I'm so sorry I went to Beatland without you,' I say. 'It would have been way more fun if you'd been there.'

She looks doubtful.

'Seriously,' I tell her. 'The whole time I was there I kept wanting to call you and tell you what was happening.'

Her face reddens as she smiles. 'Maybe next year.'

'Oh my God – yes! I'll ask Tumi to get us both VIP passes.'

She goes quiet. Pulls at a loose thread on the hem of her sweatshirt. 'I think we both know my parents won't let me go.'

'They might – we'll be seventeen by then.'

She smiles at me, eyebrows high, as if to say *yeah right*.

'Okay, so we go the year after, when we're eighteen. But we're definitely going, okay?'

Her shoulders slump. 'I want to be a normal teenager. To go to festivals and parties and have a boyfriend. But I have all

391

this pressure on me to do well in school, to get the next piano grading. To win tennis tournaments, all that stuff. It's such a cliché being the Asian girl with the Tiger Mum.'

'What's a Tiger Mum?'

'A strict Chinese mum who pushes her kids to study.'

'But it's your dad that's Chinese, not your mum.'

Chloe huffs. 'I know, ironic, right?'

'But I thought you liked that stuff. You love playing the piano. You love tennis.'

'I used to love them but practising piano two hours a day, every day, isn't fun. I hate playing piano now. And tennis sessions three times a week. And the maths tutor. It's too much. I actually enjoyed being in hospital. I got to stay in bed and watch YouTube for three days.'

I laugh. 'Hardly any kids stick to a hobby unless their parents make them. I started piano lessons at the same time as you. I gave up after a month. I wish my mum had made me keep going. How amazing is it that you can play piano? Your achievements will look brilliant on your uni applications. I've got nothing to put on mine.'

'You do now you've been working on a magazine.'

I hadn't thought of that. 'Oh yeah.'

'And you've found something you're interested in. You chose it. And you're good at it.' She pauses. 'I don't want to be a lawyer.'

'You don't?'

She shakes her head. 'I hated the work experience at my dad's office.'

'Have you told your parents?'

She nods.

'What did they say?'

'It helped that I was in hospital, and they felt sorry for me. They said there was plenty of time to figure it out. Mum said I could drop tennis, and once I get Grade 8, I can scale back on the piano.'

'Wow, they really rolled over.'

'It sounds like it, but my cousin says her parents made her drop stuff at sixteen so she could focus on her studies. That was probably their plan all along.'

'At least they listened. They just want you to do well. They love you.'

'Yeah.' She gives me a weak smile. 'Anyway. Enough about me. What have you been up to?'

I tell her everything she's missed since we last spoke. I tell her about Beatland, the interviews, losing the internship and Mum getting it back again, not being allowed to do the archive anymore, and the otosclerosis leaflet.

We talk for hours; we order pizza and when I have to get back to my grandparents' house, she invites me to stay over.

We make a pact to boycott the Leavers' Ball and go somewhere fancy instead – just the two of us.

We giggle like our old selves.

But we are not our old selves.

Chapter 82

July 2016

Emily

I'm hot off the Eurostar and I'm exhausted and hungry, but I need to see Magda.

I stop off at the florist around the corner from her flat. When I press the buzzer, her son answers.

'Is Magda home? It's Emily.'

There's a grunt at the end of the line, and I'm unsure whether it's negative or positive. I'm deciding whether to buzz again when the door hums and clicks open.

When I reach her floor, she's waiting at her door. Her expression is hard to read. I don't know how badly I've offended her.

'Come in,' she says, when I hand her the flowers.

'I won't stay long.'

But the vodka comes out and I do stay long – far too long.

She has a way of eliciting far more from me than I was planning on sharing. But it's less intrusive now. I've got used to her and I'm even starting to enjoy it. It's like therapy.

Chapter 83

August 2016

Liv

The Will Bailey I knew – Emily Lawrence

(Images, clockwise from top: Emily Lawrence, in the same gold lamé jacket Bailey wore on the cover of 'Fragments', Bailey and Lawrence at The Craic Music Festival, Ireland, 1997. Bailey playing Red Rocks Amphitheatre, Colorado, 1997 as photographed by Lawrence.)

Emily Lawrence has changed little in the twenty years since these photographs were taken. She has the same chestnut hair, the same smile, and the same dark eyes, although there are a few laughter lines around them now. Which is ironic because her eyes convey such sorrow.

Emily met Bailey when he was a busker. According to Bailey's friends, she was the inspiration behind many of the songs on the *Fragments* album. They say she was his muse.

'I don't know about that,' she says, dismissing the idea with a laugh, but the notebooks and letters he left behind suggest otherwise. Two flight cases worth. Preserved in his parents' garage, where he wrote the bulk of *Fragments* in the years prior to its release in 1996.

What is it like to have someone write a song about you?

Oh my gosh – it's surreal! The first I heard he'd written a song about me was from his girlfriend. It was an uncomfortable conversation, as you can imagine. I was with his brother then, too, so it came as a complete shock. But once you know, it's obvious. I asked him once if he hoped I'd notice. He said he *had* to write it and when it was finished, he tried swapping some lyrics, but it wasn't the same, so he left it as it was. It was a gamble, and it got him into trouble, but it also got us together.

We had been together a while when he wrote 'Intertwined'. It evolved over a few days. He played me the riff first, then the melody, and when he sang it with the lyrics for the first time, it was just . . . beautiful and heartfelt and he was so . . . *exposed* as he sang it. It took my breath away. He made me feel good about myself, he gave me the confidence to . . . be me.

I still find it difficult to listen to his songs. They're emotional anyway, but they hold so much meaning for me and there are so many memories wrapped up in them it's hard – really hard – to enjoy them. Maybe one day.

You spent three months on tour with the band. What was that like?

I was on summer break from art school and Will had the idea of me being the official tour photographer. I did a lot of photography on my course so I could take a decent picture. The pay was peanuts, but it meant we didn't have to be apart for the whole tour. This one's my favourite (top, right). This was Red Rocks Amphitheatre. It was stunning. You can tell from his face how awe-inspiring it was to play on that stage with that spectacular backdrop. When I first joined the bus, everyone was on their best behaviour because I was around, but by the end of the summer, I was one of the boys. We were like family. That was the best summer of my life. So much fun.

What was he like in private?

He wasn't like other guys. He was sensitive – he wore his heart on his sleeve. He didn't play games; he told you how he felt. You couldn't write a song like 'Yellow Feathers' and not be in touch with your emotions. Part of being creative is having this ability to tap into them. It's part of the gift, but it also means you're a little fragile, you're vulnerable. It flows both ways. If you can let it out, there's a danger you could let too much in. Being with him could be intense.

Would you say he was a 'tortured artist'?

I hate that phrase, it's *dangerous*. I mean, it implies it's okay to be struggling with your mental health as long as you're producing art. If you haven't gone through mental anguish, then your work isn't worthy.

Was Will a tortured artist? No. He was just a person. He had problems like we all do. Did he use his talent to exorcise his demons? Absolutely. Lots of creative people use their art as an outlet for their troubles, to express themselves and to deal with their thoughts and feelings. You know, I think we sometimes glamorise suicide and it's as bad as stigmatising it. A quarter of people in the UK have mental health problems. One in five people will have suicidal thoughts at some point in their life. Negative feelings are a normal part of life. Talking about them should be normal, too.

We didn't talk about mental health in the nineties, but we know now that talking helps, whether that's with a friend, or with family or a professional.

Apparently, it's common, particularly with young men, for them to make a sudden, rash decision and follow through with it before anyone even notices they're struggling. There was an exhibition on the South Bank a couple of years ago – I saw it on the news. It was photographs of all these smiling, carefree faces, but they turned out to be the last photos of people who had taken their own lives. The message was: 'Suicidal doesn't always look suicidal'.

I'd ask everyone reading this to be mindful that even the happiest, most outgoing and bubbly person in your life might be struggling right now. Reach out to your friends and ask them if they're okay. When they say they're fine – which they will – ask again. 'Are you *really* okay?'. I watched a documentary recently. A group of guys lost one of their friends to suicide and after his death, they made a pact to ask each other twice. What a lovely idea – ask your friends twice.

I didn't even ask Will once . . .

What do you miss most about him?

It's funny because we were apart for most of our relationship. I still get the urge to call him sometimes. I've got so many memories of our telephone conversations; I even dream about them. He was never in one place, and you didn't call mobile phones long distance in those days. It cost a fortune. It took lots of patience and perseverance to get through to him. But that's what I miss the most – our long-distance chats. He was funny and clever and kind.

I'll always miss him.

What was the last thing you said to each other?

I'm not sure I can talk about that . . . I don't want it to go
into—

But you'll tell me?

She nods, so I stop the recording.

'You're sure?' I ask, and she nods again.

She takes a breath. 'It was after he broke into my flat. I
think Matty told you about that?'

'He said Will cut his arm and was rushed to hospital.'

'There was blood everywhere. I went with him in the
ambulance and while we were waiting at the hospital, his
family turned up. When Mary saw me, she screamed at me to
get out. She was making a scene – I had to leave. My friend
Miranda went inside and found out where Will was. We
waited in the car park for his family to leave, then we snuck
back in. She showed me where he was. He was asleep, so I lay
on the bed beside him. I wanted to hold him.' Mum draws her
mouth into a thin line and blinks.

I give her a moment to compose herself. 'Did he wake up?'

She shakes her head. 'I lay there for ages, but he didn't
wake up. He'd lost a lot of blood. Liv, he looked awful.' Her
voice splinters, a sob escapes. 'I should have left sooner. A
nurse caught me. She was cross I was there out of hours. She
made such a fuss that she woke Will . . .' Her breath hitches.
'He said "Milly, don't go". That was the last thing he said, but
I had to go . . . they made me go . . .'

I put my hand on her arm. 'You had no contact with him
after that?'

'About a week later, I got a letter from him apologising for
the break-in and thanking me for visiting him at the hospital.'

I remember that letter. That was the one that made me think they'd slept together – that he was my dad. I got that completely wrong. 'Didn't reading it make you want to get back with him?'

She swallows. 'It's complicated.'

'Please Mum, I want to understand. You clearly loved each other . . .'

Her smile is weak. 'We did . . . but . . .'

It takes all my effort, but I try Dad's tactic of waiting until she's ready to speak.

She drags a fingertip under each eye and sniffs. 'He was so gifted, Liv. His voice, it was . . . oh, just . . .' She shakes her head, her eyes filling with tears again. 'And he'd been noticed. He was getting the success he deserved. He was living his dream. But it wasn't *my* dream . . .

'Then I got this opportunity. My art tutor put me forward for it. A residency in Amsterdam.'

'A residency?'

'They give you a studio to work in, they give you money, somewhere to live. You have all these other artists around you and mentors to guide you. I . . . I planned to go to Amsterdam and work on my art and . . . live *my* dream.

'It was already a strain trying to maintain a relationship with me visiting Will whenever I could. If I stopped doing that, that would be the end of us. I was certain. It was a difficult decision, but I took the residency. I planned to break it off with him, but when I got to Wales, where they were recording, Matty hinted that Will had been unfaithful. When I confronted Will, he admitted it, said it was a mistake, begged for forgiveness. I was angry. I felt betrayed but, in my heart, I believed him. And even though I believed him, I still let him think it was all his fault.' She falters, inhales, and finds the strength to continue. 'It was easier for me to convince myself it was his fault than to admit it was mine.

'I really believed he was better off without me, that I was holding him back. I'd been holding him back for years. He'd be happier with someone else, someone who'd follow him around the world. I was too selfish. I didn't want to give up on my dreams.'

'So why did you?'

'What?'

'You gave up on your dreams.'

She swallows. 'Dreams mean nothing when the person you love is dead. I was so stupid to think anything was more important. Nothing mattered anymore.' Her eyes swim. 'But you came along, like a little miracle, and gave me a reason to live.'

My throat is tight. I reach for Mum, and we cling to each other in tears.

Chapter 84

October 2016

Liv

I'm sitting on the right, but Mum is driving. As I sort out a playlist, I'm reminded of the car journey that ended with a lamppost in the bonnet. When this all began. This time she's wearing sunglasses and we're on a highway in Denver, heading out to the Red Rocks Amphitheatre. She is relaxed and happy – more like the girl in the photographs in Will Bailey's garage.

She catches me looking. 'What?'

'Nothing.' I fix my eyes on the road ahead.

This was my idea. Dad suggested we all go on holiday together like we used to when I was little. When he asked us where we wanted to go, I didn't hesitate. 'Colorado,' I'd said, 'where Will Bailey's ashes are scattered.'

Dad looked at Mum to check if this had upset her.

'They scattered his ashes in Colorado?' she asked.

'Yeah, at Red Rocks Amphitheatre. I thought you knew . . .'

'There's a lot I don't know.' She went quiet. 'Anyway, Dad doesn't want to go *there*.'

Dad was wrinkling his nose.

'There're loads of other things to do there,' I said. 'I only want a quick visit to the amphitheatre. We could do a road trip.'

Dad was excited again. 'Why don't we fly out to Colorado? You two do your pilgrimage to Red Rocks, then we all drive to Los Angeles? I've always wanted to do an American road trip.'

Dad is playing golf while we visit Red Rocks. There's not a cloud in the sky. I can't wait to see the view.

'Are you enjoying sixth form?' She pushes her sunglasses on top of her head and looks over at me.

'I love it. Studying is much easier when you know what you want to do. Paul says Leeds is the best uni for journalism, so I'm going to work hard to get the grades I need to go there.'

'He's a great mentor. I'm so embarrassed about the way I spoke to him.'

'What will you do when the six months is up on the coffee shop?' I ask.

'I'm starting up a business with Magda.'

'Doing what?'

'Running art clubs for kids after school and in the holidays. Magda already does one at her son's old primary school, but we've worked on a programme together and I've got two slots at your primary school now they've fired the head.'

'Mrs Taylor got fired?'

'Kay says the governors have intervened following a "safeguarding issue", whatever that means. She's on a leave of absence.'

'I hated her.'

She wrinkles her nose. 'Me too.'

'If it works out, we'll do more at other local schools. Apparently, they're all desperate for art clubs.'

'And maybe you'll get more commissions once you finish the Amsterdam one?'

'The idea is I'll work on my art when I'm not helping the kids with theirs.'

'Yeah, you can steal all their ideas.'

403

She chuckles and the sat nav pipes up: '*Take the next exit on the left.*'

We're silent for the last part of the journey and when she pulls up in the car park, her relaxed look has vanished. She has that sad, anxious expression I'm more familiar with.

'Are you ready?' I ask.

She can't speak, she just nods.

I put my hand on her knee.

She takes a deep breath, and we get out of the car.

*

There are a lot of stairs. We are breathless by the time we reach the top, but the view is awesome. Rows of steps act as the amphitheatre's seating, leading down to the stage with its craggy rock backdrop. Exercise nuts run up and down the steps; one guy is doing weird squatting jumps from one row to the next despite the early evening heat.

'Where exactly did Mary say they scattered the ashes?' Mum asks.

'Here, at the top.'

She nods.

'I'm going down to check out the stage,' I say, to give her privacy.

Once at the bottom, I take photos of the view back up the steps from the stage. Lowering my phone, I scan the rows for Mum. When I finally spot her, she's on her hands and knees on the top row where I left her. *Shit.* Is she okay? I push past the exercise freaks and run to her, but I only get halfway before my lungs are screaming and have to stop. Mum is sitting on the step now, her head in her hands. She seems more composed, so I take a moment to catch my breath before continuing the climb. As I get closer, I can see her body shaking – she's crying. I monitor her from a few rows down, sweat trickling down my face.

After a while, she lifts her head and wipes her eyes with the heels of her hands. Her shoulders rise and fall. She turns her head to take in the stunning view.

She gives a slight nod of her head and stands up.

And I'm so glad she got the chance to say goodbye.

Chapter 85

Eight Years Later

May 2024

Liv

I delete the last two paragraphs I've written and stare at the blinking cursor. What shall I do with this final chapter? This isn't fiction, it's a biography. I can't make stuff up. Will's family will want to know what the hell I'm going on about.

So, now I have to type the truth. No mention of the word 'otosclerosis'. Just second-album syndrome, crippling writer's block, the overdose of a good friend, and a devastating break-up.

I type the full stop on the last sentence. It's finished. I should pop a bottle of champagne, celebrate the colossal achievement of writing a book. All the months – years – of hard work.

But I don't feel a sense of achievement. I've betrayed my mother.

My phone buzzes on the desk beside me. The screen lights up with the picture I've assigned to calls from Mum. My seventeen-year-old self, Mum's arm draped over my shoulders, standing in the atrium of an Amsterdam hotel. We're grinning ear-to-ear with her beautiful artwork snaking up the wall behind us, reaching so high Dad couldn't fit it all in.

I can't talk to her now.

The buzzing stops, the picture disappears: Missed call: Mum.

I rest my elbows on the desk and bury my face in my hands, then flinch as a hand rests on my shoulder. Ben places a mug of coffee on the desk.

'Did you make a decision?' he asks.

'Yeah,' I sigh. 'But I'm not sure it's the right one.'

Fresh from the shower, his hair is wet and hanging in his eyes. When we first met, I couldn't keep my eyes off that Mr Whippy hairstyle as he showed me around the magazine building all those years ago.

After I left *Luminaire*, I didn't think I'd see him again, but I bumped into him in the café on the top floor during my summer internship. He said, 'You went for coffee and never came back. Was it something I said?'

Back then, I was drowning under the pressure of the *Fragments* anniversary feature and he was a welcome distraction. On the way down in the lift, he invited me for a drink after work. I told him I was sixteen, but undeterred, he offered to buy me coffee instead. He was nineteen. I remember thinking that was ancient and that my mum would kill me.

We moved in together last month.

He massages my shoulders. 'You'll feel it in your gut, if it's right or not.'

He's right – I do. I get up, grab my phone, and head for the door.

'Where are you going?' he asks.

I snatch my keys from the table in the hall. 'Research.'

*

I pull up outside Mary's house. It hasn't changed since I first arrived there with Tumi as an inquisitive teenager, and I've been here many times since then.

I remember discovering Will's last song in that house, and a few weeks later, stumbling across the leaflet about otosclerosis. Reading it suddenly made sense of the lyrics that had been puzzling me – I was certain Will must have had the disease. That day, Mum wanted me home for Grandad's birthday. I knew stopping to ask Mary about my theory would make me late, but I couldn't let it go.

I found her in the kitchen. 'Did Will have any problems with his hearing?' I asked.

'No. What makes you think that?'

'I found this leaflet.'

'Let me see that.' Mary held it at arm's length and recognised it immediately. 'Ah, no. That's mine.'

'It's *yours*?'

'Yes. I've had trouble with my ears since I was pregnant with Aidan. I had surgery but after a few years it got bad again. The consultant said surgical techniques had improved. They gave it another go, but it didn't work and surgery on my other ear was too risky, so they gave me a hearing aid. These in-ear ones are quite good if there's not too much background noise, and you can hardly see them.'

'So, Will didn't have any hearing problems?'

'No, though you'd think he would, playing all that loud music.'

'You're sure?'

'They say otosclerosis can be hereditary, but neither of my boys had it.'

'That's lucky,' I said, trying to hide my disappointment. 'Why did he have this leaflet, then?'

'I gave it to Will because I wrote that telephone number on it.' She points to the handwritten number along the top margin, the one I assumed was for the hospital department. 'Will stayed with us for a few days when he got out of hospital. This man kept ringing: a songwriter the record company wanted him to work with. Will wouldn't speak to him. He didn't want to play someone else's music. He wrote his own songs. I thought he'd thrown that leaflet away. But if he kept it, maybe he was considering ringing that songwriter fella, after all?'

'But one of his songs talks about not being able to hear the things you love,' I said. 'About music fading.'

'I don't know, love, I never understood what he was singing about. I just loved his voice.'

'Mary, can I ask you something else?'

'Fire away.'

'Reu and Matty spoke about Emily, Will's girlfriend. Do you remember her?'

Mary's face clouded, and she covered her face with her hands.

I squirmed in my seat. I shouldn't have mentioned Mum.

'Mary?' I asked. 'Are you okay?'

Mary let her hands drop. 'That girl was nothing but trouble from the beginning. She had my boys at each other's throats. She tore my family apart. Once Will got together with her, we didn't see him anymore. And after . . . she wanted to come to the funeral. Can you believe the cheek of her? As if we would want her there when it was all her fault.

'Then I heard she'd had a baby. She moved on so quickly she mustn't have cared for Will at all. She got on with her life and I'll never be able to get on with mine.'

*

I get out of the car and walk up the path to the Bailey house with its neat front garden, a blooming wisteria growing up the side of the bricked-up garage. I've kept in touch with Mary, popping over every few months to chat, but since I started writing the book, it's been more of a weekly thing. When she answers the door, she's not fazed that I've turned up unannounced again. I follow her to the kitchen, where she makes tea as though she has been expecting me.

'Have you more questions for me?' she asks, stirring milk into the mugs.

'No, not today. I wanted to ask you a favour.'

'Oh?' She puts my tea in front of me and sits opposite me.

We're sitting in the same seats as we did all those years ago, the last time I asked about Mum. Mary looks older now, her hair almost completely white.

'Do you remember before, when we spoke about Will's girlfriend, Emily?'

Her face darkens – just like it did the last time. 'Ah Jaysus, do we have to talk about her? I'll talk about anything else, but not her.'

'There's something you should know about Emily.' I'm talking about my mum as if she's a stranger. 'She didn't just move on and have a baby.'

Mary frowns.

'Their split left her heartbroken. She got drunk and made some poor decisions,' I tell Mary. 'The news of Will's death left her reeling. She was so grief-ridden and racked with guilt, she was suicidal herself. But when she found out she was pregnant, it gave her a reason to live. That baby was her only reason to live. For years.'

'How do you know all this?' asks Mary.

'Because *I'm* that baby.'

Mary's body stiffens. 'What?'

'Emily is my mum.'

A bright spark of anger flashes in her eyes. 'She sent you here? Why?'

'She didn't know about me coming here. I kept it a secret. She never spoke about Will. She wouldn't even admit to knowing him. It was her way of coping with the grief. I had to find out about him for myself. That's why I offered to help with the archive. She didn't know what I was doing.'

I tell Mary all about Mum – how she blamed herself for Will's death, how she punished herself for years: no relationships, no friends, no art – her entire life revolving around me.

'For those brief few minutes when I thought Will had otosclerosis, I knew it would change everything for Mum if she found out,' I say. 'Then you corrected me, but I couldn't shake the thought. So, I told Mum that Will had otosclerosis. I lied.'

Mary exhales sharply.

'And you know what?' I continue. 'It worked. She started living again – she let herself be happy – but only because she believed it wasn't her fault.'

Mary's expression remains stony.

'And now,' I say, 'with the publication of this book, she'll find out Will didn't have otosclerosis. I'll have to tell her the one thing that gave her a lifeline was a lie. She'll go back to blaming herself.'

Mary's jaw is set, her chin lifted, but tears threaten to spill onto her cheeks. 'She split up with him, that's why he did it . . .' she whispers.

'Nothing is ever that black and white. Matty tried to persuade her to break up with Will to give him something to write songs about. He told me himself he was worried he'd have to get a proper job. Now, that's pretty damning, but it's not Matty's fault. And Reu thinks it's his fault for overdosing on heroin, but it wasn't his fault, either. Everyone I've interviewed over the years, everyone I've spoken to, has told me they felt somehow responsible for his death. Every single one of them. You blame yourself too, don't you?'

She ignores the question. 'You lied to your mother,' she says. 'That's your problem, not mine.'

'She wasn't to blame. You know it in your heart, Mary. I know you do. I know because you've told me a hundred times how you regret the way you treated Will after they got together. You didn't expect their relationship to last, did you? He loved her! And you wouldn't let her go to the funeral. You wouldn't let her have any of his things. Even though she was the most important person in his life. His soulmate.'

'There's nothing I can do. You've got yourself in this mess—'

'There *is* something you could do,' I say. 'You have a chance to make up for the way you treated the woman your son loved.'

'It's too late. It won't change anything—'

'Let me write it in the book. Let me say Will had otosclerosis. Let my mum be happy . . .'

Chapter 86

One Year Later

July 2025

Liv

My stomach is tight, and my mouth is dry. I wipe my hands on the sides of my dress before straightening a pile of books. *My* books. I take one from the top and prop it against the others so everyone can see the cover. My favourite picture of Will Bailey: the one my mother took of him in the summer of 1997. My name is in white capital letters along the bottom: OLIVIA LAWRENCE-KING. I'm still getting used to it even though I've had it for three years now.

Ben arrives. He's out of breath from running up the stairs.

'Hi.' He kisses my cheek, then my lips, and lingers.

I bat him away. 'Pippa's over there!'

'So?'

'I'm trying to pretend I'm a professional author.'

'You *are* a professional author.'

Ben's sister Beth calls him over and puts him to work pouring glasses of fizz. This whole thing is Beth's master plan. She's in PR and insisted on organising a book launch party. Months ago, she asked me about my dream venue and who would come. I had no idea she was making mental notes. So here we are in my favourite bookshop: Cartwright's in Bloomsbury. We have the top floor to ourselves. The arched window at the end lets in the last golden rays of the day, illuminating the ancient oak mezzanine packed with books.

Beth has arranged a display of Will's guitars and on an easel beside them the *Yellow Feathers* artwork catches the light, on show at last after years in the dusty attic at Matty's parents' house.

My agent, Pippa, calls me over to sign more books.

'People are arriving,' she says, nodding towards the staircase as Dad climbs the last steps.

'This place is amazing,' he says, kissing my cheek. 'You look lovely.'

'Thanks.'

'And here it is.' He picks up a copy of my book.

'You've seen it before.'

'Not in a bookshop. Now it's real.'

There's a tap on my shoulder. It's still a shock to see Chloe's long black hair cropped into an angular bob with the ends dip-dyed blue. 'Hello, Olivia Lawrence-King.'

I throw my arms around her. 'You made it!'

'Wouldn't miss it for the world!'

She's travelled up from Brighton where she's studying psychology. Her boyfriend Dan is with her, and I hug him, too. She's much happier now she's doing what she wants rather than what's expected of her. We don't see each other as often as I'd like, but we message every day, even if it's only a stupid cat video. I pick up a book, flick to the acknowledgements, and hand it to her.

She reads the part for her:

Thanks to my partner in crime since primary school, Chloe Chan, without whose super-sleuth detective work, this book would not have been possible. And without whose friendship and support I would be lost.

'Ah, that's awesome,' says Dan, reading over her shoulder, but Chloe stares at the page in silence. A tear slides down her cheek.

My stomach lurches. 'Oh, I knew I'd get it wrong! What I was trying to say was—'

'It's perfect.' She sniffs. 'Thank you. I wasn't expecting . . . *this*.' She laughs and wipes her eyes.

I give her another hug. 'I'm so lucky to have a friend like you.'

'Shut up, Liv. You're ruining my mascara.'

I glance at the stairs. If Mum was coming, wouldn't she be here by now?

But it's Matty and Reu who arrive next, and I go to meet them.

'Wow,' says Matty, 'the book looks brilliant. I can't wait to read it.'

'Don't lie,' says Reu, 'you've never read a book in your life!'

'Well, that's because I've never been *in* one before!'

I take them to the display of guitars, then leave them reminiscing when I spot Aidan Bailey standing stock still at the top of the stairs. He loosens his collar and rubs his brow, overwhelmed by the sight of his brother's face everywhere.

He composes himself as I get closer.

'Congratulations on the book,' he says.

'Thanks for trusting me with it. This book would never have happened if you hadn't let me loose on Will's stuff.' I pause, then ask, 'Is Mary coming?'

'She's got a bit of a cold. She sends her apologies, but she asked me to give you this.'

He hands me a thin box wrapped in yellow paper dotted with tiny white birds.

'Oh, she shouldn't have.'

'Open it.'

I rip off the wrapping and lift the lid. Inside is a pen with delicate leaves curled around the barrel.

'I told her writers don't use pens anymore, but she wanted you to have it, anyway,' he says.

'It's beautiful. Perfect for signing books. Please thank her for me.'

'Maybe you can thank her in person? She loves it when you visit.'

'I'd like that. Come with me. Some people you know have already arrived.'

I take him over to Matty and Reu. 'I know you see Reu regularly, but here's a face you might not have seen for a while.'

Aidan claps a hand on Matty's shoulder. 'Long time no see, man.' Then Aidan wraps an arm around Reu's neck. 'Did this dude tell you he's godfather to my eldest?'

Matty laughs. 'I can't think of a more heathen godfather.'

Reu feigns offence.

'No, seriously,' says Aidan, 'he's the coolest godfather. I mean, who else can get Ed Sheeran to send a video message on the kid's birthday?'

Reu grins. He's a session drummer, often away on tour with big-name artists. In between gigs, he volunteers at the youth charity his sister founded. He's a genuine hero. It's hard to imagine him broken by addiction.

'Although, I'll never forgive him for buying her a drum kit,' Aidan adds.

'Come on,' says Reu, 'She's getting good, now.'

'Yeah, I admit it, she *is* getting pretty good. She's eyeing the prize at the school talent contest, that's for sure.'

I glance at the stairs as Pippa drags me away to talk to my contacts at a suicide prevention charity, but there's still no sign of Mum.

I'm mid-conversation when she finally shows up at the top of the staircase. Like Aidan, she winces when she sees Will's face everywhere. She's wearing a stylish wrap dress with a bold geometric pattern; hexagonal bangles hang at her wrist. As I listen to the charity guys, Mum composes herself, scans the room, and spots Dad. When she reaches him, she touches his arm and whispers into his ear. Whatever she's said makes him chuckle, and he kisses her on the lips. They're still like newlyweds, even though they've been married for three years. After the wedding, we all took the name Lawrence-King. It was as though the three of us made a promise to each other that day, not just the two of them.

As soon as I can break away, I go to Mum. 'I was worried you weren't coming.'

'I'm so sorry I'm late. I spilled a tin of paint in the studio as I was leaving, and I had to clean it up.'

'Was it blue, by any chance?' I ask.

'Oh no, did I miss a bit?'

I wipe the smudge from her jawline with my thumb. 'There.'

'All gone?'

'Yep.'

'Come here.' She pulls me close and whispers, 'Dad and I are so proud of you.'

I have to swallow before I can speak. 'I'm sorry I was such a difficult teenager.'

'Don't be silly,' she says, waving a hand. She picks up one of my books and turns it over in her hands. 'He would have liked you, you know.'

'Will?'

'Yes. The way you write. This book. The way you talk about music. I've often thought that . . .'

I don't want to blub in front of everyone, so I change the subject. 'Come on. People are waiting to see you.'

'Oh my *God*!' Mum cries when she recognises Matty, Reu, and Aidan. She hugs them in turn and Dad follows behind, shaking their hands.

'You haven't changed a bit,' Mum tells Reu, stepping back to take in his long black ringlets.

'Neither have you,' he replies.

'Yeah, I know . . .' says Matty, patting his gut and running his hand over his smooth head. 'I've changed quite a lot.'

We all laugh.

Mum says, 'Lovely to see you, Aidan.'

'You too.'

Dad puts his hand on the small of her back; he knows they were once lovers. Beth offers us drinks from a tray. Everyone takes a glass of champagne, except Reu, who takes a juice.

'Twenty-six years sober,' he says, raising his glass.

'That's a massive achievement, Reu. Well done,' says Mum.

Dad raises his glass. 'To Liv and her terrific book.'

Everyone raises their glass towards me. 'To Liv.'

I raise mine. 'To Will.'

'To Will.'

I excuse myself to say hello to Tumi and Paul and the team from *Amplify*, then spend the following half hour mingling. When I get back to the group, Mum is throwing her head back in laughter at something Matty is saying.

'Reu got locked in the toilet at Red Rocks just as we were about to go on stage,' he says. 'Will and I had to break the door down.'

'That was a night to remember,' says Mum.

Reu laughs. 'I wish *I* could remember it.'

I recall the magic of the place when Mum and I visited on our road trip. Everyone goes quiet. Mum's eyes look glassy and Matty gives an awkward cough.

*

The two hours we've hired the room pass in a flash. I've answered the same questions over and over. My feet, in their dainty heels, are killing me and I'm exhausted.

Mum and Dad have gone ahead to the restaurant with Chloe, Dan, and Beth. Ben's waiting for me by the staircase.

'Why don't you wait downstairs?' I call over. 'I'll be down in a minute.'

He looks up from his phone and smiles. Even after all this time, he still makes my chest flutter. He nods and bounds off down the stairs.

I sit at the table where I'd been signing books earlier and pick up the pen that Mary gave me. I roll it around in my fingers, then use it to sign one more book:

Dear Mary,
   Thank you for everything, but especially for giving my family a chance at happiness.
   With love,
   Olivia x

Before I head downstairs, I steal a minute to myself by the guitars. Next to the *Yellow Feathers* artwork sits an oversized print of the book cover. Will Bailey looks right at me. He's looking at me the same way that Ben looked at me just now. It was Mum Will was looking at when she pressed the shutter and froze that moment in time.

I study Will's face and ask him silently if he's okay with me messing with his story. His *history*. But his expression says it all. He adored my mother and if he could have spared her any pain, he would have.

I check no one's around and whisper, 'Thank you.'

And I take his blessing and skip down the stairs to my family.

Content Warning

When We Were Young contains depictions of mental health struggles and suicide.

If you, or someone you know needs help, support is available.

Samaritans
Tel: 116 123 (24 hours)
www.samaritans.org

Acknowledgements

First and foremost, thank you – to you, the reader – for choosing this book. I hope you enjoyed it.

To the troubled musicians who left us too soon – Kurt Cobain, Ian Curtis, Nick Drake, Chris Cornell, Chester Bennington, Jimi Hendrix, Amy Winehouse, Dolores O'Riordan, Taylor Hawkins, and Jeff Buckley (to name a few) – thank you for the music. Your art continues to inspire. I'm especially grateful to Matt Haig, for his powerful 2015 article in *The Telegraph* on the dangers of glamorising the suicides of famous artists.

When We Were Young references *The Last Photo* exhibition by the Campaign Against Living Miserably (CALM), which took place along the South Bank in 2022. Though the story is set in 2016, the exhibition's message was too moving and important to leave out, despite not fitting the timeline. At the time of writing, you can still view it at thecalmzone.net/thelastphoto. Thanks also to Roman Kemp, for his honest and moving documentary *Our Silent Emergency*, which taught me the importance of asking your friends twice.

To my wonderful agent, Tanera Simons, for making this dream a reality and, along with Laura Heathfield, shaping this book into something far stronger than the draft that first landed in your inbox. I'm endlessly grateful to you both for your enthusiasm, even after reading it a million times.

To my brilliant editor, Rachel Hart – thank you for

championing this book from the start. Your insight, collaborative approach, and thoughtful suggestions guided me through the bewildering publishing process and made the story better at every stage. It was an absolute pleasure working with you. And to Maddie Wilson, for picking up the baton with such passion and care – I'm truly thankful.

I'm hugely grateful to the RNA New Writers' Scheme. Without the encouragement of my two anonymous readers, this story might still be an unfinished file on my laptop. Thanks also to Angela Nurse and Laura Shepherd for their early feedback, and to *The Bestseller Experiment* podcast for connecting us. A shout-out to Kate Mueser, Marnie McKnight, Kelly Hevel, and *The Shit No One Tells You About Writing* podcast for bringing us together. And a heartfelt thank-you to Sara Naidine Cox for her help in refining my pitch to agents.

To the stranger who saw my friends and I celebrating my publishing deal in our local pub and pre-ordered the book on the spot – you made my night.

I'm grateful to Jess Zahra for her editorial input, Dushi Horti for her meticulous copy-edits, and Penelope Isaac for her diligent proofreading. Thank you, Sarah Foster, for the gorgeous cover; to Emily Hall and Jessie Whitehead for their marketing magic; and to Becky Hunter and Laura Sherlock for getting the word out. Warm thanks also to Molly Lo Re, Hannah Lismore, Angela Thomson, Emily Gerbner, Jean-Marie Kelly, Sophia Wilhelm, Francesca Tuzzeo, Joey Yau, Melissa Okusanya, Hannah Stamp, Katie Buckley, Emily Scorer, Zoe Shine, Aisling Smyth, and Ashton Mucha. The entire Avon team has been brilliant – as have my fellow Avon authors, who welcomed me with kindness and shared their wisdom so generously.

Thanks to Mary Darby for translation rights and Sheila David for dramatic rights.

To the '90s bands that shaped my love for music – especially Need, Babapapa, and Substance – thank you for the unforgettable gigs in tiny London venues, for the van rides packed in with the gear, soundchecks, performances, and post-gig celebrations. Special thanks to my brother, Carl Tiedt – the best bass player – and Grant Wilson, guitarist and songwriter extraordinaire, for the musical education and so much more.

This book is written in loving memory of all the small music venues which no longer exist – The Mean Fiddler and ULU among them. Their loss threatens the lifeblood of British music. Support your local venues (UK readers can find theirs at independentvenueweek.com), and explore the Music Venue Trust's important work at musicvenuetrust.com.

To Malika Nekhla, whose early morning texts make me smile and get me writing before the day job – without you, I would have given up long ago. And for introducing me to our dear friend Sophie Hamilton, who read early drafts with such care (even knowing there'd be no HEA for Will). You are the wisest, funniest, most generous first readers and the best (and most suitably biased) cheerleaders. Thank you for all the laughs.

To my mum and dad, for their unwavering love and support in everything my brother and I do.

And finally, to my husband, Adrian – for doing everything while I was glued to my laptop, for somehow keeping this secret despite being the world's worst secret-keeper, and for tolerating my vacant stares while I imagined scenes instead of listening. But mostly, for always believing in me. And to Sam, for making us both proud.